Books by Kate Wilhelm

City of Cain
The Clewiston Test
Fault Lines
The Infinity Box
Juniper Time
Margaret and I
Where Late the Sweet Birds Sang

Published by POCKET BOOKS

KATE WILHELM

JUNIPER TIME

PUBLISHED BY POCKET BOOKS NEW YORK

**POCKET BOOKS, a Simon & Schuster division of
GULF & WESTERN CORPORATION
1230 Avenue of the Americas, New York, N.Y. 10020**

Published by arrangement with Harper & Row, Publishers, Inc.
Library of Congress Catalog Card Number: 78-22447

ISBN: 0-671-83336-7

First Pocket Books printing June, 1980

10 9 8 7 6 5 4 3 2 1

POCKET and colophon are trademarks of Simon & Schuster.

Printed in the U.S.A.

For Jonathan With Love

1   For years Jean did not believe in the moon as a real place where people could go. When she became aware that her father believed in it, she had to accept the reality of the moon as a thing, but never as a place. Perhaps there were people already there, she thought, but no one could *go* there. It was as mythical and strange and unreachable as the kingdom of Oz.

Sometimes during the long warm summer evenings the three of them, her father, her mother, and Jean, walked to the Ice Cream Bazaar, where they made elaborate sundaes. Jean found it impossible to resist any of the toppings until in the end her dish was a palette of every color available. Her father watched with awe as she ate every bite.

"Eat it now," he said once, "because when I take you to the moon you won't find any ice cream there. Not for a while anyway."

She used to laugh at that, but in later years her laughter was muted and uneasy. She came to believe that he really would take her to the moon one day. Try as hard as she could after that to increase the size of the moon, to give it solidity, to make it a place, it remained the same pale light in the sky, now a sliver, now fatter, now round and shadowed, but never more than that.

When she was very small she always walked in the middle, holding the hand of her mother on one side, her father on the other. Sometimes, giggling, she raised her feet, and they caught her and swung her back and forth. She liked to look at her mother and father together. She liked the way they looked at each other and at her. She could not explain the feeling, but it was warm and safe. Sometimes at night she would wake up to hear their voices, and that was a good feeling. They played games together, chess, Scrabble, other word games. Later she played with them, and sometimes she even won. She especially loved her mother's low throaty laugh which was almost too soft to hear even one room away.

Her father yodeled in the shower. He said he was practicing to become a Swiss mountain climber and applicants had to yodel before they qualified. He said the Swiss mountain men talked by yodeling. She didn't believe that. She could not yodel even though she practiced. It seemed a particularly fine thing to be able to do.

One night in the Ice Cream Bazaar three teen-aged boys approached their table. Jean admired their tight jeans and their sunburned arms, but most of all she admired their sneakers. They were full of holes; one even had a piece of tape on it. She wished her sneakers looked like theirs. That was the year she started going to school.

"Colonel Brighton? Could we have your autograph, sir?"

Jean listened and watched and for the first time realized that her father really did go to the moon, that was not one of his jokes with her. She pushed her ice cream sundae away because it seemed her stomach was going up and down the way the waves did when they went out fishing in the gulf. She shivered, and when her mother asked what was wrong, she could only shake her head. She did not know what was wrong. There was no way to explain what was wrong.

On the way home she walked on the outside, putting

her father between her and her mother. She never walked in the middle again. It was the end of one phase of her childhood.

The summer Jean was ten, when they visited her father's parents in Oregon, the town celebrated the visit with a parade. There were cowboys and Indians, and a marching band, and three floats. The mayor made a speech and a tall Indian made a speech, and then her father made a speech. His speech was very funny, and she thought probably that was improper, he should not have been funny when everyone else was so serious.

"You know how we'll move the Congress, make them build roads, even a railroad, up to the moon? We'll bring back a nugget of gold and every prospector in the West, dead and alive, will hitch up a mule, buy a sack of beans, a hammer and pick, and be on his way. Won't be any way to stop them." The crowd loved him.

In his speech the Indian had called him Olalo, the Man in the Moon. When Jean was introduced to him later, he touched her hair gently and said, "Olahuene, Daughter of the Moon."

At first she had been terrified of him. All she knew about Indians was from television, and she knew they used to scalp whites in years past, expecially blond people, she felt certain. More recently they seized buildings owned by the whites and shot at people who tried to make them move. And they shot at people who tried to build dams.

Robert Wind-in-the-Tall-Trees was his name, her father said; she did not believe him, but everyone called the tall Indian Robert, so that much was probably true. Robert and her father had gone to school together, had played together, learned to hunt together. That night for hours the voices of her parents, her grandparents, and Robert mingled, rose, fell.

Jean loved her grandparents, but especially her

grandfather because she knew he was how her father would look when he became very old. His blond hair would turn gray, then white, and still look the same as now. And the many lines around his nose, on the sides of his eyes, would be like Grandpa's, crinkly, making him look as if he were smiling even when he wasn't. Her grandfather owned a newspaper and wrote for it and did many of the other jobs. He teased in exactly the same way her father did, saying things like he used to spit lead so hot that it cooked the air. He caught the cooked air and wrapped it up and took it home to roast the meat with it. Sometimes Jean tried not to laugh at his stories, but she always did.

One night she sat on the porch and listened to her father and grandfather talk inside the living room.

"How serious is it with Robert?" her father asked.

"Bad enough. He'll fight for that spring all the way. Let the damn tourists go to the ocean if they want to get wet."

"He won't win."

"Yes, he will. The drought's deepening, not easing up. One wet winter doesn't mean it's over. That spring's the difference between living and leaving for Robert and all of them. He won't give it up. He can't give it up."

For years the spring had sustained a large lake that was a favorite tourist attraction in the arid semi-desert country north of Bend. Now that the wells were going dry, and rivers were becoming dry washes, the spring had taken on an importance it had not had for decades. Jean had read about it in her grandfather's newspaper.

"If there's anything I can do . . ." her father said.

"Not yet, but it might come to that. We'll see." The talk drifted to the space station that was being built. "If you can make it rain from up there, you'll keep getting your appropriations," her grandfather said. And the talk was back on the drought and its effects.

They could not tub bathe in her grandfather's house,

and there was a toilet that did not have to be flushed at
all. Jean had eyed it suspiciously at first, but after a day
or two it had become just another item, just part of
visiting Oregon. The river below the house was still
flowing, but barely. The banks were fifty feet apart
here, but the trickle in the middle of the banks was less
than six feet wide, and the water was sluggish and
warm.

That was the first year that Jean knew how frightened
her mother was when her father was in space.
Stephanie Brighton was fair and slender. She smoked
incessantly, and when Daniel was away she chain-
smoked. That year Jean realized that she also drank
when Daniel was away. She hardly ever had seen either
of them drink anything except an occasional beer in hot
weather and wine at dinner, sometimes sipping it when
friends visited. But that time when Daniel left, calling
back to them both, "Don't wait up. I'll write if I find
any fancy postcards!" Stephanie had gone back inside
to the kitchen and poured herself a drink of bourbon;
she diluted it hardly at all with water, and drank it
down.

"I thought he was supposed to be through going up
himself," Jean said.

"He is, but all that trouble, accidents, things not
working right . . . He'll find the reason, fix it, and
that'll be that." The words were as usual, light and
quick, but underlying them, discernible for the first
time, was a current of dread.

"I used to not believe he really went to the moon,"
Jean said slowly. "I used to have nightmares."

Stephanie came to her and put her arm about Jean's
shoulders, gave her a kiss on the cheek. "I know,
honey. God, I know. I thought you had forgotten all
that."

"I had forgotten. I just remembered."

They went out to dinner that night, and a movie
afterward. It was nearly midnight when they got home,

but Jean, although so tired she could not hold her legs still, was unable to fall asleep. She got up to go to the bathroom and see what time it was, and the living room lights were on; they were still on when she got up again an hour later.

Then Daniel returned, bouncy, happy, trouble-free. "The idiots forgot that you need a screwdriver to turn screws with. Took 'em a set of screwdrivers and that settled that. Now let's go fishing."

But that was not the end of the trouble. The papers ran the stories of each accident, each miscalculation, each overrun of expenses. Every year the appropriations had been harder to come by. Each year they had been cut a bit from the previous budget. There was talk of halting the project entirely until the current recession ended, the drought ended, the stockpiles of food were replenished, and so on.

One night Jean said to her father, "If I tell you something, will you not laugh at it? It's something I don't understand, but I don't think it's funny, although it might sound silly at first."

"Profound things often sound silly when we try to explain them because you have to reduce something grand and sweeping to such ordinary words." He smiled gently at her. "I don't always laugh, you know."

She nodded. She knew he would not laugh at her now, but she still hesitated because it was hard to know exactly how to say it. "I was almost asleep," she started finally, "but not all the way, and I was already dreaming. I could feel myself not all the way asleep, and I could see myself dreaming a real dream. And I thought how my mind was like a long stretched-out snake. It was in such a hurry to dream that the front part went ahead and started before the rest of it was even there. It seems to me that sometimes you can stretch yourself out like that, just poking around, and if you decide not to go where the front part is, you don't have to go and it just comes back and tells the rest what it saw and heard where it was so you know things that you don't know how you know."

She stopped in confusion. It did sound silly after all. But he was not laughing. He was quiet for so long that she began to squirm in embarrassment. "It's a joke," she said finally.

He seemed to pull himself back from somewhere else, far away, the place he went to when he was concentrating. He had said once that everyone had a thinking place, far away, and sometimes people fooled you by pretending to be nearby when actually they were in the thinking place. Now he said, "It isn't a joke, honey. It isn't silly or funny. You've said something very profound, something that needs a whole lot of thinking about."

A few months later, a day before her birthday, he said, "I am a genie. I will grant you any wish. Speak, birthday girl!"

"I just want one thing," she said quickly. "I already know what I want more than anything else in the world. Magic. I want to be able to do magic!"

He laughed, then sobered and closed his eyes. After a moment he made a pass with both hands before her face. "It is done. You have the greatest magic in the universe."

"Hah!" She looked around the room; finally her gaze came to rest on a scab the size of a quarter on her knee. "Be well!" she commanded. Then she looked at her father sorrowfully. "You're just not a very terrific genie, I'm afraid."

"You have the magic," he said, still serious. "But you have to learn how to use it. It is language. Words. I promise you, you can do magic with words if you learn to make the words do what you choose. You can have whatever you want, make people do what you want, make them love you, serve you. You can change the world with words."

"It's like a riddle, isn't it? It's a trick like you think

you've got something but nothing changes and you find out you don't have anything you didn't have before."

He shook his head. "It's real magic, but hardly anyone learns to control it and use it. And those who do want such petty things."

She realized her father was talking to her from his thinking place. Sometimes when his voice was low and serious like this, when his eyes stopped laughing and flashing with light and became very steady and almost dull looking, he was in that far away place, and anything he said from there she should pay attention to carefully. Suddenly she thought that she was also in her own thinking place because her thoughts were flowing so fast she could hardly keep track of them and would not have been able to tell anyone about them all, but they were very clear to her, not at all confused. You could give someone a present that no one else could see or touch or know was there, she realized, and that might be the best present of all.

"Thank you," she said gravely, still in her thinking place. "I accept. You are a true and good genie."

"And you are wise beyond your years," he said, and came back with twinkling eyes and a smile on his lips.

But from her own thinking place she suddenly saw that the smile was not all the way through him, that he was concerned and preoccupied with something he did not speak of at all. Abruptly she stood up, not willing to stay in that place any longer, and when she looked at her father he was exactly as he always had been, happy, unworried, laughing at small jokes that he sometimes shared, often did not. She would never go *there* again, she decided.

That year Daniel was on tour for weeks at a time. Often there were demonstrations protesting his speeches, and Stephanie and Jean would sit side by side watching television, saying nothing, Stephanie with a drink in one hand, a cigarette in the other, Jean feeling the waves of fear churn her stomach endlessly. When her father appeared next to Colonel Cluny on stage, she always felt he was a stranger, not the man who lived with her and her mother. This man was sober and direct; he never made jokes, rarely smiled, and somehow he seemed much older than her father. Playacting, she decided, and hated it.

Once the demonstrators started a fire in the auditorium when her father was on stage, and although it was not on television, she could see every detail; she could see people getting crushed underfoot, others jamming against doors that refused to open, others huddling under chairs, under the stage, trying to escape the flames. Sixty-four people were killed that night.

There was a congressional hearing, and her father was called. He answered the questions gravely, unhesitatingly. When he stated his reasons for believing the space station should be finished, that it was a necessity, not a luxury, no one doubted that he was speaking the truth he lived with and for.

After that he spent a month in Europe, trying to persuade the French, the British, and the Russians to contribute more to the station, a more balanced proportion of the costs. They were all suffering from the drought also, not as much as the United States, but enough to make them wary of committing larger sums of money for the future.

Jean now read every word printed about the space station: the predicted benefits, the accidents that had plagued it from the start, the bickering among the four nations involved in the construction, the difficulties of four nationalities working closely together on such a technical job where every misunderstanding led to even more delays and more accidents.

Rumors of sabotage, whispered before, became louder and more persistent and ugly, and there were speeches at the UN that were scarcely veiled threats of withdrawal if the rumors did not stop. The French were insulted; the British were furious; the Russians were belligerent and issued a statement saying the Americans were trying to freeze them out of participation at this stage when at last some parts of the station were nearing readiness for use.

Many times Jean went to the backyard of their Houston suburban house late at night when there were few lights on in the neighborhood. She waited until her eyes adjusted, then looked at the sky and found the star that was the station. "Die!" she whispered at it fiercely. "Explode! Vanish!" She wished a space crab would come and eat it up, or that aliens would blast it from the sky, or that the Russians would bomb it out of existence. All the hatred she could feel was directed at that one white light in the sky.

One night her family went to Colonel Cluny's house for dinner. She had played with Arthur Cluny all her life, although he was four years older than she, but recently a strangeness had come between them, and now they were uncomfortable with each other. Everyone called him Cluny; he was seventeen that year, and had grown very tall and was as thin and awkward as a stick drawing, all elbows and knees and feet that he never seemed to know where to put.

As soon as dinner was over he asked Jean if she would like to hear some records and she said no very politely in a way that would have been ridiculous just a few months earlier. He looked relieved. Jean liked his mother very much. She was plump and short and could whistle dozens of bird calls. Jean saw the look that passed between mother and son.

His said, *I tried*. And hers said, *Not really*. For a moment Jean felt sorry for Cluny. His father muttered something about no rest for the weary and took Daniel off to his study; Mrs. Cluny and Stephanie began to talk about the food shortages and the rationing everyone expected within six months. Throughout the West electricity and water were being rationed already. Jean excused herself to get her book from the car. She had

Sid raised his head and yelled a long strident cry of

not wanted to come tonight, but her father had said teasingly that Cluny would be crushed if she didn't appear, and reluctantly she had permitted herself to be drawn along with them. Crushed, she thought bitterly, walking along the white concrete drive to where the car was parked.

She stopped outside the open study window when she heard her father's voice.

". . . won't work, Marcus. You know it won't work. We çan't do it alone!"

"Goddamn it! Make it work then! Try! They're going to close down the son of a bitch! That lousy Atherton is loaded for us. Goddamn bastard!" There was a long silence, but before Jean moved again, Colonel Cluny said in a lower, more intense voice, "You know anything else we can do? Just say it if you do."

"Shoot Atherton?"

"Maybe it'll come to that. Maybe it will. And I'd do it in a minute if he was the only one. So would you. But he isn't."

"Okay. Okay. When?"

She knew he would be slouched down in his chair, his legs out before him, the way he was after an all-day hike, or a weekend out on the gulf fishing, with too little sleep, too little rest. He sounded as tired as she had ever heard him.

"Jean, where are you?"

It was Cluny's voice coming from the back of the house.

She ran, and when Cluny came into view she was just closing the car door, her book in her hand.

"Mom sent me out," Cluny said. "She thinks I should play a game with you or something."

Jean giggled. "I know. Monopoly?"

"Yeah. I said I'd show you my telescope. It's out back. You want to see it?

She didn't want to, but she went with him anyway, because she did not want to go into any lighted room just yet. She was certain anyone who glanced at her would know immediately that she had been eavesdropping.

The next day Daniel told Jean and Stephanie that he was going back to the station one last time. "Maybe if I try hard I can get to the bottom of the trouble up there," he said, and that was the official reason given for his mission. There was a special on television about the many troubles, and then the President came on to say he personally was sending the most honored and respected astronaut of all time to investigate, to talk to the men up there, to try to find a solution to the problems that had repeatedly slowed down the project.

Lying in bed that night, Jean thought to herself, No one said anything at all. They took an hour, but they didn't say anything, not really. And she wondered if the President knew why her father was being sent to the station again. She wondered if anyone on the hour-long program knew that nothing had been said.

Four days later Colonel Cluny came to tell Jean and Stephanie that Daniel had been killed.

"He was going around the completed part in a small one-man capsule," the colonel said. "He made the turn, headed out and around the steel members, and then he just kept going. There was never any radio contact at all. He got out of range of radar almost instantly. It must have been a total malfunction of the craft. That's the only thing that could have happened." His face was gray and haggard. He looked dead. He was lying. Jean took a step toward him, another, but then her mother screamed a long, piercing, anguished wail, and Jean felt herself crumble. She no longer knew what she had intended, if anything. A doctor attended to her mother, took her away, and the colonel turned toward Jean, but she backed away, shaking her head. At the door she turned and ran. She looked up at the bright light in the sky and screamed as loud as she could, "I hate you!"

2 Arthur Cluny splurged his entire month's rations on wine the day he received his Ph.D. in astrophysics. The party went on most of the night and when dawn was a pale smudge on the horizon Cluny and a few close friends went out to find an open restaurant for eggs and coffee. It had been the first wine and smoke party for many months; none of them was sober. They all ignored the panhandlers, the women, the teen-agers' roving gangs on the streets.

Sid kept chanting a fifteenth-century call to vespers, and Roald and Murray recited Kipling's *Jungle Books*. Ralph was becoming maudlin. "They'll put you away in a high observatory on a mountaintop and nobody will ever see you again, but they will name comets after you. Cluny One, Cluny Two, Cluny Three . . ."

Murray had started a new Kipling story, interrupted it to call back to Ralph, "Maybe he'll find an asteroid with the fountain of eternal water in it!"

They entered an all-night cafeteria, where they were met at the door by a collector who demanded to see their ration coupons before they could go through the serving line. He looked bored and depressingly sober.

Murray sat next to Cluny after they had selected their food. Their choice had been limited to scrambled eggs, pies, and sweet rolls. Murray was overweight, with the unhealthy fat of one whose diet consisted almost entirely of starches. He kept adding catsup to his eggs and eyeing Cluny's three rolls. He was a biochemist, unemployed.

Virgil began to talk about the demonstration planned for the Fourth of July at the Pentagon. *"Research Water, Not Bombs,"* he said. "That's the slogan. This time we'll get in and take it apart."

Ralph made a snorting noise of derision.

"Would any of you gentlemen care to donate a water ration coupon for the refugees?" The voice was cool, the words carefully enunciated, as if the speaker knew a table of drunken students would understand nothing less than perfect diction.

Cluny looked up at her. She was tall, five ten at least, and she was very beautiful, with long brown hair done in a loose braid over one shoulder, and feathery curls over both ears. She wore no make-up; her skin was so flawless it looked unreal. Her eyes were green, with long straight dark lashes.

Cluny heard the others talking, flirting, trying to get her to join them, trying to learn her name. Virgil had his coupon book out, thrust it at her. "Take all you want, but tell me your name first. Just the name."

She tore out one water coupon and returned the book. Someone asked whom she was working for, and she answered that one. "The American Refugee Society." Everyone else was handing her the coupons she had asked for. She turned her gaze to Cluny, who shook his head.

"I don't have any more," he said and was surprised to hear his own voice. He felt he never had heard his own voice before that night. "I have food coupons," he said.

She shook her head slightly, accepted a coupon from Murray, and then she left.

She wore a pale yellow Grecian-type garment, slit on one side up to her thigh and caught at one shoulder with a butterfly brooch; when she moved, her long leg flashed pink.

"Wooie!" Virgil said then, wiping his forehead. "She could collect arms and legs and need a truck to haul them away with!"

Cluny had risen, and on both sides hands pulled him back down. "Un-unh, my boy," Sid said mournfully, tugging at him. "She's straight, a good woman, dedicated to the welfare of others. You know a good woman has been the ruin of more men than demon rum itself?" He nodded wisely. "'S a fact."

Cluny struggled, but they restrained him until he gave it up. When they left the restaurant it was full daylight; early workers were already out, along with the street people, who never left.

Sid and Murray returned to Cluny's apartment with him; the others went lurching away in the opposite direction. Later that day Cluny left his two friends sleeping on the sofa bed and the floor while he went out to find the office of the American Refugee Society. There was a single woman on duty; he remembered it was Saturday. He asked about the girl, and found he was holding his breath until the woman answered.

"Oh, you must mean Lina Davies. She won't be in until Monday. Can I help you?"

He mumbled something and left. Monday. He would wait all day Monday.

"Okay, Cluny. What now, old friend?" Sid asked that evening.

They had cleaned up the one-room apartment enough to be able to sit down without knocking anything over. There was the sofa bed, which sagged to the floor, an overstuffed chair with the stuffing completely out of one arm, several straight chairs, a tiny refrigerator and a two-burner stove built into a sink unit. Books were stacked under a small table, at the side of the sofa, and under a window. The walls were covered with posters of pop art and good prints of Kandinsky, Japanese line drawings, Michelangelo's horse studies, and other miscellany. If anyone had told Cluny that his room was a mess, he would have been surprised; he had not seen it for many months, had not really looked at it hard since the day he had taken it, grateful to have found it.

"Go work on a canal or aqueduct somewhere, I guess," Cluny said. His head ached dully and although he was hungry, the thought of eating was repugnant. Food would sink right down through his stomach.

"No," Sid said firmly. "You will not. How are you fixed for bread, dough, cash, jingle-jangle?"

Cluny shrugged. His father had had a lot of insurance, and there was the pension, which his mother expected to share with him until he could find something to do.

"Right," Sid went on as if he had answered aloud. "Here's what we're going to do, old friend. We're going up to Alpha, get it started again. You, Murray, and me. How about that!"

Cluny shook his head and the aching came in closer, began to throb behind one eye. "I bite," he said. "Tell me."

"You go back home, back to your father's files, dig out everything there. Everything—every argument, every detail, the floor plans, everything. And we make a case for going. Murray can do the kind of biological work that's banned here. I can look for radioactive rocks or something. You can set up an astronomy unit. See?"

"They've been trying that for years," Cluny said. "You know there's no money for it."

"*They* are not your father's son," Murray said then. "We think you could do it, Cluny. Probably no one else could. They might do it if only to give people something to think about instead of depressions and drought and famine, and China and Russia threatening to bang each other out of existence. If they claim it's for weather research, it could stop the demonstrations. They just might go for it."

"Do you have any idea how much it would cost?"

"No, and that's why you're to start digging in your father's files."

"But it's all on record. There's nothing I can find in his private files that isn't in Washington. Others have been through it all a dozen times."

Murray and Sid were both shaking their heads. Murray said, "He was a dreamer, Cluny. You know he was. It was his baby all the way. His and Brighton's. They pushed it down Congress's throat, made the government accept it and then finance it. They got the others to go in, France, England, Russia. You know how much manipulating they did, just to get it started? What's on record is what was finished. What we think you'll find are your father's dreams, his plans, and that's what we need now."

"Hell," Sid cut in. "Half the stuff's been classified, and it's not on record. But I'd be willing to bet my mother's gold teeth that you'll find it in his files. You don't give away all your baby's records. You make copies, fudge a little here and there, and you keep the important ones yourself. You'll see."

"What about Brighton's stuff?"

Murray answered. "Mrs. Brighton became a lush and the kid went to live with her grandparents. Mrs. Brighton signed a release for the government to take all her husband's stuff out. No one seems to know what happened to any of it after that. Probably in a Quonset hut somewhere, molding away."

Cluny went to the window then and stood looking at the street below. Nothing he saw registered in his consciousness. He might have been looking at a blank wall. Jean, he thought. And what happened to Jean after that? He didn't ask. He doubted that they had followed up that part. No reason for them to have wondered what happened to little Jean.

"How long have you been planning this?" he asked, turning toward them again.

"A year. We wanted to tell you sooner, but you were

too busy and it was important that you have the Ph.D. Doctor Cluny carries a hell of a lot more clout than Arthur Cluny, student."

"You've been waiting for me to grow up," Cluny said, his voice heavy with self-mockery. "Now I put on the long pants and do a man's work, is that it?"

Sid nodded. And Cluny knew his mocking words had been true ones.

Sid looked hung over, and deadly serious. He was a slightly built man, going bald already although not yet thirty. He had been Cluny's space geology teacher at Harvard several years earlier, and they had become friends during the course, and afterward the friendship had cemented. He lived with Terri Ruthchild, taught, and made model spaceships for a hobby. And Sid cultivated friendships that would pay off, Cluny found himself thinking.

Sid was watching him. "I didn't think of it until a year ago," he said, as if privy to the inner workings of Cluny's head. "In fact, something you said started it. One night you said the only place to study astronomy was in space. Everything else was working through a smoked glass. Remember? You thought the same thing I did then, but you put it aside. Now I'm bringing it out again. That's all."

"Okay, okay," Cluny said irritably. "I'm going home next week. I'll see if Dad had anything at home. I'll have a look at it if he did."

Murray stood up then. "Jesus, I had forgotten what wine does to the head," he complained. "I'm going. Cluny, after a couple weeks, give Sid a call, okay? I've got nothing better to do. I'll come down and help you go through the stuff."

Cluny nodded. He and Murray had been friends for nearly ten years. His mother liked Murray. There would be no problem in having him around for a while. And if it was a waste of time, it would not matter anyway, since Murray had nothing here to hold him. He and the rest of the biochemistry department had been fired *en masse* the previous year when it had been learned they were continuing the forbidden genetic engineering research.

Sid went to the door also. Cluny caught his arm. "You know they won't agree to anything like this, don't you? They won't spend the kind of money it would take, not now."

"I think they will. Have you ever been really desperate, down to rock bottom, and decided to do something totally foolish and more expensive than you could possibly afford? Sometimes that's the only thing to do when you're desperate enough. Gamble with everything you have left, hoping it'll pay off real big. I think we're ready to try that desperate gamble."

They left, and Cluny sat with his head in his hands for a long time, thinking about desperation. He thought of Murray living in a rat-infested rathole of a room, in Rat Cathedral, living like a rat himself, scrounging, making do, doing without. And Sid, working full time at the university, but on three-quarters pay, with new cuts foreseen, and new layoffs as the student population shrank again and again. And he thought of himself without a job, without hope for a job, without any prospect of having anything at all better than he had right now. And right now he had nothing except his mother's largesse.

It was as if he had been born in an endless world, but sometime when he was not watching, they came along and put walls on it, and every year since then, when he glanced out, he could see that the walls had moved inward a bit, until they were almost within reach, and the world had become constricted and shadowed. There was the deepening depression, shortages, and crowding as people were forced out of their homes in the Western states. If the drought did not end, there would be more crowding, more displaced people, more shortages. And there was no hope. Every day there was less hope that the drought would end before the walls came together.

Deliberately he had cultivated a functional blindness to the problems as long as he could, as long as he had been in school. He had lived with, nurtured, the belief that by the time he got his doctorate the problems would be gone, the rains would come again, and the people would go back home. He had refused to join any of the militant groups with their ceaseless demands for this program or that, and he had in fact thought them all very silly and naïve, as if the government could make it rain. Or make the grass grow where there was no water. Or provide jobs when industries were forced to close because there was no water or electricity. The times can't always be good, he had thought with disgust at some of his friends when they marched, or held demonstrations. And at the end, when reality began to encroach on his world, when his applications for jobs went unanswered, and his colleagues shrugged vaguely when he brought up the question of work, he had felt only a dull resentment and in relief had gone back to his books and his research and his thesis. One thing at a time, he had thought then. First the degree, then worry about what to do with it.

It was the goddamn helplessness, he thought, pushing his hands hard against his throbbing temples, willing the headache to vanish. Goddamn helplessness, he muttered under his breath; that was what finally made people riot in the streets and try to burn down every symbol of better times. That was what made the Westerners hate and despise the Easterners, who in turn feared and hated them and the threat they posed. That was what made the militarists want to take over, just to be able to try to do something, anything, no matter how desperate a gamble it was.

And that was what Sid had been talking about, he thought dully. Anything is better than nothing, any action better than no action. Even a bankrupt government might react with final desperation to the crushing onslaught of the humiliation of helplessness.

Ramona Cluny had gained a few pounds in her middle years, but her face was unlined, and her eyes were bright blue, youthful looking. She had been aghast when Cluny told her there had been no offers for a bright young doctor.

"They're crazy! Have they lost interest in the stars suddenly? They think they know enough about black holes and cosmic rays to do them for all times?"

Cluny laughed. Those were the only two astronomical terms she knew, and she used them whenever the conversation turned to his career. His mother had come back to Chapel Hill, where she had gone to school, where she had met his father. She had been very practical about it, saying, "There are always students who need extra money, and are willing to mow the lawn, or cut down a tree limb, or rake a yard, whatever needs doing. This crop leaves, there's a new one. I'll get by." And she was getting by quite well. At first, after his father's death, he had worried about her being able to cope with the world alone, but the efficient way she had rearranged her life made him suspect that she had done the coping for a long time and he simply had not been aware. Now she raised a garden every year to supplement her ration coupons; and she traded her surplus vegetables and berries for eggs and milk, whatever else she needed. What she could not use immediately, she canned and dried, and her trading material lasted throughout the year.

"What will you do now?" she asked.

"I thought I'd hang around here, if you can put up with me, and take a rest. I've been grinding away for a long time. And I might have a go at Dad's papers. I guess he left a lot of stuff behind, didn't he?" That was as directly as he could put the question, he realized. He never had asked before, and now he wondered why he had not, why she had not mentioned them if there were files or notebooks, anything at all.

They were sitting in her living room, drinking tea.

After dinner he had helped her do the dishes, and they had taken the tea to the porch, but a chill had driven them indoors again. A June bug buzzed at the screened door and midges flew erratically around the lampshade, inside it, out again, back inside. The single lamp drew every insect to it: midges, moths, a lacewing. . . . The little noises grew louder as he waited for his mother to answer. Finally she cleared her throat, put her cup down, and leaned forward.

"I knew one day I'd have to talk about the last years," she said. "I kept thinking you'd ask something that I couldn't answer without explaining everything, and I don't know enough to explain everything. He was not well for a long time, longer than anyone knew." Again she paused, not so long this time. "I can tell you exactly when he became ill. The night Dan Brighton died. It killed your father too, but it took him longer, that's the only difference. He might as well have been up there, in the little capsule along with Dan. He never got over it. He began to blame himself. He blamed himself for getting the station closed down, for sending Dan up that last time, for the malfunction, for everything. He became obsessed with it. He wanted to burn all his papers. We moved several times during those last few years, of course. Georgetown, then Florida. I told him his papers were in a safety-deposit box, that no one could get to them, that no one knew anything about the box. That would satisfy him for a time, but he would start it over again. He had to burn the evidence. They would destroy him. They would destroy you." Her voice had been steady, but now it wavered, and stopped. She lifted her tea and the cup clattered on the saucer.

"Why didn't you tell me?"

"What could you have done? I was terrified the Air Force would find out, give him a medical discharge. Section Eight? Do they still call it that?"

"Good God! Mother, you should have told me. I could have come home. I might have done something!"

She shook her head. "I decided," she said. "It was my decision. I made him take the early retirement. I gave him no rest until he agreed to it. I knew he couldn't pass his next medical, and he would tell them he caused the accidents, Dan's death, everything. They were looking for a scapegoat. He would have offered himself. I couldn't let him do it. He made something unique and beautiful and they would have wrapped it around his neck and strangled him with it. I know what they can do. I wouldn't let it happen."

Cluny felt he was listening to a stranger, someone he never had known at all. He remembered her on trips, whistling for the birds, being answered as if she were one of them. He thought of her quiet voice reading countless stories and books to him, how she had held him when he had been hurt, all the times he had been able to weep because she made weeping by a boy seem natural. And all those years, he had not known her at all.

"Toward the end," she said quietly now, "whenever he begged me for his papers so he could get rid of them, I told him he had already burned them. That seemed to satisfy him. I thought it satisfied him. Then the day he died, he told me to let you have them. To let you decide. We'd been deceiving each other a long time, each of us afraid the other would find out."

Cluny's throat was too tight and dry for him to speak. He swallowed tea, got up to pour for both of them, and when he sat down again, he had forgotten what he intended to say.

"But I was home off and on during those years. I should have noticed something."

She shook her head. "Sometimes he was away on trips, sometimes, often during the last two years, he was in his room and I just told you he was away. He knew, dear. Sometimes he was fine, and then he was home when you were. When he was ill, we thought it best to say he was away on business. He was afraid it would ruin your life to know. It was important to him

to have you finish school without any worries, the way
he had gone to school. That was very important to
him."

Cluny stood up and started to pace the pretty little
room. There were scattered Persian rugs on the shiny
floors; vases from China, Japan, France, were filled
with roses and lilacs. The room was cluttered with art
from all over the world. All of it was familiar; he had
grown up with it, and all of it looked strange, as if he
were seeing it for the first time. Like this woman saying
these incredible things about a man he never had
known.

"You should have told me," he said again.

"I couldn't have," Ramona said wearily. "You had
come to despise him by then. What would have been
the point?"

"That's not true!" He felt a flush sweep through him
and he kept his back to his mother.

"Anyway," she went on, "he always knew you'd
want the papers. Even when he wanted to burn them,
he knew. He was afraid I wouldn't be able to keep them
for you."

"How did you? I thought they sent someone to
collect stuff like that?"

"They did. He had a small file in his office. They took
that. The others were in my trunks, where I put them
the first night he talked about destroying them." She
stood up also then. "I've never looked at them. They're
all about the station, I think. I'm not sure."

"You hated it, didn't you?"

"We all did," she said, arranging the tea things on
the tray, her back to him. "All the wives hated it and
were jealous of it. It was like a disease, something only
men caught and never recovered from, something that
finally killed them off one after another." She straightened, holding the tray, still not looking at him. "Why
do you want the papers now? It's dead. It will stay
dead, won't it?"

Cluny found he could not answer, and after a

moment she left the living room with the tray. Presently he heard her washing their things, making too much noise with the dishes.

"Three things she does when she wants you to bug off and leave her be," his father had said a long time ago. "She'll go out and start yanking up weeds like the devil. Never saw a woman pull weeds like that in my life. Weed a whole garden in an hour when she's in that mood. Or else she'll bang the dishes as if she wants to break every last one of them. Bang, crash, bang. You stay out when you hear that. And if there aren't any dishes to wash, and it's not the right time of year to yank out weeds, she'll get out her quilting box and start counting pieces. Never quilts, never will, but she sure as hell can count quilt pieces."

Sid had been right, Cluny thought. He had guessed right about the files kept at home. And she had defied the space administration, the Air Force, the entire U.S. government, by hiding those documents in her trunks under quilts and quilt pieces.

He left the house and started walking the quiet streets. This was a hilly section of the old city, where the trees had not been cut for a hundred fifty years or longer and now were giants with intertwined arms, as if drawn together to share secrets. A distant whippoorwill called, over and over and over.

He had known, he realized. He had known more than he had been able to admit to himself. And since she had denied it, he had been able to deny it also, to pretend he knew nothing. His trips home had been infrequent because they had moved around so much, he had said, and he thought that was at least a partial truth. They had moved a lot after the station had closed down. Apparently no one had known what to do with an ex-space satellite authority. But they had discouraged visits too, he realized now. One year they had given him money to go to Europe for the summer vacation; another year they had mailed him the house keys and they had been gone, on a tour of duty, she had

said at the time. Possibly they had gone no farther than
the next town, he thought now.

All right, he told himself sharply. Enough. It was
done.

There were papers, and his father had known that he
should not have them in his personal possession. There
was that. Also, his father had thought he, Cluny,
should have them. Trunks full of dreams. Tomorrow he
would start sharing his father's dreams for the first
time. Before, when he had lived at home, when he had
been a boy, he had taken it for granted that his father
was the iron hand behind the satellite. It might have
been a bridge, or a skyscraper; it would be there for all
time. That was how he had thought of it, when he had
thought of it.

He headed back to the house. It was not like that, he
knew now. His father had built a dream, had made it
real and tangible and visible for everyone else to share
with him. And in the end, they had rejected it, and his
father had found that the dream was not separate from
him, but was such a living part of him that when it died,
the rest had to follow.

It wasn't just the death of the dream, Cluny thought
then, but the price he had paid for the dream that had
turned out to be empty. He knew exactly when his hero
worship of his father had crashed. He had been
fourteen. He remembered his own awkwardness, how
certain he had been that everyone was staring at his big
feet, his bony arms and wrists, the funny way his
clothes hung on him. If they were long enough, they
were too loose and baggy. His father had been neat and
handsome in his full-dress uniform.

"You mean that slob Mannheim's coming here to
dinner? He's a fascist pig. I wouldn't let him within a
mile of my house!"

"Butt out. It's business."

Cluny walked to the table and deliberately removed
his place card and tore it in half. "Sure," he said. ntly
and firmly that she would not do. Even then he had

Something happened that night that was never to be repaired. There was no way his father could recall the shame and humiliation he had revealed before his face set in a stony mask of rage, and no way Cluny could undo the look of contempt he had not tried to hide. How many asses had the old man kissed to get what he wanted, how many swine had he brown-nosed, how many jackasses had he bowed to?

After his father's funeral he had gone over that scene repeatedly. He had been young, too idealistic, too naïve. His father should not have been so hurt by anything a green kid blurted out. Cluny had writhed under the coals of guilt he heaped on himself, and his excuses and explanations meant nothing. Through them all he heard over and over his parting words that night: "I'll never put myself in a place where I have to eat shit for anything!"

Back in the house, he lifted the telephone to call Sid, then put the instrument down again. There would be time. Alpha had waited nearly ten years; it could wait another day or two.

He thought then of Lina Davies, so breathtakingly beautiful that he had not dared approach her after all. He had frozen, had slipped in time to his past, when, as an adolescent, he had known no girl would look at him, answer him if he spoke. It had been the same adolescent self who knew she was more perfect than a human being could be, she was a goddess, a divinity. And he was nothing. On the crowded sidewalk where he had waited all morning for her to appear, he stood rooted until she disappeared in the midst of people; then he had turned and walked hopelessly away.

Now, his hand on the telephone, he saw her again; her shoulders bare in a halter dress, her hair loose on her back, the fluidity of her walk. . . . He cursed himself for being a fool. He turned off the lamp and sat in the living room until the fragrance of lilacs and roses became overpowering, and then he went to bed.

3 The attic was hot; there was a wasp nest over the east window, and a mouse nest in a dark corner at the other side. There were four trunks, assorted furniture, discarded toys and ice skates and an archery set. There was a pedal sewing machine with a beautiful floral design on the front of the cabinet; there were two mattresses and an antique brass bedstead.

Two of the trunks held nothing but bedding, out-of-date clothes that never would be used again, and many scraps of fabric, some sewn together in patterns, other loose pieces stuck in to fill corners.

The other two trunks had bedding on top, with the contents of several file drawers neatly folded into a comforter in the first one, and into a quilt in the second.

Dreams, Cluny thought, lifting the quilt out carefully, spreading it on the floor. He left the papers on the quilt, brought out the comforter and added the piles of papers to the first stacks, and then he started to sort them.

His mother called him to lunch later, to dinner still later. He was hardly aware of what they talked about either time. Late that night, she stood in the doorway of the attic silently, and when he became aware of her, he had the feeling she had been there a long time.

"I wish to God I had let him burn them," she said. "I

wish I had burned them myself." She turned and went back down the steep stairs.

Cluny's eyes stung and his head ached. The heat, poor lighting, sitting on a trunk hunched over, seeing a life open to view, take form, develop—it all was there—made him feel that for hours he had been inside his father's head, had felt with him, schemed with him, suffered with him, shared triumph and finally total defeat.

Slowly he got up, his legs stiff and sore, his back hurting with a dull pain. He didn't bother to put away the papers, but simply turned off the light, closed and locked the door, and went down. For a long time that night, he was unable to sleep. The face his father had chosen to show the world was not the face he now saw when he drew him up before his inner eye. A dreamer, even a poet, a romantic who yearned for space, for the stars: that was the self his father had hidden so well behind the competent engineer's mask. The first fantasies of going into space had started when he was a child, and the fantasies had never changed. They had sustained him even after he realized the limits he might reach—the space station.

Asleep at last, Cluny dreamed of his father wearing a helmet and a metallic suit that gleamed when he moved; a strange weapon was in his hand—a ray gun, of course. His father was piloting a small ship against the eternal black of space, and a shadow was creeping toward him, gray against black; the shadow grew until it had blotted out all the stars, the swirling brilliant dust, the spinning galaxies. Then he was his father, or at least it was he, Cluny, who was operating the ship, which was hardly bigger than a bathtub. The shadow was still expanding, one edge of it nearly reaching the metal of the ship. Cluny knew he could not let the shadow touch him, or his ship, and began to maneuver in a darting, impossible motion that eluded the shadow successfully. There was a crowd waiting for him on the planet where he landed. He could feel his face grow hot with pleasure as they cheered; then he was not looking at the people at all, but overhead at a green sky with furious clouds of magenta, yellow, scarlet, gold, all boiling, roiling, erupting in flares and explosions. They merged and the color became a dead black, an endless black that drew him toward it irresistibly. He thought, quite clearly, "When I get to the horizon, I'll be free." The sound of his own voice wakened him. He was sweating heavily, his bed was sodden, his hair stuck to his forehead.

The next day Cluny found a notebook with pages torn out. He frowned at it, put it aside. He was not trying to read everything yet, but was sorting, glancing through notebooks, putting the papers in chronological order. There were sketches, drawings of interiors, of the satellite against the backdrop of space, detailed plans for structural work, pages of mathematics. . . .

He frowned at a cartoon. It showed a cowboy astraddle a moon lander with its four legs extended stiffly; like a bucking horse, he realized, and his frown changed to a grin. The cowboy was throwing a lasso that would land around a mountain of a meteor streaked with bands of different colors. It looked like spumoni ice cream. It was not his father's work, he knew. That kind of humor had been beyond him. He put it aside with the notebooks that had been torn— there were three by then. There were more cartoons, and he realized they had been done by Daniel Brighton. There were pages of small precise writing, also Daniel Brighton's, signed by him, or initialed by him. Letters? But they were not written like letters, rather like the notes a man makes to himself.

He put all the Brighton material aside; the stack grew as the afternoon wore on. There was a timetable in Brighton's writing, with his caricatures. The satellite at year one, a hazy, smudged blur in space. Year two, the beginning of a curve of metal. Year three, four . . . up to eight, when it was finished. Year nine showed a cable from earth to the space station, cable cars, crowded with people, some of them carrying picnic baskets. And above the station, aimed away from it toward space, there was a heavy black arrow. Brighton's dream.

Why had his father kept Brighton's papers? Why were they there? Cluny had been kneeling on the floor, all the papers in some sort of order finally, when the question occurred to him.

The Brighton stack was two inches high at least. There were the same kinds of drawings his father had done, the same kinds of sketches of the station in various stages, drafts of speeches, heavily rewritten, whole passages x'd out, the same kinds of cryptic notes about people identified only by initials.

The same initials, he realized, and began to paw through one of his father's stacks. He stopped, and leaned back on his heels. It hadn't been just one time, but repeatedly. *Talked to S—shithead! R says no, he'll come around   C has to be cut off at the pass*

He got up then. Another day had passed, more meals had been eaten, he had taken a walk, probably had talked to his mother, although he no longer could remember a word either had said.

He left the attic. It was twelve, but he knew he could not read anything else, see anything else. Brighton had been an artist, or could have been if he had chosen it, had trained even a little for it. His papers were full of doodles, decorations, complex geometrical designs. Some were so heavily covered it was hard to make out the actual content of them. They were a man's private papers, not meant for anyone else. Why were they in his father's stuff?

He walked for an hour, until a slight rain started and mosquitoes began to buzz him. At least here there was no drought. The rain was warm and soft; everything in this area was lush, green, possibly too wet. He passed a new development that had been started only two weeks ago, his mother had told him, and would be occupied in another week or so. It grew as fast as the amanitas under the live oak tree in his mother's backyard. Ugly, functional. Outside town, a dozen miles away, were the beginnings of a Newtown, hastily planned, hastily built, or so they all seemed, those Newtowns. He thought, with painful intensity, of the beautiful Lina Davies. Lina Davies, he repeated to himself. He thought of her all the way home, and while he lay trying to dull his mind enough to sleep. He wanted to dream of her, to possess her in his dreams. He dreamed of his father and the satellite and cowboys who blasted space monsters again and again with six-shooters.

Toward the end both men had become cynical, pessimistic, despairing. They had known for months, possibly years, that the station would not be completed. His father had written many speeches about it: one was an especially impassioned plea for understanding of what it meant, why it had to be finished. At the end of the speech, never delivered, he had written by hand, his writing bold and heavy in comparison with the neat typescript: "If I can't go why should I give a goddamn? My day is past." He had drawn a line through the words. On the back of the page he had written, with a different pen, finer, lighter ink: "Dan can do it."

Cluny found the notebook that had been used to prepare the speech. His father always had worked first in a notebook, then on to typescript from the handwritten ideas. The original speech in the notebook was even more passionate. There was a list of the men who had died, the kinds of accidents that had killed them. He had written about the rumors of sabotage, then at great length proved it could not have been the act of any one person, or nation, or group. A very heavy line had run across the page then, as if he had thought of something that had made him jerk his pen. Or had been interrupted, Cluny amended. Or something else had happened. He stared at the line, shook his head, went on reading. But the rest was different. There were false starts, crossed-out sections, a few pedestrian restatements of what he had already written eloquently.

The next page was torn out. Bits of paper still clung to the spiral. The speech was not continued in the notebook.

At lunch his mother said, "What are you finding out?"

He glanced at her, then looked closer. She was pale, and there was a slight tic in her cheek that he had never seen before.

"There is something, isn't there?" she said. "I always knew there was something he was afraid to have anyone discover. That's why he was so desperate about the papers."

Cluny shook his head. "Nothing you didn't already know."

His mother had not bothered to prepare a setting for herself, but had sipped tea while he ate the salad and sandwich she had made. She looked as if she had been sleeping no better than he.

"What do you think I'll find?"

"That they did it," she said in a rush. "Your father and Dan Brighton. They sabotaged the station when they realized the economy would not support it to completion. They were afraid the Russians would finish it alone, claim it, if we dropped out. So they sabotaged it."

Cluny almost laughed. "No. That's not in the papers, thank God!"

She did not respond to his relief. "It is, or it was. He hurried to Dan's house that night, before anyone else could get there, and he collected folders, notebooks, I don't know what all. He tore up and burned things for a long time. He would have finished them all, even his own, but there was an interruption, and he had to go to Washington, and there was no time. I put them away. It's there."

Cluny stared at her.

"They had been such good friends, right up till the end," she said. "Then Dan was supposed to do something big, maybe even blow it up. I don't know what. Instead he ran away, ran away to outer space. He got what he had always wanted, and your father never forgave him for it. He died hating Dan Brighton the way you hate a traitor, a betrayer. He never got over it. He blamed himself for pushing Dan to it, but he never forgave him."

Cluny stood up and shoved his chair back. Stiffly he hurried from the room, left her sitting at the table holding her teacup. In the attic he stared at the many stacks he had been making. When he moved again, his motions were mechanical. He had been caught up in the dream of the two men; now he was in their nightmare. There was nothing that could possibly confirm his mother's suspicions, he knew. Nothing.

He had put all the Brighton stuff in a box after glancing at it; now he began to read it thoroughly. By that night he was feeling uneasy, without anything to peg his unease to. Brighton had been too sharp, too intelligent and clever. An undertone of mockery, and self-mockery, underlay many of his notes. All along he had been several steps ahead of Colonel Cluny; that had become apparent early in the reading.

Cluny stopped at a handwritten page of notes for a speech; the page was heavily decorated with doodles—pyramids, stars, comets with corkscrew tails. There were bears, he realized, studying the intricate lines, and over and over, worked into various designs, the letters *S.M.K.* There were tracks made by one of the bears with the letters *US* on the left paw print, *SR* on the right. The entire body of the animal made a large *M.K.* The Russian bear, Cluny thought with a start. Of course. M.K.; the Russian bear. His father had referred to him also. M. Klyuchevsky. He searched for the list of accidents and dates. Klyuchevsky had been killed a week before Brighton's last trip to the station.

Not conclusive, he told himself angrily. Without his mother's accusation, he never would have noticed any of this because it was so innocuous. But—he found himself following the thought—what if Brighton had

been mixed up with Russia in some way? What if his
father had found out? He would have stopped him, not
ordered him back to Alpha. It made no sense any other
way. Unless, he thought, Brighton had agreed to do
something, or undo something, in exchange for silence.
Then, if Brighton had chosen to flee where no one
could pursue, that might explain his father's feeling of
betrayal and bitterness, his overload of guilt at the end.

He kept telling himself he did not believe any of this,
and all the time he was trying to convince himself of his
own disbelief, he kept searching. His father had burned
too many of Brighton's papers; nothing could be
proved now, nothing disproved. He did not want
Murray going through this same procedure he was
undergoing, however; there had been no good reason
for his father to have squirreled away Brighton's
papers. Their presence here could only raise questions
that could not be answered.

Two days later he took a large box of material
downstairs. "I'm getting some of this stuff out of the
house," he said to his mother. "I won't destroy it. It'll
be safe." She nodded. "I'll be away for a week or so,
and then I'll come back and bring Murray with me. Is
that all right?"

Again she nodded. Her eyes were fastened on the
box.

"It's okay, Mother. You can rest your mind. He was
a hero, not a destroyer. That's how he lived and that's
how he was. I'll see you in a week or ten days."

In Boston he rented a safety-deposit box and put his
burden in it. When he went outside again, the streets
were thick with people; he had not even noticed them
before. Now he thought he never had seen so many
people, and felt almost smothered before he began to
move with the surging mass. He headed for the office
building that housed the American Refugee Society.
This time, he thought, this time . . . In his pocket his
fingers kept closing over the key to the safety-deposit
box until he realized what he was doing and released it,

only to have his fingers grope for it, cling to it again and again.

Sid and Murray were waiting for him; he had told them he would be back sometime today, or tonight, but now he rushed the opposite way, trying to drive out the thoughts of Murray pacing his rat-infested room, or Sid chewing his nails at school. "A few more hours," he muttered. He felt a great resentment toward them, as if they were getting in his way physically, imposing barriers between him and Lina Davies.

4 "They told me someone had been looking for me," Lina Davies said when he intercepted her on her way from the office. "They said you were very tall and handsome. I don't usually meet men so much taller than I am. Did you know it's a myth that men average several inches taller than women? It's just that custom has always made a tall man want a woman short enough to show him to advantage."

"Will you have lunch with me?"

"Why?"

"I want to talk to you, get to know you. I've seen you before." She was regarding him as if she did not remember him from the restaurant. He was glad.

"I can't. I have to collect ration coupons. Have you contributed yet?"

He nodded, afraid that if he repeated he had none

left, she would remember seeing him drunk, with drunken friends. "Can I come with you, then?"

"That would be nice. You can help. I'll ask the businessmen and you ask the women. Women usually won't give me a thing, would you believe that? They look more like they would like to see me go to a camp to live, or like they're afraid I'm really after their men. It's a strange thing about women, some of them, how jealous and petty they can be. . . ."

She talked on and on, easily, expecting no response most of the time, cuing him neatly when she did want affirmation or encouragement. He watched her; today she was dressed in a pale green sari that left one shoulder bare. She was even more beautiful than he had remembered, her skin more perfect, if that was possible. In the sunlight, in the sultry air that made other women sweat, and their make-up look like house paint, she was lovely and fresh. Her eyes were greener than he had realized. Sea green, aquamarine green. She talked and he watched her and mused about her skin, her hair, which would feel silky. . . .

". . . and just stand there and wait. That's all you have to do. Most of them feel so guilty that they'll hand them over to get rid of you. Here we go." She flashed a smile and left him inside the doorway of an expensive restaurant that catered to bankers and stockbrokers and their clients. He realized he was blocking the luncheon traffic and moved, not toward any of the tables, but to one side, where he could continue to watch her approach the tables, speak, receive the coupons and leave, as majestically as a queen collecting overdue taxes.

She looked at him, frowned, and motioned for him to start collecting, and he moved very awkwardly toward a table where three women were eating salads. They looked up expectantly as he drew near and stopped. He felt foolish.

"I'm sorry to bother you," he began. "You see, I'm

helping out with the committee for the . . ." He could
not remember the name of the organization, and he
never had heard anyone refer to them as refugees until
Lina had done so. "The Newtowns," he blurted. "They
need more water and stuff. . . ." It was no use. The
women were now looking past him, for a waiter or a
bouncer or a cop or something. He tried to smile
reassuringly and backed away; he bumped into a waiter
who had caught the signal. "Excuse me. Excuse me,
just leaving. Sorry to have bothered you." He turned
and fled.

"I never eat when I'm collecting," Lina said, back on
the sidewalk. "It makes me feel virtuous somehow,
almost holy. The people I collect from seem to
understand that. Don't worry if those women didn't
give you any coupons. I wouldn't have got any from
them either. But you asked them the wrong way. You
were begging, and that doesn't work. . . ."

They walked, she talked, and they went into three
more restaurants, and then the luncheon rush was over.
"All through until dinner. I'll have to take these to the
office, and then we can go to your apartment for a
snack and some rest."

He thought his legs would buckle, and he had an
immediate erection at her words. In his apartment, she
began to undress as soon as the door was closed. "I'm
five ten and a half," she said, "and most men seem
afraid of such a tall woman, as if I'm a threat to their
masculinity or something."

Cluny jerked off his clothes feverishly, afraid she
would change her mind, remember something else she
had to do, or simply vanish before his eyes. She was
more beautiful than ever naked. He never had seen a
woman like her before.

She laughed at his erection. "Look what your mind's
been doing to your body. Did you know stimulation
comes from your own mind, not from external causes?"

He dragged her down onto the bed and stopped her
chatter with his mouth and she moved under him and

suddenly it was over. She sighed and when he rolled off her, she slipped from the bed and went to the bathroom. She returned a few minutes later, smiling happily. "You use my shampoo! And my toothpaste! Isn't that a coincidence!"

Cluny knew he didn't care. She could talk forever, say absolutely nothing for the rest of her life in a nonstop monologue, and it would not matter a bit. He watched her move, the play of long muscles in her thighs, the sharp curve of her breast, the way the light caught her pubic hair and glistened. . . . It didn't matter what she said, when, how often.

"Don't dress yet," he said, when she reached for the sari. "Let me look at you."

"Silly. You act like you've never seen a naked woman in your life. All eyes. If you could only see your eyes . . ."

"Tell me about you," he said. "Where you came from, how you got mixed up with the committee, where you went to school, everything."

She laughed and sat down tailor fashion on the foot of the bed. "You have to do something for others, don't you agree? I was in school, and I heard a lecture about the Newtowns, how awful they are, and all that. And how the children hardly ever have enough water to drink, and stay dirty all the time. I gave the man all my own coupons that day and promised to help for as long as they need someone. Only I couldn't start right away because I was working for Senator Dvorak—his reelection, you know? He lost, but we worked awfully hard and even he said he never had seen such hard workers. . . ."

Cluny reached for her, and she continued to talk as he petted and stroked her silky skin.

Later when she went to the bathroom, she took her clothes with her and came out fully dressed, as clean and fresh looking as dawn.

"Now, no more," she said sternly. "Two a day is my absolute limit. I think it's harmful to overindulge in anything, don't you? I mean anything at all. Are you hungry now? Do you have anything here to eat? This is a nice little apartment, so cozy and masculine. I think men's apartments should definitely reflect their tastes, be masculine and all. . . ."

She found cheese and bread and onions and made a sandwich, talking as she put them all together. Talking as she ate. Cluny could only watch her and marvel at her beauty even as she chewed. He never had seen anyone who looked beautiful eating. He told her that and she laughed and shook her head, wagged her finger at him.

"I said no more, didn't you hear me?"

He nodded meekly. "Will you come back tonight? After you collect coupons from the dinner crowd?"

"I don't know," she said, frowning. "You aren't getting up now, are you? Well, you really aren't very good at it. Not everyone has the knack. It's a gift, I think, don't you? To make people want to help and all?" The frown vanished and she laughed. "I'll tell you what. If you see me, that means I decided to come back, and if you don't, that means I didn't. If I come back, probably in a little while I'll be very hungry. Do you have any money? Can you afford to take me to dinner, or will I have to pay my own? I mean, I could, but then I would want a pretty cheap, but good, place because I'm already over this month's allowance, and Daddy will be furious as it is. . . ."

Murray had a room across town in a tenement that was overstuffed with Westerners who had come to Boston to escape the drought. He had one chair, a mattress on the floor, and a dozen cartons of books. A hot plate was on a wooden box, a few pans inside the box. He claimed a dozen rats were included with each room at no extra cost.

"Sid's coming in half an hour," Murray said, motioning toward the chair. He sprawled on the mattress.

"Want to wait for him, or tell me first and then repeat it?"

"I . . . It's there, just like Sid thought it would be. Enough to start with anyway. Do you believe it'll work? Really believe we can do anything?"

"Christ, I don't know. Sometimes I do, then I stumble over people in the halls, up and down the stairs, none of them working, just hanging on with coupons and scrip, and I know there's no way anyone's going to finance it again. But I don't know." A door slammed and a child began to scream piercingly. "It has to work," he said then, grimly.

Murray listened to the screaming child and thought, Again. He had started in a building like this, had lived in buildings like this for years and finally had escaped, only to be forced back again. He remembered the pallets on floors where roaches and rats ran freely, the unending nights of fear because this time his father might actually kill his mother. And later the nights of joining the cursing, wild melees. Lying drunk in hallways, a kid, fourteen, fifteen, bombed out of his mind . . . He had escaped once, far enough, he had thought, never to come back. But, he told himself sharply, he had done it; he could do it again. Only he needed Alpha, or something as big as Alpha. Escape had to be more complete, farther, with no possible way down again.

He looked at Cluny, a faint look of distaste on his face as the child's screams continued without letup. Cluny had had it easy, he knew. Things had appeared before him when he needed them, whatever he needed. Never had to fight for anything in his life, never had to grub, sneak a book inside his jacket, go without anything to buy the books that spelled out escape, no matter what the subject. Never made a hard choice in his life, he thought, and there was no hatred or jealousy in him. He accepted that that was how it was: Cluny had been born over there, he had been born here; so be it. He liked Cluny and recognized that his worst fault was ignorance, innocence, and he was hardly to be blamed for circumstances. But Cluny could be used, he also knew. Murray had spent his entire lifetime learning how to use people, to get them to do what he wanted and required from them. Cluny never had had any need to learn that particular lesson, had no defenses against it. He would play Cluny with all the TLC he could muster, he knew, because Cluny spelled escape again. He was likable, good looking, tall, everything that Murray was not, everything that Sid was not. And he had a magic name. He was his father's son, with a name that would automatically open doors. He would be good at the lunches, the hearings, the meetings; he would know how to behave with small groups at clubs, at expensive restaurants, in exclusive bars. Puppets, Murray thought; they were all puppets, being pulled this way and that by forces they could dimly perceive and never completely understand. He knew his past goaded him, that he in turn would spur on Sid and Cluny, who would act upon others. . . . Puppets all.

Sid arrived in much less than the half hour he had allowed. He was impatient, almost rude in his brusqueness. "What did you find? What kind of stuff?"

"His personal dreams, plans, hopes. Ways to make it pay off at the various stages of completion, to keep the taxpayers happy and make news, that sort of stuff. Detailed plans for each department, equipment lists, maximum and minimum . . ."

"How much of it's done now? Is there enough finished to be able to start using it without much more construction?"

"Yes. That's what he was pushing all the last year when they were deciding to close it down. About a fifth of it was structurally finished—not completed inside, not equipped, but ready to furnish. Opposite that section the shell is finished enough to start a slow spin."

Sid raised his head and yelled a long strident cry of

jubilation. "We'll do it then! That was what we had to know! I knew the papers had lied about it! The government lied about it! Everyone lied. Your father wasn't even called to testify at the hearings! They were so goddamn scared of the election that year. And for what? They lost anyway. Then that goddamn fascist Friedericks! Sat in the White House for eight years, afraid to go take a leak! His crew said it would take billions more and it would be years before anyone could start using the facilities! They funked out. Build canals, hire cloud seeders, build those goddam Newtowns. Pull the sheet over your head and hole up! Too scared to see past their noses any more. I knew it!" He took a deep breath and stopped for a few seconds. "Okay, now we know. When can you and Murray get back down there, dig out the facts, figures, everything?"

"Next week; a week from Sunday."

"Jesus H. Christ! Why the delay?"

"My mother has things she has to do before we set up shop there. It's her house, you know."

"All right; all right. Sorry I snapped. Excited, all that. That's okay. It'll give us time to brainstorm this from every angle we can think of, make lists of things we need to dig out, ask questions, do a lot of preliminary work. It'll make the rest go faster in the long run."

"I won't have much time," Cluny mumbled, not looking at either of them. "There's something I have to take care of. You and Murray can do that, can't you?"

Sid remained silent, and when Cluny finally glanced at him, he was scowling. "Woman?"

Cluny nodded.

"Is it something you'll be able to take care of during the next week? It won't hang you up longer than that?"

"No way," Cluny said. "A week from Sunday we'll be on the train, everything here finished." His hands clenched painfully as he spoke.

"Goddamn it!" Murray snapped. "This isn't something you're going to be able to do now and then when you have a spare minute or two."

"I said a week from Sunday!" Cluny muttered.

After he had gone Murray cursed heartily. "Why now? I'd like to drive a truck over her, whoever she is!"

"Take it easy. Simmer down. So he wants a woman. He'll get over it." Sid stretched. "Or he'll settle in with her or something. Terri's not getting in the way, is she?"

"That's different," Murray said. He knew it was different, but he could not have said why he knew it, or how it was different.

The Saturday before his deadline, Cluny asked Lina to marry him.

"Everyone always want to marry me," she said, laughing at him. "But they don't really mean it. They really mean will I live with them for a couple of weeks or months, until they get tired of me, I guess. Do you really mean it, Cluny?"

"More than I've ever meant anything in my life."

"And there's a Newtown near your place in the South? I probably could get a job there, couldn't I? Teaching little kids things. Little kids like me; they'll listen to me and do what I tell them. Someday I'd like about three or four children of my own, but not very soon, because I think a person should have more experiences, be more mature when they become parents, just so they will understand—"

"Will you marry me?"

"Oh, I thought I told you. Yes, you silly thing. I think it's because you're so tall. You must be the tallest man I ever met who liked me, really liked me. Most of them like shorter women. Have you ever noticed how it's the little short men who love tall women? I think it's . . ."

Cluny stopped listening and instead watched the way the light ran up and down her cheek when she spoke, the way her beautiful green eyes shadowed and light-ened as her gaze rested on him, then darted away, came back, examined the ceiling. . . . There had never been another woman like her, he knew, no one as beautiful, as desirable, as thrilling to love. It had to be marriage; nothing else would satisfy him. Marriage in the Biblical sense, where a man possesses a woman wholly, completely, forever. He couldn't bear the thought of another man with her. No more, not ever again. She would be his alone, true to him, a goddess for him to adore and worship and love forever. To see her for the first time each day was to suffer again the agony of dread that she would go away. Touching her made him ache with a desire that he never had believed in before. Having her was prelude only, always prelude. There was nothing he could not do now, he thought suddenly. He had conquered a goddess, made her his own, and there was no other difficulty in life that could affect him at all, not after this. He knew he was undeserving of such luck, and that he had to prove himself in order to keep it. A goddess needed a god at her side, a world-changer, someone who could shape the world just as surely as she was shaping him, changing him. Alpha, he thought. He would give her Alpha, and then the stars themselves.

He knew he could never tell anyone the thoughts that raced through his head that night, but he had made a pledge. Fate had arranged for him to be at that restaurant on that one night; the only time in his life he had been there, fate had sent her there too. Everything seemed as inevitable as the tides, as irresistible as aging. For a moment he felt a wash of fear at the idea of anonymous fate reaching down through infinity to touch him, to arrange his life, but the moment passed quickly. It had happened against odds that would make statisticians squirm, and now that it had happened, there was only the one direction to follow, the one path to take, the one goal to reach. And he was on the path.

For the first time he began to think seriously of Alpha, visualizing it as his father had seen it years ago: a beautiful gleaming wheel in space, the first wheel of the chariot to carry them to the stars.

5 For four hours a day, five days a week, Jean worked for Dr. Leopold Arkins in the Linguistics Department. She also taught two freshmen classes and one sophomore class in linguistics, and although she was a Ph.D. candidate, she knew she would not make it that year. Perhaps never, she thought, squaring her shoulders, ready to face Leo Arkins for the first time since his dismal reception at a national conference in Atlanta. Corinne Duland had brought copies of the devastating papers half a dozen different linguists had presented, virtually destroying his work, with innuendo and implication where there were no facts and counterresearch.

He would in turn flagellate her, Jean knew. Leo Arkins was a small man with a paunch; he had masses of black hair that covered his forehead down to his eyes, and a congenital deformity that caused him to limp slightly and had arrested the growth of his left hand when he was a child. He had no family, no interests in anything other than his work. He detested weakness, would allow himself none at all, and found it in everyone else.

She entered the language laboratory and didn't realize how tense she had become until she saw that the room was empty; a long sigh of relief brought relaxation to her diaphragm. The door to his office was closed, as was the door to the reception room. Quietly, hoping he would not hear her during the next four hours, she approached the desk that had a computer terminal, sat down and prepared to work. The room was small, with only two desks—one with a typewriter, the other with the terminal—and one extra chair. Arkins's secretary had quit recently, the third one to come and leave since Jean's arrival two years ago, and this one had not been replaced. Jean often worked through without seeing anyone at all. She turned on the terminal, identified herself—Brighton, slave laborer for Arkins, was how she privately decoded the series of numbers and letters she used; the computer acknowledged her right to access. She typed in the directions and the printout picked up where it had left off the day before.

While the printout continued to accumulate in a stack of papers, all precisely folded, all with numbered word combinations from top to bottom, Jean withdrew another stack of similar printouts and began checking the word groups. Some were clearly nonsense, grammatically correct but with no intelligible content. Others had content, but were ungrammatical or irrelevant: *wheat takes me, I take home dock, I am to there, he is dock here, food brings home* . . .

Every once in a while she circled a sentence and typed its number on the input keyboard. After a time her eyes began to burn and she had to stand up and move around the tiny office for a few seconds. The computer kept sending out phrases, folding the papers, apparently able to go on forever with the few dozen words in this program. She sat down again and read the next collection of words: *grain gets to me,* and the next and next. *I have no food to take home.* She felt a mild flicker of interest and circled the sentence, and when she typed in the number this time she added another key, signaling that this one took priority.

"Why do you give some of them higher priority than

others?" Arkins had demanded early in the first months that she had worked for him.

"I don't know. You told me to if it seemed warranted."

"Yes, but why those particular sentences? They are no more correct than others in the series. Why those?"

"I don't know," she had repeated helplessly. "Should I stop doing it?"

"No! You idiot! I want the reasons for your choices! We must program them into it. Think, woman! Why?"

But she was not a woman to him, not then, not now. She was a part of the complex machinery that finally was proving his theories that any language, even the most difficult coded languages, could be understood and decoded by a computer if only it was programmed correctly. The universality of unconscious grammars would yield to the computer, he argued. And during the last two years he had been able to show the first evidence of corroborative proof.

Suddenly she knew he was in his office, without being aware of having heard the hall door open and close, or any other sound from the room behind her. She closed her eyes briefly, then went on down the list of words, some of them making sentences, others not, and tried to ignore the definite noise he was making now. Something slammed, something else fell to the floor, a chair thumped against the wall. Her door was flung open.

"Brighton, haven't you got it yet? What have you been doing? Didn't you even bother to come in while I was away? Do I need a policeman to keep watch?"

His voice was high-pitched, shrill at times, and his words were all clipped and hard, spat out in a way that made him sound furious even when he was in a good mood.

"Still working on it," she said, keeping her voice as neutral as she could.

"Still working on it," he repeated in perfect mimicry. He was very red-faced and his tiny left hand clutched his coat in a white-knuckled grip; veins stood out on the back of it. Jean was fascinated and repelled by that small hand. Sometimes when he was having a tantrum his deformed hand seemed to lead a life of its own, trembling, then clenching, flexing its fingers. . . . Sometimes, when he was in a jovial mood, the hand patted his chest, rubbed up and down his coat lapel, or worked with a button. He appeared unaware of it. Sometimes Jean had the feeling that the grotesque hand was reaching for her. She had had nightmares about that hand.

"You will plan to work until six until further notice," Arkins screeched at her. "I will have this finished before April! You hear me? Before April! And if we have to work until seven, or eight, or however long it takes every day, we'll do it!"

"You know I have three classes a week," Jean protested, but she knew it was usless. And there was no one over him to whom she could complain. He was the department head.

"Then teach them, you simpering idiot! Until six! Starting now, today. This is to be completed in the next three months!"

He wheeled about and left, slamming the door behind him. For a moment Jean didn't move, then she went to the other desk to call home, to tell Walter she would be late.

She could quit, she thought, walking home in a freezing rain. She could go to a different school and get her Ph.D. and laugh in his face. She could find a job teaching at a junior college or high school, something. She forced herself to stop thinking of alternatives that were clearly impossible. She hated herself for playing fantasy games when her frustration overwhelmed her and her helplessness became almost a physical burden. There was no school where she would be accepted, especially if she simply quit working under Arkins, who was the authority in the field. And there were no jobs, none at all. She repeated this to herself twice, forming the words, as if to make certain all of her mind got the message she was sending it.

She had studied under Arkins, doing her work for her master's degree here at Michigan State University. He had required a paper from his dozen students that year, giving detailed plans on how to go about developing a computer program to decipher coded messages. Jean had suggested starting with children, ten-year-olds, and recording their conversations for a period of time, feeding the words into the computer and using them as the parameters of the probable message, thus limiting the possibilities, which were infinite without some such limitations imposed from outside.

"Why children?" he had demanded.

"Because they tend to use uncomplicated grammatical constructions."

"Set it up!"

"But I haven't finished my thesis yet. When?" It was April, her thesis was due in May.

"Give me the damn thesis. It's finished enough. I'm going to be your Ph.D. adviser, and you'll be a TA, working under me, in my department."

"I have no money to go on. I was going to quit this year."

He had looked at her for a moment, then said with fury that he did not even try to control, "You will do exactly what I tell you, do you hear? Quit! To work in a restaurant? To have a baby? Don't you even know what I'm offering you, you miserable little woman?"

She had hated him then, she hated him now, but because she did know what alternatives she had, she did the work that she did not believe in, that she thought was futile and a dead end. He snapped his whip and she cringed and the work got done, results started to appear, and she hated him more than ever.

And every time she felt she could not bear it another day, she forced herself to recall Mesa and the last time she had gone there, to her mother's house.

Jean had watched the riots on television in the dorm lounge. Mexicans, Chicanos, Indians, whites . . . They burned down the municipal buildings, the courthouse, the city hall; they blockaded the streets with flaming junk cars and barrels and packing crates, and when the fire engines came they doused them with gas and fired them.

Mesa had escaped the mobs, the announcer said, and refugees were streaming into that suburb, fleeing downtown Phoenix. They were bringing violence with them, he had gone on to say, demanding shelter, demanding water, demanding the Mesa police join forces with the downtown police, who were clearly unable to control the mobs. The National Guard . . .

Jean had stood up numbly. "Mother," she whispered.

The announcer was recounting the growing emergency, which had started when the government had curtailed water service to fifty percent of the metropolitan area, urging the people to store their furniture, leave the area until further notice. As the dwindling water supplies made further curtailments necessary, the first mob action had taken place in the ghettos of the city, where the Mexican-Americans took to the street. . . .

There was no phone service to Phoenix that night or the next day, and on the day after that Jean caught a plane and went to force her mother to leave her house on the edge of Mesa, Arizona.

Few people were going to Arizona, many were leaving. The roads were filled with cars, trucks, army transports. It looked like a disaster scene. The city was quiet now, almost normal, except for a low-hanging cloud of smoke. Jean caught a bus from Phoenix to Mesa. The traffic was bumper to bumper, all heading away from Phoenix. Nowhere was there anything green; every lawn had turned back into desert, every park was barren, every palm tree lifeless, every shrub and bush from every exotic land was dead. Only cactus plants looked untouched. They had seen it all before, they seemed to say.

Jean had to walk six blocks from the bus stop to her mother's house. Most of the houses were vacant, windows boarded up, sand drifted around the doors and foundations. The subdivision streets were buried in sand. The houses in this subdivision all cost one hundred thousand and up, her stepfather had told her, and added that his was on the up side. His name was Teddy Caro, and he was president of the Caro Realty Company; he had left the area nearly a year ago, when electricity was first rationed.

Jean stared at the expensive house, hating it, hating the idea of it, hating her mother for being here, for having married Teddy Caro, a chiseler who had become rich selling desert land to wide-eyed Easterners who wanted a bit of sunshine and freedom.

The house had twelve rooms, a three-car attached garage, a swimming pool with a plastic cover strong enough to park a bus on, and it was all hideous, garish, with fake bricks on the house front, and fake herons in the sand, which had been a lush velvety lawn that had required a truck load of water to be dumped on it three days a week to stay green.

She found her mother in the living room, staring at the television set, which had not worked for months. The house was as hot and airless as a sunbaked tomb; there was no water, no electricity, nothing at all to drink, although there were empty liquor bottles in the kitchen, dining room, Stephanie's bedroom, the living room. Stephanie looked at Jean without recognition, and then turned her gaze back to the television set. She was gaunt, hollow-eyed, and feverish.

"Mother, get up. We're leaving now. Come on, you have to get dressed."

Stephanie shook her head, frowning, as if she were being interrupted while watching her favorite show. Jean sank down on the floor by her and put her head on the couch, not weeping although she knew there were tears to be shed.

"Why are you doing this?" she whispered. "Why, Mother?"

Stephanie might not have heard; she made no response. Finally Jean had to haul her up from the couch, drag, shove, and push her into the bedroom, where she dressed her as if she were a child, and then they started walking toward the bus line. "I'll put you in a hotel," she said, not to inform her mother, she knew, but to break the terrifying silence that pressed in on her just as the heat and sun pressed against her.

"I'll arrange for storage for your furniture and pack your things for you. But where will you go? Where's Teddy?"

Stephanie walked obediently, and never spoke all that day or the next or the next, while Jean made the arrangements for her possessions. When she did break her silence, it was to scream, "You've stolen everything I have! Where are my jewels? Where's my mink coat? What have you done with my cars?" She screamed until the hotel manager sent a doctor to the room and he administered a sedative.

"She's very ill," he said to Jean afterward. "She needs professional care."

Jean looked out the window at the city, still burning in places because there was no water to spare for fire in that section of town, and suddenly she began to weep. Not for her mother, not for anything personal at all, she thought, but she could not stop. She was weeping for the city, for all of them down there, for everything and everybody. She was weeping because no matter where she turned she could see no hope that it wouldn't all burn just as it was burning here.

Behind her the doctor was talking about her mother and drugs and alcohol and a slow process of self-destruction, and Jean could not respond because she was weeping too hard.

All those people driven out of Arizona, Utah, Nevada, California, Oregon . . . They had all been as desperate as she, more desperate. Since that day she had had four years of relative security. She knew she was very, very lucky.

The rain stung where it hit her face; it was blowing almost horizontally. At least it kept the thugs off the street, she thought, huddling down in her coat, ducking her head as low as she could and still see at all. The university grounds were nearly deserted; it was dinnertime in the dorms, and the night classes had not started yet. Across a wide ice-glazed lawn she could see all of Mac Hall, and King Hall, both lit up from top to bottom. The refugees from the Western cities had arrived that week, had taken residence there, and already they were making a difference on campus. Every day now there were strangers on the walks, eyeing the professors and students alike with bitterness and hatred. Some of them crowded into classes, sat on the floor in the backs of the rooms or lounged against the walls, muttering at times, holding private conversations. Three young women had sauntered into Jean's class on Monday, had listened for ten minutes to her lecture on transformational grammar; then, with loud obscene remarks, they had left again.

Jean had been one of the group to campaign for the opening of all public buildings to the refugees. In principle she still knew it was the only thing that could be done as more and more people were forced from their homes and farms. She still argued their cause when it came up, as it inevitably did at any social gathering, but she admitted it was shitty in practice, if noble in intent.

At least, she thought, turning a corner into the full blast of frigid wind, she did have a job that paid enough for her to live on, with a possibility of a future if she could endure the present.

The apartment complex was on campus; recently a steel door had been added, and all the windows were now barred. A security guard greeted her and continued his rounds as she fitted her key into the door. She walked up the three flights of stairs to the apartment she shared with Walter Hasek and as she climbed she felt her day sliding off her shoulders, her brief encounter with Arkins fading from memory; the sight of the steel door and bars and the thought of refugees waiting in the shadows to gang rape her all slipped from her mind as if they were all of no consequence. Within those three rooms there was no icy rain, no paranoid Arkins, no problem.

Walter didn't get up when she entered the apartment. He was grading papers at his desk, and simply smiled at her. It was the smile that she always thought of when she brought him to mind at work, or walking home, or in class, wherever she happened to be. His mouth did not curve upward, but widened until it seemed to be a line separating his face into two sections. His black hair was so curly it almost frizzed, and he kept it very short; his eyes were as black as obsidian, his features as regular and perfect as those of Michelangelo's David. He was nearly fifty, she kept reminding herself; he had been married twice, and had lived with neither wife more than a few years, but had not lived alone since his adolescence. She was one of an incalculable number of women in his life. But she was the only one now, she always added almost smugly.

She went to him and kissed his head above his ear. He was reading an essay answer and she didn't interrupt, but went on by him to hang up her wet coat and take off her boots.

Dinner was simmering in a pot, coffee was made—their one luxury—the apartment was warm and fragrant with good food smells. She poured coffee and wrapped both hands around the mug, and then sat down on the couch to watch him and wait for him to finish.

The apartment was very small, the kitchen not big enough for two people to enter at the same time; the bedroom was hardly bigger, and the living room had the couch, his desk, a card table, three straight chairs, and Walter's music system with its components all over. There were books everywhere—on makeshift shelves, on real shelves that were from floor to ceiling on one wall, on every flat surface. There was a brown oval rug on the floor, a gift from Jean's former roommate, who had lost her job and moved back to Chicago. The rug had been a gift to her, she had said, and it seemed it would go with the apartment forever since it was too hideous to move anywhere else, and it was warmer than the bare floor. There were two high windows in the living room, where Jean had hung bright woven tapestries from Paraguay.

"Let's eat," Walter said then, and left his work spread out on the desk. He went to stir the stew, and she set the card table, and soon they sat across from each other, eating.

"Old tyrant his usual sweet self?" he asked, pouring more coffee for both of them.

"You know it. They slaughtered him in Atlanta; he's in a foul mood."

"He'll get over it. He always does. He knows exactly how far he can push you. . . . I'm going to start regular group counseling on Thursday nights. The new people."

She groaned in sympathy. They had known it was coming, but had kept hoping someone else would get the first shift. The new people desperately needed counseling, and again it was fine in principle, and shitty to be caught up in it.

They finished the stew, talking easily about their day, about the next day, the coming weekend. Then Walter returned to his paper work, and she did the dishes, since he had cooked. She cleared the table and got out her own work and they were both quiet until nearly twelve. She finished first and sat back, watching him go over the papers line by line, word by word. He was a better teacher than she, and she knew it. She had too little patience with her students. To her, language was filled with mystery and magic; words were the long-sought body/mind bridge. She wanted to force her students to grasp the wonder and the power of words when they were understood and used correctly. Her students seemed to want nothing more than a passing grade with as little effort as they could apply. Walter accepted that attitude without the fury she could not avoid. He allowed them to correct papers, which he always graded on content and grammar, and if his students returned the assignments completely corrected, he raised the grade to the next higher one. They might not learn a hell of a lot about psychology, he said, grinning, but they learned about commas and paragraphs and how to look up words in the dictionary. Jean thought it was all a waste of time. They learned nothing.

Walter looked up and smiled at her; he put down his pencil. "Let's go to bed."

She nodded. She went first to brush her teeth and get ready for bed, and then she shivered under the blanket, waiting for him. The heat was turned down to fifty-five at ten every night, and the bedroom, on the north side of the building, cooled off almost instantly.

Then Walter was beside her and it was all right again. He brought with him such warmth that she forgot the icy rain pattering against the window, forgot the cold apartment with its ugly furnishings, and the computer terminal spewing out endless reams of paper for her to check. . . . There was only the warmth of his body and his gentle hands that knew all the secrets of her body.

After they made love, Walter kissed her eyelids, and got out of bed again. "Go to sleep," he said softly. "I have a little more work to do."

He put on his robe, paused at the window, then said, "It's snowing."

Jean dragged the blanket off the bed and stood by him wrapped in it, watching the snow. The wind had died completely. The flakes were large, the kind that drift in any breeze, but now they were settling down like horizontal curtains falling endlessly.

Walter patted her bottom and left to finish his papers, and she stood looking at the snow. For a moment she imagined she was one of the flakes, starting to earth from an immeasurable distance away. At first, drifting downward, searching, she was herself, but distinct from all others, apart, eager for something, anything; then the quick descent in the upper layers, in a hurry to reach a goal, gathering particles as she raced downward, and finally braking with the realization that when the goal was reached, she no longer would exist, but would be one with everything else. What she had taken to be distinct, unique, was simply a variation; each was drifting slowly, inexorably, unable to stop, to reconsider, to pause and reflect on larger causes; each was destined to join the great white mass of everything. A violent shudder seized her and she hurried to bed and drew up her legs, trying to get warm again.

It was always like this, she thought suddenly. He knew her needs and never failed to satisfy her, but then he withdrew, left her alone again. He was . . . kind to her, she thought. Indulgent. When he should have been passionate, he was indulgent instead. She blinked hard.

They had met when she volunteered to be a subject in the research he was doing in depression. He had needed people in all stages of depression, he had announced in her psychology class, stopping in only long enough to ask for subjects. And he had needed people who had been depressed and were over it. All stages, pre, during, post, he had said, grinning.

He had not used her. During the first interview she had said, "I have no great talent, I know that. I'll get a degree and go into teaching linguistics. That's all I want. I want to be self-supporting, and I know I am competent, but not brilliant."

When he learned that her serious period of depression had been ten years before, he had told her gently and firmly that she would not do. Even then he had been kind and indulgent, she thought, hugging her knees to her body, seeking warmth.

She had not seen him again for nearly a year, and during that time she had earned her master's degree, and had begun to teach, and work for Leo Arkins.

The next time they had met, each had been heading for the administration building and they had reached the door together. She had remembered him vividly, and was surprised and delighted when he remembered her.

"Jean! How are you?"

"Good. How's your research coming along?"

"Never ends, you know how that goes."

They went in together, chatting, and when she turned toward the office, where she had an appointment with the housing administrator over problems in the dormitory, he had asked:

"Can I buy you a coffee later?"

Taken off guard, she had nodded silently. He was twice her age, established, tenured; she had not thought of him that way.

It had started so simply, she thought. Everything always started simply. Simple surfaces, complex depths. As long as she had been able to accept the surface as everything, life had been easy. Then she had learned that there was a surface tension to everything and everyone that was highly reflective, and it was safe to skim near it without disturbing it at all. All that one saw with the surface tension unbroken was what one chose to see, what could be understood, because it was the self reflected back. But once the surface had been stirred, one was drawn into the vortex of currents, cross-currents, riptides, and nothing was clear or simple or manageable.

For months it had remained simple with Walter. They had seen each other now and then, for drinks, for dinner a time or two, to go to a concert together. Then she had moved into this apartment, Janice had moved out, and suddenly nothing was simple any more. The first time Walter had made love to her, the surface tension had vanished, and she had been caught in the whirlpool ever since.

It was her fault, she knew, because she loved him too much, too foolishly, childishly. And she knew that he loved her. She tried to be more like him—calm, kind, thoughtful—but she could not keep it up. The adolescent romantic girl in her yearned for mystery, excitement, passion, and would not settle for indulgence and beef stew.

Her muscles ached now, and she straightened her legs, feeling the chill of the sheets, shivering again. Distantly the chimes in the chapel struck two.

Leo Arkins was less furious than he had been the day before. He paced the tiny office and gave a detailed summation of the conference. He recounted the speeches others had made, refuting them point by point.

"Of course," he said, "Ollifant was good, but he relies too heavily on statistics, mathematics. They all fall asleep as soon as he brings out his charts and figures. I fall alseep. And they hissed Murchison off the stage." He laughed maliciously. Murchison always managed to bring in his origin-of-speech theory no matter what the title of his paper was; he brought it in as a footnote if it did not fit anywhere in the text. They always hissed him off stage.

Jean finally had finished checking the sentences and sentence fragments offered up by her terminal. The hundred or so that she had singled out for further consideration were now being processed, and although it had been only a minute or two since she had started this new processing, already the paper was flowing out, folding itself, on and on. Now there were two lines of print: the sentence she had chosen, and the one the computer chose to follow it. Again, most of them were nonsense. She wanted to get back to it, to finish her day's work and leave. The snow was six inches deep, the sky leaden with low-hanging clouds threatening to add another six inches by morning.

She could smell coffee. Sometimes when Leo Arkins was in a very fine mood, he offered her a cup of his special brew. Now she sniffed it hungrily, but he ignored her, and continued to talk about the conference.

He was a genius, she reminded herself. He had made many breakthroughs in the field of linguistics; he was the acknowledged leader in the field. But he could also be wrong, she thought. No genius was right every single time; why should he expect to be?

". . . leave Wednesday evening. Thursday and Friday we'll work with Schmidt—"

"I'm sorry, Dr. Arkins. You said we?"

He glared at her. "We, my dear Brighton. You and I. We! Is this how you spend your time? Staring vacuously into space?" His voice rose to a screech, then with an obvious and very deliberate effort, he controlled it again. "I said I am taking you to Northwestern with me tomorrow, Wednesday. We shall return on Saturday morning. Did you hear me this time?"

She was shaking her head. "I can't. I have classes every morning. To do what?"

Speaking very slowly, as if to the idiot he often called her, he explained that Schmidt was trying once more to replicate his work. "If we go, help him set up the conditions, have you train his aides, there is no reason he should not get identical results. He has to get results!"

And that was the hitch. No one was able to replicate Leo Arkins's results. As he talked, she began to think about Walter, and she realized she wanted to go away briefly. He took her so much for granted, she thought. He would be lonesome without her; on her return they would recapture what they had had so briefly in the beginning. Arkins did not wait for her acceptance, but

returned to his own office as soon as he finished telling
her the details of their trip, which would be by train
leaving the next morning at eight-thirty.

That night when she told Walter, he nodded. "I'd do
the same thing," he said. "Sometimes it's the only way,
and you may never even know what the one factor was
that you corrected in setting up the experiments
somewhere else."

"Don't you even care that I'll be gone four days?"

He looked surprised. "Of course I'll miss you, baby.
You know that."

She shook her head impatiently. "That isn't what I
mean. He tells me I have to do this, and you say, that's
right. Then he makes me do something else and you
think that's okay. Doesn't it even bother you that I
have to do whatever that man tells me?"

"Ah," Walter said then. "You want a knight in
shining armor to come to your rescue. But I told you,
honey, I'm not the guy for that role. I let my armor rust
away to nothing before you were born, and I have no
power, no influence, no money, nothing to intervene
with. It's a job. That's all."

"I don't want you to do anything, just care!"

"I care, baby. I care. But what changes when I say
that? You still go to Chicago tomorrow. We still live in
this apartment. I still have so many debts I won't be out
of hock until I'm ninety. But I care."

He was laughing at her, she knew, and for a moment
she wanted to hit him. Then suddenly she was laughing
also, and the moment was over. "You win," she said.
"It's the nine- or ten-year-old me, isn't it?"

He nodded, laughing out loud now. "Let me tell you
what frightens me, Jean. I can see you meeting a tall
young virile man, a man with money and a car and a
six-room apartment. I can see you falling in love with
him so hard and fast that you forget about me instantly,
and when you finally remember, you say what a funny
old man he was indeed."

"Mm. Poor old thing. Poor old ex-Casanova, decrepit, used up, a has-been, can't cut the mustard at all these days . . ." She caressed him as she commiserated, and then giggled when she felt his erection against her leg.

"Witch, witch," he murmured in her ear as he picked her up and carried her to the bedroom.

She snuggled against him contentedly and played with his ear lobe.

6 Jean and Leo Arkins stood side by side watching the computer printout. It was late, nearly eleven, neither had had dinner, had thought of dinner. Jean felt dazed and hollow and weak as she read the message.

They took food from dock. Not enough money. Not enough grain (corn) (so) men came back to burn buildings. Government sent army . . . troops fired on people . . .

Arkins read it slowly, his voice wavering with excitement. "Are you sure?"

"I can't be certain. I think so. There are some obvious mistakes, but I think it's all I can do with it right now. There are blanks, six or seven words, but we should be able to get them with a simple Markov formulation. They in turn may help with some of the rough spots. Two or three more days, if it's right."

Arkins tore off the printout; his hand was shaking hard. "Call!" he whispered hoarsely. "Call! Read what we have."

"But it isn't finished."

"If this much is right, we've made it. Brighton, don't you understand? We've done it!"

Tiredly she moved to the other desk and dialed the number of his assistant in Boston. She didn't think about the time until Grunwald's wife answered the phone sleepily. Grunwald came on and she handed the phone to Leo Arkins.

"You have to check it now!" he screeched. "Take it down and go check it!" He read the brief message, muttered something incoherent, and hung up. "He'll call back in ten minutes. He'll get the message from his safe and decipher it, then call back. Ten minutes." His little hand was racing up and down his coat front, pulling at buttons, twisting at them.

It was closer to half an hour before Grunwald returned the call. Jean watched Arkins as he listened. He blanched, and she thought he would fall down. She moved closer to him, to catch him if he should collapse. At first she thought his reaction was due to disappointment, but then she realized that he was nearly hysterical with excitement, that Grunwald had confirmed the message. They had translated a foreign language message without a clue, without a key, without a Rosetta stone, which was the third factor.

Repeatedly she had told her classes there was no way to decode an unknown language without the third factor. "You have to share certain common assumptions," she had said. "Things you can point to, in a sense. The Rosetta stone was such a factor. If you have an unknown language, and even a partial translation of it into another language that you do know, then you can translate it into your own language, if there is enough text to work with. The third factor." She could almost hear her own voice saying this to her classes, but had she told them wrong? she thought wonderingly. And even though the proof was there, she still could not believe in it entirely, not yet.

Arkins hung up finally and turned to her. "We'll start working on the missing phrase; it must be a relative clause, no more than that. We'll find it. We'll find it. It can't elude us now."

"I can't work any more today," Jean said. "I'm too tired. Tomorrow, the next day . . ."

"Tired! Tired? How can you be tired! You still don't know what we've done here! You still don't understand! Get out! Go home! Fool!"

"It's just guesswork," she said to herself, walking down a deserted corridor that was gloomy with infrequent lights too dim to do more than add shadows. The building was very musty, as if decay was already setting in. It was her guesswork, she added. No one else realized how unscientific this project was, how much she relied on twitches and even boredom when she selected one phrase over another, one sentence over another equally likely. Walter often berated her for not forcing Arkins to add her name to the papers he published, add her name to the research grants he received regularly. Of course, Arkins would never agree to any of that, but even more important, she did not want her name on it; she did not believe in what they were doing, in what she was doing. She was performing for pay, she thought bitterly, doing well enough to keep her job and security and the apartment and Walter. Arkins had turned down her proposed research, had forced her to keep on with his work, but one day she would go back to her own projects and forget this crackpot theory, she told herself grimly. Her interests, she had tried to explain to Walter, were in the hidden communications language made possible; how people used words understood by both parties to say things that had no connection with the spoken message. She believed it was common in all language groups, and had done preliminary work to demonstrate it in English. "If you use the dictionary and define the words, you see that often that isn't what you mean at

all," she had said one night. "It's a face-saving device
that lets us talk without the risk of exposing ourselves
too much, endangering ourselves to ridicule or disgust
or something like that." Walter had listened patiently,
but then had gone back to what he wanted to talk
about—Arkins, his work, her place in it, the need for
her to assert herself, the benefits she would receive if
she was recognized as a partner, not merely a graduate
student.

At the outside door she waited for the security guard
who would escort her home. No woman was permitted
to walk on campus alone after dark any longer. The
new people had taken over three more halls during the
spring, and now numbered over a thousand bored,
restless, hate-ridden people with nothing at all to do
most of the time.

At home Jean told Walter about the breakthrough,
and he shared Leo Arkins's excitement. "He'll get his
new laboratory now. Sky's the limit for success."

"What with?" she asked, too tired to care, though.
She ate cheese and bread and sipped her milk and
thought about the paper work she had not yet looked
at, thought about the spring midterms she would have
to give and then grade.

"Government money will flow like water now,"
Walter said. "Army money, Pentagon money. Whatever he asks for."

She felt her face stiffen and had trouble swallowing.
"You really think so? With money as scarce as it is?"

"Honey, money's never scarce when something big
comes up that needs it. The Army isn't getting
short-changed. . . . What's the matter?"

"I'm tired." She stood up, leaving the food on the
table without a thought, and went toward the bedroom.

"Not just tired," Walter said, catching her, holding
her at arms' length to examine her. "What did I say?"

She shook her head. "The Army, secret services,
CIA, FBI, all of them. They'll snatch it up, won't they?

I won't work for them. I went out of my way to find a place where I'd be removed from all that, where I'd never have to think about them, and you say they'll come here. I won't work for them."

"Come sit down," he said quietly and led her to the couch. "Stay put while I mix us a drink. You can use something."

She sat obediently and when he put the drink in her hand she sipped it, not wanting it, not wanting to talk, wanting only to go to bed and be in a deep sleep for a long time.

"Listen, baby, you can't shake your head and say you don't want to do this or that. Not any more. We're all past that stage in our lives. And you know it. Honey, listen to me."

She realized she had been looking dreamily at the wall of books, paying scant attention to his words.

"You are in a position to make Arkins pay off finally. He needs you, honey. He can't do this without your active participation. And he'll have money to throw around. He'll have to grant your doctorate on the basis of this work. This research is as good as a thesis; better. More money, and a bigger apartment. Think what it could mean, honey. A real job, a professorship. Tenure. He could get tenure for you."

She shook her head slightly, trying to stop his voice. She drank again and emptied her glass; he took it from her and put it on the floor.

"We need all those things, baby," he said. "You know we do. We could do some of the things we'd both like to do. Travel. You could travel with Arkins' blessing now. He'd see to it that you got ration coupons, clearance, whatever you need. He knows damn well that you're responsible for his success. We could go anywhere."

"You don't know how I feel about them," she said and now she wanted to weep. She had had nothing to eat all day, except three bites of cheese and a sip or two of milk, she wanted to tell him, and the drink he had made for her had not been very little, and now she was feeling weepy and drunk.

"Have you thought for a minute what the alternatives are?"

She remained silent. She did not want to talk about any of it now.

"You'll be out of a job. They won't let you stay here in the apartment, and since it's your lease, I won't be able to stay either. We'll have to find someplace to live, and you know what that's like. We couldn't afford the rent on an apartment in town. And there's no work. Nowhere. You'll be blackballed as a teacher, they'll see to that. No work, period, no matter where you go." He shook her arm. "Do you understand?"

During the next two weeks Arkins was busy making calls to all parts of the country. He flew to Washington twice and the second time he returned he was jubilant. Arkins never confided in her, but she knew he was working on his paper to be given before the International Society of Linguists in New York the second week in April.

Walter had never been more solicitous, more tender, or more loving than he was during those weeks. He brought her small surprises—a bunch of crocuses, a box of goat-milk fudge that one of his students made, a scarf for her hair. One of their problems had been money from the beginning. Walter and his second wife had gone very heavily into debt, and when he left her, he had assumed the entire burden of paying off their creditors. Walter had taken several cuts in salary, as everyone had done, except the security forces. Jean's salary never had been very large to start with.

She knew any little gift that he bought her now would come out of his personal expense allowance, that he would do without something to please her. She was so touched that she could not even thank him when he gave her the scarf. Tears burned her eyes as she fingered it. And when he caught her up in a fierce embrace and kiss, she knew that this was what mattered, not what happened in school, in the laboratory, or anywhere else. Only this mattered.

In April one of the dormitories was burned down and there was a riot on the far side of campus. Jean could see none of it from the Linguistics Department, or from her apartment, but all day sirens wailed, and crowds surged back and forth over the grounds. There were no classes that day; people were told to stay inside, and she waited, very frightened, until Walter came home from his early class. They stood at the window in the bedroom and watched the activity below, thousands of people running this way, then that, and in the distance the billowing black smoke.

"We could leave here," she said suddenly. "We keep telling ourselves there's no other choice, but there are choices. We could work on a farm somewhere, or get jobs waiting table somewhere. There's always something."

He shook his head, his arm hard about her shoulders. "We live as close to poverty as I can stand as it is," he said. "This won't go on. It's the spring weather that got to them. They want to go home and get on with life."

"So do I."

He released her, almost flung her away from him. "You don't know what you're talking about. You're a naïve child, talking as if the world you knew as a kid is still there waiting for you to come back to it. My parents live in a Newtown, outside Indianapolis. You didn't know that, did you? I never mentioned that little fact, did I? I went there last year. You know what it's like for them? Two rooms, smaller than these, made out of plywood and cardboard. Someone sneezes a block away and every apartment shakes. The elevators were condemned before they were ever operated. They pay as much rent there as we pay here, did you know that? No hot water in their rooms. A communal shower. One electric light per room, period. And God

help them when it rains because there aren't any storm
sewers, and the buildings are flush with the ground.
They had a nice house, a pretty yard and garden, trees,
and now they have two hundred square feet, and share
the bathroom with three other families. You want to go
to that? You think you could stand living there?"

She stared at him helplessly. He had never mentioned his parents. She wondered if that was part of the
debt he had assumed, helping them survive. She did
not dare ask.

Two days after Arkins returned from his trip to New
York, where he had been received with respectful
skepticism, he told Jean their work had been classified
by the government.

"No more papers, no more demonstrations, no more
sharing ideas with Schmidt or Grunwald or anybody
else. We can't talk about it except during working
hours. You are to give up your classwork entirely,
devote your full time to this project. . . ."

He was broken, she thought with a rush of sympathy.
He looked old, ill, exhausted, and frightened. His
looking frightened was the worst of all. His small left
hand clutched his coat spasmodically.

"Can they do that? We're not in the Army or
anything."

"They can do it," he said. "I thought they would give
us money to expand, to hire more people. . . . I
thought they would encourage others to pursue this
inquiry. . . . I thought it was a breakthrough in knowledge, but it's just another weapon."

"What if we won't do it?"

"They control the finances of this department, every
department, every university. There's no choice."

He looked at her despairingly. "Poor little Brighton.
That you too should be caught up in it. I'm sorry,
Brighton."

She found herself shaking her head. "It isn't my
project. They can't make me stay. I won't do it, Dr.
Arkins. I won't be a party to it."

His little hand opened wide, then closed on his coat again. He nodded. "They can't make you stay, of course. You are a student only. I told them that and they believed me. You can leave." He turned toward his office, then without looking at her again, he added, "I lied to them. I shall lie again. I shall make them accept that you are a student only, of no consequence. But my one paper is public now; others know. They'll be working on it too; no one can stop that. They'll do it quietly, without publicity. You should know that, Brighton. It will go on. Although of course here it will die."

"You will continue." She knew he had to. He was the work. He had no other existence.

"I worked for five years until you came, and for five years I got no results. You were the key. Somehow you were the key and I never could learn what it was that you did, how you made it work. I promise you, they will not know that. You are free to leave when you choose."

"What will you do?" she asked. She did not know how to speak to him now, how to respond to this new face that she never had seen before. It was like meeting a stranger.

"It's none of your business! I'll do what I decide to do! Now get out of here! Just get your things and get out of here!"

She was almost relieved to hear the familiar screech, the furious words spoken so fast they blurred together. He rushed into his office and slammed the door. She looked around the office, but there was nothing of hers in it. Only her purse, her sweater.

She walked home slowly. Today the walkways were crowded with students and outsiders, who were always immediately identified by the sullen expressions on their faces, or the way they glared at the students and teachers. As she neared her apartment she moved faster, almost running by the time she reached it. She felt as if a burden had been removed from her, something so heavy it had been bending her lower and lower for a long time. Now she felt buoyant with relief.

"Walter!" she called from the doorway. "Walter, are you there?"

He came from the bathroom. "Hey, what happened? You got a raise? Arkins came through for you?"

Laughing, she shook her head. "He told me to get out while I can! He's human after all. He cared enough about me to tell me to go now, because later I might not be able to."

Walter had been moving toward her; he stopped, only a foot out of reach. "He told you what?"

"The Army's taking over. Classified the work. I was supposed to start working full time, give up my classes, all that. Arkins told me. He said he'd lie for me, tell them I'm only an insignificant student, nothing more, no one at all important to the work."

Abruptly Walter went to the window. He yanked the tapestry aside and stood looking out. "You can't do it," he said after a moment. "Nothing's really final, is it?"

"What do you mean? I have done it. I took him up on it. He knew I would. He knew I didn't want to work for them, especially not like that. He won't either. He'll go through the motions, that's all."

"You can still go back?"

"No! Walter, I can't. I won't. He understands that. Why can't you?"

"I can, baby, but I don't want to. We come down to the hard choices, baby, really tough ones, don't we?"

She reached for the doorknob, for the wall, something to support her, because she had a strange feeling that she was drifting above the floor, that she was not anchored to anything.

"Just say it, Walter, whatever it is. Just say it."

"Let's sleep on it first. Maybe things will look different in the morning."

She shook her head. "Just say it."

"I already told you. Nothing's changed. I can't support you, honey. It's that simple."

"We've paid the rent a month in advance. We have that much time for me to try to find something else."

Now he looked at her. "You won't find anything. There isn't anything. Ask them in one of the dorms what's available. A month won't make any difference. It's just putting off the inevitable and that's always a mistake. You have to learn to grow up and face the consequences of each and every little decision you make in this life, honey. You've decided, now you see the consequences. This hasn't been a bad place. I rather hate to leave it."

"What do you mean, leave? Where? Where can you go?"

"There's an apartment I know about, a student I know. She invited me to share it anytime I want to. Guess it's time now."

"You've been seeing someone?"

"Not really. She just wanted me to know."

"When are you leaving?"

"Tomorrow, the next day. No big rush. I just can't afford to wait a month."

"Now, Walter! Get your things and leave now, today!"

"Look, honey, don't pull a scene. It's been fun with you, I've enjoyed you tremendously. Maybe I even love you; I can't really tell. I guess I don't know much about love, but you've been wonderful and I've liked living with you better than with anyone else ever. . . ."

Jean twisted the knob and the door opened. She ran out and kept running for a long time. When it started to get dark she went to her friend Corinne Duland. "May I stay the night? On a chair, anything?"

Corinne asked no questions, but fed her dinner, and then gave her a pillow and blanket and left her while she went to teach her evening class. Jean huddled on the couch all night, and at ten the next morning she returned to her apartment and found that he had taken his possessions and had left. She closed the door and locked it, and then she sat in the silent room and stared at the book wall, now almost empty. She might weep later, or throw things around, or become hysterical, or react in some way, but not yet. She felt numb and had trouble remembering where she was or why she was staring dry-eyed at the wall before her.

She tried to visualize Walter, but his face did not appear. She could not think how his voice sounded. Instead she kept seeing Colonel Cluny that night he had come to tell her and her mother that her father was dead. How gray he had been, how wounded looking, sick. "They've done it again," she whispered. And although the words did not seem to make any sense when she heard them, even repeated them, she knew they really did.

7

Corinne Duland was a heavy woman with steel-gray hair, snapping black eyes, and a wide full mouth. She was handsome in her midye s; somehow everyone forgot she was twenty pounds overweight, and that her hair was gray. She made no attempt to hide her years, and as a consequence they seemed insignificant.

"Are you positive you can't go back to Leo?"

"Positive. It's all Army intelligence now. And Arkins. He told me they had planned to dismiss me if he hadn't done it first. As far as they're concerned, I don't exist, except as one of his students." Often during these past few weeks she had caught herself wondering if this was why she had never wanted her name connected with his research, if she had realized, and repressed, that this could easily become government business, army business.

"You have to do something, dear," Corinne said again. She had brought cheese and crackers and a bottle of wine, and they had finished off everything. "How long do you have? Five days, six? They won't give you an extra minute. If you're not out, they send movers and throw your stuff into the street and then charge you with littering."

Jean nodded. They had been over it all half a dozen times already, and there was nothing left to say. Her mother was ill and was living with her only sister and her husband, two children and one grandchild. She could not go there. They would not welcome her, she knew. Her grandparents were living in a mobile home settlement on Whidbey Island, north of Seattle. Also impossible. They had held out in Oregon until the hospital closed and the doctors left. There were two or three cousins, but they were from San Bernardino, and wherever they had found to live, she was certain she did not want to live with them. There were no jobs in Lansing or East Lansing, or anywhere else, as far as she knew.

"I'll sign up for canal work," she said.

"Nope. What are you, five two? One hundred pounds on a good day, and there haven't been many good days lately. You have to go to your aunt, Jean. There's always room for one more."

Jean shook her head. She couldn't even become a prostitute, she thought bitterly. There was too much competition already among the displaced women.

Corinne had not offered to let her move into the studio apartment. Jean was glad. Admitting there was a possibility of sharing the room, even if it was only a gesture, would have raised guilt and resentment. Their friendship was not deep enough to have survived, and Jean needed a friend now. The two women and Corinne's many callers, who more often than not spent the night—it was almost funny enough to laugh at. Jean smiled to herself, thinking how she could hide behind a screen while Corinne entertained.

The silence grew, until finally Jean said, "I guess I'll just have to be a guest of the government for a short time." For two weeks she had denied it would come down to that. She had sent out dozens of applications for jobs, had written to everyone who might know of a job, and each day she had fought with herself not to call her mother, her grandfather, someone to come help. They couldn't help, she thought clearly. No one could.

Corinne was nodding thoughtfully. "Okay," she said. "Which one? Some are worse than others. Not in the Northeast; too goddamn cold. Around here?"

Jean shook her head.

"Chicago? That might be the best. They were first and have had time to get some kind of organization anyway. Don't take anything that you want to keep. Only your clothes, toothbrush, comb, stuff like that. Anything you want stored, I'll take care of for you. Including any money you have. And I'll send you cash each week; you'll need it for little things. And for God's sake don't tell anyone you have a cent!"

Jean looked at the small living room with its pretty tapestries, the books she had loved. "You take it all," she said, dismissing everything in the apartment. "Anything you want, take. The rest can be tossed in the gutter."

"Don't be ridiculous. We'll have a sale. Saturday. I'll put your money in my safe at the office. When you want it, it'll be there. I expect in a couple of weeks you'll be ready to go to your aunt's house. We'll have to make an inventory of your stuff. . . ."

Her room was nine by eleven. It was painted tan. There was a bed, a chair, a built-in dresser with four drawers, and a plastic mirror bolted to the wall over it. There was a wood-dowel clothes rod with no hangers.

A narrow window had a green shade with a triangular hole in the lower right corner.

She sat down on the bed and stared at the window. "I'll pretend it's a dorm room," she whispered. "I'm a freshman again, starting all over. I'll get a curtain."

Then she lay down and stared at the window until the light behind it faded. She could hear people on both sides of her cubicle. A woman and a man arguing on one side; a woman and a child giggling madly on the other. When the child stopped chattering and laughing, the woman started to weep. Her head must have been only inches away from Jean's, the thin wall separating them. There were other sounds, from the hallway. Ever since she had entered the room, they had continued unabated; people going one way, then the other, back again. Running feet, dragging feet, plodding feet; voices laughing, scolding, crying; sometimes scuffling noises, a fight two times, something breaking with a crash that made the walls shake. . . .

There was a cafeteria, where scrip was accepted. Dinner was at six and Jean missed it on her first day. Breakfast was from seven to eight, and when she got to the building, there was already a line that extended farther than a city block.

She got in line behind a woman with three children who kept darting away first in one direction, then the other.

There was mud everywhere, around the buildings, between them, oozing over the sidewalks made of wood chips, cinders, and crushed stones. The children became muddier and muddier as the line straggled toward the door of the gray building. The woman didn't try to stop the children, nor did she pay any attention to them as they swooped back to her, then away, over and over again. She looked at Jean once, an appraising scrutiny that seemed to dismiss her almost instantly; then she looked straight ahead, oblivious of everything around her.

A couple in line behind Jean, a middle-aged man and woman, argued in soft voices all the way up to the door.

"We can find it this time, I know we can," the woman was insisting, pleading. "I dreamed where to drill, and I know we can find it this time."

"There ain't nothing to find. We tried a hundred times. It ain't there."

"But we didn't try back behind the garage, in the corner under the fence. That's where it is. . . ."

Jean tried not to listen. More people had joined the line behind them, and it seemed the line would stay the same length forever, no matter how many people finally reached the door and vanished inside.

For breakfast there were dried eggs, scrambled with too much water, a piece of white bread, and watery coffee. The room was like an army mess hall, or a prison dining room. Gray walls, long tables with an aisle down the middle, benches to sit on. There was mud all over the floor, some of it still wet and treacherous, some dried like old blood.

Jean tried not to look at the people as she ate, but again and again she found herself gazing at them. Some wore good clothes, some were in rags; some had watches, wedding rings, most had no jewelry at all. But they were alike, she thought, all of them were alike. They all had deep circles under their eyes, and they all looked haunted.

Close to her ear a voice asked, "New here?"

She jerked around to see a young woman, dark-haired, haunted like all the rest. She nodded.

"Thought so. You don't even smell like the rest of us. Where you from?"

Without a thought Jean said, "Oregon."

"Tried to hold out? Some are still trying, so I hear. You through? Come on, guided-tour time." She led the way out, saying over her shoulder as they walked, "Maggie. I'm in G building, room 421. Been here a year. You got any cigarettes?"

"Sorry," Jean said.

"Didn't think you would," Maggie said cheerfully. "Never hurts to ask."

They stood outside the cafeteria and looked at the Newtown. The streets were twenty feet wide, the buildings twenty feet apart and six stories high. There were no trees, no grass, no bushes, nothing but the mud and the poor sidewalks sinking into it. The buildings stretched out in all directions. The streets were crowded now and there were children everywhere, screaming, yelling. One hundred fifty thousand people lived in this one Newtown. Most of them seemed to be on the streets, Jean thought.

"Where are they going?"

"Nowhere. Nowhere to go. Anything's better than the prison cells. You'll see. Come on. Laundry's over there. This one's ours, for this section. You have to sign up to use it. Don't forget or you'll get pretty filthy in no time at all. This goddamned mud was built in."

"Is there a library?"

Maggie gave her a curious look, shrugged, and led the way. The library building was a copy of the cafeteria, down to the line stretched out in front of it. "They give you ten minutes, no more. One book, if they have any by the time you get there."

Maggie took her to the rec building, where people were crowded together playing cards, checkers, chess; there were Ping-Pong tables, but no equipment for them. There was a piano that someone was banging on in another room; dancing, Maggie said. Large wall television sets were on. They were badly focused, loud, with dozens of people before each one. They left the building to continue the tour.

There were a few shops with toilet articles, some magazines and paperback books. Each shop had a police officer stationed in it. There was a movie theater.

Jean scowled at the goods. The scrip issued was exactly enough for meals and laundry. Anything else had to come out of meal money, or whatever savings the people had hidden away.

"You like to fuck?" Maggie asked suddenly.

Jean stared at her. "Why?"

"You can pick up some spare jingle-jangle that way. Make them pay for it—quarter, dollar, whatever you can get."

"Where do they get money?"

"That's their business. You want to start up a little on the side, give me the word and I'll pass it around."

"I don't think so; not yet anyway."

Maggie shrugged. "They'll take you anyway; might as well make them pay something."

They walked to the playground, and it was like the rest of the complex, overcrowded, too much screaming and yelling and crying, too much mud, not enough equipment. There were schools, but they were like everything else, Maggie said. Jean decided not to look in on them.

"What do you do all day every day?"

"Nothing. Hang out. Fuck around. Go to town sometimes, look at the stuff in windows, panhandle a little."

Jean remembered the new people who had entered her classes, empty looking, haunted, obscene, full of hatred for her and everyone else who lived in apartments or houses, worked and made a living. Her head began to ache and she went back to her room, leaving Maggie near the rec building.

All afternoon Jean lay on her cot, staring at the hole in the green shade. The woman and child returned next door and began laughing at something. She admired the woman and wished she would shut up.

Finally the thought of going without food until morning drove her from her room, out to the muddy street, past the two gray buildings between her own and the cafeteria, and back into the line.

Maggie was lounging near the door, laughing with three other women, all very young, all with muddy jeans, two of them barefoot. Maggie could not have been more than eighteen or nineteen, the others

probably a bit younger, Jean thought, watching them
flirt slyly with the men in line. There were very few
men, she realized, and for the most part they were
either middle-aged or older, or teen-aged. She remembered what she had read about the Newtowns: the men
were the primary source of friction, the article had
said; consequently they were put to work if and when it
was possible. She felt her hands tighten as she looked
around at the haunted, empty women. Maggie saw her
in line and hurried over to introduce her friends, Rosa,
Susan, BettyJean.

"Honey, I forgot to warn you before. Don't wander
around after supper if you're alone. You know?"

"We'll be in the rec room; come on over after you
eat. You play cards?" BettyJean asked. She was the
youngest of them all, probably no more than fifteen,
and she was very pretty, with light brown hair that was
cut so short it looked babyish.

"I'll come over," Jean said. "What kind of cards?"

"Canasta. We'll snag a table and you can find us. See
ya."

Jean could not identify the foods on her plate that
night. After three bites, she put her fork down and
drank her watery coffee.

"I got cheese and some dark rye bread and even a
little wine, over in my room," a man said in a low voice
behind her.

She looked around. He was about sixty, with lank
gray hair and stubble on his chin. He looked at her
throat, down her body, back to her throat. He didn't
look at her face.

She shook her head and turned away from him.

"Even some chocolate," he mumbled.

"Leave me alone."

"Wouldn't hurt you or nothing. I don't mean no
harm. . . ."

She looked at the people across the table from her,
three women in a row, all studiously staring at their
plates. On one side of her a man ate, talked now and

then to a woman companion. On the other side three children whined and ate and quarreled with each other. No one paid any attention to the old man and Jean.

Throughout the hall there were the sounds of forks hitting the tables, cups being put down hard, feet scuffling, bare feet padding on the dirty floors, voices that merged and became a noise altogether different from human voices, more like the indecipherable sounds of the surf. A child began to cough in a harsh, whooping-cough way.

The man was still there, staring at her, she knew. Her hands were shaking too much to lift her coffee now, and she knew she could not stand and leave without bumping into him. Maybe that was what he was waiting for, for her to rise and for one moment to have her body against his. Maybe he would seize her arm, touch her. . . .

At the far end of the dining room someone began to scream, and there were shouts and cries. The old man behind Jean's chair shuffled away toward the excitement. She jerked up her tray and hurried to deposit it at a counter, and ran from the dining room. Outside she stopped. It was still bright with sunlight, and now people were streaming toward the rec building; the children shouted and cried and yelled and played in the mud. A group of teen-aged boys came toward Jean, three abreast on the walkway, arms linked. They didn't slow down as they drew near her; they were thirteen, fourteen, not yet mature enough to shave. Their faces were particularly childish, she thought, and she knew they would trample her if she did not back up, or step into the mud to get out of their way.

Behind her several women's voices suddenly were raised, and one of them shouldered past her, a thick woman with a long pole in one hand. She strode past Jean without a glance at her. Jean looked at the others then, all middle-aged, all staring grimly at the boys, who stopped, then broke and ran off the walkway through the mud toward the rec building, yelling obscenities as they went.

She moved aside to allow the other women to pass, and then followed them gratefully until they turned in at a building two short of her own. She knew she could not go to play cards that evening, perhaps never. She didn't even know how to play canasta.

She almost ran to her own building and up the stairs, afraid now of every sound, of every person who approached. By the time she reached her own door she was breathless.

"Are you all right?" a soft voice asked. The door next to her own was open a few inches, revealing a woman's face.

She nodded, groping for the key chain on her neck, her fingers trembling and awkward.

The woman hesitated, then opened her door a bit more. Now Jean could see a small child standing behind her, a little girl. The child suddenly smiled at her.

"I was starting out," the woman said, "and heard someone running, so I waited to make sure it was all right. I thought someone was after you."

The little girl said, "My name's Melinda. What's your name?"

Jean smiled at her then. "Jean."

"I'm five years old. How old are you?"

Now Jean laughed. "I'm much older than that. I'm twenty-six. You are very pretty, Melinda."

"I have to go to the toilet."

"I'm Virginia Petryk. She has the manners of a princess, don't you think?"

Jean nodded. Princess, she thought; that was exactly right. "I'll go with you," she said.

Virginia and Melinda came all the way out now, and Virginia carefully locked her door, tried it to make certain, and then took Melinda's hand in hers. "I usually wait until I see someone I know, at least by sight, before we come out," she said. "Especially in the evenings. You've been warned?"

"Yes. How long have you been here?"

"Eight months. My husband is looking for a job. He's an accountant. We're from Sacramento."

"I can read," Melinda said.

"That's wonderful. Do you have any books?"

"I have four books, and we always get more from the library."

"I was a teacher," Virginia said. "Elementary school, third grade."

"Are you working here?"

She shook her head. "No jobs. We go into Chicago, go to the library. I have a friend's card. So far no one has bothered us. It won't last, I guess, but we're making the most of it as long as it does."

The rest rooms were crowded; they had to wait in line. Half an hour later they returned to their rooms. Jean had offered to watch Melinda while Virginia used the toilet, but after a hesitation so brief it might not have been there at all, Virginia had shaken her head, smiling her thanks. Walking back to their rooms, she explained, "I promised myself that she won't be out of my sight while we're here. Isn't that the very model of an overprotective mother?"

Jean looked at the child skipping along by her mother's side and shook her head. "I'd do exactly the same thing," she said grimly.

At their doors Virginia asked shyly, "After a while, after Melinda's sleeping, would you like to come over and talk?"

"I'd love to. Tap on the wall. I'll hear you."

She felt almost light-hearted when she entered her own room then. She could hear soft laughter through the wall, and she smiled.

The two women talked for two hours that night, until Virginia began to yawn. "I'm used to such early hours," she apologized. "We get up at dawn, nearly first in line for breakfast every morning. Sorry."

The next day Jean looked for them everywhere. She knocked on their door two times without success, and then in the afternoon she went for a walk around the perimeter of the Newtown. Everywhere it was the same, although the different areas were sectioned off from one another by streets twice as wide as they were in other places. Section 1, Section 2, Section 3 . . . all alike, even to the squalling children and the insolent, bored teen-agers and the tough middle-aged women. Abruptly she turned her back on Newtown and started across the field west of the settlement. It was the only way she could walk; the other three sides were bordered by highways. The field stretched on before her endlessly. It was high in grass and weeds, and completely flat. Already, in May, the sun was very hot, and the wind was steady, dry, and warm. Soon the mud would be gone, and there would be dust everywhere. Her legs were starting to throb when she came in sight of the fence that marked the boundary of Newtown. Beyond it she could see ocher and tan and brown houses, a subdivision. The fence was well above her head, eight feet high. She did not approach it, but stood and looked at the houses, with shrubs and trees in the yards. Some children came running around a house, stopped when they saw her, stared, then turned and ran away again.

"Watch out or the Newtown monsters will get you," she whispered.

After a long time she bowed her head and returned to Newtown and to her room. She heard Virginia and Melinda when they got home, but now she did not bother to knock on their door. They had a life here, they were busy doing something, they could laugh and giggle at night. She felt she had no place in their lives at all.

Then she heard a soft tapping on her wall and she sat up so fast that she felt almost ashamed of her relief that they had not forgotten her. She tapped back.

"Are you home?" Melinda's voice came through the wall.

"Yes. Are you?"

"No!" The child laughed hard and Virginia shushed her.

"Have you had dinner yet?"

"No. Have you?"

"No. Want to go now?"

Jean nodded, then said, "I sure do. I'm ready."

That night Virginia told her how they spent their time. "We go to town," she said. "But we don't get on the bus here. You know they stamp your hand, make you pay the round-trip fare if you board in Newtown. The mark of the beast," she added. "We walk through the field, go through a hole in the fence and over to the subdivision and catch a regular bus there, pay our fare like anyone else. We come back on the Newtown bus so we won't have to walk so far both ways. No one cares if you come back without the stamp, as long as you pay. We window-shop, go to the library, eat our lunch in a park, pretend we're visiting royalty. There are museums and exhibits and church music sometimes. If you aren't stamped, they let you in those places, if you don't look too Newtown-like, that is."

The next day and frequently after that Jean went with them. She bought a notebook and began to make notes on her thesis, and she wrote in detail everything she knew of Leo Arkins's work, her part in it, her doubts about it. She tried to apply for work, for volunteer work in the school, the clinic, anything, and there was nothing. The waiting list was pages long. She tried to keep pretending she was in college again—it was tolerable if she could keep up the pretense—but sometimes it was not possible and the pages stared at her defiantly, her mind a blank.

Every day there were fights and robberies and murders and rapes. The weather got hotter and the violence increased. The streets turned to dust, and the wind blew the dust constantly, coating everything with it. Soldiers came in trucks and spread oil, and that was even worse because now fresh oil was blown also when the harsh prairie winds howled through the streets.

The grass in the field turned brown and withered, and someone set fire to it. It burned with a great roar and when the lightning-fast fire died the field was a stubble of charred spearlike points. For days Virginia was afraid to take Melinda across it to go to town.

Jean's grandmother died that summer. She had had several heart attacks, and her death was no surprise. Her grandfather wrote to her. He enclosed the deed to his house in Bend. "It's yours, little Olahuene. There's a little money to go with it; not much, I'm afraid. Never was a good saver. The water will be there again one day. I'd go back now, but somehow it doesn't seem the same, me there alone, so I guess I'll go fishing instead. All my love, all my love."

She felt frozen when she finished reading the letter. Going fishing. Then she wept for her grandfather. A week later she received an official notice that he had been lost at sea in a small boat while fishing.

"I'm going home," she said that night to Virginia. "Please come with me. He said he would go back and that means there's enough water to live on, enough to drink anyway. He was telling me there's enough to drink. That's what he meant." She was pleading, she knew, and could hear the desperation in her own voice, but did not stop.

Virginia simply shook her head. "I was there a year ago—oh, not right there, but Sacramento. Even if there's a well, the smallest trickle of water, you couldn't have it. They need it for agriculture. They made all non-agriculture people get out; why do you think they'd let you go back?"

"There isn't any agriculture, not to speak of anyway, in that part of the country. It wouldn't be taking water away from anything else."

Virginia looked at her sleeping daughter. "I don't blame you," she said slowly. "If I were alone, I'd go too. But I'm not. I wouldn't care if I starved or died of thirst—it would be better than this—but not for her. Not for her."

Jean wrote to Corinne and then remembered that she was going to be gone for part of July, visiting her brother in Delaware. The days dragged, and she saw

with horror how hideous the Newtown was, how
degrading life had become for everyone here, and she
marveled that she had been able to close her eyes to it
for so long.

Now that she knew she was leaving, she could hardly
bear staying. Every afternoon she checked the post
office, desperate for Corinne's reply, for the money
that would buy her a ticket away from here.

The walk home was hot; she was covered with dirt by
the time she got back to her building. Everywhere she
turned there were the listless dirty hopeless people;
heat drove them from the buildings, the blowing dust
drove them back inside.

She waited in line for a shower and then started back
toward her room at the far end of the hallway. It was
nearly a hundred degrees inside her building; already,
still wet from the shower, she could feel sweat trickling
down her back.

She started to unlock her door, dully aware of three
men shuffling toward her. At the other end of the hall
voices broke out in a loud argument. She pushed the
door, and at the same moment one of the men grabbed
her with one arm around her waist, one hand hard over
her mouth, and shoved her inside the room with his
body. The other two rushed in and slammed the door
and turned the lock. While one man yanked down the
shade, another began to tear off her clothes. She tried
to kick and the man holding her squeezed so hard she
could not breathe and she felt herself suffocating,
fainting.

He took his hand away from her mouth and something else was stuffed in, gagging her, and then they
threw her onto the bed. Her hands were yanked above
her head, tied to the rail; her legs were spread open,
both feet tied to the rail at the foot of the bed.

One had already dropped his jeans; he lunged at her.
She tried to draw up her knees, jerked her body, tried
to get away from him, and he lifted her head by her hair

and slapped her face hard, first one side, then the other. She stopped struggling. She would have screamed with pain then when he entered her; in her mind she could hear her scream.

They all raped her, but she was hardly conscious of them any longer. There was only pain. Distantly she felt them pulling the cords from her ankles, releasing her legs. Her hands were still bound together, tied to the rail of the bed. She was turned over and one of them tried to enter her through the rectum. When he couldn't, he beat her with his belt, again and again and again. She knew her body was twitching with pain, but it was almost as if it were someone else's pain, not hers. The gag was yanked from her mouth and she knew: that too. She began to vomit. She felt the belt cutting into her back again, and then, nothing else.

8 "I'm going to release you," the doctor said. "But you'll need counseling. We have a service; groups, of course, but a good doctor. . . ."

Jean shook her head.

"My dear child, you may not recognize the symptoms yourself, but you have suffered a trauma that is not only physical, but mental as well, and I can do nothing about the mental damage. Your stitches are out, you are healing nicely, but you have not spoken since your arrival. Your psyche is wounded perhaps even more than your body was."

"I'm going home," Jean said. "It will be all right."

The doctor sighed. "Ah, you speak to us. And you have a home you can go to. That's good. That's very good." She smiled at Jean then, patted her arm, and moved on to the next bed.

Jean stared at the ceiling and thought of Walter with his pseudo-paternal concern, drawing her out, reassuring her that this ordeal was over, that she was strong, she would recover. . . .

On the bus, pulling away from the endless suburbs, she kept thinking to herself, It will be all right as soon as I get home. Through the prairies she repeated it over and over, and when the dust storms slowed the progress of the bus so much that a running child would have beaten it, the phrase echoed and reechoed in her head. They crossed the aqueducts, bordered on both sides by green fields of corn that were being savaged by the blowing dust. It would be stunted, someone said to someone else. She did not look around at the speaker; the words were meaningless to her.

In Seattle she made the transfer to Portland and learned there that the next bus to Bend would leave in two days. She nodded and walked to the nearest hotel, where she registered, paid in advance for a room and bath, and went up the stairs without even seeing the lobby. In her room she lay on the bed. The rhododendrons were gone, she thought suddenly, and stood up to look out the window at the city below. It looked much as it had when she and her grandparents had come here during the time she had lived with them. There was traffic, buses, people, but no rhododendrons. And the Columbia was now a small river, she thought, remembering, although when crossing it she had paid no attention.

There had been something else, she thought then, and began to shake. Something she had seen, had refused to see. A Newtown. The bus had passed a Newtown south of Seattle. Her shaking increased until she felt as if she were having a convulsion. She went to the mirror and gripped the dressing table hard, staring at herself. Nothing showed, no mark, no scar, nothing at all. She knew her back had scars, would always have scars, but now, studying her face in the mirror, she looked exactly the same as always. Her shaking stopped gradually and she went to the bathroom and showered, staying under the water for a long time even though a posted notice advised that there would be a surcharge added to her bill if she used more than twenty gallons a day.

Her room was costing her one hundred five dollars a day; her dinner of a sandwich, a glass of milk, and coffee cost fourteen dollars. She didn't care. Two days later she paid the remainder of her bill, and the surcharge, and left to catch the bus to Bend. She was nearly home, she kept thinking. Even here the drought had changed everything, she realized, seeing the land-scape now. The ferns were gone from the roadside. No moss grew up the trees, and many of the trees stood starkly naked, defoliated by insects or disease. A wide-ranging fire had blackened thousands of acres of forest land; the denuded hills looked like the aftermath of a holocaust. As the bus climbed the mountains to go over the pass, the greenery returned, but only for a short distance. On the eastern slopes, the undergrowth was gone, the ponderosa pines looked pale and lifeless, and long before they should have yielded to junipers, they were dead, and small clumps of junipers had sprouted here and there.

The desert was claiming the land very fast on the lower slopes of the Cascades; sand had blown up to nearly cover a barn; the house had burned; the land was barren and very quiet. No other traffic was on the road, no cattle grazed in fenced-in fields, no life stirred anywhere.

They approached Bend from the north in the eerie, silent world of desert. On the outskirts of town, where there were fast-food restaurants, gas stations, and shopping centers, everything was still: boarded-up stores, barricades across driveways, emptiness everywhere. The bus turned off the highway into town, and now there were some people. Half a dozen Indians were on the side of the street before the bus station. There were national guardsmen there also. The bus stopped and Jean and one other passenger rose to leave it. The other person was an old Indian man. Jean had not noticed him before, had not noticed anyone else on the bus until now. There were three other Indians, two white men. They all stared at her curiously when she got off; she forgot them instantly.

"Miss? Are you sure this is where you meant to go?"

A national guardsman approached her, frowning. She knew they were stationed in all the abandoned towns, to prevent looting, to maintain order for the people to come back to when the drought ended. She nodded at the man. He was no more than thirty, and she suspected he had welcomed this duty because it was a paying job after all, even if it was in the middle of the great nowhere the West had become again.

"Ain't nothing here, ma'am," he said doubtfully. "No stores, no gas, damn few people. You got a place to stay?"

Again she nodded.

He glanced at his companion, who was grinning slightly, evidently willing to let him get himself out of the predicament her arrival had caused.

"You see, ma'am, nobody's allowed to come here unless they have a reason, a place to stay, water, all that. You from here?"

"I own a house here," she said then. "I've come to straighten out my grandfather's papers. He died a few weeks ago."

The two guardsmen exchanged glances and the second of them came near. "We'll have to see some identification, miss. It's the law, you know. Only residents can come back, and they ain't likely to because there's nothing left."

She produced identification and the deed to her grandfather's house, and finally they returned the papers to her. The bus driver had been waiting; now he got back behind the wheel, the door whooshed closed, and he started the bus, drove away. The Indians were gathering up large packs the old man had brought with him. There were other packages, boxes, crates on the pavement. Her suitcases were there. She went to them and picked them up.

"May I go now?"

"Sure, Miss Brighton. Look, there's no lights or anything here. You need anything, you just let us know. Wood, oil for a lamp, stuff like that. We can help you out for a couple of days, I guess. We're at the Federal Building. Know where it's at?"

"Thank you," she said. She left them and started the walk home. The trees had been dying ten years ago; now most of them had been cut down. All the imported plants were gone, and only sagebrush and junipers lived here now. Miss Lottie's Art Store was boarded up tightly; sand had pitted the paint, starting the peeling process that would leave bare siding that finally would turn silver with age, just as all living things seemed to do eventually.

Briscoe's Garage had a sand dune edging up the side of it. Artie's Magazine Store, boards for windows, a padlock on the door . . . There was no sound in the town, no wind blew, nothing rattled or creaked or moaned. The ghosts of this particular ghost town were at rest, she thought, and was pleased at the idea. It was fitting and proper that they should be at rest.

Along the river, now a wadi with water-patterned stones marking the final course, the grass that used to stay so green all summer had vanished, and erosion of the soil was well advanced, exposing the skeleton framework of the bluff that had given the appearance of a gentle slope. Across the dry river the mansions stood revealed as the alien structures they had always been. Unsoftened now by shrubbery and graceful trees, they rose too tall and too ornate and too fancy for a desert. Desert dwellings should be low, should blend into the sand and rocks, not stand out like sentinels, she thought, surveying them with satisfaction, as if she had always wondered about their secrets and now knew them all.

Her grandfather's house was untouched by the changes in the climate. He had used sagebrush and junipers, instead of the imported plants, and his plantings were as always. Wide wooden steps led to the house through spreading junipers. She started up the steps.

"How can they live?" she had asked once, not here, but out on the desert, speaking about the tough mesquite.

"On dew and moonbeams," he had said, and she had believed him. She still believed they endured on dew and moonbeams. It was enough.

The house was two stories, but it was built into the hillside and its height was not apparent. The cellar was cool in the summer and warm in the winter, she remembered. She was approaching from the front of the house, although the road was on the opposite side. The house overlooked the river and the foothills of the Cascades beyond it. There was a wide porch, with deep shadows now that the sun was dipping down behind the Sisters' peaks. The sky was cloudless; there would be no fiery sunset that evening. There were long, timeless twilights here after the sun went over the mountains, but the day was not yet finished. During the hot summers this had always been the best part of the day; the air would lose its heat, and the light change, become softer while losing none of its clarity. She unlocked the door, but did not immediately enter the house. She looked at the hills, and if she focused her eyes on the more distant ones, they looked unchanged, the dead trees disappeared, and there were the long shadows she remembered, and the fuzzy outlines. Soon the wind would start blowing, she told herself, and a moment later a breeze touched her face, whispered in the junipers.

Satisfied, she entered the house, left the door open, the screen door unlatched. All the years they had lived in Bend, they had never locked a door. She knew she could not lock them now. She put her suitcases down and walked into the living room. It was as her grand-parents had left it, as she remembered it. They had taken nothing with them except their clothes; they had expected to come home again.

There was a mammoth fireplace on one wall, with bookcases built around it. Firewood was in a woven basket by the hearth. There were large wooden chairs with plump cushions covered with Indian print materi-al. An oval rug, a gift from Robert Wind-in-the-Tall-Trees, covered the wide plank floor. The sofa was brown leather, very soft and supple, always warm to the touch, as if it touched back. She opened the drapes on the casement windows and looked again at the hills across the river. The illusion was perfect; she had walked into her own past, ten or twelve years ago. The breeze had turned into a steady wind, and already the evening air was cooling.

She went through every room of the house, touching those things she remembered particularly well, feeling the cabinets, the oak table where she had done her homework, the cherry table in the dining room. She ran her hand lightly down the china cabinet, careful not to touch the glass and leave smudges there. Then she went upstairs, carrying her two suitcases with her. She went to her own room and put the bags on the bed and opened the larger one. Folded neatly on top were her two Paraguayan tapestries. She took them out and shook them to release the wrinkles. With them over her arm, she went to her grandparents' room. She paused outside the door, not actually listening, but rather as if

allowing herself time to summon their faces, their
forms. She entered the room then and went to the large
high bed with its white wedding ring comforter.

"I brought you something," she whispered. "I knew
you would like them." She arranged one of the
tapestries on her grandmother's side of the bed, then
went around it and put the other tapestry in place. They
looked very gay and pretty against the white. She
looked around the room for another moment, then left
it and quietly closed the door behind her.

It was growing darker now, and before night came
she had to fill an oil lamp. She went down to the cellar
and found the cans of kerosene where they always had
been. She took one up with her and filled two lamps,
and then returned the can to its proper place. Again in
her own room, she unpacked her possessions and put
them away neatly in drawers and on hangers in her
closet. Many of the clothes she had worn here were still
hanging, covered with dust wrappers, waiting for her
return. Finally she went to her father's room and this
time she sat down in a chair at his window. The
mountain peaks were visible from here, black and
sharp against the fading violet sky.

She sat still until the sky was inky blue and the star
patterns were visible. How many times had her father
sat here to watch the stars turn on? There was so much
she would like to tell him. All the years since then,
everything she had done, the things she had not done.
How she loved this room, she thought. Over there he
had made model spaceships and space stations; he had
drawn mazes, more and more intricate and complicated
as he grew older. He never had lost that love for
puzzles and mazes and tricks. Two bookcases were
filled with the books from his childhood—fairy tales,
fantasies, adventures with knights and dragons, and
later Sherlock Holmes and Nero Wolfe. Books of
puzzles, limericks, games, tongue twisters . . . He always had loved words, language.

She had spent many hours here in this room when

she had come to live with her grandparents. They had known it was all right, it was what she had needed. Sometimes her grandmother had come in also, and had sat on the stool before his desk, which filled one wall. Grandpa had made the desk for him, and he kept outgrowing it, she had said once.

Jean had become very thirsty. She picked up her oil lamp, looked about the room to make certain she had disturbed nothing, then left it and closed that door carefully also.

Next to the kitchen was a pantry with a pump that drew water from the cistern. There had been city water here, but her grandfather had wanted his own source of water also, and he had kept the cistern clean and the pump working. She began to pump slowly, rhythmically, the way he had taught her to work it, and finally, after a long time, she heard water gurgling as it rose in the pipes. She filled a kettle, making sure she caught every drop, and took it to the kitchen. After a long drink of the cool, sweet water, she laid a fire in the stove. The dry wood blazed instantly. She measured out two cups of water into the teakettle and started to prepare her dinner. She wanted little if anything to eat, but she knew she had much to do the next day, and she got out the cheese she had brought, and the bread and dried fruit. She put the fruit in a pan, added water and put it on the stove until it came to a boil, then she moved the pot from the heat and covered it. When her tea was ready, she ate the cheese and bread, and by the time she finished it, the fruit was ready, and the tiny fire was dying. She cleaned up the kitchen, carried the kettle upstairs, and prepared herself for bed.

She left her drapes open in order to catch the rising sun on her face, her own alarm clock in this house, this room. She slept deeply, and remembered no dreams when she awakened. She felt better than she had for a long time.

She washed with the remaining water in the kettle, then dressed in her old boots, blue jeans, a long-

sleeved shirt, a scarf. She carried her wide-brimmed
hat down with her. She ate a scant breakfast of cheese,
bread, raisins, and water, and then filled a leather
water bag. When she was done, she left the house as
untouched looking as it had been when she arrived. She
locked the door this time, and after a moment put the
key under a planter on the edge of the porch.

The sun was high when she stopped to rest and nap.
During the morning she had skirted all signs of
habitation, even though she had known the houses,
barns, all the ranch buildings had been abandoned.
Now she was on a mesa where a clump of junipers
provided shade for the hottest part of the day. The
wind was steady and hot; her face felt scoured by it; her
eyes burned from the unaccustomed glare, and her feet
hurt even though her grandfather had kept her boots
well oiled. She was not used to walking.

She sank to the ground under the gray-green needles
and rested her head against the trunk. After a moment
she drank a little of her water. Now that she was out of
the sun, the wind felt less hot, and it cooled her,
evaporating the sweat as fast as it formed. Her feet
throbbed but she did not dare take off the boots, or she
might not be able to get into them again. Nothing
moved in the midday heat, no birds, no small creatures.
The sky was deep blue, cut raggedly on every horizon
by mesas and mountains, fading to a paler color
overhead, where the sun finally burned a great white
hole in heaven. She closed her eyes; presently she took
off her hat and put it on the ground, rested her head on
it, and slept.

When she awoke there were shadows to lead her
once more, and she pushed herself away from the
ground stiffly. She sipped her water, adjusted her hat,
and continued to walk eastward. But now her progress
was slower as fatigue claimed its toll. She made herself
examine the landscape, tried to ignore her aching legs
and swollen feet. The world seemed to pulse before her

eyes, keeping time with her own heartbeat. It brightened, dimmed, brightened again.

It was the same desert. Exactly the same as always. She had known it would be. "Deserts and oceans care nothing for droughts," she said, and heard the words although she had not realized she was speaking aloud.

There were the mesas, the cliffs, the sharply defined rimrock, the great granite and basalt and obsidian upthrusts and flows. Jasper gleamed in the sunlight, a rich chocolate brown that looked wet. Here a side of a cliff had been blasted out to expose a band of blue agate, streaked with white. Rock hounds had hammered at rocks, their marks clear, untouched by the years since anyone had had the time, energy, enough faith in the future to care about pretty rocks.

She crossed a fence line where the rancher had rolled up the barbed wire, lashed it securely to a fence post before he left. He must have loved the desert, she thought; his final act must have been to release it from a promise that somehow included fences. And he would be back, he had said when he lashed the wire so securely to wait for him there. It would not rust, not for eons; it would wait, and meanwhile the creatures, if any endured now, would come and go freely, unaware of the promise and the threat the roll of wire symbolized.

Half an hour later she overlooked a ranch where a row of poplars had died and now stood like spears left by giants. There was a dam that bisected barrenness; the shallow lake bed was crisscrossed with black cracks. She veered slightly to the south, unwilling to pass close to the house and yard being reclaimed by the desert.

She became aware of a long dark shadow that moved before her, and stopped in bewilderment, and then realized it was her own shadow. She could remember no thoughts at all for a very long time; it seemed almost as if she had kept walking, although she had fallen asleep. She reached for her water flask and remembered that she had emptied it. The flask swung at her hip, now slapping her thigh, now sliding against it. From a distance she heard a clear fluting bird cry and she looked for the source, but could find nothing. Another bird answered from a greater distance, and she started to move again. She no longer ached, and the world had stopped throbbing and was very steady in the stillness of the late afternoon. The wind had quieted. The drowsy time of day, her grandfather had called this. Now small creatures sniff the air, he had said as they sat together under an overhanging shelf of a high cliff. The little creatures waited for the heat to break, they emerged from their siestas very hungry, sometimes so hungry they forgot to be wary. He had pointed out a hawk circling high overhead. She looked up now, and there was a hawk. She smiled. It was as if this day and that were merging. She had known they would.

Now she turned to look at the Three Sisters, to gauge the time remaining before the sun crawled over their peaks and vanished. There was no snow on any of them; all the glaciers had melted, leaving rocks and craters that testified to the fiery birth pangs of this mountain range. Soon, she thought. Half an hour. She studied the landscape, and turned southward again, this time hurrying toward a mesa that rose almost perpendicular from the desert floor.

Before she reached it, she saw a gorge, a narrow fault that cut the desert in half here. It looked velvety black from where she stood, so deep were the shadows. No longer needing to hurry, she walked toward it, and at the edge she looked down at the tumbled rocks at the bottom, hundreds of feet below her. She let a rock fall and it bounced against the side, then rolled and bounced the rest of the way. She began to walk along the edge, following it eastward. Finally she could look straight down without seeing the side of the cliff below her. She dropped a rock and watched it fall to the bottom. She could not see it hit among the boulders;

the gorge was deeper here than where she had started following it.

The bird call sounded again, closer this time, and she wished with impatience it would just get on with it, find a mate and build a nest, or whatever it was that was on its mind at this time of year. She backed away from the gorge to wait for the return of the profound silence.

Only then did she sit down and start to unlace her boot. Her feet were very swollen, and it was difficult to get the boot off, but there was no pain. She pulled the sock off and stuffed it down inside the boot, then started to unlace the other one. Barefoot, she unbuckled the water bag from her belt, put it down beside her boots, then added her belt, and took off her jeans, folded them and put them on the pile. She unbuttoned her shirt, aware that her hands and her neck were sunburned, but not aware of them as painful. It was as if she were watching someone else ritually undressing. When she was finished, she took a pile of clothes to the edge of the cliff, then went back for the boots and water bag, the things she had not been able to carry in one armload. She was near the edge when she heard a voice.

"The desert has not called you, little Olahuene."

She dropped the things she was holding and took a step forward.

"You must not go to the desert unless you have been called."

"But it did," she said, not looking back, taking another step forward. "I heard it. I came thousands of miles because I heard it." She took another step.

"No. You heard your grandfather's voice calling you home. He told me you would return. I asked for help and he told me you would come, you would help. That's the voice you heard."

She stopped, shaking her head. "No," she whispered. "You are lying to me. Don't stop me now. Not now."

"Turn around, Olahuene. Look at me. You know I'm not lying to you. Your family and mine have been linked for many years, for four generations. We're linked today. I've come to take you home now."

She bowed her head and watched her feet. She tried to take another step; her foot did not move. So close, she wanted to cry, so close!

Now his voice was somehow touching her. She felt it as a warm air on her skin, soothing her flesh, acknowledging her pain and still denying it. "When the desert truly calls, little sister, you will go to her and feel her embrace. But the time has not yet come."

She felt a light weight settle on her shoulders, and then she was being wrapped in a blanket and lifted as if she were a small child.

He held her in one arm and rode easily, letting his horse walk home in the long, timeless twilight.

9 Lina Davies's father had turned up at Ramona Cluny's house two days before the wedding. Mr. Davies was five feet six inches tall and weighed nearly two hundred pounds, his hair was brown and soft like Lina's, and his eyes the same shade of green. He looked like a dwarf next to her.

"Want to talk to you," he had said brusquely, standing in Ramona's living room, showing no awareness of anything or anyone except Cluny.

"Yes," Cluny said. "Please, sit down."

"Let's take a walk."

Cluny glanced at Lina, who shrugged helplessly; he went to the door with her father and followed him out into the yard, then to the sidewalk.

"She has an allowance," her father said without preliminary. "And I don't aim to increase it. But I don't guess I'll stop it either. What she does with it is her business. Just want to let you know now, before everything's set, how it is with her and me."

"Yes, sir," Cluny said, still waiting for the reason for this walk.

Mr. Davies stopped and looked up at him. "I'm a rich man, but don't count on spending it, son. Don't count on it for a hell of a long time. She's all I've got, and someday it'll be hers, but I'm fifty-two, and I aim to hang on for a good long time."

Cluny nodded. "That's fine, sir. I hope so."

Mr. Davies scowled, but as he studied Cluny's face, his own features relaxed. "You care for her, don't you, son?"

Cluny could only nod again.

"You know anything about me? Where I'm from? Anything?"

"No, sir. She started to tell me a couple of times, but she gets off the subject easily. I should have pressed it, I suppose. I'm sorry."

Mr. Davies laughed, and still chuckling, began to walk slowly. "It doesn't matter, not a damn bit. She's not like other women, Cluny. You know that by now. She's not dumb, she knows everything she needs to know, but it went in scrambled sort of, and it comes out cockeyed. Don't be misled by that. She won't live by the same rules that others do, either. Don't expect her to. Never did, never will. I don't know what kind of a wife she'll make. She's been a hell of a daughter. I've wanted to kill her at times, but when she comes back home to visit, I forget. I always forget it all when she's around. She can do that to you."

They walked around the block, Mr. Davies talking

about Lina, Cluny bobbing his head like a great
long-legged bird. When they got back to the gate
outside Ramona's house, Mr. Davies stopped and
asked, "What is this project of yours?"

"We're trying to revive interest in Alpha, the space
station."

Mr. Davies chewed his lip for a moment, then said,
"Tell me about it after supper."

"And did you order my poor baby to be good to me
and love me always and never be cross and make me
scrub his back? Is that what this little walk was for?"
Lina advanced across the porch to meet them. "If
you've scared him off, Daddy, I'll never speak to you as
long as I live. I swear it. Cluny, don't you pay any
attention to him. I never do, and he doesn't even
notice. Have you ever wondered how it is that some
people never seem to know when they're being repri-
manded? They just seem so used to being right all the
time, they can't consider that once in a while they could
be wrong. . . ."

Cluny caught her father's look and tried to stiffen his
face, but it was hopeless. He knew he melted down like
butter in the sun when he was with her; he accepted it
now and hardly ever gave it a thought. He was
surprised when Mr. Davies suddenly put one arm
around him, the other around Lina, and hugged them
both. Mr. Davies was crying, he thought in wonder.

Lee Cavanaugh Davies had made a fortune squeez-
ing sugar out of grapefruits, one of the magazines had
once written of him. He had used his wealth shrewdly
to raise himself to a position of strategic importance in
the corporate world of economics. Without his financial
and political support the project would have died
stillborn. It would not have been enough to write to
people, remind them of the glories of space; visits had
been demanded, speeches had been demanded, hearings had been demanded. And they had done them all.
Surprisingly the various intelligence agencies had

proved to be their most eloquent spokesmen. To forestall the Soviet test of will and strength that was inevitable as the United States wrestled with depression, discontent, a demoralized populace, they argued, it was necessary to initiate a project that would display the still-potent power of the country, belittle its present, and temporary, troubles. Cluny and Murray sometimes discussed the strange fellows they traveled with those days—militarists, ultraconservatives, reactionaries. Cluny had long denied politics in his world view, but even an apolitical scientist had to wonder about the reason for the support they were getting. Sid refused to be drawn into the speculation. "They think they're using us for something or other," he said coldly. "In fact, we're using them. I'd welcome the support of the devil himself. Your father-in-law will do until *he* shows up."

Cluny never did get familiar enough with Mr. Davies to pretend to understand him and his motives. Very early Mr. Davies had talked politics with him, and afterward had dismissed the subject entirely, in much the way a parent rejects trying to discuss philosophy or economic theory with a not too bright child. Cluny was relieved and never initiated any conversation that could easily be turned into a political discussion. He knew Lina's father was far right, probably a militarist, although he never said to Cluny that he believed the Army should take over for the duration of the crisis.

During those early years, Cluny, Murray, and Sid had been together most of the time for interviews, panels, discussions, conferences. After the business was over Cluny always had Lina to return to, while the other two men planned the next weeks and months. He left all the planning to them.

Once Murray said to him, "Your problem, kiddo, is that you believe love and devotion, even passion, can come only from the gonads. Wrong."

"What's that supposed to mean?"

"You're playing a game and we're not. Sid and I are

dead serious about Alpha. That wheel's gotta roll! One guy gets between me and it, I'd knife him. I'd drop a bomb in a mob if they got in the way. I'd put a bullet in the President himself if I had to." He was grinning but Cluny knew he was telling no more or less than the exact truth. He also knew Murray had carried a gun from high school age on, still carried it.

"I still don't know why you think I'm not as committed as you are. What haven't I done that I should have done?"

Murray looked across the room to where Sid was talking to Morgan Whaite, who would interview them on TV in five minutes. "When I look at him," Murray said, "I see a guy with a green monkey on his back, whip in hand, spurs dug in. I've got one just like it, know exactly how it feels. But you sidestepped it back there in the beginning. All we can think of right now is how to get as much across as we can in the few minutes they'll give us. And you, all you can think of is how long is this going to take and when can you get back to Lina? Right?"

He was a shrewd son of a bitch, Cluny thought. He was a grace-sniffer; he knew instinctively who had faith and who did not. But no one could fault his, Cluny's, performance, not then, not anytime. Even Murray had admitted it would have been impossible without him; it still might not take off, but doors were opening, people were seeing them, and they had Cluny to thank for that much. They all knew it. Cluny and his father-in-law.

The interview went well; by the time the program ended Morgan Whaite had stepped into their camp, had become a supporter. They made a hell of a team, Cluny thought, comparing Sid and Murray. Equally determined, dedicated, even fanatical, both were driven by forces they could only yield to. Outwardly they were so different that few people would ever suspect they shared the same devil. Murray reacted visibly; he emanated daemonic energy; it almost glowed around him like a crackling aura. Here, one might say, was a man clearly possessed. He was like an irregular pulsating star whose unpredictable surges and flares could either annihilate or mutate those too close to him. Sid was a black hole. He was cool, remote, unknowable, deceptively calm, so self-possessed that nothing escaped for analysis. Those who distrusted Murray's ebullience turned to Sid, unaware, until captured, that his sphere of power was so far-flung, or so strong. Those he caught seldom realized they had crossed a threshold and could no longer turn back. Quietly, gently, inexorably he drew them in and held them fast. He had a secret, he seemed to say, and his opposition leaned closer to hear it, to see it through his eyes, and later, converted, now his proponents, they seemed to feel they shared his secret although none of them could have given it voice.

Perfectly complemented, Cluny thought, the ultimate ideal couple. And his place in their scheme? A doorman. He was their goddamn doorman. He knew this and accepted it without real rancor because he had no intention of losing himself in the maze of their inner sanctum.

Sid had been right, Cluny acknowledged often. Everyone had been so desperate that they had been willing to try anything. Maybe the scientists would find some answers up there, was the general comment, and there were few protests when the President announced that after the long moratorium on building and manning the space station, scientists from four countries were to resume their work there in a joint effort at solving the many and varied problems besetting most of the world. This announcement came five years after the three young scientists had started their drive.

"For you, of all people, to argue for free will is ludicrous," Alex Bagration was saying heatedly. Although he was fifteen or twenty years older than Cluny, they had become good friends. He was in charge of the astronomy section of Alpha.

They were in the common room, where every day the hydroponics people brought in a few plants in containers and set them around here and there to try to make the place less alien. They did not succeed. It was alien: all plastic furniture, plastic floor coverings, plastic wall coverings, done in soft greens, rich golden yellows, with splashes of red here and there; but it was alien. Few walls on earth came together in angles that were either oblique or acute, as they did here. And nowhere on earth did round windows look out on true space without a surrounding atmosphere to soften it, to add a bit of color to the blackness. Nowhere else could people look out on the multitudes of stars, or see the moon's face in such stark relief, and then the Earth misty under cloud covers, blue Earth, green Earth, like a highly colored floor of malachite, almost within reach.

Cluny seldom really saw it any longer, unless it hit him like a jolt of an electric shock, and at those times he felt he should pinch himself, or hit his head against a solid wall, or find someone else to help him from his dream. That night, he and Alex had worked together for hours, and then had come to the common room to have a beer before going to bed. There were others in the large room relaxing after duty, or before their shifts started. The hum of conversation was pleasantly low and behind it was Stravinsky's *Firebird*.

Cluny knew that Alex, probably most of the other people on Alpha, gave him too much credit for reactivating the station. Alex should have known better, he thought. His government had been as anxious as the United States to reopen the station, start collecting some of the overdue benefits. They had put no obstacles in the way. He looked at his friend in amusement now; Alex would rather argue philosophy than drink beer or sleep.

"And for you to argue that decisions were not made, each step of the way, is equally ludicrous. At every point one is free to say yes or no."

"Twiddle-twaddle. Free to feel free to choose is all. Illusory freedom. Mankind has never been free; it is not in his genes to be free. Only the illusion of freedom is real."

Cluny laughed. "Next we'll argue souls. Or astral states."

Alex smiled also. "You are very like your father in some ways," he said. "He also would not continue an argument he knew he could neither win nor have won by another."

"I didn't realize you knew him."

"Not well. I was very young, very insignificant when he came to Russia. I sat in the back of the room and watched him with the Chairman and our cosmonauts, and I envied him more than I could say. Later, on another trip, I was aide to Dr. Klyuchevsky, and I was in the same room with them when they talked, just them, interpreters, and several aides. We were all so proud. How we strutted at being in on such weighty matters."

"What happened, Alex? We've had very little trouble this time. Why was it such a disaster then?"

Alex shrugged. "You know the story of Babel? Men from the four corners of the earth came together to build a tower. They wanted to talk to God, I think. Imagine if they had come together after God talked to them. Each babbling in a different tongue, trying to fit stones, trying to supply food and drink . . . The men from post-Babel tried to build this tower to heaven, and it could not work."

"Building a tower uses no language of its own," Cluny said. "Science does. Is it really that simple after all?"

"Many times you speak such riddles I cannot comprehend your meaning," Alex said. "And I have studied English for all my life. Still I find many things unclear. But when we are in the observatory, or the lab, I know exactly what you mean at all times. The language of science is very clear."

"Well, I'm going to hit the old hay and grab forty," Cluny said, grinning at the frown that crossed his friend's face.

"You did that on purpose," Alex called after him as he left the common room.

Cluny walked easily now in the slightly low gravity, although it had not been so at first. All of them had found themselves reeling into walls or each other unpredictably as they overcompensated time after time. The original plan had called for paint on all interior walls, soft colors, nonreflective flat surfaces, to minimize the feeling of alienness. Only in the common room had this been done. The other walls were all steel and plastic, all gleaming, reflecting eerily, distorting bodies, door shapes, everything visual. A few of the first people had not been able to adapt to the visual distortion, and had been relieved of duty. Their symptoms had been nausea, dizziness, inability to sleep, deep psychological stress. . . . Cluny could understand how the station could do that, and he tried not to see his reflections, egg shaped, sometimes minus a head, as grotesque as any monster ever to appear in nightmares.

One fifth of the station was finished enough for use. In two months they would increase the spin that would create earth gravity. Us and God, Cluny thought; toss off a little gravity here, a new life form there. He passed the genetic research section. There were the long curving corridors, the laboratories on the outside of the curve, the sleeping rooms, dining rooms, rec rooms on the inner curve. One spoke connected the section to the center, which contained the docking facilities, the power plant, and the master computer. Outside, the construction workers were tethered to the wheel, or to scaffolding. Beams, wall sections, steel sheets were tethered, silently towed along in the slow spin. Shuttles made their runs, back and forth, back and forth, bringing supplies, replacements, taking home construction workers, each as rich as Croesus, taking the scientists back for R and R.

The sleeping room side was on four levels, with stainless steel stairs at intervals in the corridors; there were poles to slide down, a slow-motion descent that was so dreamlike that all of them at times went to the top level simply to slide down, over and over again, like small children playing on an escalator.

He was directly below his own sleeping quarters on the top level, but he was not yet sleepy, simply restless. He looked in on the observatory, and for a long time stood gazing outward. Peter Bellingham and Anna Kersh were on duty; they ignored him, as everyone on duty ignored the others who often came in just to look. Sometimes one of them would stand unmoving so long that someone else finally would gently bump into the entranced one, murmur an apology, and move on. Nowhere else in the station was there such a wide-open view of space. Thirty feet of wall had been finished with glass that could be shielded with metal, but seldom was.

It had not been necessary to have so much unobstructed viewing area, but the original planners in the astronomical section had wanted it and no one else had questioned it. Everyone who worked that unit now was grateful. For the first time they could truly see their work; always before it had been as if an astronomer were a doctor trying to diagnose a patient who was concealed behind a screen that permitted vague outlines to show and little else. And the patient was mute.

The telescopes were outside the satellite, lonely detached eyes peering into distances so great no mind could comprehend them. Inside, the astronomers worked with computers, with printouts, with pictures, and now and then stood beside the wide windows and gazed outward.

Cluny looked until his eyes watered, and he wanted to look longer, as if he thought that if he could look long enough, hard enough, with the exactly right mental set, he would be transported through that glass wall, out there somewhere else.

Space was blacker than any drawing had ever shown it, blacker than any camera had ever revealed. Space black was a new concept, never realized until now. In his mind the points of light began to move, some swelling into real shapes, with radiating points that pulsed in rainbow colors. Galaxies spun in a space dance to unheard music; he knew he would have to be out there, in that somewhere else, to hear the music, and he did not doubt that out there he would hear it.

More than anything else, it was the size of space that held him before the windows day after day. Another new concept. No one who had not been here, had not stared into the depths as he and his fellow workers had done, could have any idea of the size of space, he knew. They had guessed, down there, and had come up with the word "infinity," but without knowing what it meant, with no feeling for it, just an intellectualized symbol that stood for something they could not grasp. Only here could one understand what infinity meant.

He remembered the first time he had looked through a good telescope, a twenty-inch reflector. It had been a cold January night, the sky flawless, without a shimmer of haze. While awaiting his turn he had spotted the Big Dipper, Polaris, Cassiopeia, Orion. . . . Then, looking through the telescope, the obscuring curtains of time and space had been rent and the sky was filled with stars. The Milky Way became a highway of light, beckoning, welcoming. . . . The Ring nebula became a smoke ring in space, tangible, graspable if only one could get close enough. The unrelieved blackness of the lesser coal sacks were chutes through eternity.

Another memory came. He had been reviewing a series of photographs that had been analyzed already by the computer. He had thought, with a terrible longing, how wonderful it would have been to have counted the moons of Jupiter for the first time, to have been the first person to see the rings of Saturn, to have predicted and then found Pluto. He had looked at the astronomy laboratory then with hatred: one wall filled floor to ceiling with computer components; automatic film-processing equipment; the intricate computer-run camera mechanism and clock drives that aimed the giant eye, blinked, froze an image on film and went on, endlessly, tirelessly, without comprehension of the awful, compelling, terror-filled beauty out there.

That had been his last week at the observatory. Back in school there had been more mathematics, more physics, more computer analyses and simulations, and somehow, somewhere in the years of work toward his degree, the image had been lost, the dazzling spectacle forgotten, replaced by theories and formulae.

He had watched an interview with a pianist once, and although he no longer remembered the man, he recalled his words: "You have to be one with the music, feel it, concentrate on it, be it. The piano no longer exists. If you ever change your focal point of attention to the keys or your hands, you lose the music."

Somewhere back there, Cluny knew, he had changed his focal point and he had lost the stars. Here on Alpha he had recaptured the excitement and awe, and until now he had not realized he had lost it before. He had forgotten. It frightened him that not only had his mind erased the thrill and its memory traces, but also it had erased his awareness that once it had been his.

"You can't sleep?" Anna asked softly.

He started as if from a dream and shook himself. "I'm okay," he said. She nodded and returned to her work.

For four months one of their tasks had been to measure cosmic radiations undistorted in any way, with the incalculable benefit of having intelligence direct the research. Here for the first time they could return to an area of puzzlement, linger over a particular segment of space if they could find no answers to their questions.

The unmanned satellite observatories had been excellent as pointers, directing them with decades of preliminary work to probe here, then there. Finally someone was following up the clues, finding few answers, always more questions.

Sid had said, joking, but not altogether clowning, "So a black hole is eating up the cosmic radiation, and that means a drought on Earth. So what do we do, go snare it and make it behave?"

Not a theory, still a hypothesis only, or a suggestion even. And if they could find proof, could they reveal it, knowing as they did that there was nothing to be done about it?

He left the observatory, and finally climbed the steps to his own room. Because there were only fifty-seven scientists in this section, each had a separate room, spacious enough for two or even three when the station became fully operational. He closed his door and looked around to see if he could detect anything out of order. He never could, but he always made that one quick, almost involuntary survey. Out of fifty-seven people, no one knew how many were intelligence first, science second. He had papers on a small desk, a computer terminal, his single bed, two chairs. Better living accommodations than most people on Earth had right now, he thought, and was sorry the Earth had intruded again. His problem, he decided, was that he missed Lina so much it had become a physical ache, like a toothache that was not acute, but did not go away either. With each new turn of the head, it became manifest; allowing himself to think of her now made the pain flare, like probing the tooth with an icicle.

He sat on the side of his bed and stared at the papers on his desk. It was a long time before he was ready to sleep.

Two days later Alex and Cluny were in the common room, talking about the coexistence of infinite alternate worlds. As always they took sides, arguing heatedly, contentedly.

One of the Americans on Alpha beckoned to Cluny. "Hey, do you know how long the Edsel was in production?" Benjamin Rausche was in the astronomy division; he was twenty-four, a Ph.D. for three years already. Alex lifted his eyebrows expressively and excused himself as Benjamin continued. "Sid is trying to collect on a bet with nine months. I think he's confusing it with childbirth." Alex was laughing as he moved away and sat down with a different group, where a chess game was being kibitzed.

"More than that," Cluny said, and he marveled at the light tone he managed to bring to the words. Edsel was their signal that something was amiss. "Where is he?"

"In his room, playing it cool, feet up, music on, a cognac in his fist. . . ."

"Come along, children," Cluny said. "No public bickering, no fistfights, no brawls. We gotta maintain class."

He left with Benjamin and Joe O'Brien, who was in space geology with Sid. Outside the common room he glanced at Joe, but was met with a slight frown. Benjamin continued to talk about Edsels.

Sid was playing Scott Joplin very loud on his tape recorder. "Hell," he said over the music as the three men entered, "You think I'd let Cluny be the arbiter?"

Benjamin and Joe went to one side of the room and talked about Fords and Edsels as Sid handed Cluny a sheet of paper with a handwritten message on it:

"Joe found this in orbit today. Don't say a word. He smuggled it back and I haven't left it a second since."

With a flourish he pulled back his bedcover and revealed a slender cylinder that gleamed like gold. He motioned Cluny closer, then twisted the end of the cylinder and removed it and withdrew a tube which also gleamed like the finest Egyptian gold. He unrolled the

tube reverently to reveal a scroll with figures, sym
something embossed on the surface.

Cluny sat down hard on the bed, no longer hearing
the inane conversation taking place behind him, or the
ragtime piano, no longer aware of Sid, or anything else.

Sid sat down and put the scroll between them, and
slowly Cluny reached out to touch it. His hand
trembled. How beautiful it was! The figures, all curved
lines, were precise, unlike anything he had ever seen
before. The edges of the scroll had been polished, the
corners rounded slightly; there was no sharpness
anywhere. It was uncanny, perfect, alien. He stared
until the curved lines shifted: raised, sunken, raised.
. . . His vision blurred. He felt the gold sheet between
his fingers, flexible, yielding, warm, no thicker than
heavy vellum stationery.

Stationery fit for a god, he thought. We built a tower
in the sky, and this time we got a message back. Alex
was wrong to scorn; he was premature. Not from God,
but a message from someone out there.

But why like this? he wondered suddenly and
withdrew his hand from the scroll. Why would anyone
leave a message out here? Why not on Earth? Why a
message, why not a real contact? He heard the Joplin
rag again, and the continuing discussion about cars, and
he looked up to see Sid regarding him soberly. Is it
authentic? he mouthed. Sid lifted his eyebrows and
shrugged. A hoax? Cluny looked again at the scroll.
Now he saw it as very human, just different enough to
raise the possibility . . . But gold? His thoughts raced
back and forth and he knew there was no way he could
decide. What if they announced it, only to have it
revealed as a tremendous hoax? Or what if they hid it,
only to learn it was real? What if it contained a threat?
A doomsday warning? Who should announce it? He
began to frown; Sid was nodding grimly.

"What now?" he mouthed, barely whispering the
words.

"We have to decide."

Cluny looked again at the cylinder. It was too smooth, too clean. "Why isn't it pitted?"

"Exactly," Sid said.

For the next hour, mouthing words in a hushed whisper, they tried to decide their next move. Finally they agreed that Sid should snip off a few grains of the scroll and the cylinder, that Cluny, who was due for a rest period in ten days, should take the samples back with him, and photographs of the message, and let Zach Greene, an undersecretary of the Space Agency, go on from there. No one suggested the secretary himself should be told yet.

"Where can we hide it?" Cluny asked then. There were no places to hide anything on Alpha. Fifty-seven men and women here and only the four of them who could trust each other with this, he thought bitterly. And he was not absolutely certain about Benjamin Rausche, who had a case of hero worship now, but who could outgrow it at any time, and afterward be an unknown factor. No room was safe; they all knew various intelligence agents entered and searched freely. No one had mentioned it ever, but it was as certain as the sunrise.

"Back where we found it," Sid said finally. "Six hundred kilometers from the station. Or back in one of the other areas that have been gone over and recorded."

Reluctantly they nodded. There was no other place for it. Sid's group was making a detailed study of orbiting junk—old satellites, orbiting rocks, abandoned space monitors of all sorts. At least only nine people were likely to come across it out in space, better odds than fifty-three.

The next ten days were a nightmare to Cluny. He knew he gave himself away to Alex many times over. He became morose and noncommunicative, hoping his dark mood would make others shy away from him. Alex joked about it. "So close yet so far from the beautiful Mrs. Cluny," he said. "One might think you worried about the reunion. Ah, three months with nothing to do except love, exercise, rest. I don't blame you, my young friend. I would be edgy also."

No matter how much Cluny learned about space flight and the mechanics of the shuttle, he knew it fell to earth and at the last possible moment spread its wings to brake the fall. He was terrified of the landings. This time was no better than any of the others he had experienced. He knew his face was green, and his legs too stiff, his voice too controlled when he got up to leave the ship. The pilot laughed openly at him, then waved good-bye and busied himself in the cabin. Others departing also looked frightened, but Cluny felt none of them had been as afraid as he had been and the thought was shaming to him.

An Air Force plane flew him to Washington, and he was debriefed by a pair of security agents for the Space Agency. Then he reported to Luther Krohmeier, the secretary, a politician who had not looked inside a book of science since the ninth grade. He was a thick-set man with a small head that was exactly the circumference of his neck. Caricaturists loved him.

"What's this nonsense about a black hole?" he demanded.

"It's not firm, sir. Probably nothing at all to it. We're trying to account for the decrease in cosmic radiation that has been apparent for the past ten years or so. Someone suggested that a passing body could have screened some of it. We're investigating that also."

"What about the black hole?"

They always kept harking back to that, Cluny thought impatiently. Because it sounded mysterious, and God knew it was mysterious, but also because it wakened something slumbering in the minds of everyone who heard it. There was always someone who felt compelled to make a big show of denying them as phenomena, the way some people denied ghosts.

"Someone suggested that possibly a black hole in this neighborhood of space might be responsible. Its gravitational pull could be capturing a portion of the cosmic radiation."

Krohmeier laughed rudely. "Crap! Show me one and I'll believe in it, boy. Until then, no more talk about black holes and cosmic radiation theft. No talk with reporters or anyone else. Information comes out of this office, nowhere else. And we have a statement from you all ready to go. You're resting; keep it that way."

"Yes, sir," Cluny said.

"Snead will give you a copy of the statement to read. If anyone asks about it, you have no comment, period. Right?"

"Yes, sir."

"Good. Doing fine work up there. Real fine work. Nice seeing you again. Keep in touch."

The assistant gave Cluny the statement, in which he was quoted as saying there was a definite hope that the work being done on the station, focusing microwaves on the Arctic ice packs, would alleviate the drought in the very near future.

He handed it back to Snead without comment and stalked away, not looking up Zach Greene now, knowing everything he did and said within the building would be watched and noted.

He was free to go home. He was aching with fatigue, his legs throbbing. He had called Lina already and told her to expect him before midnight. An Air Force plane would take him there. They would go to Bermuda, he thought, or Brazil, someplace where there were no refugees, no Newtowns, no space agency goons. He turned in at Murray's office. Murray had been denied space. He was an overweight medical risk with high blood pressure and a heart that did tricks now and then. But his efforts had not gone unappreciated; he had been given an office and a staff, and absolutely nothing to do, he complained bitterly. Actually he was

Zach Greene's top aide, and they ran the agency while
Luther Krohmeier drew the salary and put in the public
appearances that went with the office.

Cluny was waved in by Murray's secretary. He
always had a drink with Murray when he was in town;
they had been expecting him.

Murray bounded across his office and grabbed Cluny
in a bear hug. "You son of a bitch! I thought you'd be in
the air flying home by now, under your own power if
the plane was held up. How're you? How's Sid? How's
everything?"

"Great, not so good, great. Sid's having a running
fight with Joe O'Brien over trivia, things like how long
the Edsel was in production. Come on, let's grab a
quick drink before I take off. Might not have another
chance for three months."

Murray's face changed subtly. The beaming smile
altered, vanished, and returned so fast that no one not
looking for a change would have caught it. Now the
smile he wore was his stage smile; his eyes were hard
and probing. He opened the door behind Cluny, took
his arm, and walked through the reception room.
"Anyone calls, tell 'em I'm out getting drunk with my
old friend Arthur Cluny. Hope the President calls," he
added, winking at his secretary. His hand was very
hard on Cluny's arm.

Cluny's legs were so weak he had trouble keeping up
with Murray's near trot down the corridor, then out to
the street, a block to a dim bar. He was breathing
heavily by the time they were seated in a dark corner.
He waited until they had drinks before them, and his
heart had subsided, and his breathing was less labored.
He felt like a rabbit being watched by a snake, he
thought suddenly, and he told Murray about the
cylinder and scroll.

"I don't believe it," Murray said softly, showing
relief in the way he changed again; he lifted his drink
and took a long draught from it. Now he looked like a
benevolent uncle out with his favorite nephew. He

grinned at Cluny and shook his head. "You've been taken, kiddo."

"Maybe. I almost hope so. But it's a complication that's got to be handled. Sid thinks it's dynamite." By the way Murray's eyes narrowed and a frown suddenly creased his forehead, he knew his friend had started the same line of thought that he and Sid had covered. He became silent, waiting.

"It's got to be a plant," Murray muttered a few seconds later.

"We think so too, but we've got to make sure. We have to get those samples to a good metallurgist who's also safe. We didn't know what else we could do. And I've got to deliver the film to Zach. How can I see him?"

"You can't. Forget that. Luther's so paranoid, if he knew you'd been talking to Zach alone, he'd shit his pants. And probably fire Zach. I don't count; we're just drinking buddies from way back. Let's think."

Neither spoke; the waiter drifted back, left again. Cluny sipped his Scotch then, but Murray was using his glass to make circles on the table.

Finally he looked up. "Where's the stuff now?"

"On me. It's been on me ever since that day."

"Keep it on you. Look, take Lina up to New York—shopping, the shows, the sights, the whole bit. I'll get Zach up there and we'll get in touch."

"You'd think we were conspiring to blow up the Pentagon," Cluny said in disgust.

"It's almost that bad," Murray admitted reluctantly. "Sid's right about this; it's dynamite. If I had strychnine capsules I'd hand you one. Anything to keep it out of Luther's hands. Well, isn't life interesting, old buddy?" He remembered his drink and lifted it in a salute. "Back to work. On home with you. See you, Cluny." He picked up the tab and they left the bar together, to part on the street.

Cluny had no realization of the politics behind the agency, Murray thought, watching him walk away.

Cluny hated Luther, but that was a visceral reaction, not political. The real battle was going on within the agency day after day, week after week; in that battle he was a general, as was Zach, and the goal was to keep Alpha neutral, an international scientific venture, and not let it become the newest weapon in an arsenal he suspected no one could comprehend any longer. And the message might blow it all up. Real or fake, it could be the fuse. He scowled at the sidewalk. It had to be fake, but why? Who? How? How did they, whoever they were, intend to use it? And how could he stop them?

He often thought of Alpha as his child, the fruit of his own labor. While Sid and Cluny had been able to go up there and do the things the three of them had dreamed about, he had been committed to the home base, the controls, and he knew his was the more important operation. He had put it there and was keeping it there, almost singlehanded, he thought often, and tried to laugh at the nearly paranoid delusional system he was constructing, with him as the master of the universe. The laugh always sounded hollow, forced. Only because he was in reality one of the two most important men in the agency, who knew exactly what was at stake up there, and how fragile it was, he admitted to himself at those times. He had given up everything for Alpha, he had no life of his own beyond it, no interests, nothing else at all. Everything else paled to insignificance beside it. And now this damned message that was almost certainly a fake.

Item, he thought. It's not a joke. The cost of the scroll and capsule could have been managed, but not the delivery. Twenty-five thousand to make, couple of million to deliver. Not an individual joke. No way. And governments don't make jokes. He nodded to himself.

Item. Not France or England. Neither could win anything through such an elaborate scheme. They could gain only if the status quo was maintained.

Item. Russia or the U.S. Us or them. Them or us.

He remembered the eagerness of the various intelligence agencies to sponsor the reopening of the station, and he knew it had been the same in the USSR. The army had been behind them from the earliest days also. Somewhere men had sat and talked—over vodka or bourbon—and the outcome of that talk had been a gold capsule and a message, and a spook to deliver it. The opening gambit had been played; it had to be answered. He didn't understand the rules of this game, or who the players were, or what the game strategy would be, but he knew the goal: Alpha. Who controlled Alpha could control the world.

He knew also that any attempt to change the status quo, any attempt to affect the neutrality of Alpha would be followed by war practically instantly. And whoever had planted that capsule knew it too.

Did they know it had been found? Were they waiting for the answer to their opening? He understood that it was not the opening that determined the course of the game, but rather the response to it. Somewhere men were waiting, pretending not to know, pretending to believe in the neutrality of the science laboratory, pretending to believe in the benefits to everyone and all the while planning their next move. If they do this, we do that. If they announce it to the world, we say this, go to Game Plan A . . .

If we simply sit on it? He shook his head. That was probably Game Plan C, or D. And the clock was running.

He had dismissed the possibility of an actual message from the start, without really considering it. Now he made himself think of that, and found that he could not. It was too big, too awesome. If they were capable of traveling through the galaxy, what would be denied them? He could think of nothing. Would they be to us, he thought, as we would be to knights in the middle ages? He turned away from those thoughts with a disquieting unease. Schemes of men, Machiavellian as they might be, he could contemplate, even admire, but aliens able to travel through the galaxy, a thousand years of technology behind them? His head was starting to ache mildly. It had to be a hoax, he muttered.

But what if it wasn't? He made himself return to that line of thought, and found he could not think of aliens in terms of their effect on Earth, only how it would affect him personally. What if they came? He would be in the frontline. One of the first to deal with them, make the first contact with an alien race. He felt his heart skip, then race, skip again. He dug a pill box from his pocket and took out one of his nitroglycerine pills, swallowed it. Calm, calm, he told himself. Easy. You're a young man, Murray, with many years ahead of you. They'll know how to fix a bad ticker, cure it, operate on it. Make it a superheart. He caught himself in the fantasy and cursed briefly, but the vision was pleasant and would not fade.

10 As he approached the house, Cluny heard children's voices raised in shouts and wailing. It was nearly ten at night. He hesitated momentarily, then opened the door and entered. There were three youngsters in short yellow pajamas rolling on the living room floor in a fight, a girl and two boys, none of them more than eight years old.

"Lynette, Michael, Jason, stop this at once! You hear

me—at once!" Lina appeared in the doorway from the hall, carrying a tray of cookies and glasses of milk. She saw Cluny and nearly dropped the tray on a table.

"Cluny! Mother—he's here!" She ran across the room and threw herself at him. "Cluny! You're home! You're really home! You've grown! I never knew you could keep growing after you get to be thirty. You look so tired. . . ."

He held her hard, with his eyes closed. He was swaying with fatigue, and he wanted to weep although he did not quite know why. He heard the children's voices again, and opened his eyes. His mother was making the kids take the cookies and milk to the kitchen. She came to him and hugged him and kissed his cheek.

"Sit down, both of you," she said. "I'll bring you a drink. And make the children go to bed." She did not look at Lina, but he felt she was directing the remark to her in spite of that.

"At least let them come in and meet Cluny," Lina said quickly. "I promised them they could stay up and meet you. You're a hero, a real hero, and children all need heroes, don't you think? I mean, it's important for them to have models, someone they can aspire to emulate. They know all about space. . . ."

"Tomorrow," Cluny said quietly, nodding at his mother.

Ramona left and soon there were sounds of children being sent upstairs, protesting loudly. One of them started to cry again.

"Who are they? What are they doing here?"

"Orphans from Newtown," Lina said, tears in her eyes. "Aren't they the most pitiful things you ever saw? We just got them last week. You have no idea how it is in the Newtowns. Their mothers were all murdered. Raped and murdered! That's all they do over there. They begged people to take some of the children, one, two, three, as many as you can, because otherwise they'll probably all just die. Lynette is pretty, isn't she? And Michael . . ."

"Lina, why now? You knew I'd be here. Why couldn't you wait?"

"How could you even ask! Orphans! They need someone to take care of them and give them milk and cookies and take them for walks and read to them. . . ."

"It could have waited a couple of months. My mother isn't able to take care of them. She's too old, it's too hard on her. I don't want to share you with three strange kids. Do you have any help with them?"

"Of course! There's a girl who comes in every day to help, and they go to school and all. It isn't like they'll be underfoot all the time. Except it's summer vacation now, but they can go to the park and let you get some rest. . . ."

He drew her down on the sofa beside him and put his arms around her, his head against her breast. It was ridiculous how he had to fight back tears, he thought angrily. It was fatigue, of course; they warned everyone returning after a tour of duty. Earth gravity would be hard to get used to again, and until they did, they could expect serious problems with fatigue. This was not the homecoming he had anticipated day and night for months, he kept thinking.

His mother returned with the same tray, now holding three tall fruity drinks. He remembered his mother's mixtures of fruit juices and rum; nourishment and degradation, his father had said of them; they sneaked up on you because they tasted like something you would gulp down for breakfast.

His mother looked exhausted, he was exhausted; only Lina looked radiant and as lovely as ever. Perhaps she was even more beautiful than she had been when he met her; maturity was adding grace and charm in subtle ways—the slight curve of her lips, where she used to grin like a jack-o'-lantern. Also she now glanced at him from the corner of her eye instead of straight on, and that was new and different, and charming.

She was talking about the children, how they wanted to help with the garden, but pulled out all the wrong things and didn't seem aware of new seedlings until after they had trampled them. "It isn't as if they were trying to get out of their share of work, nothing like that, but they've been in Newtown for so many years, they've forgotten how to behave in company and everything. And Lynette, she breaks my heart crying for her mama. Sometimes I just have to leave for an hour or two because I can't stand it any longer. Isn't that right, Mother?"

Ramona nodded, tight-lipped.

Cluny could feel the tangy drink bubbling in his head pleasantly, easing the strain of muscles long unused to such hard work as it was to stay upright. He finished off the drink and put the glass down on the table. Lina was talking about her father now. Gently he put his fingers over her mouth.

"Listen, honey, we have to place those kids in some other house. You and I deserve a vacation and we can't leave them here with Mother. Day after tomorrow I want to take you to New York for a couple of days, do some shopping, and after that I want to go to a sunny beach where we can lie all day, paddle a little, eat fabulous food, sleep. . . ."

Lina pulled away. "I can't do that!" she cried. "It would be criminal to let those children start to feel a touch of security after so many years and then snatch it away from them again. You have to think of someone besides yourself, Cluny. I'm devoting myself to them. I've dedicated myself to helping out these three little orphans. . . ."

Very gently Cluny said, "Tomorrow, honey. I'm too tired to talk tonight. Tomorrow. Let's go to bed."

She continued the argument in their room, and he tried to turn off her voice, but this time he could not do it. One of the children began to cry; she left to see about it. Cluny undressed and waited in bed for Lina's return. He felt himself drifting off to sleep and started to sit up, but it was too great an effort, and he turned over instead, burying his face in the pillow, and without moving again fell asleep.

"It isn't as if you never went away before," Lina said the next day. "You're acting as if this was the first time you just took off and stayed for weeks and months at a time."

"Never this long and never this far," he said. "Lina, we have to get away to be together. I have to have the right kind of exercise and enough rest and food. It isn't just a whim of mine. You said I'd grown, remember? I have. Joints have a way of stretching a little in space, and muscles atrophy a little. We're sent home for a period of rest and rehabilitation and the rehab is just as important as the rest."

"You just don't care a bit about those little children."

"I care in principle. I care about them all in general, but I don't care about these three in particular. How could I? I don't even know them. All I can see is that they are standing in the way of our being together. And my God, Lina, I can't bear that! I've dreamed of you, of being with you. Night after night I dream of your body, your hair, your mouth. I love you so much it drives me crazy!"

"All right, Cluny honey. We'll go to New York for a week. Is that all right? I can bring in Dolores for a week so Mother won't have to do anything at all. And we'll pretend it's like it was when we first got to know each other. Remember how you'd get an erection every time you saw me? It was so pathetic and touching and beautiful."

The children came through the house like a whirlwind then, ending their talk.

They took a taxi from the airport to Manhattan. Taxis

and buses were the only traffic, it always seemed at first glance, but then the limousines became noticeable, and the expensive imported sports cars. The city was crowded, as always, and there were more refugees than ever, all out on the streets now that the weather had turned warm. Cluny felt their hostile stares as the taxi crept along, slower than the passengers could have walked. He felt himself cringing inwardly at the noise level, and every muscle in his body was tense. New York was an endless horn and scream. It had been a mistake to come here, he knew. This was a nightmare of noise and filth and crowds.

Lina's eyes were bright with excitement; she had been ticking off the excursions she had planned for them. Museums, theaters, movies, shopping, cocktails with old friends, bookstores . . .

The doorman of the Park Plaza opened the taxi door for them, nodded to a bellhop to get the luggage, and then ushered Cluny and Lina inside the hotel. There was a heavy barred door that was never left unguarded. Only guests with reservations were accepted, and they were admitted by the three doormen, who worked in shifts. Cluny and Lina had stayed here many times; there was no delay in checking their identification, or passing them through security to their rooms.

A whisper-quiet elevator deposited them before their suite on the fifth floor. Within the building the carpeting was very deep, the doors heavy, all the walls thick enough to be virtually soundproof. It was an oasis of peacefulness after the insane cacophony outside.

Cluny got rid of the bellhop and locked the door, bolted it, and attached the chain lock. Then he looked at Lina. She was nearly undressed already, leaving a trail of clothes on the floor of the sitting room. He remembered that first time in his one-room apartment, and suddenly he was seized with the same frenzy he had experienced then. They fell onto the bed together in a heap and their lovemaking was explosive and almost

violent. Then, exhausted, Cluny lay on his back holding
her in the crook of his arm, waiting for the wild
thumping of his heart to subside before he tried to talk.

"I knew it was temporary, Cluny baby," she was
saying. "I mean, anyone could come home from space
with something not working exactly right, you know? It
didn't even surprise me. . . ."

He did not argue with her. Both nights he had fallen
asleep waiting for her to come back from doing
something with the kids, and throughout the day there
had been no time. She had been busy with the children
all day long, taking them here and there, getting
Michael's hair cut, shoes for Lynette. . . .

It was a honeymoon again, better than the first one
had been.

The first day they slept late, went to an art show, had
lunch, back to their room to make love and nap. Then
shopping, dinner, back to bed for a celebration, sleep.
The next day was a repeat with only the minor details
different: a museum instead of an art show, cocktails
with friends instead of shopping. They spent hours in
bed, recapturing the past. Cluny had never been so
content. For hours at a time he forgot completely the
envelope he carried. When he was with Lina everything
else always faded, became insignificant and hard to
recall in any detail. If she was on the phone, or in the
bathroom, or busy with her nails, his thoughts were on
Alpha, the scroll, the message, and sometimes he
caught a visceral twist of excitement that echoed palely
the feeling he had had when he stood in the observatory looking out the wide windows at space. Then she
came back and the other thoughts were wiped out of
existence once more. He was Jekyll and Hyde, he
thought; sometimes the bright, not so young any more
astronomer doing great work in the space station; then
again a lovesick boy who forgot to tie his shoelaces
when his lover was near. He veered away from such
thoughts forcefully, unwilling to follow them through,
bewildered by them, by the duality he found in himself

which seemed able to separate him into halves so thoroughly.

On the third day they went to a matinee, shopped for books for the children, returned to their room and made love, then went to dinner. At ten, as they were leaving the restaurant, Murray and Zach were entering.

Zach Greene was an ageless, narrow man with white hair and a pink complexion. His face was unlined, his eyes very knowing, and few people had ever seen him react with surprise at anything that happened.

"For God's sake!" Murray exclaimed. "The lovebirds! Lina, you're the most beautiful woman on God's earth. You still have my number? When you get tired of him, remember me. I'll be waiting, if it takes forever."

Zach shook hands with Cluny, bowed slightly to Lina. "Will you folks join us for a drink?"

"Lina?" Cluny glanced at her.

"Tell you what, honey. Just put me in a cab and I'll go on home now. You won't be long, will you?"

He couldn't believe it was going to work out like this: a chance meeting, Lina so cooperative. They would get it over with in ten minutes and he would be out from under the weight of the envelope that suddenly was hot against his chest.

"You sure you won't mind?"

"Don't be silly. I'd be bored to death listening to the three of you talk about spaceships and shuttles and stuff like that."

Cluny turned to Zach. "Suppose I join you in a couple of minutes. I'll just get a cab first."

He saw Lina off and returned to his friends. Murray looked worn and worried and Zach was glum. "It has to be a hoax," Zach said. "But why? And who?" He fell silent as the waiter appeared with their orders. "I told him Scotch and water for you. Is that all right?"

Cluny nodded and they remained silent until the waiter had left again.

"Tell me," Zach said then.

Cluny reported everything. He took a quick look

about the restaurant, withdrew the slender envelope from inside his shirt pocket, and handed it across the table to Zach, who held it below the level of the table and opened it. For a long time no one said anything as he studied the pieces of gold. The film was in a separate opaque envelope.

"Thirty-six shots," Cluny said. "Sid took care of that part. He's a damn good photographer. And Joe O'Brien got a roll of it before he hauled it aboard his scooter."

"Right. I know who can analyze the metal. Where will you be, Cluny, three days from now?"

"I don't know. Here or back in Chapel Hill."

"Delay it if you can. Stick around. We'll run into you again. Or arrange something else. Once is a coincidence, but again . . . ? We'll arrange something. You'll hear from me."

He returned the gold pieces to the envelope. "It's got to be a hoax, but goddamn it, how?"

"Who and why?" Murray added. "It could blow up in our faces, whichever way it goes from here." He drank. "Let's split. See you, Cluny. Thanks, old buddy. Thanks a whole bunch."

Cluny took a taxi and when it got stuck in traffic a block from his hotel, he left it and walked the rest of the way. There was a police car double-parked outside the hotel, and a large crowd of people, including a dozen or more yelling refugees. As he got closer he saw that the doorman and a bellhop were arguing with a refugee, and another man was sprawled on the side-walk. Two policemen were there, one kneeling by the man on the sidewalk, the other handling the crowd. Cluny edged around the crowd and entered the hotel, feeling sickened by the incident. Panhandlers, desperate enough to try to get past the doorman. No one was in the lobby; they had all gone to watch the excitement, probably. He took an elevator up.

Lina opened the door to him, then turned her back

and flounced away before he could embrace her, kiss her. He followed her to the bedroom.

"Oh, Cluny, how could you do that to me? Pretend we're on a vacation and arrange a rendezvous like that? Send her away in a taxi—is that what you told them you'd do when they just happened to run into us?" She swept through the bedroom to the bathroom. She was dressed in a filmy negligée and was barefoot.

"I didn't expect to see them tonight."

"You're lying! If you could have seen your face in the restaurant! Didn't expect to see them! And that little package?" She came to him in a quick motion and ran her hands over his chest. "Gone, isn't it? That mysterious little package is gone. Hadn't you better call the police, Cluny, or the FBI or someone? Isn't it robbery? All that gold must be valuable!"

"You opened it?"

"Don't be an idiot! Of course I opened it. Oh, not the film. Even I could tell it was film. Are you some kind of smuggler these days, is that it?"

She was moving between the bedroom and the bathroom as she talked, walking in fast sweeps of motion back and forth, brushing her hair, her voice rising and falling as she advanced and left.

"Lina, stand still a minute. Let me tell you about it. . . ."

"Tell me nothing, Cluny! You dragged me away from those poor little children who need me so you can play cops and robbers. I'm going home tomorrow."

"I didn't tell you to leave. You suggested it yourself. I never would have thought of it."

"One of them would have suggested it. I saw them look at each other when I took the words right out of Zach's mouth. You think I don't notice things like that, but let me tell you, Arthur Cluny, there isn't much happening around me that I don't notice. The look on your face, the way they looked at each other. It was all set up, wasn't it, every bit of it?"

Behind her the bathroom was getting steamy; she

had drawn a bath and perfumed clouds were forming. "I'm going home to those little orphans where I belong and you can stay here or come back or do whatever you want. Play cops and robbers if that's fun for you, it isn't fun for me. I have certain duties, responsibilities—"

"Lina, stop the pretense! Just be honest with me. You don't give a damn about those children. You pick up and drop charities as if they were pretty toys to play with for a short time until you get bored. What do you plan to do with them when you get tired of this new role? Leave them with my mother while you go have fun on your father's yacht, meet a couple of new men to amuse you?"

She stopped in the bathroom doorway, her hand raised, with the brush in it. "Why did you say that? Who's been talking about me? It was your mother, wasn't it? She never did like me and now she's trying to make you turn against me! I knew she would. I just knew it. And what are you going to do about it? Put on a big act? Be the injured husband? It isn't natural for anyone to be alone half the time, not for me or for you. I have feelings, emotions, needs. I feel things, Cluny, I really do."

"I know," he said quietly. "I'm sorry. I'm not blaming you for anything."

"Don't you dare act like you're forgiving me! I won't have that from you! I haven't done anything that needs your forgiveness!"

He moved to her, no longer hearing the words. They had become a great rising and falling sound without content, without meaning. He reached for her and she backed away from him, her mouth opening, closing, opening. He grabbed her shoulders and pulled her toward him, wanting only to hold her, to silence her, to feel the warmth of her body against his. She lifted the brush and hit him on the side of the head and he pushed her away, staggered back blindly, turned and ran through the bedroom, through the sitting room, out of the suite and down the corridor.

All he could think of was getting away. He had to get away. Over and over he saw her furious face, the hand sweeping upward, the brush. . . . He had to get away, get away. He felt as if something delicate had snapped in half, something had broken that could never be repaired; something beautiful and precious was now dead.

His thoughts made no sense to him; there was only the need to run away. Once, when he was six or seven, he had seen a fire consume a warehouse, and then too he had run. He had kept going until someone had found him staggering, trying to run farther, and had put him in a car and had taken him home. He had not known why he was running, where he had been trying to go, why he had needed to run away, but he was doing it again now, driven with the same urgency, the same undeniable need. He had to run away.

He stopped running when he nearly fell, and his legs refused to support him any longer. Leaning against the wall, he stared down the corridor. He did not know where he was. He had passed the elevators, had turned a corner, or more than one, and now he was in an unfamiliar section of the hotel. Ahead of him was an exit sign and he stumbled toward it. There were stairs; next to them was a service elevator. He pushed the button and waited blankly until it came. At the street level he left the hotel through a service door that opened at a touch. He walked a block, another block, he didn't know how far. He could feel his heart pounding, and his legs were so weak that each new step required intense concentration. He lurched and his foot slipped on a curbing; he plunged headlong into the street and dimly heard a squeal of brakes.

He had to tell them the car had not hit him, he thought, but he didn't move. He could fall asleep here, now, with all those people standing around him, talking, watching. He heard a woman's voice saying she had not hit him, she knew she had not hit him, and he thought again he should reassure her that she had not.

Finally he knew he could not sleep there and he began to push himself up. Hands tried to hold him down.

"An ambulance is coming. Just stay still until it gets here, okay?"

"I'm all right," he mumbled. "I fell down. I'm all right."

Now the hands were helping him, and he sat up. A policeman was there, holding his arm, looking at him anxiously. "You're sure, Dr. Cluny? Just take it easy and wait for the ambulance."

He blinked. They had had time to find his wallet, identify him? "I don't need an ambulance," he said, sounding the words slowly, with great care. "I slipped on the curb and fell. Must have knocked the wind out, or bumped my head, or something. But I'm all right now. Help me stand up, will you?"

The officer helped him and he stood upright, swaying just a little bit. He looked at the woman who had not hit him and said apologetically, "It was entirely my fault. Sorry." Then he asked the officer, "Is there anything I should do, sign, anything to show I don't blame anyone?"

"Guess not, sir." He nodded to the woman, who got inside a low cream-colored Porsche and drove away very slowly through the crowds of people who had collected.

"If you could help me get a taxi, I'll go on to my hotel," Cluny said.

"Which one?"

"Park Plaza."

"It's just around the corner," the officer said. "Come on, we'll take you." Another officer had appeared.

He helped Cluny into the squad car, radioed a report and canceled the ambulance, and drove around the corner, to stop again. "You in any shape to get up to your room?"

"It's space fatigue," Cluny said. "It hits you in the legs, makes them turn to rubber. We've been walking too much, I guess."

"Yeah, I read about that. I'll just see you to your room, and then I won't have to worry about whether or not you made it. How's that?" The second officer nodded his approval.

Cluny was not at all certain he could walk alone through the lobby to the elevators, and then to his room after he got to the fifth floor. The doorman came now to investigate the police car and exclaimed over Cluny, making a big fuss. Cluny found he needed no support, only steadying. It was as if he were back on the station again, he thought, reeling into walls, unable to walk a straight line. He was telling the officer about that when they got to his door and he opened it.

"Thanks," he said then. "I guess I wouldn't have made it alone. Tomorrow I think we'll take it easy, watch television."

"Forget it, Dr. Cluny. I wonder if I could bother you for your autograph, though. If you feel up to it, I mean. My kid would love to have it. All he thinks about is going off to space someday. He'd sure love it."

Cluny motioned him inside. "Sure thing. Wait a minute. I've got some station maps. . . ." He went to the bedroom door and opened it cautiously.

"Lina? It's me." The room was lighted, the bed still made up with the spread in place. He frowned, then saw that the bathroom door was not closed. He went to it and looked in. Lina was draped over the bathtub, half her body inside it, her legs drawn out in a twisted way on the floor.

It was handled very quietly and expeditiously. The officer who had been with Cluny gave his testimony. Murray and Zach came forward to give theirs. The doorman testified that no one had entered the hotel unnoticed; no stranger could have entered. The service door opened one way only, from the inside. No signs of a struggle, nothing taken, no forced entry, all indicated it was the simple accident it appeared to be. She must have been brushing her hair, turned to adjust the

water, or feel it, and slipped. Her bare foot on the wet
tile . . . They found a smear of blood on the tiled wall
where she had hit her head when she stumbled; her
hairbrush was in the tub. Lina's father came and
claimed Cluny as his son and wept openly.

Through it all, even the funeral in Jacksonville,
Cluny moved and walked and talked like a zombi. Deep
shock, a doctor said, and prescribed complete rest. Mr.
Davies gave Murray keys to a house on a small island
he owned in the Florida Straits, and Murray and Cluny
were flown there in Mr. Davies' private airplane.

Mr. Davies had called a housekeeper, who would be
there every day from ten until after dinner, and besides
her, there would be no one but the two men and the
caretaker on the island for as long as Cluny needed it.
When the plane left them, Cluny started toward the
house, with Murray following. In the shade of a grove
of black cypress trees Murray caught Cluny's arm.

"You can't keep this up, old friend," he said. "For
Christ's sake, say something."

"I killed her."

"I know," Murray said.

11 Cluny stopped. "Why didn't you tell
them? Were you and Zach having me
followed? That's how you happened to
meet us?"

"Sure we were. Look, Cluny, if that scroll is a fake,
someone else might be following you, and if so, we'd

like to know about it. Our man, Zach's man actually, watched you go inside and thought you were down for the night. Then he saw you go inside again. No one else saw you the first time; you couldn't have been there more than five minutes. I don't know how it happened and I don't give a shit. It was an accident."

"We were arguing about something, meeting you and Zach, I think, and I tried to touch her, just to hold her. She hit me with her hairbrush, and I don't know what I did. I was lost in the hotel after that, and then I was walking and trying not to crash into windows. I missed the curbing and fell down. . . . I don't know what I did, Murray. It was like being hit by your mother, or being struck down by your God. I don't know what I did!"

"Nothing," Murray said. "Maybe you gave her a little shove, a reflex. There weren't any footprints on the tiles, Cluny. Only her bare feet. The tiles were wet; footprints would have shown up, left some kind of mark, either on the tiles or that fluffy rug. Hers were on it, no one else's. Believe me, old friend, they looked for prints."

Cluny shook his head helplessly. "But I don't know."

"Okay. You don't know. So you live with it. Now listen to me, Cluny, No talk like this in the old man's house. No talk about the scroll, nothing at all. Get me?"

"Davies?" Cluny stared at Murray and then nodded. "Right."

"We talk on the beach, out under the swaying palm trees, but not inside. And for the next week or so, we don't do much of that, not until those marbles in your head turn into eyes again. Let's go see our digs. It looks like a hell of a vacation coming up. Look at that house!"

It was days before Cluny actually saw the house and by then he had grown used to it without awareness and he accepted it without awe. The house was low, white, with a red-tiled roof. It was a large U shape, with a swimming pool between the two wings. Every room

had a view of the ocean or the pool and many looked
out on both. The rooms were spacious and cool, with
only enough modern furniture to be functional; there
was nothing extra anywhere.

By the end of the first week Cluny's heart no longer
pounded when he swam the length of the pool, and he
could even snorkel a little without being afraid he
would sink and never rise again.

Murray turned off all talk about the scroll during this
time. At the end of the second week he began to talk
about the new wave of hostility that had become
evident on the space station; even the daily papers were
starting to print stories about that.

"Sid says his room's been searched a dozen times or
more. The Russians are complaining about our intelligence interfering with their work. The French and
English are at each other's throats over intrusions. The
Russians asked for a new security precaution: a complete search of everyone arriving and leaving."

Both men stared out at the sparkling blue water. In
the distance there was a traffic lane, and ships passed
continually—tankers, freighters, fishing boats, yachts.
In the other direction they could see the Keys, a low
irregular horizon not identifiable as islands at all.
Between them and the Keys pelicans were diving in the
shallow water, plummeting in bone-jarring falls to hit
with great splashes that sent waves high into the air.

"It has to be a hoax then, or how would anyone have
known anything was up?" Cluny asked finally.

"Not sure. But Sid says the scissors he used to snip
off pieces of the scroll and the container have vanished.
No doubt they had traces of gold on them. Might make
someone wonder a little."

"It's actually gold?"

"Yeah. The container's hardened a little with silica
and ferrous manganese."

Cluny turned to study him. "Even that doesn't clinch
it?"

"'Fraid not. There've been several hundred people in

and out of space in the past twenty-five years or so. One of them could have brought back raw materials, or could have made it on one of the satellites, in fact. The scroll has minor impurities; any of them could have been from Earth or the moon, a meteorite, or an asteroid. Back to Go and start over."

Cluny bit his lip. The analysis should have settled it, he thought aggrievedly.

"Do you have the reports?" he asked then.

"Nope. Zach has them. I saw them. You've got to be a metallurgist to read them. The computer is doing a rundown on the possible locations of that particular gold, assuming it came from Earth. And they're doing an analysis of lunar rocks that were brought back, checking to see if anyone swiped one of them, stuff like that. But how it looks right now is just what I've told you. A draw at best."

"Did the Russians do it?" Cluny asked, not as if expecting Murray to answer, but as if he had put off the question as long as he could until now it emerged of its own volition.

"Could be. The scenario goes like this: We can't disprove it's legitimate and we announce the first extraterrestrial message. Their boys come up with the definitive proof that it's from Earth and accuse the U.S. of skulduggery. Their hardnoses get sore and heat up the old cold war to a boil and start the shortest war ever to be started."

"Yeah," Cluny agreed. "That's the one I kept coming up with. But it's pretty crude, maybe too crude for them."

"Maybe. Try this one: We announce it, as before, and get linguists busy on it. They come up with something like the aliens are communists and want a unified one-world government to greet them when they arrive in x number of years."

"Good God," Cluny said in disbelief. "Who dreamed that one?"

"Yours truly," Murray admitted modestly. "There's

a dozen more. Want them one by one, one a day, all in a heap?"

"Let's stick to the first one. They say it's a hoax and we come back with: You must have done it then. And they say no we didn't, and so on. And meanwhile the hardnoses on both sides are getting hot and sticking burs under the generals. . . ."

"Yeah," Murray said. "Same thing."

"What if we did it?"

"No matter where you start, the ending's the same," Murray said. "We've been over it a hundred times and we keep coming out in the same lousy place."

"I don't follow that. They couldn't prove it a hoax if we did it and were pretty damn careful."

"So we're a couple of Russian scientists, and someone tells us the Americans have found this orbiting gold scroll with a message; you could set it to music, head the top forty in a week. Anyway, we do the same analyses that Zach's having done now and come up with the same results. A draw. That leaves us heads or tails. Fake or real. Since it's the Americans who found it, and we know how power hungry they are, we opt for fake. What are they after? To prove to the world they talk to God? To gain superiority when they're slipping badly economically, and it's even in doubt if they can survive. Ah ha! we say. This is why they pushed to reactivate the station at this time. To spring this little joke on the world. It must be, because we all know they shouldn't have spent the money on it now. They should be home digging canals and building aqueducts and trying to house and feed displaced people. Even if we don't know exactly what they have planned as a follow-up, we don't believe them, and we agree with those who say they must be stopped before they do whatever it is they are planning to do."

"So it's a no-win game no matter what anyone does," Cluny said after a few moments. "Maybe we should put a firecracker on its tail and send it away so no one will ever find it again." He didn't look at his friend, but continued to stare at the line of boats in the distance. "But what if it's legitimate?" he nearly whispered then.

"Yeah," Murray said heavily. "It could be for real."

Cluny thought and then said, "So we have to try our damnedest to prove it's a hoax, and if we really can't, then find it again, but next time with a mixed crew, Russian and American—something like that?"

"Welcome back to the gang," Murray said, patting his arm. "That's it. What else?"

What else? Cluny thought later, walking along the beach alone. Nothing else. The night was heavy with clouds and the waves lapping the shore sounded dull and sullen, hitting heavily at random intervals. A storm was moving in from the west and already he could see the lightning in the distance. Not yet as strokes, but as a general cloud glow that flickered off and on, revealing mountainous piles of cumulus clouds each time.

All that water, he thought, wasted on the gulf and this lousy island. For what? To keep the oleanders sunshine yellow, and the hibiscus scarlet? A white heron lifted silently a few yards in front of him; it flew around him and landed at the edge of the water again. A ghost, he thought. It was a ghost. He would not permit himself to turn around to see the bird. Ghost, as silent as a ghost, as ethereal, as unafraid. That was the real difference between people and ghosts. People were afraid. Three times he had come to the edge of the water and stared longingly at the horizon. When he regained more muscle power, he had decided the first time, and the second; the third, he had not even pretended to himself that he would start swimming toward the unreachable goal. He was afraid to die, he thought with disgust. It would be so simple to start swimming. How long could he last? Ten minutes, fifteen? At first he had known that when he foundered, he would still be in shallow water, and that would have been humiliating, to try to drown oneself in water so shallow that a man his height could simply walk out again. It would have been the equivalent of a scratch on the wrist, a Band-Aid to cover it with, sympathy from friends and relatives. He wanted no sympathy from anyone.

He had not told them at first because it had seemed so apparent to him that they would know. They should have known. To have spoken of that last scene to strangers would have been unthinkable. How could he have told anyone without telling everything? How he had worshiped her from the start. How he had dreamed of her body every single night he was away from her. How he had been able to see her and feel her and not be bothered by the endless chatter that flowed from her lips. He had known from the beginning that she was unfaithful when he was away, and yet he had known that that woman was not his Lina. His Lina was his alone forever and ever; she did not even exist when he was gone. Another soul took over her body then, did things with it, took it places; his Lina's existence began and ended with his presence. He had wanted to tell them, but there had been no way to begin, no way they could have understood. No one had ever understood how much he had loved her. If he had not been so far away, he thought, probably he would have told them. But he had been millions of miles from them all, had heard them as if from a great distance; it had been like a telephone connection that was bad and scrambled everything but the most direct, clearly pronounced syllables. He had heard and understood them so imperfectly. They had told him to sit down, and he had not known what they meant until someone had taken his arm and guided him to a chair.

The lightning flared closer and this time a rumble of thunder rolled across the sky like a train. He should have told them, he thought bleakly, so they could punish him. They had not punished him, and he could not punish himself. He stood and waited for the lightning to strike him, but the storm veered away from the island altogether and finally he went inside, where

Murray was waiting with a nightcap laced with a sedative.

He looked at the glass and then put it down on the table. "Not this time. I'll sleep or I won't. Eventually a body does fall asleep, isn't that the theory? Eventually."

Murray nodded.

Two days later Cluny decided they had to leave the island. "I can't stand it much longer," he said. "Overnight it's become a fancy prison, and I'm tired of salt water and sun. Let's go to your place."

"Thought you'd never ask. Would you believe I can be ready in five minutes? I was beginning to look for Friday's footprints on the beach."

Cluny heard himself laughing and was shocked into silence again. Murray was grinning approvingly at him. He called his office and got travel priority and a booking, and the next day they met the housekeeper on the dock. "Turn around, madam; we're going to island-hop today," Murray said to her. How much she understood was problematical; she had never spoken a word of English to either of them, but she shrugged and waited until they got in her little outboard motorboat, then she turned it toward the Keys and sped back across the water.

Cluny and Murray jogged along the Potomac to the rendezvous with Zach, and then sat down, breathing too hard, next to him on a park bench. Cluny's legs throbbed; but he had kept up, he thought with a grim satisfaction. He had his legs back now; his heart was functioning normally; he was an Earther again.

Zach was holding a long tether attached to a wire-haired terrier that was running in excited bursts of speed after birds. Zach looked more tired than ever.

He nodded and said, "Cluny, are you fit now? Are you well enough to travel, take part in this mess?"

"Yes, of course. To do what?"

"I have half a dozen men in on this by now," Zach said disgruntledly. "I don't like it. And Samuelson, our metallurgist, is howling for a look at that can. The chances of a leak increase by a factor of ten with each new person. No more. We need someone who can visit several linguists and see if that goddamn message can be translated. I can't go to the CIA or the FBI or any other service with it. They have to be independent and they can't be told a damn thing. Can you handle it?"

"How about travel priorities? Can you arrange that?"

"Doc Weill is going to have you in for a check. He'll say you're heading for a breakdown and recommend VIP treatment, including priority papers. They'll get you aboard anything moving at any time. I'll send an itinerary for you to follow. You'll have a tail, a couple of tails; pay no attention to them. One of them will be mine. God alone knows who else will stick to you. Murray will bring you the message. Okay?"

"Was someone else following me . . . that night?"

Zach nodded, watching his small dog.

"Then they, whoever it was, know too," Cluny said softly. "Why haven't they told the police? They've got a time bomb to play with. Or blackmail."

"Exactly," Zach said. He stood up. "You'll need a cover story. You're looking for your childhood sweet-heart, Jean Brighton. Murray will bring you her dossier to fill you in on the past fourteen years." He whistled to the dog, tightened the leash, and walked away with his head bowed.

That night Murray insisted that they watch the television news. It was the first time Cluny had paid any attention to the current news in months.

The lead story was the continuing coverage of the destructive fire in Cincinnati Newtown, in which ninety-eight people had died and three thousand had been seriously burned or overcome by smoke inhalation.

Russia was experiencing a disastrous drought in its

western plains and had issued directives to the farm cooperatives not to plow millions of acres for fear the damage from wind erosion would be irreversible.

The fourteenth desalination plant would open in ten days on the California coast. The price of oranges was expected to rise by fifteen percent and rationing was being tightened on all produce starting immediately. . . .

There were congressional hearings, and there were refugee demonstrations, a riot in Kansas City, and a picnic for the Newtown outside Atlanta. Cluny tried to stop hearing any of it and partially succeeded; he was jerked back to full attention by the last story. The first fatality among the scientists had been reported by Alpha. Claud Frankl had died in a docking accident. Frankl was one of the geologists working under the direction of Dr. Sidney Oberlin. There were no details yet concerning the cause of the accident. Murray cursed fluently and turned off the set. "That was due for release tomorrow, or the next day," he said. "We've got a real sieve down there, old friend. A real holey sieve."

"Why didn't you mention it to me?" Cluny asked angrily. "Can't trust me?"

"Don't be an ass! What would you have done about it? We're waiting for details. He was out alone and lost pressure. No one seems to know why. Goddamn it!"

He stamped across the room to a small bar and made drinks for them both and handed Cluny one. His face was an ugly mottled red. The apartment was very likely bugged; or the possibility was so great that they acted as if they knew it for a fact and said nothing in the rooms that they weren't willing to share with half a dozen other people.

"I'm going to bed," Murray said abruptly and left Cluny alone in the living room.

Cluny read through the dossier on Jean Brighton and could not connect anything in it to the scrawny kid he had played with on the Florida beaches. It made little difference, he thought; her trail led him to Arkins, and that was his target. Arkins could translate the message if anyone could. Jean had moved on; he would stop with Arkins. For a moment he was overwhelmed with a memory of swimming in the rising surf of a high tide pushed even higher by the first winds of a hurricane still far offshore. Jean swam beside him, her thin body nut brown, taut with the effort of body-surfing a cresting wave to shore. He yearned to go back, to have those few good years over again, to know them for the good years, savor them minute by minute. . . .

Restlessly he tossed the folder down.

The apartment had two bedrooms, a tiny kitchen, and a large living room. It was luxurious by most standards. Cluny found himself thinking of Murray's tenement room, where the three men had decided they could seize the moment and make Alpha come alive again. Rags to riches, he muttered to himself and turned off the light. He went to the window and stood there with his drink, looking at the great city twenty stories below. Not as brightly lighted as it used to be, sprawling more than ever, swarming with refugees demanding rain, demanding an end to the drought, a return to the good life that was becoming a myth in their minds.

But worse than the crowding and the fear was the perpetual threat that swung lower with each motion of the pendulum. He remembered a study he had used once in a college paper for history, or sociology, or something. The study had detailed the reactions of masses of people to unendurable stress: first came anger, a positive reaction even though it often included violence; next came stoicism, the manifestation of the intention to wait out the situation; then came apathy, the helplessness of repeated frustration. Following this stage inevitably there was an outburst of insanity—behavior that was not suitable for problem solving, the study had worded it discreetly. They go nuts, Cluny thought. And they go on a rampage. And the whole world was sitting on the verge of apathy and madness. Most of the demonstrations were quiet and controlled and filled with hopelessness and despair, not with the wild excesses that had taken place in the sixties. That would be welcomed now, any show of life would be welcomed now. But they came with dull eyes and stood silently, and then left again, hungrier and tireder and somehow dirtier than ever. Their shame was evident on their faces, in the way they moved, the way they could not bring themselves to shout now; they were ashamed for having been driven from their land by an enemy they had never tried to placate or understand. They had no god to turn to for help; their government was futile in its efforts to bring water to the parched land and keep the green sprouts thriving through the hellish summers. The canals and aqueducts were like fragile green veins in a vast bone-white corpse.

Bewilderment, humiliation, and apathy, those were the masks people wore, and it was terrifying. They were ripe for a messiah, or a dictator, or anyone who was forceful enough, strong enough to be heard. And if they started to move, there would be no way to stop them again. He was frightened, everyone was frightened, everyone who thought at all. And they were helpless. Nothing could be done. He knew it, everyone who thought about it came to the same realization: Nothing could be done.

"What we need is a good strong virus that'll wipe out about half the people overnight," Murray had said once. Joking? Cluny had not known then, did not know now. "With half the people we could manage," Murray had gone on. "There's enough of everything for about half of us, and we could kiss off the deserts and not give them a thought again. A modest proposal," he had added, grinning, but not with his eyes. His eyes had remained somber and frightened. Standing at the window, Cluny thought about such a virus and almost wished it could be developed overnight, used the following day. Within a month the shock would be gone, and the survivors would be able to start over again. Maybe that was what the militarists were after, he thought with a start of revelation. They never came out and said it blatantly as Murray had done, but the effect would be the same. Halve the population, be certain you were in the right place, and then resume a real life. They would buy it down there, he thought with a chill. Everyone would assume he would be in the right place and the others would go. They would buy it. It almost made sense.

He finished his drink, but continued to stand at the window, and now he was thinking of all the things he and Murray and Zach had not said to each other out of fear. The same fear that prevents a child from trying to anticipate Christmas too hard lest it should somehow evaporate kept them from saying anything about the possibility that the message was real. Any other civilization that had been able to cross interstellar space to leave a calling card would have an advanced technology that could handle a world-wide drought, they would have said, if fear had not stalled the words in their throats. That civilization would have gone beyond the petty wars that again and again had sidetracked Earth from its own future, had manacled nations in hatred and blood when they might have been growing, becoming capable of meeting advanced beings as equals. Cluny rested his forehead on the window and clenched his glass hard, and after a moment he realized he was praying. He did not know to whom or what he was addressing his prayers, but they existed, anguished pleas for help, for assurance that the message was real, that fate was intervening at a time when without help Earth was certainly destined to engage in the war that everyone knew would not be won. "We can't be on the top of the ladder," he whispered to the dimly lighted city below. "This can't be as high as we get. It can't be."

12 It had been a year since that first morning when Jean awakened slowly, dragging herself from a deep sleep with great effort. There were strange noises and smells, and the bed she lay on was hard and unyielding, altogether unfamiliar. She thought she was back in her university apartment, sleepily reached for Walter beside her, and then jerked into full wakefulness.

Now she remembered the day before, the night before, when women had bathed her and tended her cut and bleeding feet; someone had fed her broth, and someone else had very gently rubbed ointment on her face and hands. Dully she stared at the ceiling. All that effort, she thought, all her aches and sunburn and cuts for nothing. Her face was painful, and her hands hurt. When she moved her toes a sharp pain raced up her arch, up her leg. She did not try to move again, not yet. There was a soft noise, not like the other noises people were making in the early gray morning. She could hear low voices, the sound of a pan on a stove, the dull clang of an iron stove door being shut. . . . The new sound came again, a faint scratching at the door. She turned to look at it, and as she did, it opened a crack and a small face appeared. It was a girl with eyes as bright as sunlight on diamonds. The child slipped inside the room, holding her finger to her lips. She was no more than six, perhaps five, and very tiny. She flashed gleaming teeth and approached the bedside quickly, whispering in an unfamiliar language, speaking very fast, now and then giggling or chuckling between phrases.

Jean shook her head and said softly, "I can't understand you. Do you speak English?"

The child giggled again, and she jabbered in Wasco, or Warm Springs, or Paiute, or a tongue she made up on the spot.

Jean shook her head and said clearly, "I don't speak your language."

The child laughed as if she had told a joke, and continued to speak rapidly.

Jean shook her head again, pointed to herself and said, "Jean." She pointed to the child then.

"Olahuene," the girl said, laughing, pointing at Jean. "Olahuene." Then she pointed to herself and said, "Mary."

She became very still then, listening although Jean could hear nothing that had not been there before, and suddenly, as abruptly as she had come, she left.

In the room was the bed, a small table and a wooden chair with her clothes folded on it, and a chest of drawers. Jean clutched the blanket around her and sat on the side of the bed, dreading her first step. Her feet were pulsing with pain now. Finally she stood up and had to blink away tears. Vaguely she remembered walking barefoot among the sharp rocks and she shuddered.

There was a knock on the door. Jean hesitated, then said, "Come in." She pulled the blanket more tightly around herself and sat down on the side of the bed.

A woman entered this time and firmly pushed the door closed on the sound of giggling behind her. "Hello," she said. "I'm Serena, Robert's wife. I've come to dress your feet, see if you are ready for breakfast, make you welcome." She said it in a rush, as if she had been practicing the lines.

Serena, it turned out, had memorized the phrases. She had said them over and over until she had them

down exactly right. It had been five years since there
had been an English-speaking person around, and here
in the village they all used Wasco.

Weeks later Jean asked Robert, "Why are you still
here, your people?"

They were in his house, Serena, Robert, and his son
Wesley. Mary was playing outside. Wesley was twenty-
two and did not accept Jean with the ease that his
parents did. She often felt his wariness when she
approached; he watched her closely, ready to react to
any unreasonable action of hers. It was Wesley who
answered her question.

"For the same reason you are. You could be safe and
cared for in Newtown, yet you're here." There was an
aggressive edge to his voice.

Jean shook her head. "I didn't mean that. I mean,
what are you preparing for? What are you planning?
Today I went up the hill with the children and watched
Serena and Annie teaching them how to grind out rocks
to make mortars. What are you doing?"

Robert regarded her steadily for a long time before
he spoke. "We are neither Indian nor white," he said
then. "We've forgotten how to survive in our own
world, and now we're trying to relearn the old ways."

"You don't intend to go to Newtown ever?"

"Would you recommend them to us?"

Jean bit her lip and turned away from his steady gaze.
"But the water is vanishing faster and faster. The
Metolius has been dry for years, and the Deschutes has
an intermittent trickle. Your wells are gone, nearly all
your springs are dry. You can't survive without water.
No one can."

"There's enough water, if you know where to look,
how to look, and how to use it and preserve it. No more
wheat, no more irrigation. So we'll have acorn flour
instead. The mortars are heavy, so we make them
where we'll use them to grind the acorns. The oak
senses the dropping water table and sends its roots
down deeper and deeper. It will survive many years of

drought. No more sweet potatoes, no more turnips; we'll gather the camas root and the sunflower root, the wild carrots and parsnips instead. We've changed, the plants haven't. They're waiting the eternal wait; one year of no water, they shrink a little, but they're out there, and below them, deep in the ground, the water runs as always. Our grandfathers would have scorned the fear this drought has brought. For them it was always drought and cold and wind and heat. That's how life was. Our grandfathers call them the good days, the days of plenty and of no pain. But we have to learn it all over; we've forgotten so much."

It was the longest speech Jean had ever heard him make. Slowly she nodded, and her skepticism went unvoiced. Futile, she wanted to cry. Even the camas and the sunflower need some water, and it wasn't there. Where the usual rainfall had been ten inches annually, it was now three or four; where the snow melt had fed the brooks and underground streams that emerged on the distant slopes as sparkling springs, there was no snowfall, no meltwater.

"It will be easier for us than for our grandfathers," Robert said gently then, as if aware of her fears. "We have many things to make it easier for us. Guns and bullets to hunt with. Stout boots. Steel fishing hooks and nylon seines. When we have cattle to sell, we can make a call from Bend, load them on trucks, buy what we'll need with the cash. Many things are better."

She nodded, unconvinced. "You said you wanted me to help with something. I'm able to work now. What can I do?"

"For five years there's been no teacher here. Some of the children can't speak English at all, some of them only incorrectly. Many can't read. And the books are all in English. We need you to teach us English, and in turn to learn Wasco and give us a dictionary that we can keep to help those who forget again. The instructions for how to drill wells, how to build solar heaters, how to order from your catalogues, they're all in English and it must not be a forgotten language among our children.''

Later Jean walked away from the houses of the village and sat on a massive ledge of obsidian overlooking the deep gorge of the Metolius River. On both sides of the gorge thick strata of lava were visible and here and there sheer obsidian flows gleamed.

She heard someone approach, but did not look up, although she felt herself tense and felt her heart pound. At least she was learning to control the visible signs of her apprehension, she thought derisively. At first she had started at every sound, had whirled, ready to flee whenever anyone had come upon her suddenly. Now she merely tensed enough to make ulcers thrive.

"You think it's suicide, don't you?"

She turned to see Wesley standing over her, scowling. He was dressed in jeans and a white, stained T-shirt, moccasins on his feet. How ridiculous, she found herself thinking, for them to pretend they could go back to the old ways. She didn't answer his question.

"I'm supposed to tell you to come to our defense classes. Every morning at nine.''

"What are they?"

"Self-defense. Actually I wasn't supposed to tell you to come, only to tell you it's available. Robert started them because of you, what happened to you.'' Abruptly he sat down beside her. "This would have been the last generation to show even a vestige of the old stone-age memories," he said. "Not mine. I'm still a bastard mix. But the little kids, my children. And so it would have been completed, the adaptation of the savage into civilized modern homo sap.''

He raised his eyes to survey the hills to the west, the rising slopes that led higher and higher to the barren summit of Mount Jefferson, where historically there had been mammoth glaciers. "We don't even know for sure if we're supposed to be forest Indians, or fishing Indians, or desert Indians. Or some crazy combination of the three. Every day we're inventing a new tribe, new customs, new racial memories to follow." He jumped to his feet again, the sullenness returned to his face, his mouth tight. "Pretty goddamn romantic, isn't it? Classes at nine." He stalked away and she watched until he was lost to view behind a basalt outcropping.

Jean shook her head and wished she had answered his question. Suicide, she had decided. Robert was taking them to a certain death rather than face the uncertainties of Newtown.

To the west the high Cascades loomed over the reservation lands; the lower Mutton Mountains to the north were even less hospitable then the dying slopes of Mount Jefferson. The Mutton Mountains looked grim from where she sat, an irregular skyline, not high enough to catch the few clouds that passed, or to avoid the sudden changes of temperature that could make any night midwinter, any afternoon Saharan. To the east stretched hundreds of miles of high desert plateau, tortured land scarred by volcanoes and earthquakes, mocked by the ghostly dry riverbeds, and expanses of lake bottoms that were now alkali plains, where blowing dust stung and burned the skin and eyes viciously. Dry waterfalls, smoothed rocks, flow lines still visible, fossils of marine vegetation and animals still to be found, everywhere reminders of the lush periods of the past when the desert had been wet, and high forests had crowded shorelines. The fertile past derided the traveler who could easily die of thirst while searching for water that once had been there and now was far below the surface of the earth.

Jean pulled her thoughts back from the high desert country and began to consider the more immediate problem of how to teach the children a language they might never be called upon to use again. She had no doubt that they would vanish out on the desert.

Slowly she walked back to the village. A highway cut through the center of it; on one side of the road were

the agency buildings, on the other a small general store
that was closed now, and a gas station that had pumped
no gasoline for years. The houses were small frame
buildings, with privies behind them, most of the
outbuildings newer than the houses. They had been
built when the water system failed. There was no longer
any electricity, of course. The houses were silver gray,
many of them over fifty years old, too small for the
families they contained. Farther from the road were
several ancient army buildings, discards from a war that
no one could remember. Dirt roads led from the
village, wound around huge boulders or upthrusts of
basalt, disappeared in the sparse junipers and sagebrush, the bitter-grass stands. Some automobiles were
parked here and there, but most of them had been put
inside sheds or garages, out of the weather to wait for
the day of returned civilization. Many yards had
hitching posts again, and wooden troughs.

The Indians were dressed in clothes that could have
come from any Sears catalogue for the most part, but
here and there she saw handmade moccasins, an
occasional pair of buckskins. Dozens of people were
tending truck gardens, fields of beans. Buckets of water
were being passed hand to hand down the rows. A
woman carefully scraped away an inch of soil from the
base of each plant, measured out water and poured it
slowly on the exposed dirt, then replaced the protective
covering. None of it would be lost to evaporation, but
the beans looked spindly, as if they longed for a
downpour.

No wheat had been planted for two years. The
irrigation system had failed three years before, and
hand watering of wheat had been insufficient.

She turned her back on the pitiful efforts to save the
vegetables, and entered the agency building where she
would hold classes. The building was the largest on the
reservation, but it was small in comparison to any
municipal building in any town she had ever seen.

There were several offices, stripped of everything—
desks, file cabinets, chairs, all the government-issue
symbols of bureaucracy; there was a reception room,
empty; a library, with books still shelved; and there was
a large meeting room where the tribal council meetings
took place. Several hundred people could squeeze in
here. Sand was piled up along one wall, it crunched
under her feet, and several flies droned, hit the
windows, droned. . . .

Every morning she attended the defense classes
along with twenty-six Indians, most of them younger
than she. There was no class structure as such, and she
remembered the books she had read from the agency
library, studies done by whites on Indian psychology:
they had decided Indian children were very shy because
they refused to respond to the usual white programs.
But she found that they were not shy at all; they joked
and laughed and played freely; they simply did not
structure classes or respond to authority the way she
had been taught to do from infancy on. For days she
stayed in the background, watching, trying to catch
phrases of the rapid Wasco language. No one told her
to join or participate; no one told anyone what to do.
Wesley demonstrated, someone else tried it, then
another; someone approached Wesley and together
they went through the routine—this one was a simple
fending off a blow with the forearm—and presently
they were all pairing off and going through the slow
motions of attack and defense.

Gradually Jean realized that no one would ever drag
her into the lessons; they would wait patiently until she
made a motion to join them. Hesitantly she approached
a girl about her own size but obviously still a teen-ager.
The girl waited for a sign and Jean assumed the
defensive posture, legs bent slightly at the knees, feet
apart and braced. The girl smiled and moved in and
could have landed a blow to Jean's neck if she had
followed through. Jean felt a hot blush on her cheeks

and laughed nervously. The girl smiled and resumed her original position, waiting for Jean to prepare to try again. For a long time Jean felt self-conscious and awkward, patronized even, but gradually she began to think of her body, the body of the girl who could have killed her a dozen times over, and the way their movements resembled dance, the way her own movements were too slow. She began to be aware of how the other girl moved before her final lunge, and watching for the signals, she began to anticipate the next motions, be prepared for them, and move in a way that was anticipatory and not only a reaction.

She was surprised that day when the class was over, it had gone so quickly. Doris, the girl who had become her partner, smiled broadly at her and waited to walk back to Robert's house with her. Doris spoke correct but stiff English, as if she had learned the pronunciation very early from good teachers, and had acquired grammar from textbooks.

That day when her class appeared for the English lesson Jean had a book in her lap, was sitting in the middle of the floor, the chairs all haphazardly pushed against the walls. No more lines of chairs, she thought; no more calling on Mickey or Susan or Mary for a recitation. She had learned more than how to parry a blow to the neck, she realized, and could not entirely quell the feeling of victory.

Autumn was short that year and the harsh winter set in with a howling windstorm that stripped the tops from trees and denuded exposed fields of inches of soil. The temperature plummeted the first night of the storm to minus five, then continued downward for the next four nights in a row until it reached minus twenty-four Fahrenheit. The junipers cracked and groaned, turned brittle and white; the sagebrush looked like ghosts, and from the forest slopes there came intermittent explosions as trees killed by pine beetles and drought broke in the winds.

During the winter, an expedition had to be sent to Portland to buy provisions. Robert and Wesley and half a dozen others made the trip and there was gloom throughout the village, throughout the other, smaller villages and isolated ranches and farmhouses. They had counted on being self-supporting before this. They were humiliated, Jean realized, to have even this vestige of dependence.

One night while the group was gone, she was roused from a light sleep by the sound of voices in the living room. Presently she heard the front door open and close, and silence returned. Someone had come for Serena. There was so much she didn't know, Jean thought, staring at the dark window. Serena was a medicine woman, a healer, a religious leader of some sort, and everyone trusted her and sought her out for ailments both physical and mental. There was practically no mental illness here and never had been. The incidence of psychological breakdown was so small historically that it was too insignificant to consider in Indian studies. She had read everything in the agency library, all the studies, the summaries, the predictions. And they were all about the Indians as they existed in the minds of those making the studies. They were criticized because they did not make good managers, and the solution was to instill in them a sense of competitiveness, which was lacking. They needed strong leaders with authority to make decisions and enforce them. She smiled, thinking about Robert's leadership and the power behind it. His power lay in his ability to persuade and convince. She wondered if she would understand them ever, if it would take a lifetime of living among them.

Serena would come back cold, she thought then, and got up to make the fire, to prepare hot tea. She slipped on moccasins lined with fur, and wrapped a blanket about her shoulders, and then smiled at the image she formed of herself. Blond Indian squaw, still so much a

part of the world she had known all her life that even
this midnight vigil of Serena's seemed to her to be filled
with mystery, and inexplicable. Serena had no medical
training at all, no schooling past the fifth or sixth grade,
and she was as superstitious as any medieval peasant.
And Serena was a healer. Jean had seen it work; her
own feet, cut deeply, bruised, swollen, injured enough
to keep her immobilized for a week or longer, had
healed within two days, possibly three, and there were
no scars now, no traces of the ordeal. If Serena had
tended her back, she thought, it might not be scarred
now. She froze in the doorway as a tremor seized her.
She had not thought of that for many months, had
wiped her mind clean of her entire past as much as she
had been able to; she was still deliberately working on
completing the wipeout.

She forced herself to move again, stirred up the ashes
of the fire, added a log and some small pieces of wood,
and then measured out water to make tea. As it heated
she looked in on Mary, who had become her favorite in
the village. The child was all but buried under a mound
of blankets.

When Serena returned she did not speak of the
injury or illness that had taken her out in the middle of
the brutally cold night. She smiled gratefully at Jean as
she sipped her tea and edged her feet closer and closer
to the stove.

"You should be sleeping. Did I wake you up?"

"No. I don't think so."

"Often you don't sleep good. I hear you at night, at
the window, walking in your room. I hear you being as
quiet as a feather, moving like a shadow, trying to stay
still and still moving. That's not good."

Jean sat down close to the stove. "Sometimes I think
I must dream and that wakes me up, but I never can
remember what I was dreaming."

Serena nodded. "Do you remember when Robert
found you on the desert?"

Jean nodded slowly, then abruptly stood up. "No, I don't, not really. It was—I don't know what it was like. As if I knew and didn't know. I was there, but I wasn't looking. I can't explain it. I know he came and found me, but not as if it's something that happened to me really. I'm sorry. I can't explain it."

Serena simple nodded. "I know. What is the word that means not in yourself? Beside yourself?"

"Projection? Astral projection?" Jean took her seat again. Serena was shaking her head. "Ecstasy?"

"That's the word I need. Ecstasy. You were in that state. Sometime that afternoon you left yourself, turned away, and that let you walk without hurting on the rocks and fire glass. That let you heal your feet so fast. . . ."

"I didn't do it, you did. Just as you heal everyone who asks for you."

"You can't heal someone else. No one can. That night I told you to heal yourself and you refused at first, so I waited until you were beside yourself again and then told that other self it had to make your feet well, and it did so."

"I don't remember," Jean said helplessly. "I wish I could, but I don't."

Serena poured more tea for them both. The only light in the room was from a candle sputtering on the table behind the women. Now and again the screaming wind forced an entry between the door and walls, or through small openings around the windows. The tiny blasts were too frail to endure inside as wind, but they stirred the air and flickered the light and distorted the shadows before they died. Now and then the house cracked or groaned in protest when the wind became particularly violent and hurled sand or uptorn brush against it. Few of the houses had ever been painted; paint would have been a gesture of utter futility under this onslaught. Serena's voice was low, sometimes hesitant, as she searched for the right words and combinations, sometimes racing fluently with her thoughts, sometimes merging with the wind noises until Jean could hardly tell where one stopped and the other began. The scene became dreamlike, surreal, with the shifting shadows and the two voices merging, separating, joining again.

"It's hard to explain because your language is so hard," Serena said sometime during that long night. "Your words mean such tight things, only this and no more, and there are matters that can't be described with such hard outlines. Look backwards at yourself, where you're standing on the edge of the cliff; it's still there, something is there. It will always be there. You're connected to it, and if you deny it, you're denying a part of yourself. If you deny too many parts of your own past, deny yourself too many times, you become no more than a shadow moving through what is now."

"I can't," Jean said. "I try to remember, but it's too faint, too hazy."

"That's because you're in the wrong place when you turn to look. You have to step aside and then you can see. . . ."

"My father once told me about a place, he said it was a thinking place. Is that what you mean?"

Serena muttered several words to herself in Wasco, then looked at Jean and shrugged. "It's as near as I can say in your language, but that isn't really right. You can think there, but you can not-think too and just see. You can go to it without awareness and without memory of it afterward. Or you can go there because you will it and then remember everything."

For a long time neither woman said anything. Jean found herself studying Serena's broad face. How old was she? Fifty? Forty? Sixty? It was impossible to say. She was a heavy woman, not very tall, with dense, large bones, and the short-legged look so many Indian women had. Jean had thought her quite homely in the beginning, and now she realized she was thinking how calm and even beautiful her eyes seemed, and the expression on her face. Not a physical attractiveness, she thought, not to her anyway, because her entire cultural heritage said this was not the combination that made for an attractive woman, but her culture now seemed far removed, and the reality was that she did find Serena attractive, even beautiful in a way she could not define.

Serena put her cup down on a table by her side, began to loosen the ties of her moccasins. She did not look at Jean, but said to her, "Sometimes when you're sleeping you cry out. Would you like for me to come and take your hand, walk with you into the past to find what troubles your dreams?"

"No!" Jean stood up, shivering. How cold the house was! The devil wind was getting in after all, chilling the air, defeating the fire that was dying down.

"Yes," Serena said softly. "You've left such a large part of yourself in the past, you're like a shadow here. Even Mary wants to touch you sometimes to see if you are solid."

Jean heard amusement in Serena's voice and stared at her stonily, trying to still the shaking of her hands by clenching the blanket tighter about her. "That's silly."

"I agree. Many things are silly if you have to say them in such tight little hard words. Go to sleep now, little Olahuene. You have become a daughter to me, and I am a good mother who sees that her children have enough food, enough sleep, enough love."

Jean bowed her head, unwilling to return the love, unable to respond to it, and walked blindly back to her own room.

She dreamed that she was a statue, frozen in place forever, and people she could not see were hacking away at her with sharp knives, chipping with stones, hitting her with flails. She felt a terrible fear that turned to terror, then pain, and finally humiliation and shame. Semen, spittle, urine, blood. Blood, spittle,

urine, semen. She felt her own body as slimy, loath-
some, degraded beyond redemption, fouled beyond
cleansing. Fists of hatred, words of hatred, bodies,
cocks, mouths, so much hatred it eclipsed her pain, and
she suddenly felt a shift and became one with them and
their terrible hate. She could not speak, but she could
hear her own awful scream: "Kill her! Kill her! Kill
her!"

She woke up shaking. Get out of bed, she thought.
Walk, move, do something before the dream comes
back. Only then did she realize her shade had been
raised; brilliant moonlight shone on Serena, who was
standing at the window.

"Help me," Jean whispered. "Please help me."

Serena cupped her hands and let them fill with
moonlight and brought it to Jean and bathed her with
the cool fiery light. "Your spirit is shaped by your heart
and your deeds, my daughter, by what you do, not what
is done to you," she said softly. "It's your spirit that the
Great Spirit sees. . . ."

Jean heard her voice, and saw her use the moonbeams, and could not tell if she dreamed or was awake.
Later, knowing it was a dream, almost knowing it was a
dream, she thought clearly, she could see her own spirit
shining, washed clean by moonbeams, and she slept
deeply again.

The harsh winter stripped the land of everything
movable—topsoil, leaves, insecurely anchored shrubs
and sagebrush. Every day Jean held class in the agency
building, where more and more of the tribe now joined
the children. One day Doris showed up, said simply
that she could help, and after that they became
partners and friends. Doris suggested they should
recruit others and one by one began to bring them in.
The program took on the characteristics of a crash
program; there was a great urgency, even desperation,
to learn. At the tribal meetings there was much

discussion of the merits of going to the Seattle New-town in a large group. Many of them had decided to go, Jean knew, as she watched adults struggling with the language they had hated. They had forgotten much of it and had difficulty with the government forms they tried to fill out as practice. They were afraid of being classified as illiterate, afraid of being cheated out of the reservation land if they signed papers they could only poorly understand. She now had half a dozen aides to help her teach, but they all turned to her frequently for guidance, and invariably when the more educated ones came for help, it was the system they were planning to enter, not the language, that baffled them.

One afternoon in early March she took her class of younger children away from Tenino flats for their lesson, across the highway, out of hearing range of gunshots that echoed on the reservation lands. They were slaughtering the extra horses, to dry the meat, to rid the land of the unnecessary burden of providing forage for animals no one would want now. Only a week before, nearly half the tribe had left for Seattle.

The children had found a flat spot where they could sit in a circle around her and talk about the sky, about the earth, the air, each other. Many of the adults had gone to the Columbia to fish, and in another week many more would travel out to the upland prairies to find camas roots. Soon, Jean thought, she would have to make a decision also, and she was not yet prepared to make any decisions at all.

The children had found juniper berries and were gorging on them. Mary returned to Jean's side and opened her hand, full of the bitter blue berries that had been frozen all winter, and were slightly fermented now. Jean ate several, then shook her head.

"Look at your belly," she said, patting Mary's round stomach. "Soon the hawk will notice you and start thinking about dinner."

"Come on, redtail!" Mary shouted to the sky, thrusting her stomach out even more. "We'll have roast hawk!"

The other children had come back and were ready to resume the lesson. "The sun is very bright," Jean said.

"The sun is very bright," they said in chorus. There were fourteen of them, all under ten.

"What else is bright?" Jean asked, of no one in particular.

"Knife blade is bright," Jimmie said.

"Yes. The knife blade is bright."

Jimmie repeated it, adding the article this time. Jean waited.

"Is stone bright?" Miriam asked hesitantly.

"The stone is bright," Jean said, picking up a piece of gleaming jasper with a streak of white agate in it.

It went on for the next half hour and then Jean started to read to them. She was halfway through the Tolkien trilogy, which they loved. Abruptly Mike, one of the older boys, stood up, sniffing the air. He said something in Wasco, although no one was supposed to use the native language during the English lessons.

Jean asked him to say it in English, since she had not caught it the first time. He shook his head helplessly and repeated it, more slowly.

"You said the desert is coming?"

Again he shook his head. Now the other children were rising, dusting sand from their clothes. "We go back," Mike said decisively.

"Go on," Jean said. "I'll be along in a few minutes."

They hesitated momentarily, then turned and began to hurry toward the village.

Jean looked out over the desert slowly: mesas and buttes here, and deep chasms, tumbled land, broken rocks, stark black basalt rimrock, and a scattering of junipers that were low and grotesquely distorted. There was sagebrush, randomly spaced in clumps, then solitary plants low against the ground. There were stands of gray rabbitgrass; sometimes it hummed or whistled in the wind and sounded almost as if a person were coming, breaking the silence before him, but now it was quiet; there was not enough wind to move it. Farther, the ragged skyline, level enough in places to suggest lake beds, then sharply broken where the land had risen, or fallen. Farther still, the land and sky merged, became one in a blur. The sky was cloudless, the sun warm. She sniffed and smelled nothing that had not been there before: the pungent juniper berries had left a fragrance where a few had been crushed; the sagebrush had its own sharp aroma, almost astringent; the smell of stone and bare dirt. She shook her head.

For almost a year she had been studying their language, had learned it better than most students ever learned a foreign language. She could translate anything they said into English, but even knowing what the individual words meant, she had no inkling of what Mike had meant by saying the desert was coming.

"Jean! Is anything wrong?"

She spotted Robert on a bluff overlooking the flat place where the lesson had been held. She shook her head, shouted, "No." He started down toward her.

"What are you doing? I saw the children without you; I wondered."

"I'm looking for the desert," she said grimly.

He was close enough now to talk normally, although he was still higher than she. Now he looked eastward and sniffed, as Mike had done. "What do you mean?"

"Mike said the desert is coming and they scooted back to the village. Why? What did it mean?"

Robert made a snorting sound. Laughing at her, she suspected, and turned her back on him. He drew nearer. "You can't feel the change in the air?"

She shook her head. "There is such a slight wind that I don't think anyone would really feel it."

"Mike did." He was teasing her now. He squatted at her side and looked toward the northeast. "Let yourself feel the wind on your cheek. How does it feel?"

"Warm. The sun's very warm today. I'm probably getting a burn."

"Pay no attention to the sun. Just the wind. When you came out, it was from the south, and now it's from the northeast. The wind has shifted; it's caught between the warmth of the south and the cold of the north. It dances on your face if you let it."

"It hasn't changed," she said flatly. "Don't go mystic on me. Just tell me what Mike meant."

"He meant that the wind is shifting now, that it's coming from the northeast and it will bring frost and it will blow very hard in the next half hour. He smelled the Wallowa pine scent, where before there were alkali smells. He meant that redtail up there is following the frost wind because he knows many small animals will be caught outside their burrows when the shift is complete, and then redtail will feast. He meant that it's a mile back to the warm stoves and hot food, and that half an hour ago the walk back would have been comfortable, but that for every minute you delayed, the chances increased that your bones would rattle with cold before you got home."

Jean glanced at Robert now. He was smiling gently at her.

"You make a word carry a lot of baggage," she said tartly.

His smile broadened. "You resent that you can't see through Mike's eyes, feel through his senses, think with his brain. You resent that he sees a reality you don't see, and that for him, and for you, his reality is the one that decides who lives and who dies, and what happens in between. You'd try on his reality for a time if you could. And it can't happen like that, little Olahuene. You can't dive into another reality as if it were a swimming pool that can be sampled and left again. You can't live with one foot in your own reality and the other in this one. To enter our reality you have to die first, your world has to collapse, crumble, dissolve. You can bring nothing with you." He stood up again.

"But I did die," she said. She had gone through all the stages—the anger, the fear, acceptance, agonies—until she had stepped beyond them all into an eagerness to be finished with it, a sublime anticipation of the next and final step, ecstasy. "You brought me back after the hard part was over; the rest would have been so easy, so painless; release was so close. I'm dead to my world. I can't go back to it. I have nothing in it any more. I can't enter yours. I'm like a spirit stuck between two worlds, unable to enter either one, and I don't know what to do, where to go."

"What do you want to do?"

"I don't know. Tell me what I should do."

"No. The wind's going to start now. Let's go back." He looked down on her somberly. "Your anthropologists say we're all mystics, our children are born mystics. Maybe they're right. We have a belief that if you're withdrawn from death's clasp as easily as you were, it's because you have a great task waiting for you. I didn't just find you that day. I was guided to you as surely as the salmon is guided across the sea to the one river that will permit him to fulfill his destiny. You had to experience the touch of death before I reached you."

From deep within her Jean felt a chill; it grew and spread until it filled her. She would cause the weather to change, she thought; it would start with her, like a stone dropped into a lake, sending ripples on quiet waters, touching every part before they were done; this icy cold would send waves of hoarfrost and rime. . . .

"Don't be afraid," Robert said gently. "At this point you should be laughing at me for keeping such a hard core of superstition in spite of the efforts of your civilized schools."

How easily they laughed at her. The chill was gone, replaced by a flush of annoyance. "It isn't fair," she said. "I try to understand and you mock me for it."

Robert laughed heartily and held out his hand, took hers and pulled her to her feet. "Today I'll tell you what to do. Come home now. But one day you'll tell me what to do and that day you'll understand."

She scowled at him and they started the walk back to the village. Now she could feel the difference in the wind; it was frigid and biting suddenly. But she hadn't been able to see it happening; she had reacted to it after it became overt, incontrovertible. She had not been able to perceive it happening. You could see reality only from within; that was what Robert meant. And she was still apart from his reality, would always be apart from it.

The wind stung now, and they hurried back to the reservation. Later that day Jean told Serena about a dream she had had the night before. "It isn't enough to understand dreams," she said aggrievedly. "They can still be frightening."

"Maybe you don't really understand it," Serena said.

"I understand it thoroughly, and I'm afraid of it anyway. I am walking and I know something is behind me, keeping up with me. I run, but I can't lose it. I know it's still there no matter what I do. I'm in a panic now, and finally I know I have to turn, and I see that it's only my shadow. I should laugh, but instead I wake up, terrified, unable to move. That's one of the dreams that keep me up at night. And it's just silly."

Serena nodded, continued shredding horse meat. "When the Great Spirit was giving attributes to the creatures He had created, He gave the redtail wings, and redtail flew into the sky satisfied. He gave the hare speed, and the hare raced off. He gave the elk mighty legs, and the elk climbed the mountaintop. He gave man speech, and man went away talking. Then he gave coyote cunning, but coyote didn't leave. The Great Spirit said, 'What more do you want?' and the coyote answered, 'Only to see inside your basket of magic.' The Great Spirit let coyote look inside the basket and to learn what he could from what he saw, and then coyote went away satisfied."

Jean waited for her to continue, but Serena seemed to be finished. Finally Jean asked, "You mean you can get more if you ask for it?"

"Sometimes. You should always be suspicious of easy answers to hard questions."

"You mean it wasn't just my shadow?"

"I don't know." Serena shrugged. "No one understands someone else's dreams."

Jean shook her head. "It wasn't just my shadow. Something else. Like a riddle: What is always behind you and more frightening than shadows?"

"What is it you refuse to talk about or think about or use when you need it?" Serena began to arrange the meat strips on a shallow pan made of dried woven tule, keeping her attention on what she was doing.

"I don't know," Jean said, but she knew Serena would tell her nothing more. "It's the past, isn't it? That's what my dream was about." Serena now looked at her, waiting. "The past is like a shadow, always with you, ready to stretch out as far as you want, able to vanish altogether. . . . You can't step into it, but you can look at all of it. You can examine it closely without becoming part of it. . . ."

She was roused from her thoughts when Serena started to chop meat again, the knife blade falling rhythmically on the wide plank cutting board. Jean had been thinking of her father, her mother, their lives together, how his death had shattered the universe for her. She had thought of Walter, how little he had meant after all, how like her father she had thought him at first. And those men in Newtown . . . She felt drained and limp, and yet no more than a minute or two had passed surely.

"Drink your tea, my child," Serena said, her voice soft and comforting. "You've been far away, thought about many things that you have turned away from for a long time."

Outside it was dark, and the wind was screaming against the wooden house, causing it to shudder. Jean saw the cup of tea on the table before her and lifted it, sipped the steaming brew. She was weeping! She felt her cheek in wonder, then looked at Serena, who was regarding her calmly. "How long have I been sitting here?"

"An hour, a little more. You had many things to think about, and you went to your thinking place, where no one could disturb you." She smiled. "Now you can chop for a while and I'll make supper. I can hear Mary's stomach growling like a bear."

13 There were fewer than five hundred Indians remaining on the reservation now. A third group was preparing to depart, this time for the high prairies in the Ochoco Mountains, to drive the herd of cattle before them to the grazing grounds, where permanent alfalfa and bunch grass were thin and brittle but abundant enough for the long summer.

Jean watched the clouds of dust raised by the horses and cattle, hiding the Indians completely, and thought now the final dispersal time had come. They would separate into smaller and smaller groups, each with its own purpose, its own mission, and given enough time they would become separate tribes again, meeting to trade, meeting to celebrate marriages and mourn losses.

Robert's family and others would leave to follow the dry watercourses in search of berries and nuts, to hunt in the higher elevations where the stream beds finally led them. And when winter came again, they would return to the village, where they had warm houses. And so it would go; the pattern laid down by their ancestors would reassert itself and they would wander, follow the food, follow the water.

"Can I go with you?" she asked suddenly, speaking to Robert and Serena, who were also watching the clouds of dust. She asked with no hope, and they all seemed to know that. No one answered.

Wesley rode up on a brown and white short-legged horse, a quarter horse bred for endurance and intelligence, not for the graceful beauty of the thoroughbred race horses. He used no saddle; few of them burdened their horses with the extra weight of saddles.

He was happy, Jean thought, standing apart from the family, watching them all. The sullen look had vanished from his lean face, and now he was excited and happy, doing what he wanted to do, not what civilization had demanded of him. He would make a leader as wise and strong as his father one day. The good-byes were over with quickly; a clasping of hands, a quick wave, and he was gone.

A few people would remain on the reservation, elderly people, a few women and children, a handful of men. And the long timeless future would begin for the whole tribe, a future concerned with food and warmth and survival.

"I'm strong, and I can hunt or gather food as well as anyone else," Jean said later, inside the house. "What else do I have to do? Go back to a Newtown?"

Robert shook his head. "Don't be silly. You won't go back there. Our destiny was decided long ago, little sister, and for a while we were detoured on a path that wasn't meant for us. Now we're following our own future again. But our future isn't yours. You've dreamed of your own future, and you know it isn't out there on the desert, not for many years anyway. One day you'll come home, and the desert will embrace you and comfort you. But not for many, many years." He paused, then said somberly, "Unless the war starts. If that happens, come home to us as fast as you can. Promise."

She nodded. They had spoken of it before. He believed it was inevitable. "Why did you want me to stay here? You don't want a dictionary, or anything translated."

"We knew a lot of our people would have to go to the Newtown, and they were afraid. They knew they'd be treated as foreigners, outsiders, made to suffer because they had forgotten the right words. Some of the children had never even spoken English. You taught them well. You gave them the confidence they need. And you're wrong. We do want the dictionary. Not a white man's dictionary, but our own. Doris will help you with it."

"You could have taught them English. You speak it better than most people I know."

He laughed. "My tongue rolls easily over our own words—*la xwaixt wanai tat, citai lat, siksi kwi.* They sound like water falling over warm stones, singing in the moonlight, laughing in the breeze. Your words are hard and have no music, bring no pictures—*scrip, regulations, cafeteria.* They are noises, not sounds of what they are. They're like the nonsense words of small children playing their games, making up words to use and be discarded when the game ends."

Authority, she thought. He was speaking of her authority with the language. She was the cutting edge of a whole different reality that some of them had to enter to survive.

"May I stay until you have to go?"

"You may stay until you have to go," Robert said.

"And I'll write a book about you, about your decision; how you prepared for it. The world should know."

Robert and Serena smiled their pleasure and the matter dropped there, but Jean knew that now she had to decide. Now she had to step back into her own world, and there was no place for her to get a foot in again. Very early Serena had said that one day, when Jean was well, she would go back to her world, meet someone, start a new life. Jean had not been able to stop the long shudder that passed through her. Not that, she thought very clearly, but something. There had to be something for her.

She wandered through the village later, feeling its emptiness, aware of the vacant houses, aware of the silence pressing in from the mountains, from the desert. The sagebrush rustled in a slight wind, and the junipers moaned; a stone clattered as a small creature dislodged it, scurrying from one safe hiding place to another in the perpetual search for food.

She had dreamed of being in a strange place where the wind cut into her face harshly, and although she turned again and again, trying to avoid it, it was always in her face. She had found a small cave and crept inside to hide from the sharp wind. Inside was only silence and darkness, nothingness. She had become ashamed of herself, frightened by the nothingness, and finally had left it again, only to find the same wind, the same pressure, the same unyielding resistance to every movement she might make. Finally she had started to walk, keeping her head bowed, her eyes squinting, and as she moved into the wind, advancing had become easier. Slowly she had raised her head, and she was able to see around her. She walked faster, and discovered that the faster she walked, the less the wind cut and stung, the less frightened she was. And curiously, the faster she walked, the more time she had to look around and examine the strange, alien landscape, until paradoxically, running into the wind, there was no resistance at all, and she had all the time she needed to see and experience everything about her. She had wakened with no memory of the strange landscape and what it contained, but it no longer frightened ner, and, in fact, she felt an eagerness to return to it.

Serena had talked with her about the dream, and, as usual, had made no suggestions about its meaning, but had forced Jean to decipher it to her own satisfaction. It was the future, she had decided. She had dreamed of her own refusal to face the future, her fear of it, and in the dream she had overcome that fear.

But the dream was not the reality, she thought now, leaving the quiet village to stand over the Metolius River gorge, a chasm hundreds of feet deep carved through the volcanic rocks. Obsidian, basalt, pumice, tuff—she knew all the names; in her mind the land moved and shifted, the river cut deeply, the volcanoes flared and erupted masses of glowing magma. It was on a scale that made her remaining years seem pitifully inadequate; the insignificance of her own life and the tremendous importance she attached to it suddenly seemed a joke, the sort of joke that coyote would tell. She laughed aloud.

Jean and Doris stood on the bluff overlooking the Deschutes River bed and watched until the band of thirty-two Indians moved out of sight around a curve. Doris stood very close to Jean, and when the last of the ponies vanished, she reached out for Jean's hand and clasped it tightly. Jean remembered her first days in the village and returned the pressure.

"Okay," she said then, more cheerfully than she felt. "Let's see what shape the house is in."

She led the way into her grandfather's house, which was exactly as she had left it. Doris remained close to her, looking, saying nothing. For the rest of the summer, until late in fall, the two women would be alone in the house, working on the dictionary together. Robert and his group would pass by again before winter, he had said, and Jean had decided that would be time enought for the rough draft of the dictionary. She had debated staying in the village to do the work,

and it would have been better for Doris that way, but
here there was plenty of paper, typewriters, pencils, a
place to work uninterrupted. The village had too many
ghosts now, too few people; it was disturbing. And she
had to make that first step back into her own world, she
had added silently.

"We'll use the dining room table for a desk," she
said, trying to keep her voice cheerful, although Doris's
gloom was chilling. "We'll organize everything tomorrow and see how it goes here."

They went into the kitchen, the basement, upstairs,
Jean talking, Doris silent, watchful. They were upstairs
in Jean's room when they heard the sound of a motor.
They hurried down to the kitchen door. A jeep had
pulled up to the house.

Doris hung back out of sight while Jean watched two
national guardsmen approach.

"Hey, you're back!" the younger one said.

Jean was surprised by the sudden leap of her heart
when she saw them. These two were not the ones she
had met before, a year ago, but they were white; they
would know what was happening in that other world
she had thought of so seldom this year. The younger
man was hardly more than a boy, red-haired, freckled,
sunburned. The other one was older and stouter, his
face scored by smile lines; he was grinning broadly at
her.

"Come in," Jean said. "Tell me everything." They all
laughed at that, but behind her Doris clutched her
shoulder. Jean said, in Wasco, "It's all right. Don't be
afraid of them. If they try anything, remember, we can
break their arms." Doris smiled nervously and moved
away from the door as the two men entered.

"You brought a friend. Good. Too damn quiet out
here to be alone. Sometimes even if you've got
someone with you it's like being alone," the older man
said, indicating the red-haired man. "Steve Miller, and
this is Pat MacIlvy."

"Jean Brighton and Doris Walk-Away. Would you like tea?"

"No, thanks, ma'am. Where's the tribe going anyway? We been seeing them split up, heading this way and that all spring and summer."

"To the mountains to hunt, out to the desert to graze the herd, I don't know. Why?"

"Curious. Our way was to bring the goodies to us, you know—put in pipes to bring in water; put in electricity, haul the water up out of the ground with pumps; fence in the rangeland and plant alfalfa. We stayed put and changed everything around us. Their notion is to move to where the stuff is and change nothing. Two different worlds, you might say. Curious."

"What's been happening in the world?" Jean asked again.

"Too much to tell in less than a couple of months," Steve said. "Tell you what. We'll leave you ladies in peace now, finish our rounds and go back to the station and collect a stack of papers and magazines, bring 'em back later on. Okay?"

They brought more than just papers and magazines. They brought coffee, and oil for the lamps, sugar, and several cans of peaches and cherries, a ten-pound bag of flour, and a large bag full of ordinary supermarket staples—crackers, pickles, cans of vegetables, peanut butter—food that Jean had not seen in over a year. She felt her eyes burn as she looked at it spread out on the table.

Steve cleared his throat and glanced at Pat, who blushed furiously and studied the floor. "Coming up," Steve said then, "the notion came to us that you might get the wrong idea about this stuff. We don't mean nothing bad. I mean, it's not an offer to trade, nothing like that. . . ." He glowered at Pat, who refused to acknowledge the look.

"I know what you mean," Jean said, and heard the

huskiness in her own voice. "Thank you. Perhaps you and Pat will come to dinner tomorrow night?"

Both men beamed, and even Doris smiled slightly as the awkward moment passed. While she and Jean moved about the kitchen putting the groceries away, Steve finally began to fill them in on what was happening in the world.

The drought was spreading to places that had never known drought before—Ireland, Scotland, Japan. And at the same time other places were getting more than usual rainfall. It was a global weather change that no one could deny any longer. Parts of China were turning into jungles almost and China and Russia were having more serious border clashes than ever before. Russia was as water-hungry as the United States. Just a matter of time, Steve said often, with some satisfaction. And when war came the United States would be allies with China and rub Russia off the face of the earth. He said it as if it was a matter no longer being debated, but accepted all the way up through the government. Jean shivered at his words, but did not interrupt.

She made coffee and they sat around the table sipping it, the first coffee she had had in over a year, and the talk continued, but now it was about Portland, about San Francisco, places closer to home.

"They want to dam the Columbia to irrigate the Willamette valley," Steve said. "Damn fools. They'll flood Portland in the middle of the worst drought in history. Serve 'em right if they do."

And San Francisco was closing down the last remaining industries. It had held out longer than most Western cities, having been the first to realize the need for desalinization plants and built them early, but now the cost was too high. Agriculture needed the water more than the nation needed hardware and materials that could be produced someplace else.

After the guardsmen had left, Jean asked Doris, "You're not still afraid of them, are you?"

Doris shook her head. "But only because you weren't afraid."

She had not been frightened at all, she thought then, in wonder. She had been afraid of men all her life, or nearly all of it, and the fear was gone now. She felt a great relief at the thought.

Doris giggled then. "Poor Pat," she said. "Such moon eyes when he looks at you."

"The way Wesley looks at you," Jean countered, and Doris blushed. They were to be married in the fall.

The next day they started work on the dictionary. Doris went through an abridged English dictionary and wrote out Wasco translations in longhand; Jean typed them. She kept each word entry well separated from the ones above and below because she intended to cut them into strips and paste them up in alphabetical order later. After the first week they knew this would be too slow, and together they went through the dictionary marking the most important words, leaving the rest for a new edition one day.

Life settled into a routine very quickly. Work, long walks, sometimes horseback rides into the mountains, or out on the desert, chatting with the guardsmen, having them to dinner, or joining them at the station to eat their food. Jean was working on the short history of the Warm Springs Indians' preparations to resume the lifestyle of their ancestors, and this was more interesting to her than working on the dictionary.

They spent hours going through Jean's possessions, picking out gifts for everyone. A locket for Mary. Doris insisted that Jean put her own picture in it, and she searched her grandmother's scrapbooks for one, finally found her high school graduation pictures, including a group in which her own face was small enough to fit. For Robert she chose her grandfather's Oregon collection of books. For Serena . . . she could not choose. Nothing seemed appropriate, nothing good enough. Finally Doris suggested the crystal goblets in the china cabinet. "She would treasure them forever," she said, and Jean knew she was right. They would never be used, but they would be prized. She looked at Doris then. "You pick what you want from my closet; take it all."

Doris shook her head. There was one dress that she tried on, a slim pale-blue cotton shift that Jean had worn only once. "It will be my wedding gown," Doris said, turning slowly before the mirror. She was very lovely, the blue exactly the right color to show off her glowing skin and lustrous hair. Jean rummaged some more, until she found jewelry, a purse, scarves, everything she could think of that would go with the dress.

There were gifts for friends, and gifts for the tribe, and then other things that she thought they might find useful.

Weeks passed quickly; the nights began to have a distinct chill now, although it was still August, and Jean began to consider what she would do when Robert came back. Doris would go with him, and she, Jean, what would she do? The bus back to Portland, to what?

There was only the question, no answer.

Then Cluny came. They had been up in the hills overlooking Bend, and when they returned they saw a black camper in the driveway. A very tall man was wandering about the yard. They watched him walk to the bluff and stare down at the dry riverbed; moving again, they lost sight of him as their path took them behind trees and boulders on their way to Lon Speir's small corral, where Jean's grandfather had always kept a few horses. They dismounted and left their own horses there.

"Who is he?"

"I don't know," Jean said, pumping water for their horses. And yet, she thought, uneasily, he was familiar somehow. They started toward the house. For a moment she wanted to turn and follow the river to Robert's camp high in the Cascades, to hide there, be safe there forever. Her pace slackened as the thought came to her, but she put it aside abruptly and continued onward.

"My God!" Cluny cried when he saw them approach. "You are exactly the same!"

He hardly even saw the Indian girl with Jean after a swift glance at her. But Jean! He couldn't believe anyone could be unchanged after fifteen years! Her hair was shorter, and bleached almost white by the sun, but her body was still very small, deceptively delicate looking; there was the scattering of freckles across her nose, the boyish way of moving with strides longer than women usually took. Her dark blue eyes regarded him now with the same quizzical expression he remembered, the expression that had made him feel awkward as a boy, as if she knew more about him than he did, and felt a mixture of skepticism and amusement about what she knew.

Jean resisted memory briefly, then yielded, and somewhere she felt as if a door were closing, another one opening with the return of memory. "Cluny?"

"You remember me!" He rushed toward her and lifted her off the ground, swept her in a circle as if she were a child, laughing in relief and with a curious pleasure that he could not define. It was as if the intervening time had been obliterated, the unhappiness, the pain, the bitterness all erased by a simple return to a past that might have been.

And although he could not know it, and she did not examine it for a long time, this one spontaneous act of joy propelled her through the newly opened doorway irrevocably.

When he put her down, they were both laughing hard. "Do you remember . . .?" they both started, and laughed even harder.

"My line," Cluny said. "God, it's good to see you! What are you doing out here?"

She hesitated briefly, then said, "Teaching at the reservation. And you've been living in space."

With the words came unspoken words that she tried
to ignore and could not. Why had he come here? What
did they want? She had no doubt that he had been sent.
Gently she withdrew her hands from his and turned to
Doris. "He's a friend from my childhood," she said.
"And a famous space scientist, astronaut." She looked
at Cluny. "What do you call yourselves?"

He wanted to take her hands again, to laugh with
her, be children once more, but the spell was broken;
she had retreated, no longer the child she had been, but
suddenly the woman she had become, and he no longer
knew her.

14 Cluny was not alone. He introduced his
traveling companion, Ward Blenko,
who owned the van and the equipment
in it. Ward was a shy man of fifty or so,
frail looking and hesitant in his speech.

"They're writing a Wasco-to-English dictionary,"
Cluny told him. "Isn't that the kind of thing you're set
up to do overnight?"

"Not overnight, please. But fast. What are you
actually doing?"

"I'll show you," Jean said and took him to the dining
room table to explain.

Cluny waited, thinking very hard. Nothing was
turning out as he had expected. Leo Arkins had said
Jean was a rabbity little girl looking for a safe hole to
crawl into. Arkins was totally controlled by the Army
now, had hardly found time to talk to Cluny at all,

and then only in the company of a lieutenant, who had pretended to be busy with the files. And Arkins had sent him to Schmidt. He might know where she had gone to get her degree, to finish her education, he had said, dismissing the entire subject.

Schmidt had turned out to be a round-faced man who was overworked and tired but with an underlying ebullience that had shown through. At first he had not been willing to talk about Arkins, his work, Jean, anything at all. They had met in his office and he had taken Cluny for a walk on campus. Even here, Cluny had thought, no one talked where there might be listeners, bugs. The thought had filled him with a sense of depression that was not defined enough to identify, but existed as a curious heaviness of spirit, as if the air pressure had increased.

"Arkins is quite mad now," Schmidt said. "He's a prisoner and nothing's going well, the work is dead and they think it's his fault, that he's using faulty methods, or somehow sabotaging the project. It's not his fault. It never went well until Jean went to work for him. No one else ever replicated his results, no one ever will, not without Jean or someone like her. He started denying her role through jealousy, you know. But then at the end he protected her. Who can understand such a man?"

They had talked again the next afternoon, and then Cluny had got in touch with Zach. "Only two people besides Arkins know how much she was involved with Arkins' work," he said. "And they aren't talking about it. Schmidt says no one can translate that kind of a message without a key. Period. He also says Jean can probably tell if it's a hoax, and read it if it is. Do I still follow your itinerary, or go directly for her?"

"Schmidt can't even tell if it's a fake?" Zach asked in disgust.

"Maybe in enough time, and he'd be willing to try, but it probably can't be kept secret because his computer is accessed by almost everyone, and he's sure there's a running review of his work. The Army is still interested because he tried to replicate Arkins' work, even though he failed. They seem to think he might try again, with better results next time."

"Go after the girl," Zach had said tersely. "Can you get her to cooperate?"

Cluny assured him that he could, and he followed her trail to Newtown. No one in the hospital could remember her, and no one objected when he demanded the computer printout of her record. He read it through with his jaw so hard and tight it hurt for hours afterward. When he left the administration building he stood outside the door for a long time looking at the Newtown, blurred with dust clouds that rose and fell over the countless, nearly naked children playing in the streets. Two teen-aged girls eyed him, then started to approach purposefully, and he turned and strode away, filled with a nameless rage.

He went from there to visit Jean's mother. Stephanie had grown old. He remembered her as a vivacious, pretty woman, and now she was gray—hair, skin; even her aura, he thought, was gray. She had become an alcoholic, had remarried and divorced twice, had been hospitalized two times for unspecified causes. Nervous breakdowns, nervous fatigue, exhaustion . . .

She did not know where Jean was. They had not been in touch for the past few years, not enough to keep up, she said. Jean had quit her job at the university, and had gone on a trip to visit her grandparents. When Cluny told her Jean's grandparents were dead, she looked at him blankly.

Stephanie's sister was a bit more helpful. "She had some kind of drug therapy," she said, indicating Stephanie. "She doesn't remember things too well. Jean wrote that her grandfather died and left her the house on the desert. She was going out there to look it over. We haven't heard since."

"Could she have stayed out there?"

Stephanie laughed. "Exactly the kind of thing she'd do. Go hide there in the desert."

Cluny's orders had been to fly to San Francisco, to contact Ward Blenko and drive up to Bend with him to locate Jean. Blenko had listened attentively to the requirements: a computer that could be relied upon to take the programs Schmidt had given Cluny and spew out the miles of printout with variations of sentences. He had nodded and a few days later said he was ready to move. In the van he had a computer, a generator, cooking facilities, a refrigerator and space to sleep two.

"Gas could be a problem," he had said apologetically. "But your papers should get it for us, if it's available at all."

Cluny had expected to find Jean in bad shape, a recluse hiding from the world, burying herself in the past, possibly as crazy as her mother. Instead she was healthy and vital in a way he could not fathom. She looked like the girl he had gone swimming with hundreds of times when they had both lived in Florida, lean and muscular, suntanned with high color in her cheeks, her eyes very clear and penetrating.

He watched her now, sitting at the dining room table with Doris and Ward, head bent over the papers they were examining, the high curve of her cheek, her rather long neck. She looked up at Ward and laughed at something he had said. Doris laughed also, and they all returned to the papers.

"Is it something you can handle for them?" Cluny asked then, impatient for them to finish, impatient to get Jean alone and start the real business.

"No sweat," Ward said. "Doris and I can run it through in a couple of days, get it ready for the printers in a week."

Doris shook her head at him. "It's much harder than you think. Sometimes Jean and I talk about a word all morning because I want to define it by walking all around it, and in a dictionary that can't be done. There's no way to alphabetize holes. Jean finally points at the word we need. I can't do it alone."

"You prepared for company for a couple of weeks?"

Cluny asked. In his frustration he sounded sullen. To hell with it, he thought.

"Of course. There's a spare room upstairs, and we have enough to eat, enough water."

"Oh, we have everything we need in the van," Ward said hastily, his shyness returning. "I'll stay out there."

"And I'll take the couch, if that's part of the offer," Cluny said. "Ward, why don't you show Doris where you'll be working. I'll help Jean get some dinner under way."

Ward looked at Doris, then away. "Do you want to see it?"

"Oh, yes," she said, laughing. To Jean she added in Wasco, "He's a little boy in an old body, isn't he?"

They started out, but Ward stopped at the door. "Uh, Jean, don't use any of your food stocks. We have enough stuff in the van to feed an army. Let me make dinner. We'll bring it in when we come back." They left before Jean could respond.

"He just wants to show off his electronic marvels," Cluny said. "You know, you look exactly like you used to when we went swimming off the Cape?"

"Surely not. I remember myself as a scrawny kid, always sunburned, with a peeling nose."

"Just the same," he said firmly.

"Thanks," she said, dryly. "I needed that." She regarded him steadily for a moment, then moved past him to the living room and sat down. "Why are you here, Cluny? This isn't exactly the sort of place where people just happen to be passing."

She was surprised at his awkwardness. She had not wanted to know about the reopening of Alpha, but it had imposed itself upon her consciousness and she had known about it, had known that he was responsible. Yet he was as awkward as a boy now.

"You're right," he said then. "I was looking for you. I tracked you down to Bend. Simple?"

She shook her head. "Too simple. The question is why, not what you did."

"An overwhelming urge to see you? A need to rekindle the past? Loneliness?" She was shaking her head gently, not willing to play his game. "I have a job for you," he said then.

"I don't want it. I already have a job of my own."

"Wait until you learn what it is."

"It doesn't really matter. It has something to do with Alpha, doesn't it? Isn't that your life now? I'm not interested."

That part still held, he thought. She still hated anything to do with the satellite. It must also be true that she was still crazy about her father, his memory, still blamed the government, and his father, for that fatal accident. He felt a bit relieved now; he had been thrust into a situation that had turned out to be altogether different from what he had expected. He had anticipated finding her withdrawn and frightened, as neurotic as her mother, or even worse, consumed by hate and fear, and instead she was self-confident and too assured, too cool.

He had been prepared to offer her protection, he realized; he had felt pleased that he could rescue her, give her security, care for her as he would care for a little sister. He admired the defenses she had erected and at the same time knew he had to smash them down again. He knew she was hiding her fear behind this mask of self-assurance; she could not have forgotten so soon the terrible things that had happened to her in Newtown. Some people crumpled the way Stephanie Brighton had done, into neuroses or even madness, alcoholism, addictions; others built walls. He would help her in spite of herself, but first, he thought with a touch of wryness, he had to make her realize she needed his help.

"Let's leave it until tomorrow," he said. "There's time. Tell me about yourself, what you've been doing, your work with Arkins. I talked to him. He's a maniac, a prisoner, going nowhere."

"He was always a maniac. He could hide it most of

the time, but there it was, always waiting for a chance to leap out and assert itself."

The room was growing dark and an evening chill was in the air. The wind had started to whine through the windows. Jean went over and closed both windows and the door, then started to arrange dry sticks in the fireplace. "How short the days are getting," she said. "It can get awfully cold at night here." She put a match to the sticks and they caught and flared; flames leaped, danced over the large logs already in place. "The only thing there's no shortage of is wood. We do keep warm."

Cluny felt his frustration build as she continued to dominate the conversation, keep it turned toward safe topics. "I talked to Dr. Schmidt also," he said deliberately. "He thinks you were the sole reason for any success Arkins ever had."

"Is he still at Northwestern? It seems so long ago, another lifetime since I thought of all that."

"I went to the Chicago Newtown along the way," Cluny went on, but she seemed not to be listening now.

She looked at him, smiling. "Do you remember that time on the Cape that we got past the guards and went down to the beach? Past all the stages of rocket launchings? Right back to the stone age of space flight, where they had the holes in the ground and bunkers with slits to watch through. Remember that gunboat that spotted us, how someone stood on deck watching us through binoculars all the time we were there until they came for us in the jeep? I was so afraid they'd put us in jail. I wrote my will that night, thinking they'd come for us the next day. I remember changing the part where I had left you my stamp collection. I decided if you were in jail you'd have no more use for it than I did, so I left it to Peter Middleton instead. I thought we'd die in jail. I thought everyone did."

"I thought my father would kill me," Cluny said, laughing with her. "He said we had been swimming on

Shark Bar, where every shark in the Atlantic congregates in the summer. You were only a kid, eight, nine. I tried to get you to stay behind, remember?"

"I thought that was unfair. But I was a little mad at you for making us jail bait."

"Remember that reception where you wore your bathing suit under your long white dress? And I got mustard on my lapel and all day I had to hold my hand over it?"

"You looked like someone ready to pledge allegiance at the drop of a hat."

"And you itched. You kept scratching."

"My bathing suit was wet; sand was under it."

They became silent for a few moments, lost again in the shared past.

"My father used to talk to me about you, about spending too much time with a little girl, and I tried to make him understand that you weren't a little girl. I don't know what I thought you were."

"We had a lot in common. We could talk. My father understood that, I think."

"Yeah, he probably did. He was looser than my father was."

This time the silence lengthened, and was broken by the sound of the back door opening, closing, and Doris's voice.

"Jean, you wouldn't believe the machine he has! It's like a magic box. And he has food like nothing I've ever seen. It comes in tiny pouches and it looks like . . . like . . ." She stopped, then finished in Wasco: "Like dry cow dung."

Jean laughed.

Ward looked pleased with himself. "Freeze dried," he said. "We have here a gourmet meal for four, to be served instantly."

There were asparagus spears in butter, veal cutlets with mushrooms, creamy potatoes, hot rolls, a raspberry tart and coffee. They scraped every dish clean.

Cluny lay on the couch watching the fire across the room. The flames were very low, hissing, now and then showering the fire screen with sparks. The room was warm, but it would be cold before morning, Jean had said, tossing two blankets onto the couch for him. She had said also that probably they would awaken him in the morning, and if he was not yet ready to get up he should roll over and sleep some more. There had been no hint of apology in the words; it had been a statement of fact.

Probably she was up there lying awake wondering what he wanted, he thought, and even as he thought it, he decided he was wrong. She was asleep. Doris was sleeping, maybe Ward was, and only he, Cluny, was awake in this entire forsaken dead land where the wind and the coyotes made more noise than anything in downtown New York.

He tried to separate the various coyote voices one from another and was listening for the one he had decided was the closest when he lost track and drifted off, and was surprised to hear noises in the kitchen, more surprised to see the pale gray morning light in the room. It had been a long time since he had slept through an entire night.

Jean and Doris worked on some of the words that had stumped Doris the day before, and then Ward appeared and asked Doris if she was ready to start. She left with him.

"Can we go for a walk?" Cluny asked.

Jean nodded, slipped on a light jacket, and went out before him. "Hills or desert?"

"Hills. I can't stand that dead land out there."

She looked surprised but made no comment and they started to walk toward the hills west of Bend. Now, she thought, it would come. The reason they were willing to give computer time to an Indian girl and her tribe, the reason for Cluny's pursuit of her across the countryside. She walked steadily, leading the way that she knew would not be too fatiguing and still be an interesting walk.

"I'm amazed that there's still water," Cluny said, his legs starting to throb already although they had walked less than fifteen minutes so far.

"Oh, there's enough if you just use it for drinking and keeping clean. There isn't any for irrigation or any kind of industry. It's cistern water."

She had led him down to the riverbed, up the other side, and past the deserted mansions to a rising hill that already overlooked the entire town. Up higher was a smooth basalt flow, where she planned to stop and let him rest. She noticed with amusement that he was grimly determined not to ask.

"How have you lived out here for a year?" He kept up by ignoring the aches in his legs and the pain in his chest. Pick up a foot, put it down. Now the other one. Again . . .

"I lived on the reservation. I taught the children English and learned Wasco, their language, one of them anyway. They took good care of me."

They reached the basalt and she took off her jacket and sat on it. "Look, out there—that road is the dividing line. It's real desert south of it and to the north it's high plateau prairie, but there's not a whole lot of difference right now. Just more alkali in the south."

"It's as bleak as the moon," Cluny said, hating the naked land that showed every scar, every change.

"Have you been to the moon?"

"No. Just looked at it from the satellite, and through the telescopes."

"You showed me your new telescope the last time I saw you," Jean said, remembering.

"I wish I could show you the ones we use now. They're not inside the satellite at all, but out in their separate little orbits, transmitting pictures back in to the astronomers inside. It's . . . it's something that can't be described," he said helplessly.

"Try," she said.

And somehow he found himself able to talk to her again, just as he had been able to talk to her years ago. He told her about the satellite, the people there, the many views of space, his own work with cosmic rays and the theories about the weather change as a result of the decrease in them. . . .

"We don't know enough," he said. "That's always our problem. We think the cosmic rays affect the Van Allen belt, and it in turn affects the jet streams. But it's all just hypothesizing still."

Suddenly he realized the sun was almost overhead. It had become very hot; they had been out for hours. "I'm sorry," he said, meaning it. "You should have stopped me."

She shook her head. "I'm glad you got what you wanted. I'm glad you told me about it."

"And you? Did you get what you wanted?"

"No, but it isn't surprising. I wanted a negative—not to be bothered, not to have to do things I didn't want to do, not to be involved with anything at all. You can't achieve a negative, I think."

"What will you do now?"

"Write a book about Robert and his tribe, how they worked to relearn things they had forgotten. I'll try to publish it, and I think I may turn it in to Dr. Schmidt and see if he'll allow it for a doctoral thesis. He might."

"Jean, I seriously have a job for you. Schmidt thinks you're the one for it."

She started to get up and he caught her wrist, held her.

"At least listen."

She seemed to relax although he thought she had not really gone tense, and she thought how vulnerable he had left himself during that moment. She looked out over the rooftops of Bend. Many of them could have stayed, she thought, but they had been afraid. No electricity, no telephones, no doctors, no gas . . . They had been unwilling, or unable, to return to the Bend of a century ago, when all that those people had had was sand and juniper and sagebrush and the will to make it become more. Strange how most people thought it would be shameful to live as their ancestors had. And it needn't be that drastic, she thought, remembering what Robert had said about boots, fishing hooks, guns. They could take essentials from today. . . .

Cluny found himself hesitating, not knowing exactly where to start. "Do you follow world politics at all?" he asked finally.

She shook her head.

"Okay. You must know about the cold war that followed World War Two. I know they still teach that in school. Then came the rise of the multinational corporations and the cold war slipped into the past without a murmur. No one wanted war any longer. War was bad for trade, bad for business. Then came the drought, and everything changed again. The corporations were losing money, with markets drying up, production drying up, governments no longer willing or able to subsidize them. And somehow out of this the militarists began making a comeback. No one has proven yet that they are financed by the corporations, but no one can prove they aren't, either. And they're getting money somewhere. Suddenly these past six or eight years it's been the cold war all over again, only hotter than it was before. It never was completely dead. Our boys wanted the Russians out of the satellite from the start, but now there's a lot of talk about who can make the bombs and where, and how they can be transported to where they have to go, and so on. Half the government wants the satellite, all satellites, to be war machines; the other half is holding out for science and the good of mankind, ta da, but they're sounding weaker every day."

Jean thought of the national guardsman, Steve Miller, and his eagerness to get on with it, obliterate Russia, and Robert's belief in the major war. . . .

"Now the satellite," Cluny said. "It's international, but we developed and built the shuttles. We own them.

Neither we nor the Russians could put in the kind of money it would take to do that over. Russia has dozens of smaller satellites in orbit and we do too, but this is the big one. This is the one that could be turned into a super war machine overnight. There's enough material in orbit to finish the rest of the satellite, practically. It's also enough to make a fleet of killer satellites, killer drones, that could sweep the sky clean of everything that isn't ours. Or if they get it, they could do the same. Then they, whoever controls it, would control the world. Literally control the world," he said again slowly.

"Make the world safe for democracy," she said.

"Or communism, or big business, or whatever."

She nodded. "Presumably you don't want me to stand up and tell them all to stop immediately."

He glanced at her bitterly, then turned to look at the dead world spread out below them. It could all be like this, he thought. Dead, unable to sustain any life at all.

"We found something," he said coldly. "It could be a hoax, or it could be a message from another civilization, aliens. We don't know. It could be the *Maine*, or an assassination in Yugoslavia, or Pearl Harbor. It could be a straw, or a life preserver. Schmidt says you can find out which it is. He says probably no one else can do it fast enough. We're afraid time's running out awfully fast."

"You mean you might have a real message from outer space? There must be hundreds of people in government who can tackle something like that. And there are people like Schmidt, a dozen others. Even Arkins. He's crazy, but not in a way that interferes with real work. This is silly. There's never just one person who can do something. That's too melodramatic. I don't believe you."

"Schmidt can't do it because we don't know who has access to his work. He doesn't know. Arkins is under Army wraps. We can't turn it over to any of our own agencies. It would be headline stuff before morning. If it's real, it has to be an international project, but if it's a hoax, there's too much money and technology involved to dismiss it as a boyish prank. We don't dare let it break until we know. Schmidt and Arkins think you're the one to tell us."

She stared at him incredulously, ready to laugh. But he was serious, deadly, coldly, furiously serious. She curbed her first reaction and said reasonably, "You're wrong. I can't do it either. Schmidt is wrong about that. No one can do it without months, years, computers, help of all sorts. If it isn't readily apparent whether or not it's real, it will take a long time."

"You can at least tell us if it's a hoax. That's all we're asking for now, and then we'll give it the time it'll need for translation or to find the hoaxers, whichever."

"You don't realize what you're asking. The experiments I worked on with Arkins were all setups, every one of them. We controlled the content of the messages. I never had any faith in what we were doing. It was all phony."

"Not the last one. The one that brought in the Army, put Arkins in solitary confinement."

"It was phony too, and a fluke. I tried to tell Arkins a dozen times that the line of investigation was without value, that no one could replicate it, it was meaningless. It was guesswork. You don't make scientific advances by guesswork. Eeny, meeny, miney, mo'. That's all it was."

"Then guess again."

"No. You need chemical analyses of the materials it's on, a computer analysis of the age, carbon dating, all that. You have people who can do that."

"Nothing positive one way or the other has come out of it," he said. He stood up and looked down on her. "You have to do it, Jean. There's really no alternative."

"What do you mean?"

"I know what you felt about your father, how much he meant to you. I have proof that he was in on the sabotage of the satellite during those last years. He

committed suicide by heading out into space rather
than being exposed. I'll expose him, smear his name
through the news, the history books. It'll kill your
mother the rest of the way."

15 Jean watched Cluny stumble back down
the trail toward the house. "If you care
anything at all about the Indian girl,
keep her out of this," he had said just
before leaving. "This has the highest possible security
rating. We'll talk about it again tonight."

See what they do to you! she wanted to cry after him,
force him to acknowledge. She sat unmoving until he
was out of sight, and then she got up and climbed a
little higher, sat down again with a boulder at her back,
a straggly jack pine casting shade on her head.

It was not true about her father, of course, but did he
believe it was? That was the question she could not get
out of her mind. And if he believed, why? Gradually
Cluny faded from her thoughts and she was in the past,
reliving her childhood with her parents, seeing one
incident after another, a faint smile now and then
playing on her lips, her eyes unfocused as she looked
inward. Something had happened during her father's
last few months; not what Cluny believed, but something. Her father had developed a new urgency, a new
intensity; he had been worried and it had shown when
he thought no one was watching him.

She did not try to force meaning now, but rather saw again those days, weeks. The past is more mysterious than the future, she thought, and remembered the words as Serena's. "We think we understand the past," Serena had said, "and that makes it dangerous because we are changing it to conform to what we believe now. Not accepting that we have little understanding of what it was."

Everything that is, Robert had said, must be. Every cycle must be completed, must lead to the next cycle. He had talked about times when the desert had been drier than it now was, times when it had been lush and wet, and there had been no question in his mind that this too must be.

All her dodging, her withdrawals, denials, intentions to remove herself from the satellite, and everything it meant, had come to nothing after all. Now she was in the center. Thinking she was choosing the least likely subject to involve her in anything more pressing than the development of language, her training had been uniquely designed to thrust her into this particular pattern, this cycle that had started a long time ago and must be completed.

Cluny thought she had to protect her father, she realized, and shrugged the thought away. It did not matter what Cluny thought. He no longer existed as a person, but had become a part of a large machine that had no need for souls or consciences or feelings. The machine worked because parts moved and caused other parts to move without awareness, without regard for consequences. As soon as he used a weapon that could have injured her beyond repair, he had stepped out of the world of persons and into the world of machines. A year ago his words might have cut her so deeply she could have gone into a paralysis of shock; they would have threatened her past and through destruction of the past they would have challenged her right to exist in this present.

She understood his threat thoroughly. It was not aimed at her mother; her mother was beyond hurting any more. The threat was aimed directly at her, Jean. She was surprised that he had enough understanding to strike so unerringly at this vulnerable spot. He had expected to find Stephanie's rejected daughter, Arkins's cowering slavey, the brutalized victim of Newtown, but instead had found her living totally in the present, not denying, but also not wallowing in, the past.

"You can accept it and examine it, use what is valuable from it; or you can return to suffer again and again in whatever misery you've already had," Serena had said. "Or you can forget it and be ruled by it in ways that you'll never understand."

She had not finished, she knew; there was the whole last year or two that she had lived with her mother that she had not been able to accept yet, but it would come also.

There were snatches of memory, nothing whole and completed from start to finish. Glimpses of her mother sprawled out on the couch, too drunk to get up . . . Her mother scrambling eggs, letting them burn to foul-smelling unrecognizable lumps while she stared at nothing, tears streaming down her face. Her mother with a strange man, a second strange man, another . . . And the moves, from apartment to apartment, city to city, searching for something that could never be found again. The cramped hotel rooms, the furnished apartments with their wobbly chairs and stained dishes, an expensive suite in an Atlanta hotel, and always the men.

Carefully Jean turned away from those months. It was like a jigsaw puzzle to her, bits and pieces strewn about, few of them joined yet. She would put those pieces together, but not yet. She felt too near the terrible fights they had had then, the terrible things they had screamed at each other, the torrents of guilt and shame that had dissolved her into a sobbing incoherent child.

She felt she was gathering all the pieces together again, storing them away, gently closing the door on them once more. Not yet.

She would try to unscramble Cluny's message, she thought, not because he used empty threats, but because she now recognized the pattern of her own life from the time of her thirteenth birthday, when her father had given her the magic of words. She had been preparing for something like this all that time. Once she had tried to heal a scrape with her magic; now she would try something else with it. Strangely, she felt that her magic was real, just as Serena's healing magic was real.

She stood up and stretched, ravenously hungry. She retraced her steps to the house, where Doris met her and examined her face.

"I have found out what they want," Jean said in Wasco. "I have to do a job for them, but we'll finish the dictionary first."

Cluny jumped to his feet as they spoke; she ignored him, went into the kitchen to find something to eat.

Doris followed, speaking in Wasco. "Is it something dangerous? Cluny is upset, nervous. Ward knows nothing about why they are here. He questioned me about it. He's like a small boy being taken here and there by a parent who won't answer questions."

"He's probably ignorant of the reason. I can't tell you, and that grieves me deeply, but it could be dangerous. I'm sorry."

Doris nodded, then said in English, "We kept soup hot for you. Out of the magic pouches."

Cluny was glaring at them helplessly as they began to chat now about the work on the dictionary.

He had expected Jean to return defiantly, to demand proof, to argue. Or, alternatively, he had expected to see evidence of fear. He saw neither. When the women

sat down at the dining room table to go over the words
Doris had not been able to define succinctly, he
stamped out of the house and headed toward town.

Dinner that night was a silent, glum affair. Ward did
not have enough social grace to try to fill in the silence,
and Cluny was too baffled, too uncertain of himself and
Jean's reaction to his words on the hill. He found
himself studying her again and again as she ate with
good appetite, as much at ease as Doris was. Who are
you? he wanted to ask her, demand an answer. As soon
as the meal was finished, Doris said good night and
went upstairs. Ward mumbled something and disappeared out the back door.

"I'll clean up in here and you fix a fire," Jean said,
starting to clear the table. "Then we'll talk."

Cluny glared at her, then wordlessly went to the
living room. Pretending, pretending, he muttered. Still
pretending, but deep within he did not believe there
was any pretense in her, and that was even more
disquieting. The first big flare had settled down to a
steady fire when she came from the kitchen and
arranged herself in one of the cushioned oak chairs. He
sat opposite her; before he could speak, she started.

"I don't know how much you understand about what
Arkins was doing," Jean said. "He was a leader in the
field of psycholinguistics, the most respected linguist in
the field for a long time. Then he got the idea that any
message can be translated, without the Rosetta Stone
key. He was obsessed with the idea. When I went to
work with him he had been trying for years to prove his
theory, without any success, but he hadn't yielded a bit.
He argued that with modern high-speed computers it
was just a matter of time until he found the proper
method. Where the code is a simple transposition of
letters, by whatever method you choose—displacing
the alphabet by a random number, or scrambling letters
and putting them in the numerical places, anything like
that—the computer can break the code without any
difficulty. But so can any schoolboy."

Cluny held up his hand. "You mean where a *t* is used instead of an *a*?"

She nodded. "There must be dozens of ways you can transpose letters, run them together, even break up words and signal where by inserting a random letter. All this was pretty basic stuff. Anytime you have a variation of the alphabet, the code is fairly simple to break. You go from *A* to *B*, back to *A*. Your language to the unknown, back to your language. But the problem with translating a language is different; the hieroglyphs, for example, or petrographs, or pictographs, stand for a word, or even a phrase, that goes from *A* to *B* to *C*, not back to your language but to the thing or concept itself. Those are the ones you need a key for. Those were the ones he was determined to decipher."

Cluny thought of the lines on the golden scroll and wondered if they were letters or symbols of words. He was afraid of what was coming now.

"When hieroglyphs were first used," Jean went on, as if lecturing to a beginning linguistics class, "they were all little pictures. You can almost tell what they mean by studying them. But they became more and more stylized until most of them lost all visual cues for meaning. It was necessary to have a key, or to have memorized each one in order to translate them. Statistically the problem is clearly impossible. If you call the unit of uncertainty a bit, where there are two equally likely alternatives, then there are four and a half bits of uncertainty about the first letter of the first word in any string of unknown words. Twenty-six equally likely first letters. Statisticians wouldn't even try to work with such uncertainty. And that's dealing with a known quantity of allowable units, the English alphabet. When you come down to symbols representing words, the quantity is infinite, if you allow that words are infinite in number."

"I don't get any of this," Cluny said impatiently. "The important thing is you got results."

"Yes, by fudging. I suggested that if we taped the normal conversations of ten-year-old boys and fed their dialogues into the computer, that would put a finite number of probable words in the program to start with. And we did that. We had pairs of boys in the waiting room; we introduced them to each other, and asked them to wait for an experimenter to explain what we wanted them to do. We left them and taped everything they said. Eventually the assistant instructed them in the use of codes and secret messages and asked each one to send a message to the other. We called it code, but they were really inventing a language. By bracketing the allowable words even in this crude way, we reduced the statistical odds against translation by some astronomical figure. And finally we did begin to translate messages. But it was guesswork. It required the phony setup to limit the probable words. And it needed someone to read the sentences and sentence fragments the computer spat out and choose which ones to select. When we got a phrase that might have worked, we put it back in as a possible key to the rest of the message, using the Markov process, which says the probability of a certain event changes depending on the preceding events. It was guesswork all the way."

"Your guesswork."

She nodded. "And I told Arkins I was guessing, there was no reason to select one sentence or phrase over another. I closed my eyes and stuck a pin in, so to speak."

"Tell me about the last experiment."

"Okay. Remember we always used people who were strangers to each other. That was so they couldn't send a message dealing with things they both knew very well. Nothing like *Susan took Mark to Grandma's for lunch*. Again, it was a limiting factor, phony. The last message was sent by one foreign-language speaker to another. We did specify that the language must be one of the five major European ones, but no more than that. And also, the men could not know each other. We began by putting headline news in the computer—strikes, airline crashes, threats of war, all the usual stuff. That was our limiting factor. Strangers would be unlikely to use personal materials, and they would probably use newsworthy events they both would be familiar with. Again we drew our own parameters, and of course with real messages that would not do. Real messages might deal with material we would never dream of including. That's why it was worthless, a waste of time."

"We wouldn't expect you to be able to decipher it, not without help. But you could discover if it's a fake. If it turns out to be something you can decipher, we'll assume it's a hoax. Is that it?"

She shrugged. "I just don't know. What are the parameters? How to limit the possible languages? It could be Japanese, or Chinese, or Swahili, or one of several thousand languages spoken by fewer than a thousand people each." He was scowling at her and she added, "If there's a repeating word, it's nice to be able to rule out articles, if possible. Many languages don't use them, and if it's a code in one of those languages, they won't be there. And the grammars are different," she went on. "Syntax is different in different languages, combinations of words. Unless we can limit the possible languages, there is really no way to start."

"Limit them to Russian, English and French for openers," he said harshly. "I would have thought that much was apparent."

She nodded. "The original builders. That's as good a starting place as any." She stood up. "I'm going to bed. I'm not used to staying up past sundown."

"When will you start?"

"As soon as the dictionary is finished."

"Damn the dictionary! Haven't you understood a thing I've said? It doesn't make any difference to the world beyond this goddamn desert if your precious Indians live or die. They've chosen to die. Okay. Let

them. I won't have any more delay with this message,
because it does matter! It's the only important thing
there is right now."

Jean went to the staircase. She looked back at him and
said slowly, "I don't know how long you've had your
message, but it seems you've actually missed its signifi-
cance. If it's real, then it will matter very much what
happens to these Indians, and it will matter more and
more as time goes by. Good night, Cluny. Sleep well.
Or do you sleep much these nights?"

He listened to her footsteps, up the stairs, very
faintly in the hallway, then fading out entirely as she
entered her room. No, he wanted to call back to her.
He didn't sleep well, or much; his sleep was chaotic
with dreams that left him muscle-sore and headachy.
He should not have threatened her, he thought glumly.
Someone else should have come out here, someone
who knew how to persuade a woman to do something
she did not want to do. There wasn't enough time for
diplomacy, to sweet talk his way into her confidence.
They needed results immediately, not six months in the
future. . . . He heard the hollowness of his excuses,
and stopped. His threat had not changed her mind, he
realized. She had not asked anything at all about her
father; she had rejected the threat entirely and that was
why she was not afraid. She had changed her mind for
reasons of her own, reasons he could not fathom. He
felt baffled by her, angered at her self-containment, her
assurance. Worst of all, he felt excluded.

All he had accomplished was to turn her into a
stranger. There would be no more shared reminis-
cences about their childhood; no more shared memories of swimming together, the picnics their families had
had, the fears they had confided to each other when
their fathers were in space. . . . Maybe that's why he
had done it, he thought suddenly, to close a door on
that past, to continue the sealing-off process he had
started with Lina's death. He shut his eyes, but her

image did not come this time; in his mind's eye there was only the void he had been glimpsing more and more frequently as the weeks and months passed. When it was there every time he shut his eyes, he would have achieved his goal, the complete obliteration of the past.

Upstairs, Jean felt herself drifting already. She was very tired and her room was quite cold; the warmth of the blankets soothed her. She made herself resist sleep long enough to pursue a thought that had flittered through her mind earlier when she and Cluny had been talking. Now she had it again. It would prove nothing, she realized, if she, or someone else, did manage to translate his message. A hoax that could not be read would be pointless, self-defeating. It could say something like: *Destroy your weapons before summer when we shall arrive,* or *We come in peace,* or almost anything else. But it would be understandable. Even if it was real, it would have to be decipherable, or again it would be pointless. Presumably it had been left where it would be found without too much trouble, meant for Earth people, to be read by them. Why code then? Perhaps the aliens had been watching for a long time and knew of the schisms, the many jealous factions, nationalities, religions, and had found a way to bypass them all, to code a message that would not seem to favor any one group. The language might be Esperanto, or a dead language, or in symbols from mathematics or music or art.

She heard a coyote's laughing bark close by, and she smiled to herself and turned over and let sleep take her.

Cluny listened to the coyote that seemed to be just outside the door; a shiver passed through him. It was the most lonesome wail he had ever heard. How did the creatures manage to live out there? No water, nothing but sand and stones and lava, dead and dying trees and bushes. Finally he slept also, and he dreamed of Lina. She was out of reach, dressed in a filmy gown that hid nothing. When he reached for her, she was always slightly too far away; he advanced again and again, reaching, grasping nothing. She was opening and closing her mouth, speaking rapidly, and he could hear nothing that she said.

Jean and Doris worked together the next morning, their soft voices rising and falling, the sound of pencils on paper like whispers. Then Doris and Ward vanished into the van, parked now in the shed behind the house, and Jean joined Cluny in the living room. "I'd like to see the message," she said.

He took his sunglasses from his pocket and, using a tiny screwdriver, took off one of the temples. A tightly rolled piece of plastic dropped into his hand when he held the temple upright. He opened his suitcase, which he had brought in the first day, and removed a box of stationery and from the bottom of the stack of paper he drew out a piece of cardboard. He unrolled the plastic and smoothed it down on the cardboard, where it clung as if bonded. "Wait a minute," he said. As they watched, the plastic began to show faint marks that gradually grew darker until they could be seen easily, black against the white cardboard.

The markings were all curved lines, nine groups across, nine groups down, equally spaced in both directions on the cardboard. At first glance Jean could not see any repeating characters, but she knew she could not trust her eyes alone for this. Many of the curves were so nearly alike that there might have been no difference between them at all.

Some characters were made up of two or more of the curved lines, not touching, but very close; some were like quotation marks, others curved off in two directions, another had a short curve above a longer curve, with a third curved line at the side, as if enclosing them both; another was like two sides of an apple, with a stem sticking out the top. . . .

"Can you tell me anything about the original?" she asked, examining each character now.

He described the scroll and its container. "None of the tests have proven anything one way or the other."

"Where was it found?"

"There's a lot of junk in orbit around Earth," he said. "Meteorites that have been captured by Earth, held in orbit. Sometimes they are close enough together to be considered a mine, a possible source of minerals, heavy metals, whatever. We've been making a study of them, classifying them, cataloguing, all that. The gold can was found parked in the center of such a group."

"Hidden?"

"No way. A group is not packed together. It just means a bunch of them in a close vicinity to each other. Anyone approaching this particular group would have spotted it shining in the sunlight."

"Why wasn't it found before, then?" Jean had turned from the message to watch Cluny.

"I don't know. Because of the numbers, I guess. There are thousands of them, millions. Here on Earth there are a million visible meteors per hour by naked-eye observation as they enter the atmosphere and burn up. There are up to a thousand times that many visible to telescopic observation. Forty thousand tons of meteoritic dust lands on Earth every day of the year. It was chance that let this be found at all. It could have gone undetected for years, or centuries. It might never have been found."

She was frowning at him, puzzled by the implications of his words. "Why leave a message without making certain someone will find it?"

"We found it, so maybe it wasn't that tough."

She turned again to the message, still frowning, bothered by something she could not identify.

"What do you think?" he asked several minutes later. She looked at him absently, with no sign of recognition or interest. Without replying, she returned to the message. Cluny stood up, presently walked outside. The wind moaned in the junipers, and he stood shivering on the porch.

16

"You're crazy!" Cluny snapped.

"It's the only thing to do," Jean said. "I can take time to bind the book in Grandpa's shop downtown, or you can take it to Portland and have it set in type and printed professionally. I'll have to learn as I go, so it'll take a long time. I don't care which it is. I have plenty of time."

The dictionary was finished. Two thick stacks of printout were on the table. One stack would be bound as it was, the other would be printed on fine paper. It was too simple, Jean knew, too scant, but it could be added to, it was a start.

"Let Ward take it."

"He's going to teach me to operate his magic box," Jean said. "And he should be on hand in case I need help. It's only a week, Cluny. You're just in the way here."

Cluny scowled, but could think of no good reason to refuse. Ward was certain no one had followed them into Oregon, and there had been no strangers in town, according to the national guardsmen. Cluny had talked to them, had told them a story about Russian agents, deepening the suspicions of both men that the Russians were intent on doing away with the Americans on the satellite and keeping it for themselves. If anyone showed up, he would be stopped and the guardsmen would hold him for further orders. And God, he thought, he was bored with this goddamned desert! Doris and Ward were busy; Jean was a cool polite stranger; and he had never been so bored and lonesome in his life.

He would catch the bus the next morning and return in one week. He began to look forward to the city, restaurants, life. Any sort of life. "Okay. But I want the message in the computer before I leave."

The van was about twenty feet long; on the outside it looked like another pleasure camper, something that very few people could afford to operate any longer. But inside it was a miniature computer laboratory. The computer took up most of the space, floor to ceiling, fifteen feet long, nearly the width of the van, with a narrow aisle and fold-down seats before the input keyboard and screens. Storage cabinets, a tiny stove, hooks for hammocks, a toilet and shower filled the rest of the available space. Not a square inch had been wasted.

Ward turned pink with pleasure when Jean exclaimed over the arrangement. "Had it made to my specifications," he said. "When they shut down the power plants, it left a lot of people hanging. They'd got used to letting the computer do part of the work. This way I can go to them up and down the valley." He patted the console, then pulled down two seats and motioned Jean to take one.

"Nothing is stored in the computer itself," he said. He pressed a button; a panel opened, revealing a row of narrow black boxes. He pulled one out. "Everything goes into the cassette here. You put it in at the start, take it out when you're through. And you select a key word to access the cassette so no one else can transfer the material back to the computer. Say you choose your name, *Jean*. And you have several days' work stored. If I try to learn what you're doing, or even if I accidentally insert it and try to access, unless I use the proper identifying word, *Jean,* everything in the cassette is automatically scrubbed. Keep it in mind. You'll erase it yourself if you forget."

She inserted the cassette into a slot near her screen. The computer printed: *Number?* She typed in the number of the cassette: *127.* The computer printed: *Identify please.* She typed in her name and was told to proceed. She nodded. It was simple, and it appeared fail-safe. She scrubbed the cassette, ready to start in earnest.

"You keep the cassettes," Ward said. "I don't want anything to do with them. It wouldn't matter actually, since no one but you will be able to use them, but it might be reassuring. If you run out of space—not likely to happen, but possible—the computer will inform you. Start with the same identifying code on the next cassette, and number it two, and so on. For example, you would say, *Jean two."* He glanced around, as if checking to see if he should instruct her about anything else. "I'll tell Cluny to bring the stuff now. Okay?"

"Okay." She typed the number again, and added, *Olahuene,* and then waited for Cluny to bring the message.

He watched the visual scan process; the message began to appear on the screen. When it was completed Jean took out the original and handed it to him. He put it in the stainless steel sink and touched a match to it. It burned explosively to a fine gray powder, which he lifted out with a Kleenex and tossed into a trash bag.

"You all set? I'll be leaving in an hour."

She nodded. "I'll try to have something by the time you get back, but you shouldn't count on it."

"Yeah." He turned to leave. At the door he looked

back at her; she looked diminutive against the complex face of the computer. "Jean, I'm sorry about that day up on the hill." He left fast, before she could reply; he was furious with himself. He had not intended to say that; it had not crossed his mind that he should, or that there was any real reason to apologize. Still angry, he stamped into the dead, deserted town and chatted morosely with the guardsmen while he waited for the bus.

Jean worked all morning until she was interrupted by a soft knock on the door. It was Doris.

"Will you stop for lunch? For a short walk? It's not good for you to stay cramped up in there all day."

"In a minute," Jean said and returned to the computer. She signaled the end of the work, added the code, *Olahuene,* and took out the cassette.

"Look," Doris said, pointing, when Jean walked into the yard. "Snow on the Sisters!"

A faint white haze covered the peaks, brilliant in the sunshine. Jean caught her breath; maybe the weather would change now, maybe the drought would end.

"Robert will be coming back soon," Doris said. "Before Cluny returns, possibly." She was gazing at the snow, the first sign of the approaching winter, the reunion of the tribe—Wesley from the Ochoco prairies, Robert from the Cascade slopes, others from the banks of the Columbia. . . . Her wedding would take place soon and there would be a week-long celebration: singing, dancing, a religious ceremony that would be a blend of Christianity and paganism.

They ate lunch, Ward, Doris, and Jean, and by the time they were finished, the snow had vanished and the peaks were once more stark and barren. The wind shifted and blew in from the south, bringing the smell of alkali and blowing sand; the sun was very hot.

"I thought I might take Ward to see Lava Butte," Doris said, turning away from the mountains. "He's never seen anything like it."

Lava Butte was a five-hundred-foot cinder cone with a perfect crater in its summit. "Why don't you take the horses," Jean said, leaving the kitchen. "They haven't had enough exercise these past few weeks."

She returned to work. She was still incorporating Dr. Schmidt's program in her cassette; it was slow, boring work, and she was anxious to be finished with this phase. English, Russian, French, she thought, studying the message as the computer silently, invisibly copied one tape onto another. English, Russian, French. Someone had written out a message in a natural language, and then coded it into those curved lines, eighty-one words or phrases. No hand had engraved those lines on the gold sheet; they were too precise, too perfect. A computer had guided the tool. Curves, arcs, pieces of circles . . .

The computer signaled that she needed a second cassette. She inserted another one next to the first. Schmidt's work duplicated what she and Arkins had done; she was familiar with all this material. Words, phrases in the three languages she would try first. Several thousand words; too many, she thought, but how to limit them?

She studied the message intently on one screen, while the one next to it ran a continuous display indicating copying was being done.

She blinked; the curves were starting to slither. She closed her eyes and rubbed them gently. Then she tried to get lines of identical sizes in groups, and there were none. All different? She tried for a gradation, starting with the longest line, going down to the shortest, and this came on the screen quickly. It looked like a schematic of a sound wave, a sonar reading. But the lines were too irregular in places, some curved more sharply than others. The transfer was completed then and she stopped playing with the lines and turned her attention to the next step in the program.

It was no use, Jean thought that night in her room,

too tense to go to sleep immediately. Eighty-one
different symbols, no repeats at all, and she still didn't
even know if the groups of curves were single words,
phrases, or paragraphs. Or nothing.

The warm weather continued the next day, and the
next. Doris was restless, bored with inactivity, anxious
for Robert's return.

"It was all right when it was just you and me," Doris
said unexpectedly. "You are different, but not that
different. At least you try to see the same things I do."

Jean waited, almost understanding what she was
getting at.

"But Ward," Doris went on, struggling with the
ideas, with the words she needed, lapsing into Wasco,
back into English. "He looks and sees something that I
don't think is there. Or he doesn't see what I know is
there. I don't understand it. He asks questions all the
time, but they are the wrong questions. He makes me
feel . . . inadequate? Something like that."

"I know what you mean," Jean said. "They come out
here and bring their culture with them and expect you
to conform to it. It's like Ward's food. He would be
horrified if he had to switch to your food. He'd get a
bellyache."

Doris nodded soberly. "And he asks too many
questions. All the time questions. Sometimes the same
one with new words, as if I failed to satisfy him the first
time. He thinks I don't notice."

Jean felt a rush of anger with the realization that
Ward must be treating Doris like a child, or a savage.
"Turn the tables on him," she suggested. "Stop trying
to answer his questions. Ask him things instead. Ask
why it's better to freeze-dry instead of sun-dry food
when people have been doing it for thousands of years
without that elaborate equipment. You'll think of
others once you start."

A glint of amusement lighted Doris's eyes and they
dropped the subject. She had been treating him as she

would any guest, suffering his nonsense silently and politely, Jean knew, but if she put aside that role, Ward would do some of the squirming.

At lunch that day she asked Doris if she would start writing what she could remember of tribal life from her earliest childhood, and, more important, the things she had learned to do in the past four or five years, preparing for a return to the old way of life.

"Hell," Ward said, disconsolately. "I'll type up what she writes. Sure isn't a very lively place around here, is it?"

Jean laughed. "This afternoon you two go down and play cards with Steve and Pat. But not for money," she added. "Doris already owes Steve about a million dollars."

They were eating baked apples for dessert, and she sighed. What good food Ward had brought with him. Apples. She thought of the trees blooming up near Hood River, fluffy, so pale that the flush of pink looked like a shadow on the white. And later, the apples like ornaments on the trees, thick enough to hide the foliage; and biting into an apple. Cutting one in half and smelling that delightful spiciness . . .

Suddenly she dropped her spoon and stood up.

"Jean?"

She was hardly aware of Doris and Ward. She saw without thought that Ward put his hand on Doris's arm, restrained her. She heard his soft, "Leave her be a minute."

She saw them then, saw Ward's look of understanding, and the look of bewilderment on Doris's face. "I . . . You two go on. I'll see you later," she said in a rush and hurried from the kitchen, ran up the stairs to her room and closed the door.

She opened the second drawer of her chest of drawers and started to rummage through her belongings there. Her mother's few letters and postcards to her . . . Her grandmother's string of agate beads . . .

A small box that held a necklace her father had given her for her thirteenth birthday, never worn, hated all these years, hidden away, forgotten. When she reached for it, she saw with detachment that her hand was shaking. She took the small box to the bed and sat down before she opened it. Inside was a pendant he had designed for her, crafted out of gold and silver. She stared at it and heard again his voice, light and amused, and underneath very serious: "I know you don't like anything about the satellite, honey. Put it away and one day you'll get it out and decide it's not so bad after all."

The silver was rough, like rocks, two irregular and lumpy crescents, one smaller than the other, like the sides of an apple, and between them was the gold stem, not touching either, held in place by wires so thin it was hard to see them. The three pieces were wired together to form a single object, an artifact no larger than a marble.

Two sides of an apple with a stem sticking out. One of the words in the message.

He had known, she thought, staring at the pendant. He had seen it. Abruptly she slipped the chain around her neck, the silver and gold pendant tucked away under her shirt. She replaced the box, picked up her wide-brimmed hat, left the house and started to walk, following the meandering riverbed. Was he the one who put it there? Was her father the one who had hidden the message among the rocks in orbit?

She walked until the shadows filled the canyon, and the air was chill on her skin. Absently she noticed that clumps of blackberries were bearing now; the berries were small and tart. They should be gathered and dried. The shadows were like rising water in the canyon, cooling the stones, creeping up silently. It was not a message, not in the usual sense, she decided. It would be pointless to hunt for words. She tried to visualize the curved lines, but they moved and changed and slithered away like snakes. She hastened her pace,

eager now to return to the van, to catch those shifting
lines and make them hold still long enough to reveal
their secrets.

When she got back to the house Doris and Ward
were there already; dinner was ready and waiting. Jean
had been gone for hours although she had the feeling
that she had walked out the door and then back in with
hardly a pause outside.

"Ward is teaching me to play chess," Doris said. "I
like it. The board is like the desert. . . ."

"She's a natural for chess," Ward said. "It's a matter
of focal point. You can see a piece and not the whole,
or see the whole and let the pieces go and somehow
they get where they have to be. Most new players just
see the individual pieces but she sees the whole
pattern." His eyes were very knowing, sympathetic
when he looked at Jean.

That evening, into the night, she studied the individual symbols, searching for another one as definitive as
the two apple halves had been. When her eyes blurred
too much to see, she went to bed. Early the next
morning she started again, filling every screen with
curved lines, comparing them, searching for patterns.
Late in the day she extracted all the curves that were
similar to those in the one meaningful symbol. She
joined them in a continuous line, and an irregular oval
appeared. Apples to eggs, she thought; it was a grocery
list. She turned to one of the other screens to see where
the pieces had come from, where there were holes now,
and a new pattern seemed to be forming as she
narrowed her eyes and concentrated. There were other
clusters of three. She extracted the center curved line
from one of them. The outside lines fell apart,
regrouped with other curves. She returned to the first
one, the apple, as she thought of it, and studied it
again. The outside lines seemed to be falling away in
the next two spaces diagonally downward; by the third
space they had re-formed with other lines. The stem,
the piece extracted, was not represented in any of the

following spaces. She had the computer extract the next set of like curves, then join them: another oval, smaller than the first. She repeated this two more times and had four ovals and four lines left over. She stared at them stupidly; they were bobbing up and down. Finally she signed off. It made sense, she knew, but she was too tired to understand it.

Ward was a huddled mass of blankets on the couch. She felt a flicker of sympathy for him as she tiptoed through the living room and went up the stairs. She entered her own room and closed the door softly, then stiffened when she heard a whisper from her bed.

"Jean? Is that you?"

Doris was lying across her bed, rousing now, pushing herself up. She was a faint shadow among shadows. Jean went to her and sat down.

"Are you sick? What's the matter?" She found that she was whispering also.

"I wanted to say good-bye. I fell asleep."

"Good-bye? Why?"

"Ward said you had to leave in the morning. A plane is coming for you. He said you're made too sad by telling people good-bye. And I'm made sad also, but not as sad as I'd be if you left without saying it."

Jean groped for the candle on the nightstand; nothing was making any sense, she thought, too blank to try to cope with anything but sleep right now.

The flame seemed very bright, causing Doris to shield her eyes from it. She had not undressed.

"I don't know what you're talking about," Jean said. "I'm not going anywhere in the morning. You must have heard him wrong, or something."

Doris looked frightened. She shook her head. "We walked to the station after dinner. We left after a few minutes, but Ward said he had forgotten something and went back. Instead of waiting, I followed him and I overheard him telling Steve and Pat that Cluny is sending a plane for you at dawn. He said there's a job only you can do and it's very important. He said you don't like to tell people good-bye and you asked him to do it for you. I left then and pretended I didn't hear. Then I decided to wait for you because sometimes it's better to say what you feel and taste the sadness than to try to avoid it. I didn't mistake what he said."

Jean felt a hollow dread growing in her chest. Cluny! She thought of Arkins, a prisoner in his own office, forced to work at a project that would never be released, but used only for the Army.

"You heard right," she said grimly. "Only I'm not going. Get some warm clothes on. We're leaving."

Doris nodded, and there was a gleam in her eyes. She slipped from the room without a sound. Jean dressed quickly, changing the moccasins for boots, her light-weight shirt for a woolen one. In a few minutes they were both ready. Jean put her finger to her lips and led the way downstairs. The fire still lighted the living room faintly; in the shadowy light she could see the blanket-covered form on the couch. At the foot of the stairs she paused momentarily, thinking of her boots on the wooden floors, visualizing where the rug started.

"Shit!" Ward said suddenly, his voice regretful, not at all sleepy. "Christ! I hoped she had fallen asleep." He turned on a flashlight and caught them in the glare.

"Come on in and sit down," he said. "Doris, put another log on the fire."

Jean turned her face from the light and entered the room, with Doris close behind her. "What are you doing, Ward? What does all this mean?"

"Put the log on so we can have some light," Ward said. "And then you both sit down in the big chairs."

"We're leaving," Jean said. "Give the tapes to Cluny, do whatever you want with them. But I'm leaving now with Doris."

Ward moved the light away from her face briefly and the glare caught a flash of metal in his other hand. He was holding a gun, not pointing at them, but toward the floor. He lifted the light again, keeping her pinned by it, and said, "I won't shoot you, Jean. You're valuable. But I'll shoot her, and I don't want to. I like her. She's an innocent kid. Don't make me do it."

Jean moved toward the chair he had indicated. "Put the log on," she said to Doris, and she sat down.

The log blazed, and Ward turned off the flashlight. He remained on the couch across the room from the two women. Jean studied him thoughtfully. A slightly built, middle-aged man, tired-looking. "You lied about Cluny, didn't you? He wouldn't have anything to do with threats like this."

"He killed his own wife," Ward said.

Jean shook her head. "Another lie. You think I've found something. You have a radio in the van? You must have. You called someone and received orders to sneak us away from here before Cluny gets back. Who do you work for, Ward?"

"How much of what you've discovered have you told Cluny?"

"I had barely started when he left, as you know."

"Why is he in Washington?"

Jean stared at him, then shook her head.

"Our people lost him in Portland, and then he turned up in Washington. We'll find out why, but it could take time, and meanwhile it changes everything. What if he doesn't come back alone, but brings reinforcements? What if he comes back by plane to take you? Too many unknowns. It was decided that I should make certain you were safe, somewhere away from here, and then see what he's up to."

Jean leaned back with her eyes closed, trying to fit the pieces together. She began to suspect there was no way she could do that. It was like being caught in the center of a Kafka novel, she thought; or at a masquerade where everyone wore layers of masks and each unveiling revealed only more mysteries.

"I thought of you as a gentle man," she said then. "A peaceful man who wanted only to work with the computers he loved. A man who wanted to show off a little, with cause, because he had things to be proud of. I would have put treachery so far down on your list of attributes that it would have been off the page." She kept her eyes closed, thinking furiously. She and Doris could take him, she knew, if he gave them the chance. Had Doris told him about the defense classes? She didn't know. But as long as he kept the room between them, as long as he sat with the gun on his knee, there was nothing to do but talk.

"I am exactly what you thought," he said eagerly. "You're a wise woman, wiser than you realize. You're brilliant with the computer, your ability to write a program so quickly with so little effort. Some people have that intuitive understanding of what to do, how to make it perform. I have it. So do you. I respect you for that."

"Another lie," she murmured. "You've been able to access everything I've done."

"I didn't lie," he said stiffly. "I just started a program first with instructions to include all subsequent tapes."

"You didn't lie," she mocked. "You are a peaceful man with a gun, ready to shoot an innocent child."

"You can't have peace with an armed enemy pointing a gun at you," Ward admitted. "That isn't peace; it isn't even a truce. It's a waiting period, never knowing when he'll pull the trigger, wondering every day if this is the day he'll shoot. I want space too, just as much as Cluny does. I've dreamed of deep space beyond Jupiter, beyond Pluto, the wonders and mysteries out there. I want to do good work, help make that come true, work that will mean something, that will live on after me. And I could, I could, Jean, if only I weren't afraid of that armed enemy. I don't want my work used in a bigger death machine, or blown to dust, or vaporized. The threat has to be ended! We can't keep on living with it. This may be the last generation with enough strength and will to do it."

Jean looked at him now. "I don't understand you at

all," she said, "You want peace, you hate war, yet you're the one with the gun. I don't understand.

"If that message is a hoax, it means the Russians are behind it, getting ready to make their final move. But it isn't a fake, is it? Jean, think! If we can communicate, when they come . . . Think what it would mean to all of us! They can't find us an assortment of armed camps, ready to bomb each other out of existence. It has to be settled, over with, put behind us, before we're mature enough to deal with an alien civilization that has achieved interstellar flight!"

"I've been hearing talk like that all my life. That's been the backdrop for everything we've ever done, all of us. We play our little games against the background of destruction until we can't even see the canvas any more. It's lost all meaning; it's only a taking-off place for men with such hunger for power that they would risk total destruction to satisfy themselves."

Ward nodded. "Not only here, but also in Russia. Remember that, Jean. Also in Russia. Don't you think they're going through the same kinds of processes? The same reasoning? The same conclusions? If it were just here, I wouldn't be part of it. I'd tell Davies and Barneveldt and Halprecht and all of them to go play war games somewhere else. But it's happening everywhere. They have wind of the message also. They're working on finding it. That's why it's imperative to get you to a safe place and keep you where they can't reach you. Don't you see?"

"Have you read anything about the first transactions between the Indians in this area and the white traders?"

Ward shook his head.

"There were no chiefs to speak for the Indians," Jean said. "Whenever a situation arose that demanded a decision, whoever was most qualified to act in that area assumed leadership that was temporary. When the situation was cleared up, finished, again there was no leader. Even then, the only power the leaders had was

advisory and judicial; they could enforce nothing.
Every village was autonomous. That was an impossible
state of affairs for the traders to deal with. They had to
make deals, to bargain for pelts, write up contracts.
They forced the Indians to consolidate, to select chiefs
in order to have one person to deal with and not every
village, every tribe independently. They began forcing
changes the day they arrived, and the Indians couldn't
resist. They had no experience to draw on to strengthen
themselves with. Step by step they were forced to
change, to adapt. That's what you're proposing now.
The first step toward what? You don't know. No one
knows. And they aren't even here, may never be here.
But the pressure is here already." She yawned. "I'm
very tired. As you must be. Shouldn't we all get some
sleep?"

Ward stood up. "We'll make coffee, have a snack,"
he said. "I'm afraid we'll have to stay together the rest
of the night. At dawn we'll go down to the airport and
wait."

There was no chance to get at him during the next
hour as they made a fire in the stove, prepared coffee,
found crackers he had supplied and a meat spread. He
was wary of Doris, not allowing her to approach him at
all, watching her closely whenever she moved. So Doris
had told him about the defense classes, but probably
she had not mentioned that Jean had participated also.
Jean, after all, was like him, one of his kind; it was the
other, the alien, he had to watch. Ward sat at the far
end of the table and motioned them to sit together at
the other end. Jean wished she had put her watch on.
She had taken it off that day over a year ago when she
had come home to take her final walk on the desert.
She had left it upstairs in her drawer that day, and it
was still there. She yawned again.

"What time is it?"

"Four-thirty."

"My God! No wonder I'm tired."

"Have some more coffee. You'll be able to sleep all day. A nice quiet room of your own, with running hot water, all the luxuries."

"Ward, I want to talk to you alone."

He shook his head. "We stay together."

"Let her go, Ward. She doesn't know anything about all of this. You know she doesn't. Let her go find her people."

"It's not my decision," he said.

Jean turned to Doris and put her hand on the girl's cheek. "I'm sorry," she said, near tears. "You are my sister and I'm responsible for all of this, for the danger you're in. . . . You are . . ." In the same tone, with no change in emphasis, she said in Wasco, "When we clear the table, stay on that side. Be ready." She bowed her head and withdrew her hand.

"What did you tell her?"

She shook her head, not looking at him. "It's untranslatable. I said that she'll soon join her ancestors, that it's my fault, that if she can forgive me . . . I can't translate it." She stood up, picked up her cup, began to walk around the table toward him. "They'll kill her, won't they? What use will they have for a poor Indian girl? She'll just be in the way." She heard the desperation in her voice and knew it was convincing, because it was real. Now, she knew. Now or never. She reached for his cup, not looking to see where Doris was, what she was doing. He was pushing his chair back, starting to rise, when she suddenly flung her remaining coffee into his face, and hooked her foot around his chair leg, gave it a hard yank, upsetting it. He fell with the chair and Doris leaped on him from the other side and hit him in the throat.

They tied him up with his own belt and a clothesline. He was starting to moan before they finished.

"Listen carefully," Jean said then, in Wasco. "Get the horses. You go find Robert and tell him what happened here. Tell him he has to stop the bus and get

Cluny off before it gets to Bend. Tell him to tell Cluny
where Skeleton Cave is. I'll hide the van and the tapes
there."

"Why can't you come with me? Robert can hide you
so no one can ever find you."

"No. I'll take the van. I have to hide it so they won't
find the tapes. They'll think we're trying to escape in it.
They'll be searching the roads. It'll give Robert time to
get Cluny off the bus. After I get rid of the van, I'll go
to Wesley's camp. They won't find me on the desert."

As they talked Jean hurried into the pantry and
picked up two water bags; she collected a packet of
dried meat and another of dried fruit. Four days, she
thought. She added the chocolate bars that Steve and
Pat had given them. She swung her backpack off a hook
and was ready. Her hat. She raced upstairs and got her
wide-brimmed hat. Doris had gathered a few packages
also, and they left together. Ward was struggling
feebly. Jean embraced Doris quickly and kissed her,
then they parted.

Ward's keys were on the van dashboard. She drew in
a deep breath and turned the key. The motor started
instantly.

Ten minutes, she thought. They had killed ten
minutes already. It would be daylight in an hour.

She had dismissed the idea of going to Steve and Pat
for help as soon as it occurred to her. They would be
totally ineffectual against men like these, she knew.
Also, she could not have the van on a road when a
plane arrived; the search would be over before it even
began.

She drove through the back streets until she reached
the highway, and then turned south. She felt too
conspicuous with the headlights on, but when she tried
driving with them off, she could see nothing at all. The
dirt road she sought was four or five miles out of town,
and she had to drive very slowly to find it. There were
driveways, subdivision entrances, businesses with their

drives and parking spaces . . . all dead and black now. All the mouths opened to the highway looked alike.

Just when she decided she had passed her turnoff, she saw it, with a boarded-up Dairy Queen on one corner, a gas station opposite. She turned and she was glad it was still dark, for the cloud of dust her wheels raised pointed like an arrow. The next turn was onto a ranch road, narrower, dustier than the county road; it was a zigzag course among rocks and boulders, now following a dried stream, now crossing the rocky bottom, making a steep climb up the other side. . . .

The road wound upward steadily. She had not remembered that it was this far to the next turn, or this steep, the curves this sharp. Hurry, hurry, hurry! she thought. There was the next turn, another ranch road, even steeper, even narrower. Her hands started to hurt from clutching the steering wheel too hard.

Straight ahead, the gaping hole of Skeleton Cave came into view. On the eastern horizon there were streaks of silvery gray. She passed the cave, made a sharp right turn and saw the overhanging cliff where her grandfather had taken her years ago. He had driven his truck under the rocks into shade where they had had a picnic lunch. She drove in now until she felt the van scrape the side of the cliff, and then she stopped and pulled on the hand brake.

As far as any searchers would be able to tell, the van had disappeared. No amount of searching would reveal it; only hikers, or someone driving by the opening of the overhang, would ever see it here.

She went to the entrance of the shelter and sat down cross-legged and watched the rising sun. The silver streaks had yielded to broad bands of gold, rose, vermilion, pale green, and marine blue. The colors flared, turned the desert into a land where gold became pink as if by magic, with no transition period. The desert glowed, pink with magenta shadows, gold highlights. The sky was alive with color in motion.

Then the sun climbed the cliff of the horizon and called the brilliant colors back to itself. Jean closed her eyes and felt the first rays on her skin like a kiss, like a benediction on this, the most holy moment of the new day.

 "Cluny, what are you doing here?" Murray asked impatiently. They were walking along the Potomac; the day was very warm and still, the sky solidly overcast.

The signals were all wrong, Cluny thought. The sky was like a winter sky, the day like a summer day, and at this time of year neither was right. He kicked a stone. "I told you. I was bored. I wanted to know what's happening."

"Okay. So read a newspaper. Watch the nightly news."

"You know that isn't what I mean."

"On Alpha? Nothing. Not a goddamned thing."

"What about the draft? Will it pass?"

"It looks like it. Bledsoe has his forces lined up in tight formation. He's got the votes."

Cluny kicked another rock, harder this time. Two men approached from the opposite direction, and they all passed each other silently. They would wire the paths, Cluny thought. How many decisions were being made these days along the banks of the scummy

Potomac? How many classified secrets were passed? How many careers started and ended?

"I want to go back to work," Cluny said then and was surprised at his words. He had not thought of returning to the satellite for weeks.

"I thought so. Can you deliver the girl first?"

"Where, when?"

"We'll have to arrange something." He glanced at Cluny thoughtfully. "You know Alpha is where it'll all start."

Cluny nodded. Whoever made the first move would make it there, try to seize Alpha, rid it of the others. "When?"

"I wish to God we knew. Before Christmas, that's the word. We need that message, Cluny. Real bad."

"She doesn't think she'll make anything out of it for months."

"Change her mind then. Cluny, you know that if either side makes a move, we're all in it, every man jack of us, with no holds barred. If either side takes Alpha, it's going to be bad, but it'll be worse if the Russians do it."

"So what else is new?" Cluny said bitterly.

"I've got to get back," Murray said then. "See you in the apartment later." He turned to retrace their steps, then paused again. "Almost forgot—your father-in-law left a message for you to call him if you showed up. See you, Cluny."

Cluny watched him walk away, a pudgy man with a bad heart, bad coloring. Murray thought they had lost already. It was evident in his walk, his speech, his manner, his eyes, which had become wistful and too sad for a man rising in his chosen career as he was doing.

He called Mr. Davies from a pay phone and was invited to dinner that evening. Davies was in town for a month, he said; there were affairs to be discussed, things to be settled, if Cluny felt up to it. From time to time Cluny had received papers from Mr. Davies'

lawyer, and he had signed them with little or no
interest. When he had been informed that he had
inherited over four hundred thousand dollars from
Lina's estate, he had not grasped the meaning of the
words, still had not fully realized what they meant. It
wasn't his money, would never be his money, but it was
in his name—stocks, bonds, cash, certificates of deposit. He hoped Mr. Davies had the proper papers for him
to sign to return it all.

Mr. Davies had a permanent suite in the downtown
Ambassador, six rooms on the top floor with a magnifi-
cent view of the city from three window walls in the
oversized living room. There were several other men
already in the room when Cluny was admitted. He
recognized Senator Bledsoe and General Barneveldt,
but had met neither of them. He felt his stomach
tighten when he saw Luther Krohmeier standing at one
of the floor-to-ceiling windows, talking to Roderick
Gris, whom he also knew slightly. Roderick Gris was
on the President's science advisory staff.

Mr. Davies met Cluny effusively, introduced him to
the people he didn't know, put a martini in his hand,
and then resumed a conversation that had been in
progress when Cluny arrived.

"It's the logical thing to do, Senator, even if it would
rouse them to wrath, as you suggest." He turned to
Cluny. "Don't you agree that we need to draw up new
lines of representation now that half the states west of
Ohio are virtually uninhabited?"

Cluny shook his head. "Hadn't given it much
thought, to tell the truth," he said. Bledsoe was very
red-faced. Texas, Cluny thought, or Arizona. He
couldn't remember which state Bledsoe represented.

"And let BLM take care of it all?" Gris asked. "The
bureau would love it, I'm sure." His voice dripped
irony.

This was all phony, Cluny told himself. They were
playing with him, biding their time to get to the real
reason for this dinner party. He sat down to wait them

out. Or, he thought, perhaps he had not been planned on, perhaps they never would get down to business this night. He sipped his drink and listened to Mr. Davies make a case for turning the West back over to the Bureau of Land Management. He made a very good case.

Cluny studied the men. Bledsoe was the silver-haired debonair man of charm who always looked so good on television that he was one of the first to be called for whatever came along: debates on treaties, the draft legislation, his view of the Russians' sudden increase in armaments. . . . And Bledsoe was deferring to Davies.

The general also was well known. He had the knack of being in the right place at the right time to gain publicity, with no effort on his part. Ex-presidential adviser, ex-NATO commander, ex-chief of staff of the Joint Armed Forces Command, he could call a news conference with the same aplomb as the President himself, or he could duck forever under the National Security blanket. He was six feet tall, every inch military, from his posture, to his steady bright blue eyes, to his sandy hair, which would always be just a trifle shorter than fashion dictated but noticeably longer than the military demanded. It was simply the toss of the political coin that had made him ex-every post of importance at this time. He had backed the wrong man in the last election. Next time he would be on the right side again.

Roderick Gris was one of the bright lights from Harvard, called from his cloistered halls to advise this President in these trying times. But that was only the popular version, Cluny knew. Actually Gris was adviser for so many committees and think tanks and special commissions that he had put in more time on government business than the senator himself, who boasted of thirty years. Gris was fifty, author of a string of popular science books, politically an eel who could slip under any door to land in the midst of any group without discomfiture.

Cluny didn't once look at Luther Krohmeier, who in turn was studiously avoiding him.

Dinner was a buffet. Davies hated servants and waiters fussing about him while he ate. The food was excellent, cold dishes in bowls of crushed ice, hot dishes on warming trays, an assortment of wines on the sideboard. Nothing of consequence was discussed at dinner.

When they returned to the living room, coffee service had been arranged on a side table, and there was brandy and glasses on the coffee table between two leather-covered couches. It was like being in the Beast's castle, Cluny thought, with invisible hands arranging everything before them. He was pouring coffee with his back to the others when Davies said:

"This week we reinstate the draft, Cluny."

Cluny turned. "We?"

"Oh, I helped a little bit with it. Not much, not enough, but a little bit, talking here and there with people I know."

Cluny nodded.

"Actually you might consider this a recruitment committee right here in this room," Davies went on. He glanced at the other men sitting now with coffee or brandy, or both. "Our own first little recruitment committee. We want you, Cluny." He held out his hand, pointing a finger straight at Cluny, and they all laughed.

"I'm afraid you're being too subtle for me." Cluny took his coffee to a chair where he could see them all and sat down.

"I think you understand," Davies said. "The time's come when you choose sides. It's that simple really. We say we have to hit first, take home all the cake. Others say not now, wait. They'll still be saying that when the bombs start to fall, while they're frying in their snug little houses. We need people like you with us from the beginning."

Cluny shook his head. "But my natural inclination is

to say not now, let's wait. I don't believe the Russians will start a war, unless they're driven to it."

"If it's handled right, there won't be a war," Bledsoe said smoothly. "A few orbiting satellites get knocked out, a display of power, that's enough in this modern age. Both sides know what's to be expected if certain steps are taken swiftly enough, enough power exerted at the beginning. We won't start the war, there's no need to. But if they move first, we have no doubt about the next countermoves. That would be the holocaust we all want to avoid."

"With all due respect, sir," Cluny said, "I think it's a mistake to think we'd fight back but the Russians wouldn't." He shook his head slightly. "I don't think you understand what Alpha really is—a scientific laboratory, that's all. It's not a weapon, it can't be defended or used as a weapon of war. The people up there are scientists."

"And what about the ongoing experiments with the microwaves melting the ice packs in the Arctic? If the satellite were shifted in orbit, the beams focused elsewhere . . ."

"There are safeguards built into the system," Cluny said flatly. "That was considered and guarded against."

For the first time that evening Luther Krohmeier spoke to Cluny directly. "People who won't cooperate won't be there. Others can undo all the fail-safes. We're going to decide who's up there and who isn't when the time comes."

"Luther! No threats!" Mr. Davies cried. "We don't have to use threats with men of intelligence. Cluny and I have other business to discuss tonight. I'll talk with him further on this matter. We don't demand an immediate response, my boy. Think of it. Later I'll try to explain our position. But now, there's vintage brandy and excellent Celebesian coffee, and my God! wasn't that dinner superlative!"

He had given the cue and the others knew it. Within half an hour they finished the coffee and brandy, shook hands all around, and left Cluny with his father-in-law. Mr. Davies poured more coffee for himself and waved generally toward the silver pot. A servant had brought in fresh coffee as the other guests had prepared to leave. The ashtrays had been taken away, the empty glasses, the brandy. Now the coffee was on the low table that served both couches. Cluny sat opposite Mr. Davies.

"You know I'm politically neutral," Cluny said slowly. "I really won't take sides in this. I think what you're doing is dangerous beyond comprehension."

Davies seemed withdrawn now, deeply thoughtful. All former traces of joviality had been erased. "I know about the message," he said. "We've known for a long time actually. How you brought it back with you, the gold, everything."

"Did Lina tell you?"

"Remember that talk we had, when we first met? I told you then she wasn't like other women, other daughters. She used to tell me things no daughter should tell her father. I never knew what to do about that. She'd come home and tell me about her men, what they did, what they said, everything. I think she did it to torment me. She looked very much like her mother, you know. She knew what it did to me when she told me those things."

His voice was still very remote, and he looked at the coffeepot, not at Cluny. "She told me about the stuff you had and I sent a man around to collect it, make a copy while you were sleeping. We've been working on it too, with no success. But our people don't have the special talent that your Jean Brighton has. She's getting something. According to my reports she'll be the one, if it can be done. It'll prove to be a Russian trick, of course. Maybe she can demonstrate that. You went straight for the best, didn't you. I admire you for that. You have an eye for the best there is."

There was a cold lump in Cluny's chest now. It made breathing difficult and swallowing something he had to do very consciously. "You still haven't got to the point," he said, and was surprised to hear the steadiness in his voice.

"Yes. Of course. I almost had you killed when you went to the island. I sent you there to kill you. I didn't want to do it while you were still in shock, you see. I wanted you to be aware. And then I didn't do it. I'm still surprised that I was able to have second thoughts. For a whole week all I could think about was how I'd do it, but then I realized that you wanted it too. I'd be doing what you were too cowardly to do for yourself. And I made new plans, better plans."

The lump vanished as swiftly as it had formed. At last, Cluny thought, it was out. They both knew. He cleared his throat, but Davies waved him silent, regarding him through narrowed eyes, as if he never had looked at him before.

"I know how you must have felt," he said. "I could almost sympathize. Almost. I wanted to kill her many times, but I didn't, and that makes the difference."

"I didn't want her dead!"

"But she is dead, and you're alive. You killed her and I can prove it, Cluny. We know when you got back that night, both times. She told me how trusting you were, how you called her a goddess, thought her pure and chaste. She thought it was very funny that you were so idealistic and naïve, and she was touched by it. She was very perceptive, you know. She knew that you didn't love her, not as she really was. The woman you loved didn't exist. She told me that. And she said that if you ever really saw her, you'd kill her. She wrote me a letter saying just that. That's the difference between us, Cluny, you and me. I knew what she was and loved her, and when you found out you killed her."

Cluny felt frozen to the couch, unable to move, unable to look up at Davies. She had told her father everything he had said, everything he had done. He felt very tired of trying to move, tired of listening, of trying to understand.

"You'll do what we want you to do, Cluny. Whatever we want. And I'll watch you doing it, watch you change and become something else, watch you wishing you were dead over and over, watch you living and wanting death. You'll do your own work, come and go to Alpha when you want to. And we'll know, you and I both, that when I snap my fingers, you'll jump as often and as high as I say. So I will kill you, but it will be very, very slow, and every day you'll know it's happening."

Now Cluny looked at him. "Do you really think I care if you tell them? I'll dial the number for you."

"I know. I know, Cluny. But I wouldn't do it. Someone else will, and I'll protest and try to protect you, and get you declared mentally unstable and see that you get medical treatment. I'll treat you just like my own son, pay for private hospitals, everything. There are drugs that do strange things to people, make them very docile and tractable for hours at a time, and then when the effects wear off, full memory returns. You'll have a lifetime to experience them, Cluny. Fifty years? Forty? You know I can do it, my boy. You know it."

Staring at him, Cluny did know it. He stood up and walked away from the couch, away from the table, away from Mr. Davies.

"Two days, Cluny. You have two days, and then we go on from here."

There was little traffic, but people on foot were as thick at eleven as they had been at noon. Cluny walked with his head bowed, seeing little, looking up when he was accosted by women who were selling themselves, by men who were begging, by boys who offered whatever he wanted. He stayed in the downtown section, where the dimmed lights made it like a late overcast afternoon with hordes of shoppers on the prowl. Every corner had two policemen, or soldiers. The windows were all protected by wire cages, or steel bars. He walked to the corner, crossed the street,

turned and walked back the way he had come, turned
again, then again and again. He had to think, had to
think, had . . . His mind kept returning to Lina.

He shook his head angrily. Davies, he had to think of
Davies and what he represented, what they could
accomplish. The message was a catalyst, he thought.
No matter what it actually said, if they ever learned
what it said, it had served this other purpose already:
the unexpected pressure it had exerted had brought to a
head a long-festering boil. Without it the boil might
have stayed sore and tender for another generation; it
might have come to a head alone, but also it might have
gone away again, might have been reabsorbed.

He did not realize when his thoughts shifted, but
when he became aware of them, he was again in bed
with Lina, remembering. . . . He stopped, looking
about him. He was still in the downtown section. It was
twelve-thirty.

Jean had to announce that it was real, he realized. It
was the only way to buy time now. He tried to think of
Jean inspiring the kind of blind love he had had for
Lina, and he knew it could not happen. Jean was too
honest. She would force a lover to look at her, to see
her and know her. Love with someone like Jean would
not be a total loss of self, not the way he had lost
himself. Love with Jean would be a finding of self, a
growing larger than self. With a sense of guilt, he tried
to banish the thoughts. "I did love her," he muttered,
and the words were ignored as he thought about Lina
and what he had felt for her.

Davies had been right in saying that his was the real
love. He had known her, accepted her exactly as she
was, and still had wanted only her happiness. And if
that was the definition of love, he admitted, he had not
felt it. But he knew there was more than that. His
passion had to mean something, had to account for
something.

Davies must realize that Cluny would not join forces
with the militarists. He was too shrewd to miscalculate

about that. Cluny was bumped into from behind before he became aware that he had stopped walking. He moved to stand before a barred show window, and for the first time that night he was seeing himself as Davies must have seen him. Passionate, infatuated, blindly loyal, totally selfish. Davies must also think he had the same attachment to Alpha, to his work there.

Davies believed in Cluny's blind devotion to his work, to Alpha and his place on it; that was why he had brought in Luther Krohmeier with his threat of keeping Cluny off Alpha, and the general who had reinforced that threat. That was why he had counted on the weight of his own threat of daily brain death by drugs and a lifetime of torture through not being able to continue in his work. And it was all empty.

What had driven him was Lina, from start to finish. He had done everything for her, to show her that he was deserving of her. No one had known that, not Lina, not Murray, not Sid, not Mr. Davies. All the passion he had brought to Alpha, getting it running again, getting his own position there—it had all been to demonstrate something to her.

He started to walk again. Intellectually he could form the words and say them to himself: he had not been in love; it had been a blind infatuation, longer lasting than most, but of the same nature as any adolescent boy's blind passion for an unattainable princess. In a world without dragons, he had gone after Alpha, and he had won the princess. Now the adolescence was over. Emotionally he could not accept the words he said to himself. Emotionally he might never be able to accept his rational judgment.

Maybe, he thought, on some deep level he had known that only through her death could he finally free himself from that long-sustained adolescence. What Davies could know least of all, he realized, was that he, Cluny, recognized his own need for punishment, and was willing to suffer it, even welcomed it.

But not yet, not yet. His punishment should be his

alone. Not his and the world's, not Alpha's and its
people. Not Jean's for doing what he had forced her to
do. He remembered with disgust how easy it had been
to threaten her, how knowingly he had touched the
nerve that would make her yield.

Davies thought she was getting something, he remembered, and he felt his stomach churn. How had
Davies known? He looked about him then; he was still
in the vicinity of the Ambassador Hotel. He had
walked for hours up and down the streets that bounded
the hotel. Why were all those people still on the
streets? Not as many as earlier, but still hundreds and
hundreds of them, shuffling along, huddled in display
areas, drooped in doorways. There was a taxi stand
before the hotel; he roused a nodding driver and gave
him Murray's address.

He let himself in quietly, went to Murray's room and
awakened him, holding one hand over his mouth while
he shook him. Murray struggled briefly, then permitted
himself to be dragged into the bathroom, where Cluny
turned the shower on full.

Whispering, he told Murray everything that had
happened. "I've got to get Jean," he said afterward.
"Ward must be a plant. They know what she's doing.
They mustn't suspect that I know that or they might
move before I get back."

Murray shook his head. "Put that on the back
burner," he said. "We'll take care of the girl. You've
got to go along with Davies. You can be of more use
there."

"Murray, wake up! Davies trusts me as much as I
trust him. I won't be able to do anything, learn
anything. They'll use me to endorse whatever policy
they have, no more than that. We have to protect Jean;
she has to announce that the message is real, even
translate it. Davies honestly believes it's a Russian
hoax, and they're getting ready to jump. They believe
in what they want to do. They think we're lost unless
they act now. We have to buy time with that message."

"Will he carry out his threat? Have you arrested?"

"He's too shrewd to gamble without having the cards. He will tighten the screws first, but in the end, yes."

"Good Christ!" Murray felt the shower, adjusted the heat, and then stepped under it. He stuck his head out and growled, "Go make some coffee. I'm still sleeping, remember."

Cluny put on coffee and then sat down and started writing. When Murray padded out barefoot, wrapped in a floor-length robe, Cluny handed him the paper. Murray glanced at it, put it on the table, poured coffee, and then sat down to read it. He added a note to the bottom, and for the next fifteen minutes they exchanged notes silently. Finally Murray nodded, got up and left, returned with an atlas. He turned to the Western states, studied the page, and then pointed to Boise. There would be a plane waiting in Boise for Cluny and Jean, and Doris if she wanted to go along. Murray was not happy with it, but he admitted grudgingly that it was the best of several alternatives he could come up with.

Cluny wrote a short letter to Mr. Davies, explained his job of getting the dictionary bound, what it meant to Jean. He said that in return she was working on the message, that if he didn't fulfill his part of the bargain she would more than likely simply vanish into the mountains with her Indian friends again. It was fake-sounding, he thought, reading it over, but it would have to do. He mailed the letter at the airport, and caught the seven-thirty flight to San Francisco, with a connecting flight to Portland.

That afternoon he picked up the dictionaries. He ordered twenty more copies, paid for them in advance, and gave instructions about mailing them to Robert at the reservation.

The following day he caught the bus to Bend. There were a dozen other passengers for the first part of the trip, but most of them got off before they reached the high Cascades. They were people who had defied the government's orders to leave the countryside, and they were clinging to a precarious livelihood in the mountains just as the early settlers had done.

The bus started down the eastern slopes, then slowed and came to a stop in the middle of the wilderness. On the road were many Indians on horseback; others were on the side of the road.

"What the hell's going on?" the driver yelled through his open window.

One of the Indians approached the bus and called back, "Is Arthur Cluny aboard? I have a message."

Then Cluny saw Doris and he rushed to the front of the bus.

"Bring your belongings," the tall Indian called again.

He grabbed his suitcase and the parcels he had brought and left the bus high above the deserted village of Sisters.

They stayed in the woods all that day. In the evening the group split, most of them heading north toward their homes in the reservation. Their horses were loaded with game, berries, nuts. Robert and three other Indians remained with Cluny at the edge of the pine trees, waiting for dark. All day they had listened to the airplane going back and forth, back and forth. While they waited for darkness, a slender boy of twelve or less appeared at Robert's side and spoke briefly to him, vanished again.

"They've sent more men, more cars to patrol the roads," Robert said. "They know you're with us; there are men at the reservation waiting for you."

Cluny said, "And Jean? Have they found Jean?"

"No. They won't find her. They, like you, would never think of looking for her on foot in the desert."

Cluny had protested vehemently, had urged speed in finding her, had insisted on riders spreading out to search for her. Robert had shaken his head, saying only that her plan was wise. The wind started to blow at sunset and by the time they were ready to move it was a

howling, cold, demon wind. Cluny thought of Jean out
there on foot alone, and he shivered.

"Don't try to force the pinto," Robert said at the
beginning. "He'll follow my lead." He mounted and
two Indians took places on each side of Cluny, the last
one followed behind, and they moved steadily over the
rough ground. They should not ride at night, Cluny
thought, visualizing the dropoffs, the sheer canyon
walls, the treacherous scree of loose gravel and obsidian and lava. He could see so little that he was
effectively blind; he could tell no difference in the trail
where they slowed to a painstaking crawl, and the
places where Robert let his lead horse break into a trot.
When they crossed the highway, they could see the
taillights of a car moving away from them, heading
north. They rode parallel to another road, and several
times they were within shouting distance of cars on slow
patrols. They had to use the road to go down a steep
cliff at one point, and they waited under juniper trees
until the patrol car passed, and then let the horses
gallop after it, pacing it down the hill into a valley.
When the car's red brake lights came on, they returned
to the scant cover of the rocks and trees. The car turned
and went back up the cliff. One of the Indians laughed.

At the far end of the valley, they returned to the
road. No patrol cars were coming out this far, and now
they made good progress. The road was pale in the
starlight, but when the moon rose at midnight, its light
was bright enough to reveal the landscape in startling
detail. It was black and silver and white, and alien.

Cluny had found the desert ugly in its apparent
lifelessness; the signs of death had been everywhere,
but now in the moonlight it changed, it became the land
of fairy tales and dreams. He would come back one
day, he thought, explore this relic of prehistory. This
was a land of scars, of brutalizing forces whose marks
were not erased by forests and meadows, but left there
to be examined and pondered. Earthquake country in

the distant past, volcanic country in the more recent past; mesas stood in sharp outline against the light sky, cones could be seen in the fragments that the wind had not yet succeeded in wearing down, pinnacles and upthrusts jutted high from the floor. Raw, unequivocal power had shaped this land, was still shaping it; nothing was hidden here.

The wind bit into his face and neck, chafed his hands and wrists, blew through his clothes. Again he thought of Jean on foot, huddled somewhere in the shelter of a rock, waiting out the long night.

They left the road for a ranch road, and then left that for a fire road that started to climb up a mountain. Here there were trees that blunted the force of the wind, and although they had to go slower, Robert was satisfied. They had made very good time.

Cluny had been too cold to feel his muscles, but now they started to ache, and the last two hours seemed endless, tortured hours that were distorted and really stretched out into days, a lifetime. When they got to the camp, he had to have help in getting off the horse, and he groaned when he stood up. Robert took him to a clearing, where there were several men talking in low voices.

"Wrap up," Robert said, handing Cluny a blanket. "Sleep now. We won't build a fire to call attention to ourselves, but soon it'll be morning and warmer and we'll eat then."

At first when Robert had told him Jean would join them in the mountains, he had believed. People could walk sixty or seventy miles; they did it all the time. Then he had ridden over the ruined land and belief had faded, and now, as he stood in the shadow of a pine tree, belief was gone. Robert had brought him by way of roads, rough dirt roads for the most part, but they had been graded somewhat; the road engineers had found the easiest ways to follow. For Jean there were no roads. As far as he could see looking southwest, there were gorges and sharp buttes and cliffs, but no roads.

She would walk in the early morning hours when there were shadows to hide her, Robert had said, and again in the late afternoon. In the midday she would rest; she would not move at night when it would be too perilous on foot. She would arrive today, Robert had also said, and Cluny did not believe it.

He heard the airplane again and knowing he was not visible from the sky, he still did not move. Damn them, he thought over and over. Damn them! Even if there were roads she could use, they made it impossible, skimming a hundred feet off the ground, searching, searching.

"Don't worry," Robert said earlier, his voice surprisingly gentle. "They're searching like white men and she's moving like an Indian. Two different realities. The restrictions they impose on themselves will prevent their seeing her."

The wind blew and the sun slipped lower in the western sky, lengthening the shadows again. Now she would be moving, if she was able to, if she was not already dead, or dying. His jaw ached from being clenched so hard, and he tried to relax against the tree trunk. The sun was hanging on a peak of the distant Cascades; it balanced like a ball on the sharp nose of a seal, and then began to slide down the other side. It looked as if the peak were growing as he watched, hiding more and more of the great ball. He started when he heard Robert's voice.

"Look," Robert said, pointing.

He saw her then, a miniature figure skirting a twisting riverbed, walking down into it, up the other side. She vanished behind an outcropping, appeared again, closer, but still too far away to see her features.

He pushed away from the tree. "I'll take a horse down; she must be exhausted."

"No. If the plane came back, they'd wonder why we were moving at dusk. Let her finish alone."

She was starting to climb now, and Cluny could see a glint of pale hair that had slipped from under her hat. It was the color of the moon. The sky was rapidly turning violet and in the east there was a reflection of a sunset, dimmed, quiet, done in pastels. There were no clouds in the west, no sunset there, only the luminous violet sky. The wind screamed, the only sound.

He looked at Jean again, walking faster now. Her shoulders were straight, her arms moving freely with her body motions. She moved like a dancer. How small she was.

The plane came back and he felt his heart thump when he spotted it, close enough to see blue and white markings. He looked for Jean and could not find her. Robert was smiling faintly, also watching. The plane left, heading north, and when he looked at the fire road, Jean was there, moving steadily, easily.

Robert whistled a low, sweet bird call; Jean raised her head, and without slackening her pace, whistled back. It sounded very faint and distant. In her faded jeans, tan shirt, cowboy hat, boots, she looked like a very young boy. Cluny rejected that. No, she looked like a dancer, with grace that was completely unself-conscious. She moved like something totally free, not male, not female, not adolescent, but all those things and something more.

"She moves like the moon floating over the eternal sky," Robert said. "Let's go meet her at the end of the road."

They crossed the high meadow, where Robert spoke briefly to his son. Wesley grinned. "We'll prepare her a feast," he said.

They went on to the first turn of the road that was being reclaimed by the land so fast that it was hard to say where it began and ended. They stopped. Before them the road curved again. There were no shadows now under the deep violet sky and on this side of the mountain the wind was a faraway wail, like an echo of itself.

She walked around the curve and smiled, as if she had been expecting them. Cluny wanted to break and run to her, but when Robert didn't move, he resisted the impulse and waited also. She walked faster and Robert held out his arms for her. She went straight to him.

"My little sister. My daughter. I am very proud," he said, holding her tight against him. For the first time Cluny realized that Robert had been worried and afraid for her. Robert and Jean drew apart and he held her shoulders and studied her face. "The desert treated you well," he said huskily.

"Yes. I'm well."

Looking at her, from her to Robert and back again, Cluny knew something very important had passed between them, something both of them understood and held in reverence. He sensed a new relationship between the tall Indian and the tiny blond woman. Robert was deferential in a way Cluny could not quite grasp. He watched, bewildered, as Robert removed her hat and touched her hair very lightly, let his hand rest on her head momentarily, and then smiled at her.

Jean turned from him to Cluny. "I'm glad you're here. I knew you would be. Did Doris tell you all about it?"

They walked into camp, but Cluny felt baffled and excluded by something he could not identify or comprehend.

That night they all sat around a small fire. Jean was wrapped in a blanket that covered her entirely, leaving only her face showing.

"Will you tell us about your trip?" Wesley asked.

She nodded, and with no trace of self-consciousness, began. "The sun was coloring the day, preparing the sky, and I sat down and forgot and was one with the desert and the sun. At first it was very warm and gentle on my eyelids, then it was in me, and then it went through me. . . ."

Cluny half listened to her; he was very sleepy, so tired he felt dopey and leaden. Her voice was low and musical, soothing, as his mother's voice had been when she used to read to him. . . . He roused with a start and glanced about to see if anyone had noticed. They were all listening intently, their gazes unwaveringly fastened on Jean. He blinked; her face was floating, he thought; it looked like the moon floating in the black sky.

". . . shadows like caves," she was saying, "and the caves hid me from their airplane. My sleep had refreshed me, and I knew the desert was no longer hiding. Redtail flew close to look at me, and a lark sang to me. . . ."

Why was she doing this? Playing this game? But more important, why were they listening like that? Raptly, reverently. She was going to describe every rock, every lousy juniper tree, every rotten sagebrush, every living creature. . . .

". . . across the valley was the ranch and I thought it would be good to spend the night under the roof, but the wind led me along the butte and then the plane came back and if I had been down in the valley, they would have seen me. . . ."

Cluny drifted, returned, drifted further, came back. She had been talking a long time, he thought sleepily, listened again.

". . . sat as still as possible and on the other side of the juniper tree I knew coyote was sitting still also. He didn't laugh again, but he waited, and finally I began to tell him about the work I was doing, and he listened very quietly. The moon rose and put out the stars and I kept talking to him, explaining it all, not to make him understand, but to help me understand. I couldn't see coyote, but I could almost see him, see a shape there. I waited for him to say something for a long time and I was getting sleepy and finally I turned around to ask him to comment, and I saw that he had put a sagebrush there to fool me, that he had come and gone, laughing at me for talking to a bush. As I lay down to sleep, I heard him laughing at me from on top the butte, and I had to laugh too."

Her story finally ended, and the Indians began to murmur in Wasco, asking her questions that she answered in Wasco. They would have kept it up all night, Cluny thought, if Robert hadn't said, very firmly, that they would all go to sleep now. With obvious reluctance, the Indians began to wrap themselves up in their blankets, some of them still talking in low voices.

He watched Jean withdraw into the shadow of a lean-to that Wesley had constructed for her. He wanted to go in after her, to make her drop this act, to make her be the girl he remembered from so many years ago. To make love to her, he thought with a jolt. Not to possess her or dominate her, or even use her. He wanted to know who she was. He wanted to know her.

What had happened to her? He felt certain he would have recognized her if he had run across her before she left the university, while she was still working for Arkins. Or in the Newtown. Then she had spent a year with the savages and had become a savage herself. Savages, he thought bitterly: Davies and Murray, Robert, Dan Brighton and his own father, the mobs of roving youths, Ward Blenko . . . If aliens had left the message, if they came back, if they chose to count the savages, who would they count?

Jean had said something about the importance of what happened to these Indians, he remembered, and now he understood what she had meant. For hundreds of years Indians and whites had lived in the same world, shared the same land, and they knew little about each other. The Indians were mysterious to him, unfathomable to him. How had they resisted the pressures of the conquerors? What did they know that let them endure?

What had sustained them? What had sustained Jean during her long trek across the hostile desert?

He fell asleep thinking of how she had talked about the desert, as if it had been her ally, not the hostile barren wilderness he knew it to be. She had talked as if the desert had opened a path for her, had sheltered her when she needed shelter, had provided hiding places when the plane had circled low overhead, had guided her to berries, to a spring in the dry Dog River. She had talked of a coyote keeping her company during the long nights. And they had listened with unmoving attention, respectful, assuming the same deferential manner that had altered Robert subtly. He dreamed that Jean was seated in a classroom where he was the teacher, demanding explanations that she gave over and over, patiently and kindly, as if trying very hard to make him understand, and he could recognize not a single word of the language she used.

18 "By now they must have roadblocks at every track, trail, and highway leaving the state," Cluny said the next morning. He ached and was sore, but not as much as the previous day. Jean looked untouched by her ordeal, except for a deep suntan.

"How do you think they'll proceed?" Robert asked.

"They probably think Jean holed up waiting for me to come, and when we join forces, we'll make a dash in the van. They'll be watching the places where it could travel cross-country, and all roads leading from the state."

Robert nodded. "And you have a plane waiting at Boise?"

"Yes. Until further notice. We didn't know when I'd be wanting it."

"Okay," Robert said, standing now. "We'll go to Boise."

Cluny drew in a breath to explain again, but Jean nodded.

"We should start soon," she said. "They may decide to investigate this camp at any time."

Robert spoke to Wesley briefly. The youth joined them and shook hands with Cluny, and then looked at Jean for a moment before he clasped her to his chest, as his father had done the day before. "Little Olahuene," he murmured. "Take care. You'll come back to us one day. I'll watch for you."

"I'll come back," she said. "I'll miss your wedding. I'm sorry."

In two days the Indians would start the cattle drive back to the reservation. The watchers would concentrate on them, Cluny knew. They would think he and Jean were using the dust and the confusion to cover themselves, as they would be doing, but on the eastern border of the state.

They rode in high, sparsely timbered country all that day, among junipers and pines, tan, dead-looking clumps of grass, and sagebrush. Cluny wondered how the cattle survived such a diet, how anything could live in this land. They rode single file, Robert leading, Jean last, and Cluny in the middle. He knew that he was inexperienced, that riding with no saddle was the hardest thing he had done in many years, but even more than his own discomfort, he disliked the thought of Jean as his protector. She looked like a child on her horse, had to have a hand to mount it, slid off as if from a sliding board when they stopped.

At dusk Robert selected a campsite so sheltered among mammoth boulders that when their three bodies were around the tiny fire, not a spark could be seen ten feet away. After they ate, Robert drew out the dictionary and handed it to Jean. She had not seen it yet.

"It's so little," she said in dismay.

"It's a perfect start," Robert said firmly. "We will add to it."

"Why do you even want it?" Cluny asked them.

Robert looked away from him, his face shadowed and remote. "You know all the theories about two cultures? Your people came and it was like a cloud settling over us." He moved one hand over the other, held it there. "Everywhere there was your way—your lifestyles, your science, your tools, your gadgets—and we came to doubt the value of everything of our own. Neolithic savages: we even accepted your name for us, and began the process of change that would make us like you. Our people were ashamed that they didn't look like your people, that they couldn't think like them. The very concepts were ungraspable—economics, ownership, domination over the land, superiority over the animals. All very strange, unknowable. We went to your schools and tried to learn your ways, but in our hearts we were still resisting because we found that cultural heritage is a very potent force, Dr. Cluny. Your cloud and its shadow over us obscured too many things we sensed were important, even though your people seemed unaware of them."

He looked at Jean then. "I didn't think we could live side by side ever. The two realities are too dissimilar. But perhaps we can. When the drought ends your people will come back, but this time your shadow must not smother us. We must live side by side, overlapping, no doubt, but without the overwhelming pressure to become white. We can't become white. We both have to be able to select or reject what the other offers. At first we didn't understand, and when we began to, it was too late. We'll need to be able to talk. Our children must not forget, or it will be as it was the first time. We need a written history of our people, a written dream of our future. Our children must not forget."

It wouldn't work, Cluny thought. They would be driven from the land finally, and in the Newtowns they would adapt or die. It seemed very simple, very final.

Robert stood up. "I'll check on the horses, and then we should sleep. We'll start again at daybreak."

Cluny watched him until he vanished among the junipers. "Noble savages," he said cynically, turning toward Jean.

"No. They were a dying culture. Now they see a chance to survive. They've grabbed at it. They had one of the highest birth rates anywhere on earth, and it's down to simple replacement, or slightly less. The number one cause of death in the reservation was accidents, and they aren't having fatal accidents any more. Juvenile delinquency was as high as in the slums of any major city; it's no longer with them. Alcoholism was rampant and now there's no alcohol. The shadow was killing them and now they can breathe again. They'll still die," she said softly, but with no regret. "If the desert keeps advancing it will kill them, but it's better than dying in the Newtowns. They'll be hungry at times and cold and lonely, and that's better than being fed and warm and in the Newtowns. For them it's better."

"Anything's better than death," Cluny said flatly.

"Maybe. You choose; we all choose. If the drought doesn't get worse, or if the rains start again, they'll be alive and they'll be proud of what they accomplished." She yawned. "Don't you even wonder what I found out about the message?"

"Later," he said harshly. The hope in the back of his mind that had made everything seem possible suddenly had become small and naked, defenseless. One word from her and it would no longer exist at all.

"It's real, Cluny. I know what it means, in part anyway."

He jumped to his feet, dizzy with a rush of adrenaline. Real! He looked down at her. He thought she smiled, but could not be certain because the fire-cast shadows were dancing on her face. "You said it would take months." His voice was hoarse.

"I was using the wrong mind set. When I shifted, it started making sense. It's what I said at the start: a message no one can translate is more useless than no message at all. It can be translated."

Robert returned and they all wrapped themselves in their blankets on mounds of pine needles. Cluny could not still his racing thoughts. Real! They were out there. They had left a message! He stared at the sky, where stars were visible that he never had seen without a telescope, brilliant spots that did not dance or flicker at all in the clear atmosphere over the desert. Which one? How far? When would they be back? Soon; it had to be soon. Earth could hold out, if help was on the way, he thought. And help would be on the way. Had to be on the way. The doctor was coming. . . .

He heard the wind, and closer rustlings, and then nothing until Robert called his name and the morning light was pale gray, the air very cold. Hoarfrost had turned the world into a white-edged illustration, something unreal except in an artist's mind.

That afternoon they left the shelter of the Ochoco Mountains and began to pick their way through arid hills where only sagebrush grew in widely separated clumps. The land had been twisted and faulted more savagely here than anywhere else yet, Cluny thought, feeling a disquiet so deep within him that he could not bring it to the surface where it could be shaken off.

Late in the afternoon they reached a cliff overlooking the Snake River; the sun was low in the sky, and the air was already very cold, promising another hard freeze during the night.

"We have to go down now," Robert said, "or else go

back to the cover of those cliffs." He pointed. "It
would be better to do it now when this side's in such
deep shadows."

Jean nodded, showing none of the disbelief Cluny
knew he revealed. From here it looked straight down to
the tiny, almost dry river, two or three thousand feet
below.

Robert looked at him thoughtfully, as if weighing the
odds against his panicking. He said, "It's an old Indian
trail, used by generations of fishermen. It's deteriorat-
ed a little, not too much." Without changing his
expression, but with a faint laugh in his voice, he
added, "I don't think any white man will look for us
here." He turned and started down the trail.

Cluny watched him, looked at Jean, who was waiting
for him to start, and he shrugged and followed. He
didn't know how Robert could see the signs of a trail,
how he could guide his horse this way, not that, when
both appeared equally impossible. It seemed the
longest trip he had ever taken, and yet, when suddenly
his horse stepped onto level ground, he had the feeling
that it could not already be over, finished. They had
done it.

Jean drew even with him and smiled teasingly.
"You're sweating, as cold as it is," she said.

He laughed suddenly, and she joined in, as did
Robert.

"Have you ever done it before?" he asked the Indian.

Robert shook his head. "I wouldn't come down
when my father brought me here. Too steep and
dangerous. Some of us went farther upriver, where it
isn't so steep. But I thought they might be watching
there; we had to do it at this place. And now, camp and
food. We all deserve hot food."

Again Cluny slept so deeply he heard nothing,
dreamed nothing, remembered no thoughts before
falling asleep. In the morning Jean studied him.

"You looked awful when you first came out here,"

she said. "Gaunt, haunted, shifty-eyed. You're still shifty-eyed, but now you look better, more healthy."

He scowled at her.

She laughed softly. "Today we'll be in Boise."

Climbing the Idaho side of the gorge was not as difficult as going down had been, and on the other side the country stretched out flat and barren before them. Robert let the horses run to the foothills in the distance, and they headed east. They reached Boise late in the afternoon, when the sun was going down in a colorless sunset. Robert took them as close to the airport as they could get on horseback, and then dismounted, helped Jean down.

Boise was not dead, not like Bend. There were no farms now, but there were ranges where cattle grazed, and there was traffic. There were military installations in the mountains, Cluny knew vaguely, and mines still being worked. He had studied the Boise map, and he knew where the airport was. The rest of the way they had to go on foot.

He shook hands with Robert, and watched as the tall man and the slight woman withdrew to talk in low voices for several minutes. He could hear nothing of what they said. She removed a necklace and drew it over his head, adjusted it. Then Robert and Jean embraced and she came to Cluny's side. Her eyes were moist and for the first time she looked subdued.

They were near a subdivision that appeared lifeless. There were roads and streets, but no traffic in this area. Robert would wait here for one day; if they did not come back, he would leave. If there was no plane waiting, or if they could not get to it, they would rejoin him and return to the reservation.

"Ready?" Cluny asked her.

"We might as well start."

They looked back at Robert, then began to walk on a street at the outer edges of the subdivision. The street curved and when they looked back again they could no

longer see him. For a long time they walked in silence
as the sun went down and the evening turned dark.

"There's a manufacturing, industrial section," Cluny
muttered. "Should be reaching it now if we're not
lost."

She did not reply and they walked steadily, their
steps sounding hollow and echoing in one deserted
section after another. There were traffic sounds from a
distance, and once they had to run into a yard and hide
behind a house when a patrol car swung into the street
where they were walking.

"There," Jean said, several minutes later. She
touched his arm, directing his gaze to the left, where
the industrial park sprawled. They circled the complex,
keeping close to a fence, and halfway around it they
saw the airport.

"It's a couple of miles," Jean said then. "Let's rest a
few minutes before we finish."

There were runways between them and the buildings
and the air traffic control tower. Lights were on in the
tower and in the terminal building, as well as some of
the lower hangars and shops. A jeep, or truck,
something very small and silent from where they
watched, darted from one building to another, came to
rest again, vanished when its lights were turned off.

Jean sank to the ground, drew up her knees and
hugged her arms around them, facing the complex in
the distance. "The message is real," she said quietly.

It was too dark to see her features; she was a pale
blur against the dark ground. Cluny sat close enough to
touch her. "What does it say?"

"Nothing. At least I don't think it has content.
Remember the story about the natives in New Guinea
who lived on an inaccessible mountain by a terrible
gorge that separated them from another native village?
There was never any contact between them. Sometimes
one group would signal the other by building a fire,
sending smoke signals into the sky. And there was
always great rejoicing in the other village because they

had received a message. No content. It wasn't necessary to have any content. The message was enough. I think we have that kind of message."

"Christ!" Cluny said, and Jean could hear the desperation in his voice, sense it in the way he seemed to be so rigid so close to her.

"I think it's a signal device to let the senders know that we found it," she went on. "And there are three more of them in orbit around the Earth."

His hand clutched her arm then and she could feel his fingers trembling. "Are you sure?"

"I think so."

"Tell me exactly what you found."

"There are patterns. There are four groups of three curves, two of them forming sides, like pieces of an apple, and the third is like the stem, between them, not touching either side. If you have the computer extract the stem, the cylinder, the two sides fall away in the next spaces, and finally regroup with other curves and stop moving. The computer will join all like curves to form ovals, orbits, each one slightly larger than the next, and the stems, the cylinders, are left over. Four cylinders, four messages, or signals."

His hand dropped from her arm. "It wasn't like that," he said dully. "It wasn't in a group like that. It was just in a bunch of junk, nothing identifiable as curves. We have pictures of where it was found."

"The second time," she said softly. "I think the first time it was exactly like I described."

Across the expanse of empty runways and barren, gullied earth and tumbleweeds at rest now in the quiet night, the lights of the tower went out. The airport was closing down for the day. There were no night flights any longer, except troop movements or emergency flights.

Jean stood up. "We should go before the moon rises," she said.

"What do you mean, *the second time?*"

"My father found it years ago," she said softly. "I

don't know who else knew about it, probably your
father did, maybe others. Like now, they didn't know
what to do with it, about it. And then my father was
killed, and no one did anything at all. Maybe he never
told anyone else. Or no one knew where it was any
more. I don't know. But he knew about it."

She did too, Cluny thought. There was no uncertainty in her voice. They started to walk along one of the
ruined runways. His mind was curiously blank although
there were questions he wanted to ask, had even
thought of during the long ride across the Idaho
wastelands; now the questions were forgotten. She
knew. That was enough. The aliens had come, had left
a message. That was enough.

He watched his feet, and thought distantly, they
could fix this, make the grass grow, the rain come. . . .
Only the major landing strips were being maintained.
The others were breaking up in the ground, thrust up
by freezes, buckled under the summer sun. It was
easier walking on the ruined concrete than in the
corduroy earth along it. The wind erosion was powerful
here, patiently working at the soil, loosening rocks,
moving them aside to release inches more of the
vulnerable dirt and blow it away.

As they drew closer to the clump of buildings, they
could see a 707 parked a distance away from the other,
smaller planes lined up near a hangar.

"That's it," Cluny said. "It's a USDA plane. Department of Agriculture. Come on." He turned away from
the main buildings and headed for the plane. There was
nothing to hide behind here, no trees, signs, shrubs,
nothing but the tumbleweeds, which stirred now and
then, as if testing muscles to see if they could start
rolling yet. Several hundred feet from the plane, he
stopped. "Can you see anyone?"

"I think so. There's a jeep or something parked near
it. I thought I saw a figure a second or two ago. I don't
see him now."

"Okay. We'd better not go any farther together. If anything funny happens, hightail it back to Robert. If it's our plane, I'll whistle."

Cluny approached the jeep cautiously and when he was close, he called softly, "Hey! Anyone there?"

"Keep back, mister. Didn't they tell you this plane's contaminated? You don't want to get close to it." He got out of the jeep and stretched. Then in a low voice he asked, "You Dr. Cluny?"

"Yes."

"Got something I can look at? ID?"

He took Cluny's wallet inside the jeep again and examined it by a light so carefully held that not even a glow was visible. "Okay, Dr. Cluny. You can go aboard. You alone?"

"Who sent you?"

"Zach Greene. He said you would have a companion."

Cluny turned to whistle to Jean, but she was nearly at his elbow. "I told you to wait."

"I was afraid it was a trap. You might have needed help."

"What did you mean, the plane's contaminated?" Cluny asked before moving.

"Our cover story. We had to land because a shipment of chemicals sprang a leak. We're waiting for orders from Washington. No one knows what the stuff is yet; they're checking. It's so plausible I'm almost afraid of it."

"Okay. See you later."

"The seating's been rearranged. There are a couple of couches; you can stretch out, blankets in the bins, all that."

"Right."

They hurried up the stairs, to be greeted by an odor of chemicals: they could see vague shapes of crates and boxes in the rear. Another emergency being taken care of, Cluny thought, a shipment of sprays for the

California growers. No one would question the flight, no one would interfere.

"Here are the lounges," Jean whispered, and took his hand, leading him. The two couches were separated by a table. Cluny groped for the blankets in the storage bins, handed one to Jean, and wrapped himself in the other. He could hear rustling sounds as she got comfortable on the other couch. "If only we had something to eat," she whispered.

His couch was not quite long enough. Finally he propped his head on the armrest. "Are you sleepy?"

"No. Not yet. I'm hungry."

"Me too."

"Cluny?"

"Hm?"

"There's probably a time message along with the rest of it. You know what I mean?"

"Did you figure that out too?"

"Not really. Not enough time. But there's a pattern when you start extracting the ovals, the orbits. Whoever works on it should know that."

"Yeah." He jerked upright. "What do you mean, whoever?"

"It has to be international now. It isn't ours alone."

"Jean, you know you can't go making any announcements about this, don't you? It's classified until Zach, or someone else, says it isn't. You'll go along with that, won't you?"

There was laughter in her voice when she answered, "Who'd believe anything I said? I wandered out there on the desert and got a touch of sunstroke, or had a vision. Isn't that what they'd say? But if you said it, Cluny, with your background and your ability to make people believe in you and do what you want, if you said it . . ."

"I'm under orders. I don't make the decisions."

"I know." She chuckled softly.

He tensed, then forced himself to relax. Neither

spoke again. Inside the plane it was so quiet that if either of them moved, the sound threatened to betray their presence. He could stand guard at the door, he thought, and did not move. He couldn't make decisions, he thought angrily. With any agency, any group effort, no one could preempt authority, do things alone, or the entire project would fall apart. There had to be chains of command. The alternative was anarchy. He could hear her, close enough to touch, so far away that he could not fathom her at all. She wanted him to get a soapbox and carry it from corner to corner. Childish, silly woman, no awareness of the reality of the world, the agency, the government, how they all operated, how he operated within the large complex. He could hear her steady breathing and knew she was asleep, and he felt only resentment that she could drift off like that, so easily, like a child who never has to think about the future, about anything at all.

19 They landed at Philadelphia, were rushed to a limousine and sped to Washington, where they were hurried inside a tall building through a back entrance, onto an elevator to the tenth floor. Their escort tapped on the door and Zach Greene opened it.

"Good job, Cluny," he said. "Come in, both of you. Ms. Brighton, I'm delighted."

Cluny introduced him and before he was completely

finished, Zach said, "Two bedrooms down that hall, Ms. Brighton's on the left, yours on the right. I had some of your clothes brought over, and we'll round up some for you, Ms. Brighton. Five minutes there will be food, but you'll want to wash up first, I'm sure."

Jean looked like a street tough; her clothes were the same jeans and shirt she had been wearing the day she left Ward tied up in her kitchen; her hair was dirty, as was her neck, the backs of her hands, her arms. Her skin was too taut over her bones; she had lost weight during the past week; but her eyes were clear and unwavering as she studied first Zach, then the apartment, which was pleasant and totally impersonal—no book collection, no art, no plants. She nodded and led the way down the hall he had indicated.

When she returned she was barefoot. "Do you mind?" she asked. "I've had those boots on for a week, and my feet threatened to leave if they weren't given some relief."

Zach laughed. "It's Jean, isn't it? May I?" He took her hand and put it on his arm, led her across the room. "Dinner is served."

There was a small table set in the corner of the living room. Zach had coffee while Jean and Cluny ate steaks, potatoes browned in butter with onions, green beans, corn on the cob, hot biscuits, wine, coffee, and then ice cream. Jean ate as much as Cluny did.

When the ice cream dishes were empty, Zach said, "Now. Tell me."

Jean told him everything she had learned, what she had guessed.

"Why do you think your father found it years ago?"

"When I was twelve, just before my birthday, we had a talk about language, the magic of words. He said a few words could change the entire world, make it take a new direction. I forget exactly what all he said, and at the time I didn't understand, but now I'm positive he had seen the message and realized its importance."

There was a knock on the door, and the man who

had escorted them from Philadelphia came from the kitchen to open it. A woman was admitted.

"This is Tillie Cook," Zach said, rising. "She'll get some information, measurements from you, Jean, and bring some clothes in a little while. What's that?"

Tillie was a fair woman of thirty-five or a little more. She carried a paper bag. "A robe," she said. "He mentioned you'd be tired and have nothing at all to put on." She wrinkled her nose. "You want those things in the laundry, or trash can?"

"Laundry," Jean said indignantly, and they left together.

"She'll do," Zach said.

"What's happening here?"

"I don't know if they realize you got out of Oregon yet, but they'll know by tomorrow. I've got a meeting scheduled for nine in the morning. I wasn't sure what we'd be announcing to them. Guess I didn't really believe it would be this. Laurence Tilton from the President's staff is coming over, and he's lined up half a dozen independent referees. Some of them are on the President's science advisory staff, and I'm not sure yet who the others are. One shuttle is on the ground, maintenance problem. This morning Luther ordered the other shuttle to return in forty-eight hours, bringing Sid, Brett, more than half our people back home for what he calls an extraordinary meeting. You bet it's extraordinary. They won't go back, if he has his way. That's the opening gambit, and we've got to move fast. And it doesn't help matters a damn bit that the Russians are already shuffling their people around."

"And the President? Where's he in all this? Doesn't he know the next step is a military takeover?"

"He's thistledown in the wind, Cluny. No more than that. If we blow hard enough with our message, he'll go with us. If not, he'll count on being a figurehead."

Throughout the evening, into the night, people arrived, consulted, left again. Jean huddled with computer programmers for hours, telling them exactly what

she needed, how to program the material. Her clothes
arrived sometime during that afternoon and Cluny was
shocked when he saw her in a tailored pants suit with a
frilly blouse in a soft melon color. He had not seen her
dressed up since they were children. She looked like a
little girl playing grownup.

That evening Murray arrived and drew Cluny out
into the hallway. "God, that was good work, kid!" he
said fervently. "I knew you'd deliver!" He slapped
Cluny on the shoulder, and started to return to the
room. "Oh, that guy Davies said was on your tail that
night? Heard he had an accident; hit by a truck or
something. He's the only one with direct evidence;
anything else is hearsay, worth absolutely nothing.
Thought you should know." Quickly he reentered the
room, leaving Cluny standing in the hallway.

"Wait!" Cluny yelled, but the door was already
closed. He stared at it. It had to have been an accident,
he thought, too hard, too clearly, trying to deny the
implications behind Murray's words, evident in the
tone of voice, so casual and offhand, almost as if it had
been an afterthought. He felt very cold suddenly. He
went back inside; Murray was talking to three men who
would try to determine the orbits for the cylinders.
Murray looked up, returned Cluny's gaze steadily for a
moment, then rejoined the discussion, turning his back
altogether on Cluny.

Later Cluny found himself thinking: spies, counter-
spies, agents, double agents, investigators, private
investigators, blackmail, threats. . . . There was a
lump of concrete in his stomach and his skin was
clammy. Davies would simply nod, accept this as one of
the infinite possibilities of this particular game. He
caught a flash of light on Zach's white hair. Zach would
have blinked, then opened his eyes to a new situation,
prepared to go on from there. Jean was looking at
Zach, listening intently. He wanted to go over to her,
yank her from her chair and make her listen. This is

how it is, baby! Your father played this game and so did mine. We all play the game. You're all the way in or all the way out.

She would learn, he knew. From now on she was in, all the way in. They'd see to that. She might not like the rules, or the way they kept score, but she would play her part. They all played their parts.

It was after two in the morning when everyone but Zach had left for the night. "I'll take one of the beds in your room, if you don't mind," he said to Cluny. He looked ready to collapse and when he left the living room he stumbled against a chair and regarded it blankly before continuing.

"I'm going to bed too," Jean said. "What a day!"

"Wait a minute." Cluny leaned forward. "When did you find time to discover so much about the message? You said it would take months, years even, and yet you seem to know everything about it. How?"

She looked at him with faint crinkle lines at her eyes, as if she was repressing a deep smile. "I had time," she said. "My father told me once about a thinking place, a place where you can think a lifetime's worth of thoughts in a few minutes, if you learn how to do it. I believed him, but I couldn't do it. Then Serena, one of my Indian friends, the wisest woman I've ever met, taught me how to use it, as much as she could anyway. I had plenty of time on the desert."

"You could visualize the message enough to keep on working with it?"

"There was a lot of time." She stood up and stretched. "Good night, Cluny."

He watched her go down the hall, turn at her room and vanish inside, and he could almost taste his frustration. She had told him nothing, in such a way that he had not been able to question it, and now it was too late.

Jean undressed slowly, too tired to make any strenuous effort, not even the effort to hurry to get into bed. Zach had said they would tape everything the following day, they would let a voice-stress analyst determine if the speakers were truthful, meaning her, and that would be reported along with the conclusions reached at the all-day conference. He had said it with a particular intensity, watching her for a reaction. And she had smiled at him. "I won't lie about anything at all," she had said.

She brushed her teeth and then crawled into bed with its smooth sheets and plump down pillow, luxuries she had not known for a long time. She would not lie, she thought, but neither would she tell the entire truth. She imagined herself telling them about talking with coyote in the light of the moon and, smiling, she fell asleep.

There were eleven men and women in the room, seated at a conference table piled with folders, graphs, photographs, note pads. There was a coffeepot and plastic cups. Jean was at the end of the table, speaking. To her right was Zach Greene, who never took his eyes off her. Cluny was there, as was Murray, and Dr. Schmidt. There was a woman computer scientist from MIT and two other NASA officials, and a middle-aged man she had not been introduced to, from the President's staff, a woman exobiologist from the National Sciences Board, and another woman from the Communications Center at Hastings-on-Hudson.

Jean had been very nervous before the meeting had started, but by the time the introductions were over, her computer screen placed where all could see, her terminal before her, and with Dr. Schmidt's beaming approval warming her, she had lost her unease and now spoke quietly of the work she had done.

"At first I tried to find duplications, and there are none. Although many lines appear similar, no two curves are exactly alike, no two groupings of the lines are alike. I tried arranging them according to size, and again, it led nowhere." The pictures of her attempts were shown as she spoke. A lumpy circle appeared. "No circles . . ."

She took them step by step through her work until she reached the point where she had removed the four "stems," and now ellipses appeared. "I had to go look up the definition and mathematical formula for ellipses," she said, smiling slightly, "but as you see, the remaining lines did form four perfect ellipses. I concluded they could be orbits, and that could be part of the message."

No one moved as she spoke and the computer screen flicked from one picture to the next. The original picture of the scroll appeared, with the neatly spaced groups of curved lines. It changed to a grid, nine boxes each way.

"I extracted all the groups that made up one ellipse," Jean said. "There were twenty-one of them. The next ellipse was made up of eighteen groups, and the next two had twenty-one each. It seemed significant to me that only one ellipse used eighteen, and I studied that configuration for a long time, pondering the possibilities. It is not the smallest of the ellipses, as I assumed at first, but rather the largest. I assumed from the beginning," she said, looking at them all, "that nothing was random about the message, nothing was accidental. Eighteen had to have importance if that assumption was correct. But there was no pattern that I could identify. Next I separated the grid into strips and reshuffled them, and finally I came up with this new configuration."

There was a gasp from someone at the far end of the table when the next picture appeared. It looked like a stylized plane, or a rocket ship, or possibly a sting ray. It was made up of eighteen blacked-out spaces on the grid of eighty-one squares.

"This is the message we found," Jean said, showing it again. "By dividing it into strips, three of them two

squares wide, the full length down, and one three
squares wide, I had four strips. If we rearrange them so
that the widest strip is first, we get the pattern." On the
screen the strips were separated slightly, a number over
each one. The sequence was three, four, one, two.
Three and four began to move left, off the screen; the
others moved to the left and three and four reappeared
following number two; the ship, or fish, appeared
again.

When she finished, the questions started. One of the
NASA men led off. She could remember hardly any of
their names, she realized with embarrassment.

"Why did you decide the messages are signaling
devices? I don't think you've touched on that at
sufficient length."

"Here is the entire message starting with number
one," Jean said. She pointed to one of the boxes. "That
is the original group, two sides and a stem. It suggests
an apple to me. And here"—she pointed to the
next-lower row, the box on a diagonal with the first
one—"is the next sequence. Two lines very much like
the first two, but without the stem now, and these two
appear to be falling away from each other. And finally,
here in the next-lower diagonal boxes, each line has
formed a new relationship with different lines. The
very fact that they are on the diagonal, going downward, suggests falling apart." She pointed to another
section. "The same process," she said. "First the three
lines, two sides and the stem, and then the same falling
away in the next boxes diagonally down from it." She
showed the other two sets of curves with the same
sequences. "Again, it could not be coincidence, not a
random ordering of the curves. So, if it is for a purpose,
this particular arrangement, how could that purpose be
served? Only by removing one of the parts? I thought
so anyway. And I began to think about why the other
two pieces would fall apart as they seem to do. It
suggests a force binding the three, and by taking one

out, that force is disrupted, turned off. But such a force would not be needed to keep the cylinders in place. It had to serve another purpose, and I thought possibly it would be a signal. When the relay is turned off, disrupted, a signal is sent announcing it. I could be completely wrong about that part of it," she added simply.

"You believe that there are three other messages, and you know where they are?" The presidential aide was studying her with narrowed eyes, as if judging her for market.

"If the ovals represent orbits and the farthest orbit corresponds to the finished pattern, the ship, then the one we found would be number two. There should be one closer to Earth, and two farther out. If we know the orbit of the number two cylinder, we should be able to compute approximately how far it is from the others, and so on. I can't do it, but I can see how it can be done."

"We've done it," Zach said then. "We'll get into that in a couple of minutes. Any more questions?"

"Yes." It was the woman from the National Sciences Board. Exobiologist, Jean remembered, Hazel something. Her hair was carrot red, her skin as white as milk.

"Ms. Brighton, everything you have explained seems very childish, primitive even, like a child's prank. This suggests a Rorschach test to me, where you've let your imagination play games with you. Any extraterrestrial race that can travel interstellar distances surely is not as primitive in communications as you would have us believe."

"Hell!" Marian Cassel, from Hastings-on-Hudson, said in disgust. "Effective communications demand a feedback system. We have almost fifty percent redundancy in our languages just to guard against missing the point the first time around. If you're sending a message without knowing who's going to get it, you've got no feedback. You use tricks to make it clear what you mean, because you can't rephrase and repeat if there's any misunderstanding the first time. You use universals, like gravity, to suggest falling down. You use shapes, like fish, or birds, or ships, to suggest a movement through a particular medium. You use numbers in a one to one relationship. One for me, one for you, one for me, one for you. Eighteen! My God, don't any of you see what that means? It's when they are going to move through their medium and arrive here! It's eighteen orbits of our Earth around our Sun! It's so basic it makes me sick to think of looking for E equals MC squared. There's no language because how the hell did they know which one of the various language groups would find it? No pretty picture of the sun and its planets with an X marking Earth? What the hell for? We know where we are, and so do they, and if it's important for us to know where they are, they'll tell us when they get here. No pretty man and woman with long clean limbs and flowing hair? So? Ask an Eskimo if that's his idea of homo sap. Ask a Bantu. Ask a Japanese woman. We sent those Mickey Mouse messages of ours, and you expect them to be the standard? What we have here is a straightforward message that tells us to expect company. I say let's get on with finding the other three, and let's see if we can derive any more from the one we have, and let's announce to the world that we'd better wash up because guess who's coming to dinner."

She sat back in her chair, glaring at the red-haired woman, who turned away with a look of disdain. Jean could have hugged Marian Cassel. She caught Cluny's look and smiled slightly as he put one hand before his mouth and coughed, ducking his head to hide his own grin.

Shortly before noon the first meeting ended. Zach steered Jean and Cluny to a smaller room that reminded Jean of a dentist's waiting room, with the right assortment of magazines, the same soft lighting, the standard vinyl chairs.

"For the rest of the day," Zach said, "it's going to be pretty technical. Plans for finding the other three cylinders, stuff like that. You can stay, or go back to the apartment."

"Column A or Column B," Jean murmured.

"Exactly. We've got to keep you under wraps for a while yet."

"For my own good," Jean said gravely.

"You said it. Which would you prefer?"

"The apartment. Is it permitted that I make some requests?"

"For what?"

"Books, paper, a typewriter."

"Whatever you want."

She looked at Cluny. "You'll be tied up, I guess. See you later." Then she added, "Remember what we talked about?"

He nodded. "Zach knows. He doesn't want it kept a secret either. We'll do what we can."

Tilton had gone directly to the White House following the morning conference; and until they heard something, they would go on as if they expected full cooperation. They would try to plot the orbits, locate the probable spots for the cylinders, start people working on the announcement, make contingency plans for including the Russians. . . . Dr. Schmidt was organizing a staff of experts to see if they could wring anything more out of the message they already had. He had accepted Jean's findings without question, and when Zach had demanded to know how he could be so certain, he had shrugged. "She did the impossible before under Arkins. So she did it again. Tomorrow she may well do it once more."

Although the meetings had taken place in the space agency building, and the work was progressing there, it was all done without Luther Krohmeier's knowledge or consent, and when the phone call from the White

House came finally at nine that night, he was at home. Zach hung up carefully, and turned to Cluny and Murray with a look of incredulity on his face.

"We've done it!" he whispered.

20

A tiny spacecraft edged up to an orbiting mass of space junk and matched speeds with the largest clump of meteorites; a suited figure floated away, tethered to the ship by a thread that looked like fine silk. The man on the line was like a lure being drawn through water; he examined the rocks, waved to his companion inside the craft, and slowly floated back to it. The small ship moved on.

Cluny watched the scene, gnawing his lip, until the spacecraft moved out of sight. One of the technicians made an adjustment on a control panel and the craft appeared again, started its maneuver to close in on another, similar clump of floating rocks. Cluny left the room; no one looked up.

"It'll be there," Alex said, falling into place by his side. "We'll find it."

"It's been ten months."

"We'll find it," Alex repeated. "No one who has examined the message doubts any longer. And many good people have examined it."

"Ten fucking months!"

Alex laughed and put his arm about Cluny's shoulders. "You're disappointed that you must leave before it is located. You wanted to be the one."

Cluny grinned at him, not denying it. "A needle in a haystack would be easier, wouldn't it?"

"Much easier."

"Thank God for Klyuchevsky," Cluny said fervently.

The Russian laughed. "Or Providence, or Chance, or Fate."

Klyuchevsky had seen it also. Among his belongings there had been a journal, and on one of its pages had been a solitary drawing of a crude formation, much like an apple with a stem. Klyuchevsky had not returned to Earth, but had been killed when a piece of structural steel had got out of control, had floated like a dream missile in slow motion through space to pierce his craft as it had approached the docking area.

Cluny thought of the quandary the Russian's death had placed Dan Brighton in: he had become the sole witness to the start of a new era. Brighton and Cluny's father must have gone through the same endless arguing that Sid and Murray and Zach, others, had gone through more recently, and in the end Brighton had died before they had a chance to resolve it. Had he been on his way to retrieve the message on that last mission? No one would ever know, of course, but it seemed likely now. And his father's role in it all? He would never know that either, but he had been mixed up in it, of that Cluny was certain. He must have known, without proof, without knowing where it was, and when Brighton had died, he had been left with little more than a rumor of contact, and had destroyed evidence that might have existed concerning it. Why? Finally he must not have believed in it. Brighton had been a trickster, the boy who cried wolf. Cluny imagined his father trying to believe in it, succeeding for a time, even sending Brighton back to retrieve the message. But then Brighton had died and the belief that had been possible when shared became untenable, too fragile to withstand the doubts and questions. Vehemently he had denied it then, or else why had he destroyed so many papers with such urgency? Or maybe Klyuchevsky had found it, hidden it again, and Brighton had tried desperately to refind it. . . . Cluny shook his head hard. He had gone over this ground too many times for it not to have become almost a ritual, with each thought preceded and followed by cues that determined the entire sequence, and none of it had meaning any longer.

"Even if we never find another one," Alex said suddenly, breaking into Cluny's thoughts, and yet not speaking directly to him either, but in a low halting voice, rather as if he were voicing a thought to himself, "the first one has served its purpose, if indeed its purpose was to make us prepare for an alien contact."

"And how long do you suppose that kind of peaceful cooperation is going to last without another piece of the puzzle?"

"Long enough, perhaps. Who knows? Every day is an unexpected plus, and we've had ten months no one expected to have. Who knows?"

Cluny looked at his friend curiously. Alex had not lowered his voice and the corridor was filled with other men and women; any of them might have heard. The corridors might still be bugged, probably were still bugged.

Alex smiled his peculiar crooked smile and added, "Within a year we will have accomplished a five years' schedule of space construction, Cluny. That's a lot of money committed. Few people are willing to abandon that kind of commitment, especially since it's made your economy and mine start to climb so precipitously. Who would have predicted the trade agreements your country and China have made? Farm equipment today in exchange for products when harvested. It's easier to start the avalanche than to stop it or avoid it, once begun."

"Catalytic effect," Cluny said. "It's like a marriage

broker who brings together the strangest people and then steps back to let whatever happens begin."

Alex stopped walking for a moment, his hand on Cluny's arm. "The marriage broker never marries— isn't that part of the system?"

For a second they regarded each other, neither adding anything, and then they walked again, no longer speaking. Cluny felt a flash of panic that was like the wave of anxiety at the moment the dentist first touches a drill to a tooth.

Murray and Jean sat facing each other in her one-room studio apartment in New York. The room reminded her of Corinne Duland's room at East Lansing. That seemed too far in the past to be her past, she thought, examining the memory of the room, of Corinne, the other memories that were attached to that one. She wondered briefly where Walter was now, how many women had come and gone in the intervening time, nearly two years. She could look at it now because she was not that same person, but someone made up of all the pieces of her past, and that piece was, after all, a very small one.

"You know I want to talk to you," Murray said finally. "Yeah, you know."

Through dinner they had talked about her book on the Warm Springs Indians, due out in four days now. The advance reviews were respectable, no more than that, she had told him. It had been enough for Dr. Schmidt to put her name forward for her doctorate. That would come about, he had promised her. Of course, it really was for her work with the message, but until that was made public they pretended her Indian book was the reason.

"Why haven't you gathered reporters around, spilled it all?" Murray asked.

She shrugged. "They'd think it was for publicity. No one would believe it."

"They'd grab it and run," he said. "They've been

looking for something to account for the speed of the construction, for the new focus of our efforts and the Russians', and for a reason for suddenly inviting everyone else who can use a calculator to become our partners. They'd accept it all right."

She waited. She always had to remind herself that Murray was Cluny's age; he looked so much older, so much more tired. It was not merely that he was overweight, but rather that he was burdened by a mission. He had the same absolute devotion and need for the space satellite to work as her father had had. She recognized the same distant look when he talked about it, the same unwillingness to speculate about its failure, the same relentless drive to accomplish this first baby step into the universe of stars. She recognized it without sharing it, without feeling any real empathy for it. He could have been this devoted to the worship of a strange god, or to a steadily increasing gross national product, or any other abstract she could think of. The drive she recognized in him was obsessive, unrelated to human needs, interpreted human needs as weaknesses to be purged. Another dichotomy, she thought with amusement; she had always hated things easily dichotomized. There were those whose need was for something unattainable, far removed from self; and there were others who felt an equally desperate need for the exploration of self, of humanness; the two were separate. No Conestoga wagons, but a wagon train for all that, one that would lead eventually to another solar system, other stars, other civilizations, wagons peopled by obsessed travelers who could never be satisfied because when one goal became attainable, it was immediately replaced by another, more distant one. But they were so few, she thought, and there were so many who would never go although they might want to, and even more who did not want to go out at all, who had no need for space and its elusive goals. Obsessed people didn't really care what they trampled, what they

destroyed to get where they were driven. But they had
to care! They had to leave something behind for those
whose needs were different.

"It's a lie, isn't it?" Murray said finally.

She turned to look out the window, twenty-two
stories above the streets, which were too far away to
allow the noise to penetrate. Like a silent film with
poor lighting, it was dim down there with the few
electric lights, and distance. She could see people as
moving shadows only. The government-issued statistics
dealt with percentage points, fragmentation; the reality
was down there—people moving aimlessly, nowhere to
go, nothing to do, no hope, no future. What about
them? she wanted to ask.

"I didn't lie about anything," she said then.

"No. We had our analysts go over those tapes a
hundred times, and your voice shows no stress, no lies.
But you lied. You knew what we'd believe, what
everyone would believe from what you said. You did it
so well, so skillfully, and you looked like a kid,
innocent, too naïve to try to fool experts like you had in
that room. Everyone knew you were being tested for
truthfulness. God alone knows how many tape record-
ers were in that room, how many experts have listened
to you how many times. And they all believed every
word. They still believe every word. But you never said
it was a message from aliens, did you? I've gone over it
a dozen times this past week, and you never said that.
You led us on until someone else said it, and we all
wanted to believe so fucking much! You used that
desperate need to believe the way you'd use a life
preserver to save a drowning man."

So much pain, so much hatred in his voice. She
winced. She had not let herself know it would be this
bad. She could not ask him what about them, those
living shadows on the street below, because he had no
answers. His answer was to leave them behind, let them
live and die out of sight.

"Why did you stop believing?" she asked, still at the window.

"When I was a kid, nine years old, before the world went to hell, we didn't have anything. I wanted a bike so much I could smell it when I went to sleep. For a long time I thought I was going to get it for Christmas, but then one day I realized it wasn't going to happen. No way. And I quit believing in the bike, quit dreaming about it, quit smelling it, quit looking at bikes in windows and parked at curbs."

She did not ask if he got the bike.

"As long as I believed in it," he said harshly, "I kept finding ways for it to be possible, and as soon as I quit, I found all the ways that made it impossible. As soon as I stopped believing in that goddamn message, I knew it had been a lie from start to finish. I don't know how, or who else is mixed up in this, but it's a lie."

She heard the refrigerator door open and slam shut. He poured wine and gulped it down. He had brought the wine; she had not been able to afford it. She listened to him return to the center of the room, come closer to her.

He touched her shoulder, then jerked her around. "Aren't you going to say anything at all? Deny it? Say you did it? Something?"

She shook her head.

"For Christ sake! You pulled it off! It worked. If you didn't lie about it, all you have to do is say so on a tape, and I've made a jackass out of myself."

"Not now," she said. "I didn't lie before, but I don't know any more. After tonight I'd be afraid to say anything about it."

He stepped back. "You've got it planned this far? You knew someone would finally accuse you and you planned even this?" He stared at her in disbelief that slowly faded and left his round face a mask. "Just tell me why. Will you do that much for me? Just a simple answer. Why?"

She did not flinch or lower her gaze, and finally he

turned and walked across the room, opened the door and left, walking like a very old man.

"I'm sorry," she whispered. She was shaking as if with a chill, from deep within her. Her face felt feverish, and when she touched her cheek, her hand was ice cold.

They *had* needed to believe. They had been conditioned, or had conditioned themselves, so long to believe. UFOs, movies, books, even comic books, had strengthened that belief, and when the chance came, when it seemed the fiction had become an actuality, like Pavlov's dogs, they had accepted without being able to doubt. The aliens would turn on the water, she thought; they would press buttons and turn off war, they would cure diseases, heal sick souls, turn Earth into a land of milk and honey. All that was built into the conditioning, that and more. She turned again to the window. And it was happening, she thought. All of it could happen if they had enough time. All of it.

Later that night she wrote letters to half a dozen newspapers and television news stations. It was simple: "Ask any of the following people if a message from aliens has been intercepted." She listed nine names; Murray's was not there, nor was Cluny's. She hesitated over his for a few seconds, thinking about him, about him with Murray, and she knew he should not be asked. She mailed the letters before she went to bed, where she fell asleep almost instantly, and dreamed of walking with Serena, wanting her forgiveness without being able to ask for it, or explain why she needed it.

21 "Of course she did it!" Murray shouted. Cluny sat on a window ledge in Zach's office, watching, feeling numb. He was concerned for Murray, who was the color of wet putty.

Zach also continued to study him thoughtfully. "Why?"

"To get publicity for her book. Have you read the first chapter? She isn't talking about the first contacts between white men and Indians; she's talking about aliens coming to Earth. It's as clear as crystal what she's up to. She's talking about Earth as a huge reservation. She dropped her little bombshell, and then excused herself. She had work to do. There were others more qualified to work on the message; she had done all she could with it. Bullshit! She knew she didn't dare hang around or she'd be tripped in one of her own lies!"

"How did she get from the message to the orbits, the falling away of the pieces, the whole thing? Everyone who's studied it thinks that's exactly what it means."

"Her father told her."

"When she was twelve, thirteen? Doesn't seem likely, does it?"

"Okay, I don't know how. But now she's got the press and television people on our heels. It's gone out; people out there believe exactly the way we all did that first day. You can't put the steam back in the pot."

Quietly Zach said, "Some of the greatest cathedrals were built out of belief. The pyramids. Discoveries made, explorations arranged. A few words spoken in the right place at the right time, you've got a belief system that nothing can shake, and it can do miracles."

"But I know it's a lie," Murray whispered.

"Don't you think some of the popes knew their saints were frauds? They didn't expose them, risk more than they could have gained. What would it accomplish if you exposed Jean?"

"If they find out, what will that do to the program, us, the Russians? It's a time bomb and the fuse is too short. You can't sit on something like this. Sooner or later someone will corner that girl and get a straight answer and it'll all blow."

Cluny stood up abruptly. "What are you saying?"

Zach waved him away. "He's right, of course. Her name will come into it, probably sooner than any of us anticipates. The dam is breached and the torrent will follow." He looked at Cluny and said, "We'll have to keep her under wraps for the time being."

"Where?"

"There must be places," Zach said vaguely.

Cluny had a vision of Jean walking across the desert, moving like the moon sailing through the sky. He saw her again riding by his side across the flat wastelands of Idaho, the wind playing with her hair. There would be places, he thought dully. Places where guards locked gates at night, where other guards ate meals with her, cooked for her, filled her orders for her needs, all very polite, very civilized. She would not want, he knew; everything would be provided.

"When?"

"We'll pick her up today. We'll keep her in the safe apartment where you both stayed when you first got to town. In a week or so we'll have a better place ready, out in the country somewhere."

"You're not even going to find out for sure first?"

Zach shook his head. "You don't understand, Cluny.

I believe what she said, what Schmidt confirms. I won't
see her, question her, or have anyone else question her.
I haven't asked you what you believe and I don't want
to know. Your only comment to reporters is no
comment. You and Murray both. I take all questions,
this office."

Cluny looked away from him. Banish the doubt,
don't test faith, he thought, and you were safe. He went
to the door. "Can I see her before she vanishes?"

"Suit yourself. You know where it is. We'll have her
there in a couple of hours."

Murray had spread it all out for Cluny the night
before. He had stormed, raged, stamped back and
forth at the park bench that had become their conference room.

"The Russians must suspect!" he had said finally,
and in exhaustion had dropped to the bench beside
Cluny. "I found it without any trouble. Eighteen years
ago Klyuchevsky's brother, Pietr, was tortured and
finally killed in Peru. He was accused of smuggling
pre-Columbian goodies from the country. He was
caught with a few relics, gold relics. They tortured him
to try to get information about others he had already
got rid of. He died without talking. Klyuchevsky got
them somehow, and he knew he couldn't unload them,
or he'd be hauled in. He and Brighton cooked up the
glorious idea of a hoax to end them all. Pure Aztec
gold, hardened a little, inscribed with an alien message.
Pretty!" He snorted with rage. "Other men dream of
getting rich off stuff like that. He played games with it."

Some of the Russians suspected, Cluny knew, remembering Alex. He walked through the mobbed
streets without seeing the people at all. Many were
going back to work, but the effects were not apparent
yet, and they would never catch up again with the
housing shortage. He seldom saw actual individuals,
just mobs, and when one person, several persons did
impinge on his consciousness, he hurried to get out of

the crowds. At those times he yearned to be back on Alpha, away from the noise, the smells, the press of strange bodies and their hungers and needs. From Alpha the world was calm, serene, beautiful; up there no one had to think about the pain and the despair and hopelessness that was inescapable here. Alex did not believe in the message, he thought clearly, and possibly never had. And Alex did not care. Maybe all over the world people were finding themselves becoming disbelievers, and none of them was saying anything, each one hoping no one else would puncture the balloon either. Someone bumped him hard, and he cursed, but didn't look around, didn't care if he bumped back.

He thought of the detective Lee Cavanaugh Davies had hired, how casually Murray had said that he had suffered a fatal accident. He stopped and was nearly knocked down from behind. He didn't even curse this time, but staggered slightly, started to walk again. The good guys, he thought bleakly, his side. He remembered what Murray had said once: It would be bad no matter who made the first move, but it would be worse if the Russians did. Relative good and evil: it always came down to that after all. His side, the good guys in pursuit of knowledge, swatting down opposition effortlessly without a twinge of conscience, because their goals were noble. He came to a stop again, and this time realized he had arrived at the apartment house.

Cluny stared at her furiously. Now that he faced her, there was nothing to say.

She studied him for a moment, then turned and walked down the short hallway into her bedroom, motioning for him to follow. "I don't think they'd bug their own apartment, would they?" The man who had admitted Cluny had returned to the kitchen, but she kept her voice low anyway, and when Cluny spoke he did also.

"Why?" It came out muffled, like a sob.

Her voice dipped even lower. "I thought it was real

at first when I began getting patterns. I was excited; they would come and save us, I thought, just like everyone else. They would have answers to our problems, teach us how to make the rains come again, how to have clean energy; everything we want and need, they would provide. I wasn't thinking of intelligent beings from another planet, I was thinking about God, or a pantheon of gods. In my mind it was the Second Coming. I wanted to believe. I needed to believe, and finally I did."

She became silent and Cluny waited motionless for her to go on. His fury had dissipated, his anger had turned to an apathetic resentment. He yearned for sleep, for forgetfulness. He wanted to stretch out on the bed and sink into oblivion. When she spoke again, he roused with a start.

"The first day on the desert I still believed," she said softly as if from a great distance, her eyes unfocused now, as she looked inward, backward in time. "That night I watched the stars light up the sky and I wondered, This one? That one? One we've never seen before? And I heard a coyote laugh, so close I could have touched it if I had turned around. In that instant I knew I'd been deluding myself. I'd let what I wanted take a separate reality. And everything shifted again. I knew."

"Why didn't you say it was a fake? You didn't have to lie. No one pressured you to lie." He remembered his plan to do just that, pressure her to lie about it. That would have been different, he thought angrily. Zach would have made plans for just this contingency; others would have been involved. She would not have lied to him, placed herself apart from it all as she had done. No one could stand apart, not for long. "You're part of the machinery," he said aloud, "or when it rolls, you're under it." He had to believe that, he realized, if only because he had been part of it for such a long time.

All his protestations about commitment, about Alpha assuming a hypnotic pull, about putting Lina

first, his work second: all false. How many times had he
sworn he would give up Alpha if ever it started getting
between him and Lina? For nothing. He had been away
more than he had been with her. Nothing he had got
from her equaled the gut-wrenching feeling of awe and
terror and anticipation that had overwhelmed him
again and again when he had stood at the wide windows
and stared at space, knowing it was attainable, he could
have it. Vowing never to become obsessed, he had
become obsessed, possessed every bit as much as his
father before him, her father, Murray, Sid, all of them.
He was another part of that machine, symbiote, part
technology, part metal, part human drive; the machine
would roll, he knew, and anyone who dropped off or
stepped into its path would be rolled over. Once
started, the machine would not stop again.

She sat on the bed and looked at her hands. "Ward
said something about the right moment for action. He
said there's always one right second, less than a second,
when one person does or doesn't do something that sets
up echoes across the world. He was talking about their
military takeover, of course. But he was right in a way.
One moment, one word, one phrase, and everything
reverses; what was in front is in back, what was
important is gone and the unimportant presses forward. We were on a train moving at an uncontrollable
speed through a blackness that no light could penetrate. We all knew exactly what was ahead, a chasm,
but no one tried to find the brakes, no one tried to find
an alternative. Everyone screamed and yelled and
threatened, and no one did anything. Everyone accepted it all—the Newtowns, the draft, the coming war,
famines, the drought. But the drought was here long
before the rains stopped. The aridity was here, everywhere; it had gotten into us, poisoned us, so that when
the real drought came it was almost welcomed as
something we could all point to and say, There's the
reason. No one could expect miracles when the land
itself was drying up, dying."

"And you thought you could save the world."

"Nothing so grandiose," she said, smiling faintly at his sarcasm. "I thought this might gain us a little time. Everywhere people were ready to believe anything that was stated as true, anything. Your father-in-law knew that, Ward certainly knew it. They were counting on it. If they had managed to say with authority that their way was the best, the only way, people would have believed them, the way Hitler's Germany believed. If someone else said, The aliens are coming, they were more than ready to believe that. I saw it happen with Ward, and I didn't even say it to him. How long has the buildup been going on? Fifty years? Everyone is ready to believe they'll be here during our lifetimes." She shrugged. "Maybe they will."

"And they'll find us grubbing for sunflower roots and lizards, pretending we're all Indians," he said bitterly.

Jean laughed, a shocking sound in the face of his bitterness and despair. She shook her head. "I'm not stupid," she said. "I never intended that, as you'd know if you'd read the book. I said the Indians have seized this chance to take control of their own lives again. They're gambling on survival, just as we all are, but they have better odds than those prisoners in Newtowns. There's no chance there. In South America there are the *barrios,* their Newtowns, where people live and die and never have any hope at all. In India they do the same on the streets. That's what's happening here, Cluny, but we call them Newtowns. Robert's tribe chose not to go that way. Others have to make other decisions; not to become Indians, of course— they couldn't if they wanted to—but they can say and mean no more war, no more weapons systems, use the money for life, not death. If we can't change from what we have now to something that gives us some hope, we'll all die. The change won't come from any institutions, with institutional goals, not the government, or industry, or church; it has to come from the people with human goals. And they'll need time to do it."

"You're talking about revolution," Cluny said.

"Without the aliens wouldn't it have been revolution, anarchy, chaos? Isn't that what the militarists wanted to squelch before it could get under way? They aren't fools. Anyone who's been in a Newtown knows the only possibility is revolution; not today, or tomorrow, but one night when the temperature doesn't fall below ninety inside the buildings, or too many children have been raped and mutilated, or a bunch of them realize the slop on the trays is all there's going to be forever, and that it's getting worse every day. You could hide up there in your shiny wheel in space, look at the Earth and think how beautiful, how perfect, like a carved globe hanging in the void. We could always escape behind our gadgets and machines, in our schools, our suburbs, and all the while this moment has been sneaking up on us. It's here suddenly. I sat under the juniper tree and I thought, It's here, that one moment when one person could say a few magic words and change everything. It was a chance to offer one more alternative, one of hope. You can run off into space, but you can't leave the rest of us huddled in Newtowns waiting to die. Go off to space, but put the world in order first. Leave the rest of us with reason to want to live!"

He looked at her, hating her so intensely that he felt numb. "I'm glad you got what you wanted," she had said, that first day on the hillside. He wanted to laugh, but he knew it would come out like a cry. The moment seemed frozen. Jean waited without motion. His thoughts raced, and he saw her again walking across the desert, looking impossibly small, lost among the boulders, lost in the shadows, and later, her face pale against the blackness as she recounted that long walk. And he saw himself standing at the large windows of Alpha, staring hungrily at the blackness of space, trying to still his heartbeat, his pulse, so that the music he knew was out there could be heard. Still she waited, not moving.

"Get your things," he snapped. "I'm taking you back to Robert."

"They won't let you."

"Do you know what they'll do with you now? Protective custody. Five years? Ten? Who knows how long? As long as you're a threat to the belief in the aliens, and that's as long as you live."

Her face became so expressionless, she might have fallen into a deep trance. Before he could shake her, snap her back, she said, "I can't. I understand what you're offering to do, how much it would mean to you. Thank you. But I can't."

"Listen to me, Jean. You're playing games with men who are at the limits of desperation. You can't hold out alone. You're a real threat. One unguarded moment and you could blow the whole thing. You carried it off at the briefing, but only because there weren't any really hard questions. Now there are. And they know if you're lying. The voice-stress analyzer can tell every time. They won't settle for evasions and innuendos next time. You'll be safe with Robert."

She shook her head. Cluny wanted to hit her, to make her stop behaving like a child. He caught her shoulders and shook her. "How can you be so bright and so dumb!"

"Stop it! I know exactly what I did. All my life I've heard nothing but lies from the government, from radio, television, schools, everywhere. Lies! I detested them and loathed them, and now I've done it too! Using words to manipulate people, doing it deliberately, using the magic of words, the power, to make people react in certain ways, using them as weapons, like the doctors in death camps, perverting what is good and awesome, using a fine, even rare talent to make people do something . . . I know what I did! I can't run away from it and hide."

When she stopped, the silence in the room, in the apartment, in the building, the silence in the world, pressed against her as if waiting. But there was no one she could tell she was sorry, no one who had the power to excuse or forgive her.

Neither had moved when the door swung open violently and Murray entered. He was breathing too hard, his face was too gray, and a vein stood out on his temple alarmingly.

"You're still here," he said to Cluny, but his gaze fastened on Jean and did not shift again.

"What's wrong?" Cluny asked, looking behind Murray to see if he was being chased.

"The Army's sending someone over to collect her, to ask her about Arkins' work, and they'll go over the message with a fine-tooth comb when they get her." He took a deep breath and his color improved slightly. "I was on the phone with Zach when they called. Zach didn't hang up and I heard it all. They're still being polite about it, but they want Brighton. Zach can't stall them too long."

"What are you going to do now?"

"I can't tell you. If they ask, you won't know anything."

Cluny shook his head. "No more games, for Christ sake!" He looked at Jean, who had moved to the window. "Did your friendly coyote tell you this would happen?"

"I knew," she said. "It isn't over yet."

"Cluny, come out in the hall a minute. I've got to talk to you." Murray took Cluny's arm and drew him out, closed the door behind them.

Jean turned to look out the window. In the distance she could see the line of trees that followed the river. How beautifully shaped the maples were, self-assured somehow. Suddenly she heard again her grandfather's voice talking about the junipers.

"Take an oak tree now. Any fool can tell an oak tree as soon as he's close enough to see it. And a willow, and a jack pine. You get so you can tell by the outlines against the sky, and they're easy. But the damned juniper pretends. You think it's an oak and when you get closer you see it's a juniper putting on airs. Or you see one shoot straight up with a little tuft at the top and you think, pine, and it's the juniper again. You come down from the hills and see this lush-looking pasture for your horse, knee-high graze, and it's nothing but a juniper playing it's grass. They're the coyotes of the plant world. Tricksters."

She remembered another tree, a pine tree killed by beetles and drought. She had stared at it and a shudder had passed through her.

"You see it as a terrible tragedy," Serena had said. "In every death you feel a threat. Try to think of it as simply a part of the eternal cycle. The insects eat the needles and kill the tree; they fall to the ground and are consumed by smaller creatures that live there, who are food for yet smaller beings, and finally the Earth itself is nourished. All of this, the trees, the bitter grass, the sagebrush, redtail, you, me—it's all of the Earth finally. We rise, move about, learn, and grow, and in the end return."

"It's hard to accept," Jean had said. "People who are helpless always seem to develop a fatalism. But we're more than that. We can learn to change things, not bow our heads and accept whatever happens as part of a grand scheme."

Serena had nodded. "I know you feel that. You see yourself separate from and above all this instead of accepting that you're simply a moving part of the whole."

In the hall Cluny was shaking his head. "You can't have her," he repeated. "I've already told her I'm taking her back to Robert. No one will ever find her again. You're in no shape to play hide and seek."

"No," Murray said. "You'll take orders, Cluny, just like always. Zach knows I'm here and why. You might as well go on in and tell her to get ready. Five minutes."

Murray started down the short hallway and behind him he heard the door open and close again. He stopped and fingered the old Colt Special he had owned ever since high school days. He went to the kitchen for a drink of water, spoke briefly to the man on duty there, and then slowly returned to the room.

Zach and Sid could manage Cluny. They had always been able to manage him, right from the start. Sid had known exactly how to play him. He remembered the night he had told Cluny not to worry about the man Davies had hired to tail him. All night until Murray had left, he had felt Cluny's eyes boring into his back, his head. Later, when Cluny had demanded details, Murray had said coldly, "He's dead. That's all you need to know. You don't even know his name, so forget it. We're riding a whirlwind, Cluny, but the point is we're riding it. And we'll keep riding it. We've got the momentum and we're going to keep it. That means keeping you clean; no scandals, no hints even, and we'll do it if we have to follow you around with a bucket of whitewash." Cluny had turned away, had asked nothing else, had taken it exactly the way Murray had known he would. And he would take it again. Whatever.

He went in without knocking. They were side by side at the window. He felt nothing toward her now. The hatred was gone, the resentment, everything. He didn't know why she had done it and he no longer cared. It was poison with a sugar coating, that was her gift to the world, and the world was licking the sugar greedily. When it came to the poison, the space agency would go, Alpha would go, everything that was important would go. It could be five years or twenty-five, or it could be tomorrow, if she said one wrong word. He watched her glance at Cluny and he saw her dead.

Cluny wondered at the woods in the middle of the city, and he realized that to win, to conquer it really, it had to be burned down, all of it, and covered with concrete. Jean had called it the will to live. It was never neat, she had said. Life is seldom neat and orderly. It comes in bursts, in spurts, in dribbles and gushes, and when you think it's all in order, it's only holding its breath getting ready for the next big push.

"Our time scale is too small, too petty," she had said. "Even when we think we're winning, it's no more than a pause between clashes. The clash of our urge toward control or destruction of everything natural, and its own will to live and mature. And when it's a time like now, when we can see our efforts being swept away like sand, we're filled with an insane frenzy. If we can't take it out on nature, we take it out on each other."

Cluny, looking out at the rampant green, nodded. Inevitability, fate, destiny; such handy words. His hands clenched so tight they ached, as he realized that he had fallen in love with her. And it was nothing like the frenzied passion he had suffered over Lina. He didn't want to dominate her, possess her, lose himself in her. Neither could he bear the thought of her locked up, spied on, her every movement and sound recorded. Somehow in this insane world she had found sanity and freedom. They couldn't take it from her again. But who could stop them? With an inevitability that was terrifying, the entire past had brought them here, to a place where there was no turning back, no way to leave the path they were on, no way to avoid the future.

"No!" His voice was loud and harsh, startled both of them. "I suppose anyone can look back and say it was all inevitable," he said. "It always looks inevitable in retrospect."

"Maybe. But it's not over yet. The pattern isn't complete." She turned as Murray pushed the door closed with his foot.

"What do you mean?" Cluny asked. "What pattern?"

"I don't know. Nowhere along the line have I known what was coming, or what I should do, but it always seemed to be like something that I had known and simply had forgotten when it finally happened. You know what I mean?"

He nodded.

"I just feel this is one of the steps, that there's another one up ahead, and when it's time, I'll recognize it."

There was so much he wanted to say to her, half a lifetime of events, feelings, hopes, things he had not been able to talk about with anyone else. He pressed his forehead hard against the window, his eyes closed. "Listen to me, Jean. If you go with them, if you cooperate, you'll become part of the machine. You've avoided that until now. They'll take you somewhere and just as long as there's a possibility that one day they might be able to use you again, they'll keep you well and healthy. But you'll be a disposable part and the day you become more of a threat than an asset, something will happen to you. You'll get sick and a doctor will administer a shot, or there'll be a case of food poisoning, or an accident. . . . You'll become a disposable part, no more than that."

"I know," she said softly. "But it wasn't going to be like that, was it, Murray? You weren't really going to take me anywhere, were you? It's too late already."

Cluny jerked around to see Murray standing across the room from them. Murray had a gun. Cluny nearly laughed at the preposterous picture of fat little Murray with a gun.

"What the hell are you up to?" he asked, and his voice was curiously high, unfamiliar.

"Move away from her," Murray said, looking at Jean.

"Don't be a goddamn fool." Cluny took a step toward Murray. The gun didn't shift, was pointing steadily at Jean. "Murray! Look at me! You're under a strain, tired. Give yourself a couple of days; you'll see she's not really a threat, not after she's back on the reservation."

Murray seemed not to hear him. He took a step sideways, to get Cluny out of the way.

He was going to do it, Cluny knew, and it seemed

that everything stopped. She had known, he realized; this was what she had meant. It wasn't finished yet, the pattern was not complete. She waited, willing it to happen, willing completion, order out of chaos, fulfillment.

"No!" he screamed. He flung himself at Murray and heard the roar of the gun echo over and over in his head.

Murray tried to stop his fingers, tried not to pull the trigger, to turn the gun away, to make his hand fall. Cluny's eyes held him; his scream and the report of the shot blended, became a single sound that beat its way into Murray's head, into ...s chest, where it exploded again, soundlessly this time.

Cluny was twisted, thrown backward as if a giant invisible fist had slammed him. The explosion in Murray's chest was sending shock waves through him. Somewhere he was sobbing, "Not Cluny! Jesus God, not Cluny!" He saw Jean at Cluny's side. A shock wave raced through Murray's arm; he could not feel his hand, the gun in his hand. Another wave swept up over his face, blinding him momentarily. Jean reappeared; he tried to fire the gun again, but his fingers were numb, his legs. . . . He could not get a breath. This time when the wave raced through his body, up into his head, it did not recede.

Jean knelt by Cluny and tore open his shirt. "You're here, Cluny. You're not going to die! Not yet, not like this! . . ." Someone pulled her away.

"Call Zach! Tell him to bring a doctor!"

She waited in the living room, leaning her forehead against the window, thinking nothing at all. When Zach finally came to her, she closed her eyes for a moment before she turned.

"Cluny's going to be all right," he said wearily. "Murray's dead." He sat down on the couch and put his face in his hands. "All we're releasing is that Murray had a heart attack." He looked up then. "Cluny's going to need a long rest when he gets out of here. He told the doctor you promised to take him home and take care of him. Anything to that?"

She nodded.

"We'll fly you two out as soon as he can move. A week, ten days." He pushed himself up stiffly. "The nurse is staying overnight. Get some rest." He went to the door and paused. "We'll keep everyone away from you and Cluny until he's able to go. After that . . ."

He thought Cluny would be her jailer, she realized. Coyote guarding the rabbit. But which of them was which?

"They won't find me," she said, going to the door with him. She held out her hand hesitantly, unsure if he would be willing to touch her. He took it in both of his. He looked very tired, weary. Softly she said, "It isn't over yet. It'll never really be over. But maybe we have enough time now. Maybe it'll work."

His hands pressed hers hard for a moment. "A gift of time? We'll see. We'll see." He leaned over and kissed her forehead, then left.

Back in her room, she sat on the bed. "I wanted to die," she said softly. "It would have been absolution." She imagined a faint sound, Serena's laughter, and heard her voice, mildly sarcastic: "And you have to search for another way. Poor little Jean."

She laughed at herself and got ready for bed then. She would show him the places where volcanoes had shaped the land, where earthquakes had opened chasms that time had not yet filled again. She would teach him the many things they could eat and how to prepare them, and the many other things they could not eat. They would watch redtail's soaring flight and listen to the coyotes' chorus and count stars. And perhaps he would be cured, she thought sleepily. His exile would end; he would go to the stars, and that would be good. And perhaps she would be cured the rest of the way, perhaps she would see what she was to do next.

She slept and dreamed they were running together over black, red, and green fields of fire glass. They came to a chasm and she gave herself to the wind, which lifted and carried her effortlessly over the gorge. A juniper tree formed itself before her and she sank to the ground beneath it and looked at the sky through pale gray-blue needles. She did not look to see if he followed. She would wait here, she thought lazily. There was time enough.

ACK-3766
O.O
3-26-97

Fantasy Novels

POCKET BOOKS

_____ 83217 **THE BOOK OF THE DUN COW**
Walter Wangerin, Jr. $2.50
*"Far and away the most literate and intelligent
story of the year."—The New York Times*

_____ 83148 **THE WHITE HART**
Nancy Springer $2.25
*"It has everything; a believable fantasy world…a
lovely, poignant book."—Marion Zimmer Bradley*

_____ 82912 **BEAUTY Robin McKinley** $1.95
*"The most delightful first novel I've read in
years…I was moved and enchanted."—Peter S.
Beagle, author of THE LAST UNICORN*

_____ 83149 **E PLURIBUS UNICORN**
Theodore Sturgeon $1.95
*"Grade A Sturgeon stories…a book belonging in
any fantasy library."—Fantasy & Science Fiction*

_____ 82164 **STRANGE EVIL Jane Gaskell** $1.95
*Beautiful and compelling fantasy adventure
from the author of the ATLAN saga*

_____ 83294 **ARIOSTO Chelsea Quinn Yarbo** $2.25
*"Colorful and exciting…a vivid tapestry come to
life…superb!"—Andre Norton*

_____ 82958 **THE ORPHAN Robert Stallman** $2.25
*"An exciting blend of love and violence, of
sensitivity and savagery."—Fritz Leiber*

POCKET BOOKS Department FAN
1230 Avenue of the Americas · New York, N.Y. 10020

Please send me the books I have checked above. I am enclosing $_____
(please add 50¢ to cover postage and handling for each order, N.Y.S. and N.Y.C.
residents please add appropriate sales tax). Send check or money order—no
cash or C.O.D.s please. Allow up to six weeks for delivery.

NAME_____

ADDRESS_____

CITY_____STATE/ZIP_____

FAN 3-80